Praise for Sarah Lotz's

THE THREE

"*The Three* is really wonderful, a mix of Michael Crichton and Shirley Jackson. Hard to put down and vastly entertaining." —Stephen King

"A spellbinding tale of science fiction, religious fervor, and media madness that makes us wonder who, exactly, are the monsters." —Nancy Hightower, *Washington Post*

"Sarah Lotz is a natural-born storyteller. Like the hand reaching up from the dark well, she'll drag you into her thrall. You'll come up gasping." —Lauren Beukes, author of *The Shining Girls*

"This absorbing novel seems at times like a descendant of *Lost:* an irresistible premise involving a plane crash, a superb feel for the uncanny.... Across a clever range of forms, including Skype interviews, tape recordings, and transcripts from Internet forums, the truth slowly emerges. *The Three* is nicely researched and hard to put down. Who knows? It might make a good TV show." —Charles Finch, *USA Today*

"It's reminiscent of Stephen King's *Carrie,* and *The Three* comes preloaded with praise from the master of horror himself. It deserves it: this high-concept thriller is a blast." —Alison Flood, *The Guardian*

THE
THREE

THE
THREE

SARAH LOTZ

Little, Brown and Company

New York Boston London

Copyright © 2014 by Sarah Lotz
Excerpt from *Day Four* copyright © 2015 by Sarah Lotz

Little, Brown and Company
Hachette Book Group
1290 Avenue of the Americas, New York, NY 10104
littlebrown.com

Little, Brown and Company is a division of Hachette Book Group, Inc. The Little, Brown and Company name and logo is a trademark of Hachette Book Group, Inc.

The publisher is not responsible for websites (or their content) that are not owned by the publisher.

Printed in the United States of America

Originally published in hardcover by Little, Brown and Company, May 2014
First Little, Brown and Company mass market edition, April 2015

10 9 8 7 6 5 4 3 2 1

For Uncle Chippy
(1929–2013)

THE
THREE

HOW IT BEGINS

Come on, come on, come on . . .

Pam stares up at the seat belt light, willing it to click off. She's not going to be able to hold it in much longer, can almost hear Jim's voice scolding her for not going before she boarded the plane: *You know you got a weak bladder, Pam, what in the heck were you thinking?*

Truth is, she hadn't dared use one of the bathrooms at the airport. What if she found herself face to face with one of those futuristic toilets she'd read about in the guidebook and couldn't figure out how to flush it? What if she accidentally locked herself inside a stall and missed her flight? And to think Joanie suggested that she spend a few days exploring the city before taking the connecting flight to Osaka! Just the thought of navigating Tokyo's alien streets by herself makes Pam's already clammy palms sweat – the airport had been bewildering enough. Rattled and greasy after the flight from Fort Worth, she'd felt like a sluggish giant as she slogged her way towards Terminal 2 and her connecting flight. Everyone around her seemed to crackle with efficiency and confidence; compact bodies swarmed past her, briefcases swinging, eyes hidden behind sunglasses. She was aware of every extra pound she carried as she squeezed onto the shuttle, colouring each time someone shot a look in her direction.

Thankfully there had been plenty of other Americans

on the flight to Tokyo (the nice boy sitting next to her had patiently shown her how to work the video system), but on this flight she's painfully aware she's the only… what's the word – the one they always use on the detective shows Jim likes? Caucasian, that's it. And the seats are far smaller; she's squashed in like a canned ham. Still, at least there's an empty space in between her and the business-type fellow sitting in the aisle seat – she won't have to worry about accidentally nudging him. Although she'll have to disturb him when she squeezes out to use the bathroom, won't she? And Lordy, it looks like he's falling asleep, which means she'll have to wake him.

The plane continues to climb and still the sign glows. She peers out of the window into darkness, sees the red blipping light on the wing emerging through cloud, grips the arms of her seat and feels the aircraft's innards thrumming through her.

Jim was right. She hasn't even reached her destination and already this whole enterprise has been too much for her. He'd warned her that she wasn't cut out for long-distance travel, had tried to convince her that the whole thing was a bad idea: *Joanie can fly home anytime she likes, Pam, why bother travelling halfway around the world to see her? Why'd she want to teach Asians anyway? Aren't American kids good enough for her? And besides, Pam, you don't even like Chinese food, how in the heck are you going to cope with eating raw dolphin or whatever it is they eat over there?* But she'd stuck to her guns, chipping away at his disapproval, surprising him when she wouldn't back down. Joanie had been gone for two years and Pam needed to see her, missed her terribly, and from the photos she'd seen on the Internet, Osaka's gleaming skyscrapers didn't look that different from those of normal American cities. Joanie had warned her that she might find the culture perplexing at first, that Japan wasn't all cherry blossoms and geishas smiling coyly from behind fans, but Pam assumed she'd be able to handle it. She'd stupidly thought it would be some sort of fun adventure she'd be able to brag about to Reba for years afterwards.

The plane levels out and finally the seat belt sign pings off. There's a flurry of movement as several passengers jump up from their seats and start rummaging in the overhead compartments. Praying there won't be a queue for the bathroom, she unclicks her belt, steels herself to edge her bulk past the fellow in the aisle seat, when an almighty booming sound rockets through the plane. Pam immediately thinks of a car backfiring, but planes don't backfire, do they? She yelps – a delayed reaction that makes her feel faintly stupid. It's nothing. Thunder, maybe. Yes, that's it. The guidebook said it wasn't unusual for storms to hit—

Another bang – this one more like a gunshot. A chorus of reedy screams drifts from the front of the aircraft. The seat belt light flashes on again and Pam fumbles for the belt; her fingers are numb, she can't remember how to tighten it. The plane drops, giant hands press down on her shoulders, and her stomach feels like it's being forced up into her throat. Uh-uh. No. This can't be happening. Not to her. Things like this don't happen to people like her, ordinary people. *Good* people. A jolt – the overhead lockers rattle, then, mercifully, the aircraft seems to calm itself.

A ping, a babble of Japanese, then: 'Please remain in your seat with your seat belt tightly fastened.' Pam breathes again; the voice is serene, unconcerned. It can't be anything too serious, there's no cause for her to panic. She tries to peer over the backs of the seats to see how everyone else is reacting, can only make out a series of bowed heads.

She grasps the armrests again; the plane's vibration has increased, her hands are actually juddering, a sick throb reverberates up through her feet. An eye half-hidden behind a fringe of jet-black hair appears in the gap between the seats in front of her; it must be the small child she remembers being dragged down the aisle by a stern, lip-sticked young woman just before they took off. The little boy had stared at her, clearly fascinated (you can say what you like about Asians, she'd thought, but their children are as cute as buttons). She'd waved and grinned, but he hadn't responded, and then his mother had barked something at him and he'd slid obediently into his seat, out of sight. She tries to smile, but her mouth is dry and her lips catch on her teeth and oh Lordy, the vibration is getting worse.

A white mist floats down the aisle, drifts around her, and Pam finds herself batting uselessly at the screen in front of her, fumbling for her headphones. This isn't happening. This can't be happening right now, uh-uh. No, no, no. If she can just make the screen work, watch a movie, something reassuring – like that romcom she'd seen on the way here, the one with...Ryan somebody. The plane lists violently again – it feels as if it's rolling from side to side *and* up and down and her stomach flips again – she swallows convulsively, she won't be sick, uh-uh.

The businessman stands up, arms flailing as the plane heaves – it looks like he's trying to open the overhead locker, but he can't get his balance. *What are you doing?* Pam wants to scream – has the feeling that if he doesn't sit down the situation will get worse – the vibration is getting so bad it makes her think of the time her washing machine's stabiliser broke and the darn thing bucked across the floor. A flight attendant looms out of the mist, gripping the seat backs around her. She gestures at the businessman, who meekly falls back into his seat. He fumbles in his inside jacket pocket, pulls out a phone, rests his forehead against the seat in front of him and starts talking into it.

She should do the same. She should phone Jim, tell him about Snookie, remind him not to feed her that cheap stuff. She should phone Joanie; but tell her what – she almost laughs – that she might be late? No, tell her that she's proud of her, but – can they even get a signal here? Won't using her cellphone mess with the plane's navigational systems? Does she need a credit card to work the handset on the back of her seat?

Where is her phone? Is it in her fanny pack with her money and passport and pills, or did she put it in the bag? Why can't she remember? She reaches down for her purse, her stomach feeling like it's squashed against her spine. She's going to vomit, she just knows she is, but then her fingers touch the strap of her bag – Joanie had given it to her the Christmas before she left two years ago – that had been a good Christmas, even Jim had been in a good mood that day. Another jolt and the strap leaps away from her grip. She doesn't want to die like this – not like this. Not amongst strangers, not looking like this, with her hair greasy – that new perm had been a mistake – her ankles swollen, uh-uh. No way. Quickly – think of something nice, something good. Yes. This is all a dream, she's actually sitting on the couch with a chicken mayo sandwich,

Snookie on her lap, Jim dozing off in his La-Z-Boy. She knows she should pray, knows that this is what Pastor Len would tell her to do – if she prays, will it all go away? – but for once in her life she can't think of the words. She manages a 'help me, Jesus', but other thoughts keep intruding. Who'll look after Snookie if something happens to her? Snookie's old, nearly ten, why did she leave her? Dogs don't understand. Oh Lord, there's that pile of ripped pantyhose hidden in the back of her underwear drawer that she keeps meaning to throw away – what will they think of her if they find it?

The mist is thickening, burning bile rises in her throat, her vision blurs. A sharp *crack*, and a yellow plastic cup swings into her eye-line. More Japanese words – her ears are popping, she swallows, realises she can taste the spicy noodle mess she ate on the last flight, has time to feel relief that she no longer needs to pee. Then English: *something help fellow passengers something something.*

The businessman continues to babble into his phone, it's torn out of his hand as the plane bucks once more, but his mouth keeps moving; he doesn't seem to be aware he's no longer holding it. She can't get enough air into her lungs, it tastes tinny, artificial, gritty, makes her gag again. Flashes of bright light blind her momentarily, she reaches for the mask, but it keeps swinging out of her reach and then she smells something burning – like plastic left on a stove top. She'd done that once, left a spatula on the burner – Jim had gone on about it for weeks. *You could have burned the house down, woman.*

Another message... *brace, brace, brace for impact.*

An image of an empty chair fills her head and she's flooded with self-pity so acute it hurts – it's her chair, the one she always sits on every Wednesday at Bible group. A sturdy, reliable, *friendly* chair that never complains about her weight, its seat pitted with wear. She always gets to the meeting early to help Kendra put the chairs out, and everyone knows that she always sits to the right of Pastor Len, next to the coffee maker. They'd prayed for her the day before she left – even Reba had wished her well. Her chest had filled with pride and gratitude, her cheeks burning from being the centre of so much attention. *Dear Jesus, please take care of our sister and dear friend, Pamela, as she…* The plane shudders – and this time it's joined by a thuck thuck thuck as bags and laptops and other debris spill out of the overhead compartments, but if she keeps concentrating on that empty chair, then everything will be fine. Like that game she sometimes plays when she drives back from the store: if she sees three white cars, then Pastor Len will ask her and not Reba to do the flowers.

A rending sound like giant metal fingernails scoring a blackboard, the floor convulses, a weight pushes her head towards her lap, she feels her teeth knocking against each other, wants to scream at whoever is viciously yanking her hands above her head to stop. Years ago, a pick-up had pulled out in front of her car as she was driving to fetch Joanie from school. At that moment everything had slowed right down – she'd been aware of tiny details, the crack in her windscreen, the rust peppering the other car's bonnet, the shadowy shape of its baseball-capped driver – but this, this is happening too fast! *Make it stop it's going on for too long* – she's whipped and pummelled and beaten; her head, she can't keep her head up and then the seat in front of her rushes up to her face and then white light flares, blinding her and she can't—

*   *   *

A bonfire crackles and spits, but her cheeks are cold; freezing in fact, there's a real bite in the air. Is she outside? Of course she is! Stupid. You can't have bonfires indoors, can you? Where is she though? They always have a get-together at Pastor Len's ranch on Christmas Eve – she must be out in the yard, watching the fireworks. She always brings her famous blue cheese dip. No wonder she's feeling so lost! She's forgotten to bring the dip, must have left it on the counter – Pastor Len will be so disappointed and—

Someone's screaming – *you can't scream at Christmas, why are you screaming at Christmas? It's a happy time.*

She lifts her left hand to wipe her face, but can't seem to...that's not right, she's lying on her arm, it's twisted behind her back. Why is she lying down? Has she fallen asleep? Not at Christmas when there's always so much to do...she has to get up, apologise for being so rude, Jim's always saying she needs to buck up her ideas, try and be a little bit more...

She runs her tongue over her teeth. They don't feel right; one of her incisors is chipped, the edge nips her tongue. She crunches down on grit, swallows – Lordy, her throat feels like she's been swallowing razorblades, is she—

And then the knowledge of what's happened hits her all at once, the force of it making her gasp, and with it comes a white surge of pain, blooming up from her right leg and shooting into her stomach. *Get up, get up, get up.* She tries to lift her head, but when she does, hot needles spike the back of her neck.

Another scream – it sounds fairly close to her. She's never heard anything like it – it's naked, raw, barely human. She needs it to stop, it's making the ache in her gut worse, as if the scream is directly connected to her innards, tugging at them with every wail.

Oh thank you, Jesus, she can move her right arm and she inches it up, probes her belly, touches something soft and wet and just plain *wrong*. She won't think about that now. Oh Jesus, she needs help, she needs someone to come and help her, if only she'd listened to Jim and stayed at home with Snookie and hadn't thought all those bad thoughts about Reba...

Stop it. She can't panic. That's what they always say, don't panic. She's alive. She should be grateful. She needs to get up, see where she is. She's no longer in her seat, she knows that for sure, she's lying on some sort of mossy, soft surface. She counts to three, tries to use her good arm to heave herself over onto her side, but she's forced to stop as a flare of agony – as sharp and startling as an electric shock – flashes through her entire body. It's so intense she can't believe the pain actually belongs to her. She keeps absolutely still, and mercifully, it begins to fade, leaving a worrying numbness in its wake (but she won't think about that either, nuh-uh).

She squeezes her eyes shut, opens them. Blinks to clear her vision. Tentatively she tries to turn her head to the right, and this time she's able to do so without that horrible, intrusive pain. *Good*. A bruise of orange light in the background casts everything in silhouette, but she can make out a thick grove of trees – strange twisted trees, ones she can't identify – and there, just in front of them, a curved piece of twisted metal. Oh Lordy, is that the plane? It is...she can see the oblong shape of a window. A pop, a hissing sound, a soft boom and the scene is suddenly lit up clear as day. Her eyes water, but she won't look away.

She won't. She can see the jagged edge of the fuselage, cruelly sheared from the rest of its body – where is the rest? Was she sitting in that part? Impossible. She couldn't have survived that. It's like a huge broken toy, makes her think of the yards around the trailers where Jim's mother used to live. They were scattered with debris and old car parts and broken tricycles and she hadn't liked to go there, even though Jim's mother had always been kind to her... Her vision is limited due to her position, and she ignores the cracking sound she hears as she cranes her head so that her cheek is resting against her shoulder.

The screaming ceases abruptly, mid-howl. *Good*. She doesn't want this time to be muddied with someone else's pain and noise.

Wait... Something's moving, just over by the tree line. A dark shape – a person – a small person, a child? The child who was sitting in front of her? She's flooded with shame – she hadn't given him or his mother a moment's thought as the plane dropped. She'd only thought of herself. No wonder she couldn't pray, what sort of Christian is she? The figure flits frustratingly out of her line of sight, but she can't inch her neck any further over.

She tries to open her mouth to shout; can't seem to make her jaw move this time. *Please. I'm here. Hospital. Get help.*

A soft thud behind her head. 'Ack,' she manages. 'Ack.' Something touches her hair, and she feels tears rolling down her cheeks – she's safe. They're here to rescue her.

The shush-pad of running feet. *Don't go. Don't leave me*.

Bare feet suddenly appear in front of her eyes. Small feet, dirty, it's dark, so dark, but they look to be smeared with black goop – mud? blood?

'Help me, help me, help me,' that's it, she's talking now. Good girl. If she's talking she's going to be fine. She's just in shock. Yep. That's all. 'Help me.'

A face looms towards her; it's so close she can feel the whisper of the boy's breath on her cheeks. She tries to focus on his eyes. Are they...? Nuh-uh. It's just the poor light. They're white, all white, no pupils *oh Jesus help me*. A scream grows in her chest, lodges in her throat, she can't get it out, it's going to choke her. The face jerks away. Her lungs are heavy, liquid. Now it hurts to breathe.

Something flickers in the far right of her field of vision. Is it that same child? How could he have got all the way over there so quickly? He's pointing at something... Shapes, darker than the trees around them. People. Definitely people. The orange glow is fading, but she can see their outlines clearly. Hundreds of them, it looks like, and they're coming towards her. Drifting out of the trees, those strange trees, knobbled and bubbled and twisted like fingers.

Where are their feet? They don't have feet. That's not right.

Uh-uh. They aren't real. They can't be real. She can't see their eyes, their faces are inky black blobs that remain flat and unmoving as the light behind them blooms and dies.

They're coming for her – she knows this.

The fear ebbs away, replaced with a certainty that she doesn't have long. It's as if a cold, confident Pam – a new Pam, the Pam she's always wanted to be – enters and takes over her battered, dying body. Ignoring the mess where her stomach once was, she gropes for her fanny pack. It's still here, although it's shifted around to her side. She closes her eyes and concentrates on opening the zip. Her fingers are wet, slippery, but she's not going to give up now.

The whup-whup sound fills her ears, louder this time, a light floats down from above and dances over and around her and she can make out a row of disembodied seats, the metal struts catching the light; a high-heeled shoe that looks brand new. She waits to see if the light will halt the crowd's approach. They continue to creep forward, and still she can't make out any facial features. And where is the boy? If only she could tell him not to go near them, because she knows what they want, oh yes, she knows exactly what they want. But she can't think about that now, not when she's so close. She digs inside her bag, yips with relief when her fingers graze the smooth back of her phone. Careful not to drop it, she ekes it out of the bag – has time to marvel at the panic she felt earlier when she couldn't remember where she'd put it – and instructs her arm to bring it up to her face. What if it doesn't work? What if it's broken?

It won't be broken, she won't let it be broken, and she caws in triumph when she hears the chiming do-do-do-dah welcome message. Nearly there... A tut of exasperation – she's such a messy bunny, there's blood all over the screen. Using the last of her strength to concentrate, she finds her way to the applications box, scrolls to 'voice recorder'. The whup-whupping is deafening now, but Pam shuts it out, just as she ignores the fact that she can no longer see.

She holds the phone to her mouth and starts speaking.

BLACK THURSDAY

FROM CRASH TO CONSPIRACY

Inside the phenomenon of The Three

ELSPETH MARTINS

Jameson & White Publishers
New York ★ London ★ Los Angeles

A NOTE FROM THE AUTHOR

There can be few readers who do not feel a frisson of
dread when the words Black Thursday are mentioned.
That day – January 12, 2012 – when four commuter
planes went down within hours of each other, resulting in
the deaths of over a thousand people, has joined the
annals of the devastating disasters that have changed the
way we look at the world.

Predictably, within weeks of the incidents, the market
was flooded with non-fiction accounts, blogs, biographies
and opinion pieces, all cashing in on the public's morbid
fascination with the accidents themselves, and the child
plane crash survivors known as The Three. But no one
could have predicted the macabre chain of events that
would follow or how fast they would unfold.

As I did in *Snapped*, my investigation into gun crime
perpetrated by US children under the age of sixteen, I
decided that if I was going to add my voice to the mix, the
only way forward was to collate an objective account, letting those involved speak in their own words. To this end,
I have drawn from a wide variety of sources, including
Paul Craddock's unfinished biography, Chiyoko Kamamoto's collected messages, and interviews personally
conducted by me during and immediately after the events
in question.

I make no apologies for the inclusion of subject matter
that some may find upsetting, such as the accounts of

those who were first on the scenes of the tragedies; the statements from former and current Pamelists; the *isho* found at the crash site of Sun Air Flight 678; and the never-before-published interview with the exorcist hired by Paul Craddock.

While I freely admit to having included excerpts from newspaper reports and magazine articles as context (and, to some extent, as a narrative device), my main motivation, as it was in *Snapped*, is to provide an unbiased platform for the perspectives of those closest to the main players in the events that occurred from January to July, 2012. With this in mind, I urge readers to remember that these accounts are subjective and to draw their own conclusions.

Elspeth Martins
New York
August 30, 2012

They're here. I'm... don't let Snookie eat chocolate, it's poison for dogs, she'll beg you, the boy. The boy watch the boy watch the dead people oh Lordy there's so many... They're coming for me now. We're all going soon. All of us. Bye Joanie I love the bag bye Joanie, Pastor Len warn them that the boy he's not to—

The last words of Pamela May Donald (1961–2012)

PART ONE

CRASH

From chapter one of *Guarding JESS: My Life With One of The Three* by Paul Craddock (co-written with Mandi Solomon).

I've always liked airports. Call me an old romantic, but I used to get a kick out of watching families and lovers reuniting – that split second when the weary and sun-burned emerge through the sliding glass doors and recognition lights up their eyes. So when Stephen asked me to collect him and the girls from Gatwick, I was more than happy to do it.

I left with a good hour to spare. I wanted to get there early, grab myself a coffee and people-watch for a bit. Odd to think of it now, but I was in a wonderful mood that afternoon. I'd had a call-back for the part of the gay butler in the third series of *Cavendish Hall* (type-casting, of course, but Gerry, my agent, thought it could finally be my big break), and I'd managed to find a parking spot that wasn't a day's hike from the entrance. As it was one of my treat days, I bought myself a latte with extra cream, and wandered over to join the throng waiting for passengers to emerge from baggage reclaim. Next to a Cup 'n' Chow outlet, a team of bickering work-experience kids were doing an execrable job of dismantling a tacky Christmas display that was well-overdue for removal, and I watched their mini drama unfold for a while, oblivious that my own was about to begin.

I hadn't thought to check the flight information board to make sure the plane was on time, so I was taken unawares when a nasal voice droned over the intercom: 'Could all those awaiting the arrival of Go!Go! Airlines

Flight 277 from Tenerife please make their way to the information counter, thank you.' *Isn't that Stephen's flight?* I thought, double-checking the details on my BlackBerry. I wasn't too concerned. I suppose I assumed the flight had been delayed. It didn't occur to me to wonder why Stephen hadn't called to let me know he'd be late.

You never think it's going to happen to you, do you?

There was only a small group of us at first – others, like me, who'd arrived early. A pretty girl with dyed red hair holding a heart-shaped balloon on a stick, a dreadlocked fellow with a wrestler's build and a middle-aged couple with smokers' skin who were dressed in identical cerise shell suits. Not the sort of people with whom I'd usually choose to associate. Odd how one's first impressions can be so wrong. I now count them all among my closest friends. Well, this type of thing brings you together, doesn't it?

I should have known from the shell-shocked expressions on the faces of the spotty teenager manning the counter and the whey-faced security woman hovering next to him that something horrific was afoot, but all I was feeling at that stage was irritation.

'What's going on?' I snapped in my best *Cavendish Hall* accent.

The teenager managed to stutter that we were to follow him to where 'more info would be relayed to us'.

We all did as we were told, although I confess I was surprised the shell-suited couple didn't kick up more of a stink, they didn't look the type to take orders. But as they told me weeks later at one of our '277 Together' meetings, at that stage they were in denial. They didn't *want* to know, and if anything untoward had happened to the plane, they didn't want to hear it from a boy who was barely out of puberty. The teenager scurried ahead, presumably so that none of us would have the chance to interrogate him further, and ushered us through an innocuous door next to the customs offices. We were led down a long corridor, which, judging by its peeling paint and scuffed floor, wasn't in a section of the airport typically encountered by the public gaze. I remember smelling a rogue whiff of cigarette smoke wafting in from somewhere in a flagrant disregard of the smoking ban.

We ended up in a grim windowless lounge, furnished with tired burgundy waiting-room seats. My eye was caught by one of those seventies tubular ashtrays, which was half-hidden behind a plastic hydrangea. Funny what you remember, isn't it?

A guy in a polyester suit clutching a clipboard waddled towards us, his Adam's apple bobbing up and down like a Tourette's sufferer's. Although as pale as a cadaver, his cheeks were alive with a severe shaving rash. His eyes darted all over the place, briefly met mine, then his gaze settled into the far distance.

It hit me then, I think. The sickening knowledge that I was about to hear something that would change my life forever.

'Go on then, mate,' Kelvin – the fellow with the dreads – finally said.

The suit swallowed convulsively. 'I am extremely sorry to relay this to you, but Flight 277 disappeared off the radar approximately an hour ago.'

The world swayed, and I could feel the first wisps of a panic attack. My fingers were tingling and my chest was starting to tighten. Then Kelvin asked the question the rest of us were too afraid to ask: 'Has it crashed?'

'We cannot be certain at this time, but please be assured we will relay the information to you as soon as it comes in. Counsellors will be available for any of you who—'

'What about survivors?'

The suit's hands were trembling and the winking cartoon plane on his plastic Go!Go! badge seemed to mock us with its cheeky insouciance. 'Should have called it Gay!Gay! Air,' Stephen used to quip whenever one of Go!Go!'s dire adverts came on the television. He was always joking that that cartoon plane was camper than a bus-load of drag queens. I didn't take offence; that was the sort of relationship we had. 'Like I say,' the suit flustered, 'we have counsellors at your disposal—'

Mel – the female half of the track-suited couple – spoke up. 'Sod your counsellors, just tell us what's happened!'

The girl holding the balloon started sobbing with the gusto of an *EastEnders* character, and Kelvin put his arm around her. She dropped the balloon and I watched as it bounced sadly across the floor, eventually ending up lodged next to the retro ashtray. Other people were starting to drift into the room, ushered by more Go!Go! staff – most of whom looked as bewildered and unprepared as the spotty teenager.

Mel's face was as pink as her shell-suit top and she was jabbing a finger in the official's face. Everyone seemed to be screaming or crying, but I felt a curious distance from what was going on, as if I was on set, waiting for my cue. And this is a ghastly thing to admit, but I thought, *remember what you're feeling, Paul, you can use it in your acting.* I'm not proud of that. I'm just being honest.

I kept staring at that balloon, and suddenly I could hear Jessica and Polly's voices, clear as a bell: 'But Uncle

Paaaaauuuuul, what keeps the plane in the air?' Stephen had asked me round to Sunday lunch the week before they left, and the twins hadn't stopped badgering me about the flight, for some reason assuming I was the font of all knowledge about air travel. It was the kids' first time on a plane, and they were more excited about that than they were about the holiday. I found myself trying to remember the last thing Stephen had said to me, something along the lines of, 'See you when you're older, mate.' We're non-identical, but how could I not have sensed something awful had happened? I dragged my phone out of my pocket, recalling that Stephen had sent me a text the day before: 'Girls say hi. Resort full of twats. We get in at 3.30. Don't be late ;).' I thumbed through my messages, trying to find it. It was suddenly absolutely vital that I save it. It wasn't there – I must have accidentally deleted it.

Even weeks afterwards, I wished I'd kept that text message.

Somehow, I found myself back in the Arrivals area. I don't remember how I even got there, or if anyone tried to stop me leaving that ghastly lounge. I drifted along, sensing that people were staring at me, but right then, they were as insignificant as extras. There was something in the air, like that heavy feeling you get just before a storm hits. I thought, sod it, I need a drink, which, since I'd been on the wagon for a good ten years, wasn't like me. I sleep-walked towards the Irish theme pub on the far side of the area. A group of suited yobs were gathered around the bar staring up at the TV. One of them, a florid-faced prat with a Mockney accent, was talking too loudly, going on about 9/11, and telling everyone that he had to get to Zurich by 5.50 or 'heads would roll'. He stopped, mid-sentence, as I approached, and the others made room for me, drawing back as if I were contagious. Of course, I've learned since then that grief and horror *are* contagious.

The TV's sound was up to full volume and an anchor – one of those botoxed American horrors with Tom Cruise teeth and too much make-up – was yabbering into shot. Behind her was a screen capture of what looked to be some sort of swamp, a helicopter hovering over it. And then I read the strap-line: Maiden Airlines Everglades crash.

They've got it wrong, I thought. *Stephen and the girls were on Go!Go!, not that plane.*

And then it hit me. Another plane had gone down.

At 14.35 (CAT time), an Antonov cargo and passenger plane leased by Nigerian carrier Dalu Air crashed into the heart of Khayelitsha – Cape Town's most populous township. Liam de Villiers was one of the first paramedics on the scene. An Advanced Life Support Paramedic for Cape Medical Response at the time of the incident, Liam now works as a trauma counsellor. This interview was conducted via Skype and email and collated into a single account.

We were dealing with an incident on Baden Powell Drive when it happened. A taxi had clipped a Merc and over-turned, but it wasn't too hectic. The taxi was empty at the time, and although the driver had only minor injuries, we'd need to ferry him to Casualty to get stitched up. It was one of those rare still days, the southeaster that had been raging for weeks had blown itself out, and there was only a wisp of cloud trickling over the lip of Table Mountain. A perfect day, I guess you could say, although we were parked a bit too close to the Macassar sewage works for comfort. After smelling that for twenty minutes, I was grateful I hadn't had a chance to scarf down the KFC I'd bought for lunch.

I was on with Cornelius that day, one of our newer guys. He was a cool oke, good sense of humour. While I dealt with the driver, he was gossiping with a couple of traffic cops who were on the scene. The taxi-driver was shouting into his cellphone, lying to his boss while I dressed the wound on his upper arm. You wouldn't have known anything had happened to him; he didn't flinch

once. I was just about to ask Cornelius if he'd let False
Bay Casualty know we were en route with a patient, when
a roaring sound ripped out of the sky, making all of us
jump. The taxi-driver's hand went limp and his phone
clattered to the ground.

And then we saw it. I know everyone says this, but it was
exactly like watching a scene from a movie; you couldn't
believe it was actually happening. It was flying so low I
could see the chipped paint in its logo – you know, that
green swirl curving round a 'D'. Its landing gear was down
and the wings were dipping crazily from side to side like a
rope-walker trying to get his balance. I remember thinking,
airport's the other way, what the fuck is the pilot doing?

Cornelius was shouting something, pointing at it. I
couldn't hear what he was saying, but I got the gist. Mitch-
ell's Plain, where his family lived, wasn't that far away
from where the plane looked to be headed. It was obvious
it was going to crash; it wasn't on fire or anything like
that, but it was clear it was in severe trouble.

The plane disappeared out of sight, there was a
'crump', and I swear, the ground shook. Later, Darren,
our base controller, said that we were probably too far
away to feel any kind of aftershock, but that's how I
remember it. Seconds later a black cloud blossomed into
the sky. Huge it was, made me think of those pictures of
Hiroshima. And I thought, yissus, no way did anyone survive that.

We didn't stop to think. Cornelius jumped in the driver's seat, started radioing the base station, telling them we
had a major incident on our hands and to notify the centre
for disaster management. I told the taxi-driver he'd have
to wait for another ambulance to take him to Casualty and

shouted, 'Tell them it's a Phase Three, tell them it's a Phase Three!' The cops were already on the road, heading straight for the Khayelitsha Harare turn-off. I jumped in the back of the ambulance, the adrenaline shooting through me, washing away all the tiredness I was feeling after being on duty for twelve hours.

While Cornelius drove, following in the wake of the police car, I pulled out the bergen, started rummaging in the lockers for the burn shields, the intravenous bottles, anything I thought we might need, and placed them on the stretcher at the back. We're trained for this of course – for a plane going down, I mean. There's a designated ditch site in Fish Hoek in False Bay, and I wondered if that was where the pilot was heading when he realised he wasn't going to make the airport. But I won't lie, training is one thing, I never thought we'd have to deal with a situation like this.

That drive is etched on my memory like you won't believe. The crackle and pop of the radio as voices conferred, Cornelius's white-knuckled hands on the steering-wheel, the reek of the Streetwise two-piece meal I'd never get to eat. And look, this is going to sound bad, but there are parts of Khayelitsha we usually wouldn't dream of entering, we've had incidents when staff have been held up – all the ambulance services will tell you that – but this was different. It didn't even occur to me to worry about going into Little Brazzaville. Darren was back on the radio, talking Cornelius through the procedure, telling him that we were to wait for the scene to be secured first. In situations like these, there's no place for heroes. You don't want to get yourself injured, end up another casualty for the guys to deal with.

As we got closer to the site, I could hear screams

mingling with the sirens that were coming from all directions. Smoke rolled towards us, coating the windscreen in a greasy residue, and Cornelius had to slow down and put on his wipers. The acrid smell of burning fuel filled the ambulance. I couldn't get that stench out of my skin for days. Cornelius slammed on the brakes as a crowd of people flooded towards us. Most were carrying TVs, crying children, furniture – dogs even. They weren't looting, these guys, they knew how quickly a fire could spread in this area. Most of the houses are slapped together, shacks made of wood and corrugated iron, a lot of them little more than kindling, not to mention the amount of paraffin that had to be lying around.

We slowed to a crawl, and I could hear the thunk of hands slapping the side of the ambulance. I actually ducked when I heard the crump of another explosion, and I thought, shit, this is it. Helicopters swarmed overhead and I yelled at Cornelius to stop – it was obvious we couldn't go much further without endangering our safety. I climbed out of the back, tried to steel myself for what we were about to face.

It was chaos. If I hadn't seen it with my own eyes, I wouldn't have known it was a plane gone down – I would've assumed a bloody great bomb had gone off. And the heat that was coming from there…I saw the footage afterwards, the helicopter footage, that black gouge in the ground, the shacks that were flattened, that school those Americans built, crushed as if it was made of matchsticks; the church split in half as if it was as insubstantial as a garden shed.

'There's more! There's more! Help us!' people were shouting. 'Over here! Over here!'

It seemed like hundreds of people surged towards us yelling for help, but fortunately the cops who were on the scene of the minor collision pushed most of them back, and we could assess what we were dealing with. Cornelius started organising them into triage groups – sorting out who was most in need of urgent attention. I knew immediately that the first child I saw wasn't going to make it. His distraught mother said they were both sleeping when she heard a deafening roar and chunks of debris rained into their bedroom. We know now that the plane broke up on impact, scattering burning parts like Agent Orange.

A doctor from the Khayelitsha hospital was first on the scene, doing a fantastic job. That oke was on the ball. Even before the disaster management team showed up, he'd already allocated areas for the triage tents, morgue and the ambulance station. There's a system with these things, you can't go in half-cocked. They set up the outer circle in record time, and the airport's fire and rescue service were there minutes after we arrived to secure the area. It was vital they made sure that we weren't going to have any more follow-up explosions on our hands. We were all aware of how much oxygen planes carry, never mind fuel.

We dealt mostly with the peripheral casualties. The majority were burns, limbs hacked by flying metal, quite a few amputations, lot of people with ocular issues – specially the children. Cornelius and I just went into overdrive. The cops kept the people back, but you couldn't blame them for crowding around us. Screaming for lost relatives, parents looking for children who were at that school and crèche, others demanding to know the status of injured loved ones. Quite a few were filming it on their cellphones – I didn't blame them – it provides a distance, doesn't it? And the press were everywhere, swarming around us. I had to stop Cornelius from punching an oke with a camera slung on his shoulder who kept trying to get right up into his face.

And as the smoke died down, you could see the extent of the devastation, bit by bit. Crumpled metal, scraps of clothing, broken furniture and appliances, discarded shoes, a trampled cellphone. And bodies of course. Most were burned up, but there were others, pieces, you know… There were yells going up all around as more and more were discovered, the tent they were using as a makeshift morgue just wasn't going to cut it.

We worked through the day and well into the night. As it got darker, they lit up the site with floodlights, and some-how, that was worse. Even with their protective breathing gear, some of the younger disaster management volunteers couldn't deal with it; you could see them running off to vomit.

Those body bags kept piling up.

Not a day goes by that I don't think about it. I still can't eat fried chicken.

You know what happened to Cornelius, right? His wife says she'll never be able to forgive him, but I do. I know what it feels like when you're anxious all the time, you can't sleep, you start crying for no reason. That's why I got into trauma counselling.

Look, unless you were there, there's no way to adequately describe it, but let me try to put it in context for you. I've been doing this for over twenty years, and I've seen some hectic stuff. I've been at the aftermath of a necklacing, the body still smoking, the face fixed in an expression you don't want to see in your worst nightmares. I was on duty when the municipal workers' strike turned bad and the cops opened fire – thirty dead and not all from bullet wounds. You don't want to see the damage a panga can do. I've been at car pile-ups where the bodies of children, babies still in their car seats, have been flung across three lanes of traffic. I've seen what happens when a Buffel truck loses its brakes and rolls over a Ford Ka. And when I was working in the Botswana bush, I came across the remains of a ranger who'd been bitten in half by a hippo. Nothing can compare with what we saw that day. We all understood what Cornelius went through – the whole crew understood.

He did it in his car, out on the West Coast, where he used to go fishing. Asphyxiation, hose from the exhaust. No mess, no fuss.

I miss him.

Afterwards, we got a lot of flak for taking photos of the scene and putting them up on Facebook. But I'm not going to apologise for that. That's one of the ways we deal with it – we need to talk it through – and if you're not on the job, you won't understand. There's some talk of taking them down now, seeing as those freaks keep using them in their propaganda. Growing up in a country like this, with our history, I'm not a fan of censorship, but I can see why they're clamping down. Just adds fuel to the fire.

But I tell you something, I was there, right at ground fucking zero, and no ways did anyone on that plane survive. No ways. I stand by that, whatever those conspiracy fuckers say (excuse my French).

I still stand by that.

Yomijuri Miyajima, a geologist and volunteer suicide monitor at Japan's notorious Aokigahara forest, a popular spot for the depressed to end their lives, was on duty the night a Boeing 747-400D, operated by the Japanese domestic carrier Sun Air, plummeted into the foot of Mount Fuji.

(Translation by Eric Kushan.)

I was expecting to find one body that night. Not hundreds.

Volunteers do not usually patrol at night, but just as it was getting dark, our station received a call from a father deeply concerned about his teenage son. The boy's father had intercepted worrying emails and found a copy of Wataru Tsurumi's suicide manual under his son's mattress. Along with the notorious Matsumoto novel, it's a popular text for those who seek to end their lives in the forest; I have come across more discarded copies than I can count in my years working here.

There are a few cameras set up to monitor suspicious activity at the most popular entrance, but I had received no confirmation that he had been seen, and while I had a description of the teenager's car, I couldn't see any sign of it at the side of the road or in any of the small parking lots close to the forest. This meant nothing. Often people will drive to remote or hidden spots on the edge of the forest to end their lives. Some attempt to kill themselves with exhaust fumes; others by inhaling the toxic smoke from portable charcoal barbecues. But by far the most common method is hanging. Many of the suicidal bring tents and supplies with them, as if they need to spend a night or two contemplating what it is they are about to do before going through with it.

Every year, the local police and many volunteers sweep the forest to find the bodies of those who have chosen to die here. The last time we did this – in late November – we discovered the remains of thirty souls. Most of them were never identified. If I come across someone in the forest who I think may be planning on killing himself, I ask him to consider the pain of the family he will be leaving behind and remind him that there is always hope. I point to the volcanic rock that forms the base of the forest floor, and say that if the trees can grow on such a hard, unforgiving surface, then a new life can be built on the foundation of any hardship.

It is now common practice for the desperate to bring tape to use as a marker to find their way back if they change their minds, or, in most cases, to indicate where their bodies may be found. Others use the tape for more nefarious reasons; ghoulish sightseers hoping to come across one of the deceased, but not willing to become lost.

I volunteered to venture into the forest on foot, and with this in mind, I first checked to see if there was any indication that fresh tape had been tied around the trees. It was dark, so it was impossible for me to be sure, but I thought I discerned signs that someone had recently made his way past the 'do not pass this point' signs.

I was not concerned about getting lost. I know the forest; I have never once lost my way. Apologies for sounding fanciful, but after doing this for twenty-five years, it has become part of me. And I had a powerful flashlight and my GPS – it is not true that the volcanic rock under the forest floor muddies the signals. But the forest is a magnet for myths and legends, and people will believe what they want to.

Once you are in the forest, it cocoons you. The tops of the trees form a softly undulating roof that shuts out the world beyond. Some may find the forest's stillness and silence forbidding, I do not. The *y rei* do not frighten me. I have nothing to fear from the spirits of the dead. Perhaps you have heard the stories, that this place was a common site for *ubasute*, the practice of abandoning the aged or infirm to die of exposure in times of famine? This is unsubstantiated. Just another of the many stories the forest attracts. There are many who believe that spirits are lonely, and they try to draw people to them. They believe this is why so many come to the forest.

I did not see the plane going down – as I said, the forest's canopy conceals the sky – but I heard it. A series of muffled booms, like giant doors slamming shut. What did I think it was? I suppose I assumed that it might have been thunder, although it wasn't the season for storms or typhoons. I was too absorbed in searching the shadows, dips and ruts in the forest floor for evidence of the teenager's presence to speculate.

I was about to give up when my radio crackled, and Sato-san, one of my fellow monitors, alerted me to the fact that a troubled plane had veered off its flight path and crashed somewhere in the vicinity of the forest – more than likely in the Narusawa area. Of course I realised then that this was the source of the booming sound I heard earlier.

Sato indicated that the authorities were on their way, and said that he was organising a search party. He sounded out of breath, deeply shocked. He knew as well as I did how difficult it was going to be for rescuers to reach the site. The terrain in some parts of the forest is almost impossible to navigate – there are deep hidden crevices in many areas that make traversing through it dangerous.

I decided to head north, in the direction of the sound I had heard.

Within an hour, I could hear the roar of the rescue helicopters sweeping the forest. I knew it would be impossible for them to land, and so I ventured forward with added urgency. If there were survivors, then I knew they had to be reached quickly. Within two hours, I started to smell smoke; the trees had caught alight in several areas, but thankfully the fires hadn't spread and their limbs glowed as the flames refused to catch and began to die. Something made me sweep the beam of my flashlight up into the trees, catching on a small shape hanging in the branches. At first, I assumed it was the charred body of a monkey.

It was not.

There were others, of course. The night was alive with the sound of rescue and press helicopters, and as they swooped above me, their lights illuminated countless forms caught in the branches. Some I could see in great detail; they looked barely injured, almost as if they were sleeping. Others ... Others were not so fortunate. All were partially clothed or naked.

I struggled to reach what is now known as the main crash site, where the tail and the sheared wing were found. Rescuers were being winched to the site, but it was not possible for the helicopters to land on such uneven and treacherous terrain.

It felt strange nearing the tail of the aircraft. It towered over me, its proud red logo eerily intact. I ran to where a couple of air paramedics were tending to a woman who was moaning on the ground; I couldn't tell how badly injured she was, but I have never heard such a sound coming from a human being. It was then that I caught a flicker of movement in my peripheral vision. Some of the trees were still aflame in this area, and I saw a small hunched shape partially hidden behind an outcropping of twisted volcanic rock. I hurried towards it, and I caught the glint of a pair of eyes in the beam of my flashlight. I dropped my backpack, and ran, moving faster than I have ever done before or since.

As I approached I realised I was looking at a child. A boy.

He was crouching, shivering violently, and I could see that one of his shoulders appeared to be protruding at an unnatural angle. I shouted at the paramedics to come quickly, but they could not hear me over the sound of the helicopters.

What did I say to him? It is hard to remember exactly, but it would have been something like, 'Are you okay? Don't panic, I'm here now to help you.'

So thick was the shroud of blood and mud covering his body that at first I did not realise he was naked – they said later that his clothes were blown off by the force of the impact. I reached out to touch him. His flesh was cold – but what do you expect? The temperature was below freezing.

I am not ashamed to say that I cried.

I wrapped my jacket around him, and as carefully as I could, I picked him up. He placed his head on my shoulder and whispered, 'Three.' Or at least that is what I thought he said. I asked him to repeat what he had said, but by then his eyes were closed, his mouth slack as if he was fast asleep, and I was more concerned about getting him to safety and keeping him warm before hypothermia set in.

Of course now everyone keeps asking me: did you think there was anything strange about the boy? Of course I did not! He had just been through a horrific experience and what I saw were signs of shock.

And I do not agree with what some are saying about him. That he's possessed by angry spirits, perhaps by those of the dead passengers who envy his survival. Some say he keeps their furious souls in his heart.

Nor do I give any credence to the other stories surrounding the tragedy – that the pilot was suicidal, that the forest was pulling him towards it – why else crash in Jukei? Stories like these only cause additional pain and trouble where there is already enough. It is obvious to me that the captain fought to bring the plane down in an unpopulated area. He had minutes in which to react; he did the noble thing.

And how can a Japanese boy be what those Americans are saying? He is a miracle, that boy. I will remember him for the rest of my life.

My correspondence with Lillian Small continued until the FBI insisted that she no longer have contact with the outside world for her own safety. Although Lillian lived in Williamsburg, Brooklyn, and I am a resident of Manhattan, we have never met in person. Her accounts are extrapolated from our many phone and email conversations.

Reuben had been restless all morning and I'd settled him in front of CNN; sometimes it calms him down. In the old days, he loved to watch the news updates, especially anything political, really got a kick out of it, used to heckle the spin doctors and political analysts as if they could hear him. I don't think he missed a debate or an interview during the midterms, which was when I first really knew there was a problem. He was having trouble recalling the name of that Texan governor, you know, that damn fool one who couldn't say the word 'homosexual' without screwing his mouth up in disgust. I'll never forget the look on Reuben's face as he floundered to remember that putz's name. He'd been hiding his symptoms from me, you see. He'd been hiding them for months.

On that dreadful day, the anchorwoman was interviewing an analyst of some type about his predictions for the primaries when she cut him off mid-sentence: 'I'm sorry, I have to interrupt you there, we've just heard that a Maiden Airlines plane has gone down in the Florida Everglades...'

Of course, the first thought that jumped into my head when I heard the words 'plane crash' was 9/11. Terrorism. A bomb on board. I doubt there's a single person in New

York who didn't think that when they heard about the crash. You just do.

And then the images came on screen; an overhead view, from a helicopter. It didn't show much, a swamp with an oily mass in its centre, where the plane had plummeted with such force it had been swallowed up. My fingers were freezing – as if I'd been holding ice – though I always make sure the apartment was warm. I changed the channel to a talk show, trying to shake off that uneasy feeling. Reuben had dozed off, which I hoped would give me enough time to change the sheets, take them down to the laundry room.

I was just finishing up when the phone rang. I hurried to answer it, worrying that it would wake Reuben.

It was Mona, Lori's best friend. And I thought, why is Mona phoning me? We're not close, she knows I've never approved of her, always thought of her as fast, a bad influence. It turned out fine in the end, but unlike my Lori, even in her forties Mona hadn't changed her flighty ways. Divorced twice before she was thirty. Without even saying 'hello' or asking after Reuben, Mona said, 'What flight were Lori and Bobby coming home on?'

That bitter coldness I felt earlier was creeping back. 'What are you talking about?' I said. 'They're not on any damn plane.'

And she said, 'But Lillian, didn't Lori tell you? She was going down to Florida to see about a place for you and Reuben.'

My hand went limp and I dropped the phone – her whiny voice still echoing out of the receiver. My legs buckled and I recall praying that this was just one of those sick pranks Mona had been so fond of playing when she was younger. Then, without saying goodbye, I hung up on her and called Lori, almost screaming when I was put straight through to her voicemail. Lori had told me she was taking Bobby with her to see a client in Boston, and not to worry if she didn't get hold of me for a couple of days.

Oh, how I wished I could have talked to Reuben right then! He'd have known what to do. I suppose what I was feeling right then was pure terror. Not the sort of terror you feel when you watch a horror movie or you get accosted by a homeless man with crazy eyes, but a feeling so intense you barely have control of your body – like you're not really connected to it properly any more. I could hear Reuben stirring, but I left the apartment just the same and went straight next door, didn't know what else to do. Thank God Betsy was in – she took one look at me and swept me inside. I was in such a state, I barely noticed the cloud of cigarette smoke that always hangs in the air in her place; she usually came over to me if we were in the mood for coffee and cookies.

She poured me a brandy, made me knock it back, then offered to return to the apartment with me and sit with Reuben while I tried to contact the airline. Even after all that happened afterwards, I'll never forget how kind she was that day.

I couldn't get through – the line was busy and I kept being put on hold. That's when I really thought I knew what hell was like – waiting to hear the fate of those you hold most dear while listening to a muzak version of "The Girl from Ipanema." Whenever I hear that tune nowadays, I'm taken right back to that awful time, the taste of cheap brandy on my tongue, Reuben moaning from the living-room, the smell of last night's chicken soup lingering in the kitchen.

I don't know how long I tried that same damn number. And then, just as I was despairing of ever getting through, a voice came on the line. A woman. I gave her Bobby and Lori's names. She sounded strained, although she tried to remain professional. A pause that went on for days while she clacked away at her computer.

And then she told me. Lori and Bobby were listed on that flight.

And I told her there must be a mistake. That no way were Lori and Bobby dead, they couldn't be. I would've known. I would've felt it. I didn't believe it. I wouldn't accept it. When Charmaine – the trauma counsellor the Red Cross assigned to us – first arrived, I was still in such denial I told her... and I'm ashamed of this... I told her to go to hell.

Despite this, my first impulse was to go straight to the crash site. Just to be closer to them. Just in case. I wasn't thinking clearly, I'll admit. How could I have possibly have done that? No planes were flying and it would have meant leaving Reuben with a stranger for God knows how long, maybe putting him in a care home.

Everywhere I looked I saw Lori and Bobby's faces. We had photos up all over of the two of them. Lori holding a newborn Bobby in her arms, smiling into the camera. Bobby at Coney Island, holding a giant cookie. Lori as a schoolgirl, Lori and Bobby at Reuben's seventieth birthday party at Jujubee's, a year before he started to go downhill – when he still remembered who I was, who Lori was. I couldn't stop thinking about when she first told me she was pregnant. I hadn't taken it well, didn't like the idea of her going to that place, shopping for sperm as if it was as simple as buying a dress and then being… artificially inseminated. It seemed so cold to me. 'I'm thirty-nine, Momma' (well into her forties she still called me Momma), she said. 'This could be my last chance, and let's face it, Prince Charming isn't going to rock up any time soon.' All my doubts vanished when I saw her with Bobby for the first time of course. She was such a wonderful mother!

And I couldn't help but blame myself. Lori knew that one day I hoped to relocate to Florida, move into one of those clean, sunny assisted-living places where Reuben would get the help he needed. That's why they'd taken the trip. She was planning on surprising me for my birthday. That was just like Lori, unselfish and generous to her very core.

Betsy was doing her best to calm Reuben down while I paced. I couldn't sit still. I fidgeted, kept picking up the phone, checking it was working, just in case Lori was going to call me to say that at the last moment she hadn't made the flight. That she and Bobby had decided to take a later one. Or an earlier one. That's what I clung to.

News of the other crashes was starting to break, and I kept turning the damn television on and off, couldn't decide if I wanted to see what was going on or not. Oh, the images! It's strange to think of it now, but when I saw the footage of that Japanese boy being carried out of the forest and air-lifted up into a helicopter, I was jealous. Jealous! Because at that stage we didn't know about Bobby. All we knew was that no survivors had been found in Florida.

I thought we'd had all the bad luck one family could ever need. I thought, why would God do this to me? What had I ever done to deserve this? And on top of the guilt, the agony, the crushing absolute terror, I felt lonely. Because whatever happened, whether they were on that plane or not, I'd never be able to tell Reuben. He wouldn't be able to comfort me, make any of the arrangements, rub my back when I couldn't sleep. Not any more. He was gone too.

Betsy only left when Charmaine showed up, said she was going to go back to her kitchen to make us something to eat, although I couldn't have swallowed a thing.

The next few hours are hazy. I must have settled Reuben in bed, tried to get him to eat a little soup. I remember scrubbing the kitchen counter until my hands were raw and stinging, though both Charmaine and Betsy tried to get me to stop.

And then the call came in. Charmaine answered it while Betsy and I stood frozen in the kitchen. I'm trying to remember the exact words for you, but each time it shifts in my mind. She's African-American, Charmaine is, with just the most gorgeous skin you've ever seen, they age well, don't they? But when she walked into that kitchen, she looked ten years older.

'Lillian,' she said. 'I think you should sit down.'

I didn't allow myself to feel any hope. I'd seen the footage of the crash. How could anyone have survived that? I looked her straight in the eye and said, 'Just tell me.'

'It's Bobby,' she said. 'They've found him. He's alive.'

And then Reuben started screaming from the bedroom and I had to ask her to repeat herself.

Based in Washington, NTSB (National Transportation Safety Board) Officer Ace Kelso will be known to many readers as the star of *Ace Investigates*, which ran for four seasons on the Discovery Channel. This account is a partial transcript of one of our many Skype conversations.

You gotta understand, Elspeth, an incident of this magnitude, we knew it would be a while before we could be absolutely sure what we were dealing with. Think about it. Four different crashes involving three different makes of aircraft on four different continents – it was unprecedented. We knew we'd have to work closely and coordinate with the UK's AAIB, the CAA in South Africa, the JTSB in Japan, not to mention the other parties who had a stake in the incidents – I'm talking about the manufacturers, the FBI, the FAA and others I won't go into now. Our guys and gals were doing all they could, but the pressure was like nothing I ever experienced. Pressure from the families, pressure from the airline execs, pressure from the press, pressure from all sides. I wouldn't say I was expecting a clusterfuck exactly, but you got to expect some misinformation and mistakes. People are human. And as the weeks rolled on, we were lucky if we managed to get more than a couple of hours' sleep a night.

Before I get to what I know you want to hear, I'll give you a brief overview, put it into context for you. Here's how it went down. As the IIC [Investigator-in-Charge] on the Maiden Airlines incident, the second I got the call, I started rounding up my Go Team. A regional investigator was already on site doing the initial stakedown, but at that stage all the footage we were getting was from the news. The local incident commander had briefed me via cellphone on the conditions at the site, so I knew we were facing a bad one. You gotta remember, the place where the plane went down, it was remote. Five miles from the nearest levee, a good fourteen miles from the nearest road. From the air, unless you knew what you were looking for, you couldn't see any sign of it – we flew over it before we landed, so I saw that for myself. Scattered debris, a watery black hole about the size of your average suburban home, and that saw-grass that cuts through your flesh.

Here's what I knew when I was first briefed: A McDonnell Douglas MD-80 had crashed minutes after take-off. The air traffic controller reported that the pilots had indicated an engine failure, but I wasn't about to rule out foul play at this early stage, not with reports trickling in about incidents elsewhere. There were two witnesses, fishermen, who saw the plane behaving erratically and flying too low before plummeting into the Everglades; they said they saw flames coming from the engine as it dropped, but this wasn't unusual. Witnesses almost always report seeing signs of an explosion or fire, even if there's no chance of there being any.

I immediately told my systems, structures and maintenance guys to haul ass to Hangar 6. The FAA had assigned us the G-IV to fly to Miami – I needed a full team on this one and the Lear wasn't going to cut it. Maiden's track record with maintenance had caused us some concern before now, but the aircraft itself was known to be reliable.

We were an hour away when I got the call that they'd found a survivor. Remember, Elspeth, we'd seen the press footage – you wouldn't even know a plane had gone down unless you'd been right there at the site, it was completely submerged. I got to admit I didn't believe them at first.

The boy had been rushed to Miami Children's Hospital, and we were getting reports that he was conscious. No one could believe that a) he'd managed to survive, and b) he wasn't taken by the alligators. There were so many of the goddamned things we had to call in armed guards to keep them away while we were pulling up the debris.

When we landed, we headed straight to the site. DMORT [Disaster Mortuary Operational Response Team] were already there, but it didn't look like they were going to find any intact bodies. With so little to go on, top priority was to find the CVR [cockpit voice recorder] and black box; we'd need to get specialist divers in. It was bad in there. Hot as hell, crawling with flies, the stench...We needed full bio-hazard suits, which aren't fun to wear in those sorts of conditions. Right from the get-go I could see that it was going to take weeks for us to piece this one together, and we didn't have weeks, not now that we knew other planes had gone down that day.

I needed to talk to that kid. According to the passenger list, the only child of that age group on board was a Bobby Small, travelling back to New York City with a woman we assumed was his mother. I opted to go alone, leaving my team on the scene to do the preliminaries and liaise with the locals and other parties who were en route to the crash site.

The press was swarming around the hospital, dogging me to make a statement. 'Ace! Ace!' they were calling. 'Was it a bomb?' 'What about the other crashes, are they connected?' 'Is it true there's a survivor?' I told them the usual, that a press statement would be issued when we knew more, that investigations were still under way etc. etc. – the last thing I was going to do as IIC was shout my mouth off before we had something concrete.

I'd called ahead to say I was on my way, but I knew it was a long shot that they'd let me talk to him. While I waited for the doctors to give me the go-ahead, one of the nurses hustled out of his room, careened straight into me. She looked like she was on the verge of tears. I caught her eye, said something like, 'He's all right, huh?'

She just nodded, scuttled off to the nurses' station. I tracked her down a week or so later, asked why she'd seemed so disturbed. She couldn't put it into words. Said she had a feeling that something was off; she just didn't like being in that room. She felt guilty for saying it, you could see. Said she must have been more affected by the thought of all those people dying at once than she realised; that Bobby was a living reminder of how many had lost their lives that day.

The child psychologist who was on the case arrived a few minutes later. Nice gal, mid-thirties, but looked younger. I forget her name...Polanski? Oh right, Pankowski. Thanks. She had only just been assigned, and the last thing she wanted was some gung-ho investigator upsetting the boy. I said, 'Lady, we got an international incident on our hands here, that boy in there may be one of the only witnesses who can help us.'

I don't want you to think I'm insensitive, Elspeth, but at that stage the info on the other incidents was sketchy, and for all I knew, that boy could be a key to the whole thing. Remember, in the Japanese situation, it was a while before they confirmed there were any survivors, and we didn't get word about the girl from the UK incident till hours later. Anyway, this Dr Pankowski said the boy was awake, but hadn't said a word, he didn't know his mother was more than likely dead. Asked me to tread carefully, refused to let me film the interview. I agreed, although it was standard procedure to record all witness statements. Gotta say, afterwards, I couldn't decide if I was glad I hadn't been able to film it or not. I reassured her that I was trained in interviewing witnesses, that one of our specialist guys was on the way to do a follow-up interview. I just needed to know if there was anything specific he remembered that could help point us in the right direction.

They'd given him a private room, bright walls, full of kids' stuff. A *SpongeBob* mural, a stuffed giraffe that looked kind of creepy to me. The boy was lying flat on his back, a drip in his arm, you could see the abrasions where the saw-grass had sliced his skin (we all fell foul of that particular hazard in the days to come, let me tell you), but other than that, he'd suffered no other significant injuries. I still can't get over that. Like everyone said at first, it really did look like a miracle. They were prepping him for a CAT scan, and I knew I only had a few minutes.

The doctors hovering around his bed weren't happy to see me, and Pankowski stuck to my side as I approached his bed. He looked really fragile, specially with all those cuts on his upper arms and face, and sure, I felt bad about questioning him so soon after what he'd been through.

'Hiya, Bobby,' I said. 'My name is Ace. I'm an investigator.'

He didn't move a muscle. Pankowski's phone beeped and she stepped back.

'I sure am glad to see you're okay, Bobby,' I went on. 'If it's all right with you, I'd like to ask you a few questions.'

His eyes flipped open, looked straight into mine. They were empty. I couldn't tell if he was even hearing me.

'Hey,' I said. 'Good to see you're awake.'

He seemed to look right through me. Then... and listen, Elspeth, this is going to sound as hokey as hell, but they started to swim, like he was about to cry, only... Jesus... this is hard... they weren't filling with tears but with blood.

I guess I musta cried out, because next thing I know Pankowski's at my elbow and the staff are buzzing round the boy like hornets at a picnic.

And I said: 'What's wrong with his eyes?'

Pankowski looked at me as if I'd just sprouted another head.

I looked back at Bobby, stared right into his eyes, and they were clear – cornflower blue, not a trace of blood. Not a drop.

I'm often asked, 'Paul, why did you take on the full care of Jess? After all, you're a successful actor, an *artiste,* a single man with an erratic schedule, are you really cut out to be a parent?' The simple answer is this: just after the twins were born, Shelly and Stephen sat me down and asked me to be the twins' legal guardian if anything should happen to them. They'd thought long and hard about it – Shelly especially. Their close friends all had young families of their own, so wouldn't be able to give the girls the attention they deserved, and Shelly's family wasn't an option (for reasons I'll go into later). Besides, even when they were tots, Shelly said she could tell the girls doted on me. 'That's all Polly and Jess need, Paul,' she'd say. 'Love. And you've got buckets to spare.'

Stephen and Shelly knew all about my past of course. I'd gone off the rails a bit in my mid-twenties after a severe professional disappointment. I was in the middle of filming the pilot for *Bedside Manner*, which was being dubbed as the UK's next hot hospital drama, when I got the news they were cancelling the series. I'd won the part of the main character, Dr Malakai Bennett, a brilliant surgeon with Asperger's syndrome, a morphine addiction and a tendency towards paranoia, and the cancellation hit me hard. I'd done months of research for the role, really immersed myself in it, and I suppose part of the problem was that I'd internalised the character too much. Like so many artists before me, I turned to alcohol and other substances to blunt the pain. These factors mixed with the stress of an uncertain future caused an acute depression and what I suppose one would call a series of mild paranoid delusions.

But I'd dealt with those particular demons years before the girls were even a twinkle in Stephen's eye, so I can honestly say they really did think I was the best choice. Shelly insisted we make it legal, so off we popped to a solicitor and that was that. Of course, when you're asked to do something like this, you never think it's actually going to happen.

But I'm getting ahead of myself.

After I left that horrible room where we'd been funnelled by the inept Go!Go! staff, I spent the next half-hour in that airport pub just staring up at the screen as Sky's rolling banner repeated the terrible news over and over again. And then came the first footage of the area where they thought Stephen's plane had gone down: a shot of the ocean, grey and rolling, the occasional piece of debris bobbing in the waves. The rescue boats scouring the water for survivors looked like toys in that bleak endless seascape. I remember thinking: *Thank God Stephen and Shelly taught the girls to swim last summer.* Ridiculous, I know. Duncan Goodhew would have struggled in that swell. But in moments of emotional *extremis*, it's incredible what you cling to.

It was Mel who came and found me. She may smoke forty Rothmans a day and buy her clothes at Primark, but she and her partner Geoff have hearts as big as Canada. Like I said before, you can't judge a book by its cover.

'Come on, love,' Mel said to me. 'You can't give up hope.'

The yobs at the bar were giving me a wide berth, but they hadn't taken their eyes off me the entire time I was there. I was in a terrible state, sweating and shaking, and I must have been crying at one point as my cheeks were wet. 'What are you staring at?' Mel barked at them, then took my hand and led me back to the briefing room.

An army of psychologists and trauma counsellors had arrived by then. They were busy passing around tea that tasted like sweetened dishwater, and setting up screened-off counselling areas. Mel sat me protectively between her and Geoff: my own shell-suited bookends. Geoff patted my knee, said something like, 'We're all in this together, mate,' and handed me a fag. I hadn't smoked for years, but I took it gratefully.

No one told us not to smoke.

Kelvin, the fellow with the dreadlocks, and Kylie, the pretty redhead who'd been holding the balloon (now nothing but a squiggle of rubber on the floor), joined us. The fact that us five were the first to hear the news gave us a shared intimacy, and we huddled together, chain-smoking and trying not to implode. A nervy woman – a counsellor of some type, although she looked too high-strung for the role – asked us for the names of our relatives who'd been on the doomed flight. Like all the others, she had the 'we'll update you as soon as we know' line down pat. I understood, even then, that the last thing they wanted to do was give us false hope, but you *do* still hope. You can't help it. You start praying that your loved one missed the flight, that you've got the flight number or date of arrival wrong, that everything is just a dream, some loony nightmare scenario. I fixated on the moment before I first heard about the crash – watching those kids dismantle the long-forgotten Christmas tree (a bad omen if ever there was one, although I'm not superstitious) – and found myself longing to go back there, before the sick, empty feeling had taken up permanent residence in my heart.

Another panic attack started poking its icy fingers into my chest. Mel and Geoff tried to keep me talking while we waited to be assigned a trauma counsellor, but I couldn't get a word out, which wasn't like me at all. Geoff showed me the screensaver on his smart phone – a photograph of a grinning twentyish girl, overweight but attractive in her own way. Told me that she was Danielle, his daughter, the one they'd been there to collect. 'A bright girl, went through a rough patch but back on track now,' Geoff said glumly. Danielle had been in Tenerife on a lavish hen party escapade, had only decided to go along at the last minute when someone else dropped out. How's that for fate?

I was struggling to breathe by now, cold sweat dribbling down my sides. I knew if I didn't get out of that room immediately, my head would explode.

Mel understood. 'Give me your number, love,' she said, squeezing my knee with a hand weighted down with gold jewellery. 'Soon as we know more, we'll let you know.' We swapped numbers (I couldn't remember mine at first) and I ran out of there. One of the counsellors tried to stop me, but Mel shouted, 'Just let him go if he wants to.'

How I managed to pay for my parking and make it back to Hoxton without sliding under a lorry on the M23 is a mystery. Another complete blank. Later, I saw that I'd parked Stephen's Audi with its front wheels on the kerb as if it was a discarded joyride vehicle.

I only came to when I stumbled into the hallway, sending the table we use for post flying. One of the Polish students who lived in the ground floor flat popped his head around his door and asked me if I was okay. He must've seen that I wasn't because when I asked him if he had any alcohol, he disappeared for a few seconds, then wordlessly handed me a bottle of cheap vodka.

I ran into my flat, knowing full well that I was about to fall off the wagon. And I didn't care.

I didn't bother with a glass, I drank the vodka straight out of the bottle. I couldn't taste it. I was shaking, twitching, my hands were tingling. I dug out my BlackBerry, scrolled through my contacts, but I didn't know who to call.

Because the first person I always called when I was in trouble was Stephen.

I paced.

Downed more alcohol.

Gagged.

Then I sat on the sofa and switched on the flat screen.

Normal programming had been suspended in favour of ongoing reports on the crashes. I was numb – and by that stage, well past half-cut – but I gathered that air traffic had been grounded, and more pundits than you could shake a stick at were being ferried into the Sky studio to be interviewed by a grim-faced Kenneth Porter. I can't even hear Kenneth Porter's voice these days without feeling physically sick.

Sky concentrated on the Go!Go! crash, it being the one that was closest to home. A couple on a cruise liner had caught shaky footage of the plane flying dangerously low above the ocean, and Sky repeated it endlessly. The moment of impact was off camera, thank God, but in the background you could hear a woman's voice shrieking, 'Oh my gawd, Larry! Larry! Look at this!'

There was a number people could call if they were concerned their relatives might have been on the flight, and I vaguely thought about dialling it, before thinking, what's the point? When Kenneth Porter wasn't quizzing air safety officials or grimly introducing another repeat of the cruise ship couple's coup, Sky turned its attention to the other crashes. When I heard about Bobby, the boy who'd been found in the Florida Everglades, and the three survivors of the Japanese disaster, I remember thinking, it *could* happen. It could. They could be alive.

I drained the rest of the bottle in one gulp.

I watched a clip of a naked Japanese boy being lifted into a helicopter; footage of a traumatised African man screaming about his family, while behind him toxic black smoke roiled. I watched that crash investigator – the one who looks a little bit like Captain America – urging people not to panic. I watched a clearly shaken airline exec report that flights had been cancelled until further notice.

I must have passed out. When I came round, Kenneth Porter had been replaced by a slick brunette anchor wearing a ghastly yellow blouse (I'll never forget that blouse). My head was throbbing and nausea was threatening to overwhelm me, so when she said that reports were coming in about a Go!Go! passenger being found alive, at first I thought my mind was playing tricks on me.

Then it hit me. A child. They'd found a child clinging to a piece of wreckage a couple of miles from where they thought Stephen's plane had gone down. You couldn't see much from the helicopter footage at first – a group of guys on a fishing boat waving their arms; a small figure in a bright yellow life jacket.

I tried not to get my hopes up, but there was a close-up as she was lifted into a helicopter and I knew in my gut that it was one of the twins. You know your own.

I called Mel first. Didn't think twice. 'Leave it to me, love,' she said. I didn't stop to think how she must be feeling.

It felt like the family liaison team were there in seconds, as if they'd been hanging around outside my door. The trauma counsellor, Peter (I never did catch his last name), a little grey man with specs and a goatee, sat me down and talked me through everything. Warned me not to get my hopes up, 'We have to be sure it's her, Paul.' Asked me if he could contact my friends and family, 'for added support'. I thought about calling Gerry, but decided against it. Stephen, Shelly and the girls *were* my family. I had friends, but they weren't really the type you can lean on in a crisis, although later they all tried to muscle in, eager to grab their fifteen minutes of fame. That sounds bitter, I know, but you find out who your real friends are when life as you know it falls apart.

I wanted to fly out straight away to be with her, but Peter assured me she would be medivacced to England as soon as she was stabilised. I'd completely forgotten that all European planes had been grounded. For the time being, she was being assessed in a Portuguese hospital.

When he thought I was calm enough to actually hear the details, he told me gently that it looked as if there might have been a fire on board before the pilot was forced to ditch, and Jess (or Polly – we didn't know which twin she was at that stage) had been injured. But it was hypothermia they were most concerned about. They took a DNA swab from me to be sure that she really was one of the twins. There's nothing quite as surreal as having the inside of your cheek rubbed with a giant ear bud while wondering if you're the only surviving member of your family.

Weeks later, at one of our first 277 Together meetings, Mel told me that when they heard Jess had been found, she and Geoff didn't give up hope for weeks, not even after they started finding the bodies. She said that she kept imagining Danielle washed up on an island, waiting to be rescued. When air traffic was back to normal, Go!Go! offered to charter a special plane to fly the relatives out to the Portuguese coast, which was the closest they could get to the scene of the crash. I didn't go – I had my hands full with Jess – but most of 277 Together went. I still hate the thought of Mel and Geoff looking out over that ocean, feeling a sliver of hope that their daughter might still be alive.

There must have been a leak inside Go!Go! as the phone rang off the hook from the moment it was confirmed that one of the twins had survived. Whether the hacks were from the *Sun* or the *Independent*, they all asked the same questions: 'How do you feel?' 'Do you think it's a miracle?' To be honest, dealing with their incessant questions took my mind off my grief, which would come in waves, sparked off by the most innocuous thing – a car advert showing an impossibly groomed mother and child; even those toilet paper commercials with the puppies and multicultural toddlers. When I wasn't fielding calls, I was glued to the news like pretty much the rest of the world. They ruled out terrorism early on, but every channel had experts galore speculating about what the causes might be. And like Mel and Geoff, I suppose I couldn't murder the hope that somewhere, out there, Stephen was still alive.

Two days later, Jess was moved to a private hospital in London where she could get specialist care. Her burns weren't severe, but there was the constant spectre of infection, and although the MRI scan showed zero sign of neurological damage, she still hadn't opened her eyes.

The hospital staff were great, really supportive, and they showed me to a private room where I could wait until the doctor gave me the go-ahead to see her. Still swamped with a feeling of unreality, I sat on a Laura Ashley sofa and flipped through a *Heat* magazine. Everyone says they can't understand how the world can just keep turning after someone you love has died, and that's exactly how I felt as I paged through images of celebrities snapped without their make-up on. I dozed off.

I was awoken by a commotion outside in the corridor, a man's voice shouting, 'Wotcha mean we can't see her?', a woman screeching, 'But we're her family!' My heart sank. I knew immediately who they were: Shelly's mum – Marilyn Adams – and two sons, Jason ('call me Jase') and Keith. Stephen had dubbed them the 'Addams Family' long ago for obvious reasons. Shelly had done her best to cut ties with them when she left home, but she felt obliged to invite them to her and Stephen's wedding, which was the last time I'd had the pleasure of their company. Stephen was as liberal as they come, but he used to joke that it was compulsory for an Adams to spend at least three years in Wormwood Scrubs. I know I'm going to come across as simply the most awful snob, but really, they were a walking chav cliché, right down to the casual benefit fraud, the dodgy fags they sold on the side and the souped-up motor in the council house driveway. Jase and Keith – aka Fester and Gomez – had even named their kids (an army of them, spawned by a coterie of different mothers) after the latest celebrity or footballers' kid trends. I believe there was even one called Brooklyn.

Hearing them screeching in the corridor took me right back to Stephen and Shelly's wedding day, which, thanks to the Addams Family, would be remembered by everyone for all the wrong reasons. Stephen had asked me to be his best man, and I'd brought along my then boyfriend, Prakesh, as my plus one. Shelly's mum had shown up in a pink polyester nightmare of a dress that gave her an uncanny resemblance to Peppa Pig, and Fester and Gomez had eschewed their usual knock-off leather jackets and trainers for ill-fitting off-the-peg suits. Shelly had worked hard to organise that wedding; she and Stephen didn't have a lot of cash to throw around back then, it was before they did well in their respective careers. But she'd saved and scrimped and they'd managed to book a minor country house for the reception. At first the two halves of the family kept to their own territory. Shelly's family on one side, me, Prakesh and Stephen and Shelly's friends on the other. Two different worlds.

Stephen said afterwards he wished he'd put a cap on the bar. After the speeches (Marilyn's was a moribund disaster) Prakesh and I stood up to dance. I can even remember the song: "Careless Whisper."

'Oy oy,' one of the brothers yelled above the music. 'Bum me a fag.'

'Fucking poufs,' the other one joined in.

Prakesh wasn't one to take an insult lying down. There wasn't even a verbal altercation. One minute we were dancing, the next, he was nutting the closest Adams to hand. The police were called, but no one was arrested. It ruined the wedding, of course, and the relationship; Prakesh and I split up shortly afterwards.

It was almost a blessing that Mum and Dad weren't

there to witness it. They died in a car crash when Stephen and I were in our early twenties. They left us enough to see us through the next few years; Dad was good like that.

Still, when the Addamses were shown into the waiting room by an intimidated nurse, one of the brothers, Jase I think it was, had the grace to look shamefaced when he saw me, I'll give him that. 'No hard feelings, mate,' he said. 'We got to stick together at a time like this, innit.'

'My Shelly,' Marilyn was sobbing. She went on and on about only finding out when a tabloid leaked the passenger list. 'I didn't even know they was going on holiday! Who goes on holiday in January?'

Jason and Keith passed the time flicking through their phones while Marilyn blubbered – I knew Shelly would have been horrified knowing they were part of this. But I was determined that for Jess's sake, there wouldn't be a scene.

'Popping out for a fag, Mum,' Jase said, and the other one sloped out after him, leaving me alone with the matriarch herself.

'Well, what do you think about this, then, Paul,' she started in. 'Terrible business. My Shelly just gone.'

I mumbled something about being sorry for her loss, but I'd lost my brother, my twin, my best friend and I was hardly in a state to give her any real sympathy.

'Whichever one of the girls they've found, she'll have to move in with me and the boys,' Marilyn continued. 'She can share Jordan and Paris's room.' A massive sigh. 'Unless we move into their house of course.'

Now wasn't the time to inform Marilyn about Shelly's custody decision, but I found myself blurting: 'What makes you think you're going to look after her?'

'Where else will she go?'

'What about me?'

Her chins quivered in indignation. 'You? But you're a...you're an *actor*.'

'She's ready,' the nurse said, appearing at the door and interrupting our delightful tête-à-tête. 'You can see her now. But five minutes only.'

Even Marilyn had the nous to realise that now wasn't the time to have this sort of fraught conversation.

We were given greens and face masks (where they found ones big enough for Marilyn's bulk I'll never know) and then we followed the nurse into a room designed to look like a hotel suite, all flowery sofas and state-of-the-art television, the illusion only partially broken by the fact that Jess was surrounded by heart monitors, drips and various other intimidating pieces of equipment. Her eyes were shut and she barely seemed to be breathing. Dressings covered most of her face.

'Is it Jess or Polly?' Marilyn asked no one in particular.

I knew straight away which twin she was. 'It's Jess,' I said.

'How the fu—how can you be so sure? Her face is covered,' Marilyn whined.

It was her hair, you see. Jess's fringe had a chunk cut out of it. Just before they'd left for the holiday, Shelly had caught Jess hacking away at it, trying to copy Missy K's latest half-shorn style. Plus, Jess had the tiniest scar just above her right eyebrow from when she'd fallen against the mantelpiece when she was learning to walk.

She looked so tiny, so vulnerable, lying there. And I swore, right then, I'd do anything I could to protect her.

Angela Dumiso, who is originally from the Eastern Cape, was living in Khayelitsha township with her sister and two-year-old daughter when Dalu Air Flight 467 went down. She agreed to speak to me in April 2012.

I was in the laundry room doing the ironing when I first heard about it. I was working hard to finish in time so that I could catch my taxi at four, so I was already stressed – the boss is very fussy and liked everything, even his socks, to be ironed. The madam ran into the kitchen and I could see by her expression that there was a problem. She usually only wore that face when one of her cats had brought in a rodent and she needed me to clean it up. 'Angela,' she said. 'I've just heard on *Cape Talk*, something's happened in Khayelitsha. Isn't that where you live?'

I said yes, and asked her what it was – I assumed it must be another shack fire or trouble from a strike. She told me that from what she could gather, a plane had crashed. Together we hurried into the sitting room and switched on the television. It was all over the news and at first it was difficult for me to understand what I was seeing. Most of the clips just showed people running and screaming, balloons of black smoke billowing around them. But then I heard the words that chilled my heart. The reporter, a young white woman with frightened eyes, said that a church near Sector Five had been completely destroyed when the plane hit the ground.

My daughter Susan's crèche was in a church in that area.

Of course, my first thought was that I must contact

Busi, my sister, but I was out of airtime. The madam let me use her cellphone, but there was no answer; it went straight to voicemail. I was starting to feel sick, even light-headed. Busi always answers her phone. Always.

'Madam,' I said, 'I have to leave. I have to get home.' I was praying that Busi had decided to collect Susan, my daughter, from crèche early. It was Busi's day off from the factory, and sometimes she did this so that they could spend the afternoon together. When I left at five that morning to catch the taxi to the Northern suburbs, Busi was still fast asleep, Susan by her side. I tried to keep that image – Busi and Susan safe together – in my mind. That's what I concentrated on. I only started to pray later on.

The madam (her real name is Mrs Clara van der Spuy, but the boss likes me to call her 'madam', which made Busi furious) said straight away that she would take me.

While I collected my bag, I could hear her having a fight with the boss on her cellphone. 'Johannes doesn't want me to take you,' she said to me. 'But he can go jump. I'd never live with myself if I let you catch a taxi.'

She didn't stop talking all the way there, only pausing when I had to interrupt to give her directions. My stress levels were now making me feel physically ill; I could feel the pie that I'd eaten for lunch turning into a stone in my stomach. As we made it onto the N2 highway, I could see black smoke drifting into the air in the distance. Within a few kilometres, I could smell it. 'I'm sure it's going to be fine, Angela,' the madam kept saying. 'Khayelitsha is a big place, isn't it?' She turned on the radio; the newscaster was talking about other plane crashes that had occurred elsewhere in the world. 'Blerrie terrorists,' the madam swore. As we approached the Baden Powell road exit, the traffic thickened. We were surrounded by hooting taxis full of frightened faces, people, like me, desperate to get home. Ambulances and fire trucks screamed past us. The madam was beginning to look nervous; she was far out of her comfort zone. The police had set up roadblocks to try and prevent more vehicles getting into the area and I knew I would have to join the crowd and make my way to my section on foot.

'Go home, madam,' I said, and I could see the relief on her face. I didn't blame her. It was hell. The air was thick with ash and already the smoke was making my eyes sting.

I jumped out of the car and ran towards the crowds fighting to get through the barricade they had set up across the road. The people around me were shouting and screaming, and I joined my voice to theirs. '*Intombiyam*! My daughter is in there!' The police were forced to let us through when an ambulance came racing towards us and needed to get out.

I ran. I have never run so fast in my whole life, but I didn't feel tired – the fear pushed me onwards. People would emerge through the smoke, some of them covered in blood, and I'm ashamed to say I did not stop to help them. I concentrated on moving forward although at times it was difficult to see where I was walking. Sometimes that was almost a blessing as I saw . . . I saw flags stuck into the ground and blue plastic bags covering shapes – shapes that I knew were body parts. Fires raged everywhere and fire-fighters in masks were busy cordoning off other areas. People were being physically restrained from going in any further. But I was still too far away from the street where I lived – I needed to get closer. The smoke scorched my lungs, made my eyes stream, and every so often there would be a pop as something exploded. My skin was soon bathed in filth. The scene looked completely wrong, and I wondered if I had wandered into an unfamiliar area. I was looking for the top of the church, but it was not there. The smell – like a spit-braai mixed with burning fuel – made me vomit. I dropped to my knees. I knew I couldn't go any closer if I wanted to carry on breathing.

It was one of the paramedics who found me. He looked exhausted, his blue overalls soaked with blood. All I could say to him was: 'My daughter. I need to find my daughter.'

Why he chose to help me, I do not know. There were so many other people who needed help. He led me towards his ambulance and I sat in the front seat while he got on his radio. Within minutes, a Red Cross kombi arrived, and the driver motioned me to squeeze inside. Like me, the people inside it were all filthy, covered in ash; most wore the expressions of the deeply traumatised. A woman at the back stared silently out of the window, a sleeping child in her arms. The old man next to me shook silently; there were tear tracks on his dirty cheeks. '*Molweni*,' I whispered to him, '*kuzolunga*.' I was telling him that everything would be all right, but I didn't believe it myself. All I could do was pray, making deals with God in my head so that Susan and Busi would be spared.

We passed by the tent filled with the dead. I tried not to look at it. I could see people hefting the bodies – more of those shapes covered in blue plastic – inside it. And I prayed even harder that they did not contain the bodies of Busi or Susan.

We were driven to the Mew Way community hall. I

was supposed to sign my name at the entrance, but I just pushed past the officials and ran for the doors.

Even from outside, I could hear the sound of crying. It was chaos inside there. The centre was full of people huddled in groups, covered in soot and bandages. Some were crying, others looked deeply shocked, staring ahead sightlessly, like the people in the kombi. I began to push my way through the crowd. How would I ever find Busi and Susan in this mass? I saw Noliswa, one of my neighbours, who sometimes looked after Susan. Her face was thick with blood and black dirt. She was rocking back and forth and when I tried to ask her about Busi and Susan she just looked blank; the light had gone out of her eyes. Later, I found out that two of her grandchildren had been at the crèche when the plane had crashed into it.

And then I heard a voice saying, 'Angie?'

I turned around slowly. And saw Busi standing with Susan in her arms.

I screamed, '*Niphilile*! You are alive!' over and over again.

We stood and held each other – Susan wriggling, I was squeezing her too tight – for the longest time. I hadn't given up hope, but the relief that they were okay...I will never feel anything that powerful again in my lifetime. When we both stopped crying, Busi told me what had happened. She said she had collected Susan from crèche early, and instead of going straight home, had decided to walk to the spaza for sugar. She said the sound of the impact was incredible – they thought at first it must be a bomb. She said she just grabbed Susan and ran as fast as she could away from that sound and away from the explosions. If she had gone home, they would have been killed.

Because our home was gone. Everything we owned had been incinerated.

We stayed in the hall while we waited to be allocated to a shelter. Some of us put up partitions, hanging sheets and blankets from the roof to make makeshift rooms. So many people had lost their homes, but it was the children I felt for the most. The ones who had lost their parents or grandparents. There were so many of them, many of them *amagweja* [refugee children] who had already suffered during the xenophobic attacks four years ago. They had already seen too much.

One boy sticks in my mind. On that first night, I couldn't sleep. The adrenaline still hadn't left my body and I suppose I was still dealing with the after-effects of what I had seen that day. I stood up to stretch and I felt the weight of someone staring at me. On a blanket next to where Busi, Susan and I were lying sat a boy. I'd barely noticed him before – I was too caught up in caring for Susan and queuing for food and water. Even in the dark I could see the pain and loneliness shining in his eyes. He was alone on his blanket; I could see no sign of a parent or a grandparent. I wondered why the welfare people had not taken him to the unaccompanied children's section.

I asked him where his mother was. He did not react. I sat next to him and took him in my arms. He leaned against me, but although he didn't cry or sob, his body was like a dead weight. When I thought he was asleep, I laid him down and crept back to my blanket.

The next day, we heard we were to be moved to a hotel that was donating its rooms to those of us who had lost their homes. I looked around for the boy; I had some idea that perhaps he could come with us, but I couldn't find him anywhere. We stayed in the hotel for two weeks, and when my sister was offered a job at a large bakery near to Masiphumele, I went to work with her. Again, I was lucky. It is much better than being a domestic. The bakery has a crèche and I can take Susan to work with me every morning.

Later, when all the Americans came out to South Africa to look for that fourth child, an investigator – a Xhosa man, not one of the bounty hunters from overseas – tracked me and Busi down and asked us if we had seen a particular child in that hall where we were taken. He matched the description of the boy I had seen that first night, but I didn't tell the man that I'd seen him. I'm not sure why. I think in my heart I knew it would be better for him if he wasn't found. I could see that the investigator knew I was hiding something, but I still listened to the voice inside me that told me to keep quiet.

And…he may not have even been the boy they were looking for. There were many *intandane* [orphaned children], and the boy did not tell me his name.

Private First Class Samuel 'Sammy' Hockemeier of the III Marine Expeditionary Force, based at Camp Courtney on Okinawa Island, agreed to talk to me via Skype after he returned to the US in June 2012.

I met Jake when we were both deployed to Okinawa in 2011. I'm from Fairfax, Virginia, and it turned out that he grew up in Annandale, so we became buddies straight away. Found out that in high school I'd even played football against his brother a couple of times. Before we went into that forest he was just a regular guy, nothing special, quieter than most, had a sense of humour that could pass right by you unless you were paying attention. He was a smallish guy, five eight, maybe five nine – those photographs that were all over the Internet made him look bigger than he actually was. Bigger *and* meaner. Both of us got into computer games when we were there, they're big on base, kind of got addictive. That's the worst I could say about him – till he flipped the fuck out, I mean.

We'd both signed up for III MEF's Humanitarian Aid corps, and in early January we heard that our battalion was going to be deployed to Fuji Camp for training – a full-on disaster reconstruction. Jake and I were pretty upbeat when we heard about that. A couple of anti-terrorism marines we'd gone up against at one of the game cons had just come back from there. They said Katemba, one of the nearby towns, was a cool place to hang out in; had a joint where you could drink and eat all you liked for 3000 yen. We were also hoping to get a chance to head into Tokyo and check out the culture. You don't see much of it on

Okinawa, on account of it being seven hundred clicks from mainland Japan. The view from Courtney is awesome, looks right over the ocean, but you can get sick of looking at that day in day out, and a lot of the natives on the island don't have a high opinion of the marines. Some of this is down to the Girard incident – that marine who accidentally shot a local woman who was collecting scrap metal from the firing range – and that gang rape back in the nineties. I wouldn't say the locals were actively hostile, but you could tell a lot of them didn't want us there.

Fuji Camp itself is okay. Small, but the training area is cool. Got to say it was colder than a witch's tit when we arrived there. Lots of mist, ton of rain; we were lucky it didn't snow. Our CO told us we'd be spending the first few days preparing equipment for the deployment to the North Fuji Manoeuvre area, but we'd barely settled into barracks when the news about Black Thursday started filtering in. First one we heard about was the Florida crash. Couple of the guys were from there and their families and girlfriends emailed them the latest news. When we heard about the UK plane, and the one in Africa, you should have heard the rumours that were flying around. Lot of us assumed it was terrorists, another rag-head reprisal maybe, and we were convinced we'd be deployed straight back to Okinawa. It's kinda ironic, considering where we were, but the last one we heard about was the Sun Air disaster – none of us could believe it had happened so close to where we were based. Like everyone else, Jake and I were glued to the Internet that night. That's how we heard about those survivors, the flight attendant and the kid. The connection was bad for a while, but we managed to download a You-Tube clip of that kid being hoisted into a helicopter. We were bummed when we heard that one of the survivors had died en route to the hospital. It's freaky to think about it now, but I remember Jake saying, 'Shit, I hope it wasn't that kid.' This is going to sound bad, but knowing there was also an American on board, and that she didn't make it, made the Sun Air crash seem more real to us. The fact that one of our own had gone down.

On the Friday morning, my CO said they needed volunteers from the Humanitarian Aid div to help secure the area and clear a landing pad for the search and rescue helicopters so they could get closer to the site. In the briefing meeting, he told us that hundreds of distraught family members had flocked to the site and were interfering with the operation. The press were also turning the whole thing into a clusterfuck; some of them even got lost or injured in the forest and had to be rescued. I was surprised the Japanese wanted us involved. Sure, the US and Japan have an understanding, but the locals are big on doing things their way; guess it's a matter of pride. But the CO said they'd been criticised for dropping the ball after that bullet train crash in the late nineties; didn't get their act together fast enough, waited while the wheels of bureaucracy turned, would only act when a superior told them what to do, that kind of thing. Cost lives.

I stepped up right away and Jake did too. We were told we'd be working in tandem with a bunch of guys from the nearby JGSDF camp and Yoji, this GSDF private who was assigned as our translator, started telling us about the forest en route. He said it had a really bad rep because of the number of people who had killed themselves there. Told us that there had been so many suicides that the cops had been forced to set up cameras on the trees and that the place was full of unidentified bodies that had been there for years. He said the locals stayed away from it because they believed it was haunted by the spirits of the angry dead or some shit like that, souls that couldn't rest or whatever. I don't know much about Japanese spirituality, just that they believe the souls of animals are in pretty much anything, from people to chairs or whatever, but that sounded way too hokey to be anything but bullshit. Most of us started cracking jokes, messing around, but Jake didn't say a word.

Got to say, the Search and Rescue and the GSDF guys hadn't done a bad job of securing the scene, considering what they had to deal with, but they were seriously out-manned. No way they could control the number of people who were milling around outside the morgue tents. After we were briefed, Jake, me, some of our squadron and a bunch of GSDF guys were sent straight to the main crash site. The rest of the division were deployed to secure the temporary morgue tents, help ferry the supplies and set up latrines.

Our CO told us that SAR and the JTSB guys had mapped where most of the bodies had fallen on impact and now they were bringing them down to the tents. I know you're mostly interested in Jake, but I'll give you an idea of what it was like. When I was at school, we'd stud-ied this old song, 'Strange Fruit'. About the lynchings that went on in the Deep South. How the bodies hanging from the trees looked like strange fruit. That's what we saw. That's what some of those freaky trees were holding as we got closer to where the body of the plane had landed. Only most of the bodies weren't whole. Couple of the guys puked, but me and Jake maintained.

Kinda worse than this were the civilians who were

stumbling around the scene, calling for their parents or families or loved ones. Most of them had brought offerings – food or flowers. Later, Yoji, who was assigned to help round them up and get them away from the site, told me that he came across one couple who were so convinced their son was still alive, they'd brought him a change of clothes.

Jake and I were sent to help the guys clear the trees for the helicopter pad, and although it was tough going, it was away from the wreckage and it took our minds off what we'd seen. The NTSB guys didn't make it till the next day, but by then things were far more organised.

Our CO said we were to stay at the site that night and we were assigned sleeping quarters in one of the GSDF's tents. None of us were happy about that. There wasn't a private there who wasn't feeling spooked about spending a night in that forest. And not just because of what we'd seen that day. We even spoke in whispers; it didn't feel right to raise our voices. A few of the guys tried to crack jokes, but they all fell flat.

Round about three hundred hours, I was woken by a scream. Sounded like it was coming from outside the tent. Bunch of us leaped up and ran out. Shit, my adrenaline was just pumping. Couldn't see much – the air was full of mist.

One of the guys – I think it was Johnny, this black dude from Atlanta, good guy – pulled out his flashlight and shone it around. The light was wobbling 'cause his hand was shaking. It settled on this shape a few yards from where we were standing: a figure, its back to us, kneeling down. It turned to look at us and I saw it was Jake.

I asked him what the fuck was going on. He looked dazed, shook his head. 'I saw them,' he said. 'I saw them. The people with no feet.'

I got him back into the tent and he fell asleep straight away. The next morning he refused to talk about what had happened.

I didn't tell Jakey this, but when I told Yoji about it, he said, 'Japanese ghosts don't have feet.' And he told me that the Japanese witching hour – the *ushi-mitsu*, no way can I forget that word – was 3 a.m. Got to admit, I got spooked again when I heard Pamela May Donald's message. Stuff she said, well, it sounded too similar to what Jake said that night. I guess I assumed he'd been influenced by what Yoji had told us.

The other guys busted Jake's balls about it for weeks afterwards of course. Carried on even when we got back to Camp Courtney. You know the kind of thing: 'You seen any dead people today, Jakey?' Jake just took it. I guess it was around that time that he'd started emailing that pastor down in Texas. Before then, he was never into religion. Never once heard him mention God or Jesus. Guess he must have done some Googling about the forest and the crashes, come across that pastor's website.

Jake didn't deploy with the rest of the unit when we were sent to help with the rescue effort after the floods in the Philippines; he got sick, really sick. Stomach pains, suspected appendicitis. Course, now they think he was faking it. They still don't know how he got off the island. Reckon he must've bribed a fishing boat or whaler to take him, something like that; maybe one of the Taiwanese crews who smuggle eel fry or meth in the area.

I'd give anything to go back in time, ma'am. Stop Jake going into that forest. I know there's nothing I could have done, but for some reason, even now, I feel responsible for what he did to that Japanese kid.

Chiyoko Kamamoto, the eighteen-year-old cousin of Sun Air 678's only surviving passenger, Hiro Yanagida, first met Ryu Takami on the forum of a popular online role-playing game. The majority of the players are *otaku* (slang for geeks or obsessives) in their teens or twenties, and as one of the few female gamers, Chiyoko became extremely popular.

It's a mystery why Chiyoko chose Ryu, an under-achiever and hikikomori (recluse) as her chat buddy, although this has been the subject of endless speculation. Until events overtook them, the pair messaged each other every day, sometimes for hours. The messages were retrieved from Chiyoko's computer and smart phone after her disappearance, and leaked onto the Internet.

The original was written predominantly in 'chat speak', but for ease of reading and consistency, with the exception of Ryu's use of emoji (emoticons), this has been modified. Translation by Eric Kushan.

(Chiyoko refers to her mother, with whom she had a frosty relationship, as 'Mother Creature' or 'MC'. 'Android Uncle' or 'AU' denotes Kenji Yanagida, Chiyoko's uncle and one of Japan's most celebrated robotics experts.)

Message logged @ 15.30, 14/01/2012

CHIYOKO: Ryu, you there?

RYU: (｡･ω･) Where you been?

CHIYOKO: Don't ask. Mother Creature 'needed' me again. Did you hear? The flight attendant. She died in hospital an hour ago. That means Hiro is the only survivor.

RYU: It's all over 2-chan. So sad. How is Hiro?

CHIYOKO: He's okay, I think. A dislocated collarbone, scratches; that's all as far as I know.

RYU: So lucky.

CHIYOKO: That's what Mother Creature keeps saying. 'A miracle.' She's set up a temporary altar for Auntie Hiromi. I don't know where she got the photograph of her from. MC never liked Auntie, but you'd never know that now. 'Such a shame, she was so pretty, so serene, such a good mother.' All lies. She was always saying Auntie was stuck up.

RYU: Did you find out what they were doing in Tokyo? Your aunt and Hiro, I mean.

CHIYOKO: Yeah. MC says Auntie Hiromi and Hiro were visiting an old school friend. I can tell that MC's pissed that Auntie didn't visit when she was here, but she won't say it out loud, it wouldn't be *respectful*.

RYU: Have any reporters tried to talk to you? That footage of them trying to climb over the hospital walls to get pics of the survivors was crazy – you hear about the one that fell off the roof? There's a clip of it on Nico Nico. What a moron!

CHIYOKO: Not yet. But they found out where my father works. Not even something like this, the death of a sister, is enough for him to take a day off work. He refused to speak to them. But it's Android Uncle they're really interested in, of course.

RYU: I still can't believe you're related to Kenji Yanagida! Or that you didn't tell me when we first met – I would have bragged about it to the whole world.

CHIYOKO: How would that have sounded? Hey, I'm Chiyoko, and guess what? I'm related to the Android Man. It would've sounded like I was trying to impress you.

RYU: You impress *me*? It should be the other way round.

CHIYOKO: You're not going to start all that self-pitying stuff again, are you?

RYU: Don't worry, you've got me out of that bad habit. So…what is he really like? I need details.

CHIYOKO: I told you. I don't really know him. Last time I saw him was when he, Hiro and Auntie Hiromi came for New Year two years ago, just after we got back from the US, but they didn't stay over and I only said about three words to him. Auntie was really pretty, but quite distant. I liked Hiro though, cute kid. MC says Android Uncle might come and stay with us while Hiro is at the hospital. I don't think she's happy about it. I overheard her saying to Father that Android Uncle is as cold as his robot.

RYU: Really? But he comes across as really funny and cool in that documentary.

CHIYOKO: Which one? There's like a thousand.

RYU: Can't remember. You want me to look it up for you?

CHIYOKO: Don't bother. But how you are on camera might be different to how you *really* are. I think it's a genetic thing.

RYU: What is? Being on camera?

CHIYOKO: No! Being cold. Like me. I'm not normal. I'm cold. A sliver of ice in my heart.

RYU: Chiyoko, the ice princess.

CHIYOKO: Chiyoko, the yuki-onna.

CHIYOKO: So we've established I have an ice princess genetic condition that can only be cured by…
what?

RYU: Fame? Money?

CHIYOKO: That's why I like you, Ryu, you always have the right answer. I thought you were going to say love and then I was going to be sick.

RYU: o(_ _)o What's wrong with love?

CHIYOKO: It doesn't exist outside of bad American movies.

RYU: You are not completely cold. I know you aren't.

CHIYOKO: Then why do I not care more? Listen, I'll prove it. How many people died in the Sun Air crash?

RYU: 525. No, 526.

CHIYOKO: 526. Yes. Including my own aunt. But all I'm feeling is relief.

RYU: ??(•_•*)

CHIYOKO: Okay…let me explain. Since the crash, since she heard about Auntie Hiromi and Hiro, MC hasn't been on my back about going back to cram school once. Is that a bad thing to think? That because of someone's tragedy I get some peace in my personal life?

RYU: Hey you have a personal life. That's something. Look at me.

CHIYOKO: Ha! I knew it was too good to last. Never mind, you can be my own personal hikikomori. I like to picture you locked in your small room, the curtains shutting out the light, chain-smoking and messaging me when you get tired of playing Ragnarok.

RYU: I am not a hikikomori. And I don't play Ragnarok.

CHIYOKO: Didn't we say we would always be honest with each other? I told you what I was.

RYU: I just don't like that word.

CHIYOKO: Are you going to sulk now?

RYU: _|7O

CHIYOKO: ORZ????? Neraa! How long have you been saving that one up? Do people even use that any more? You sure you're really 22 and not 38 or something? And when are you going to grow out of posting all that ascii shit?

RYU: <(_ _)> Let's change the subject. Hey... when are you going to tell me about your life in the States?

CHIYOKO: Not again. Why do you want to know so badly?

RYU: Just interested. Do you miss it?

CHIYOKO: No. It doesn't matter where you live, the world's messed up. Another subject please.

RYU: Okaaaay... The message boards are still going wild about why the plane crashed into Jukai. There's this whole theory that the captain crashed it on purpose. The suicide captain.

CHIYOKO: I know. That's old news, it's everywhere. What do you think?

RYU: I don't know. Some of the things they are saying might be true. The forest does have a history and it's miles off the Osaka route, why crash there?

CHIYOKO: Maybe he didn't want to land in a populated area. Maybe he was trying to save more lives that way. I feel bad for his wife.

RYU: *You* feel bad? I thought you were the ice princess.

CHIYOKO: I can still feel bad for her. Anyway, that Sun Air corporate drone mouthpiece said the captain was one of their best and most reliable, that he would never have done something like that. Also, they said he had no money worries, so he didn't need the insurance and his medical showed he was in good health.

RYU: They could be lying. And anyway, maybe he was possessed. Maybe he was *made* to do it.

CHIYOKO: Ha! Brought down by hungry ghosts.

RYU: But you have to admit… Why so many planes on the same day? There has to be a reason.

CHIYOKO: Like what? Don't tell me, a sign that we're facing the end of the world?

RYU: Why not? It is 2012.

CHIYOKO: You've been spending *way* too much time on conspiracy sites, Ryu. And we'd know by now if it was terrorism.

RYU: Can the real Chiyoko come back now please? You are the one who is always saying the government and the press use us like pawns and lie to us.

CHIYOKO: Doesn't mean I have to believe some half-baked conspiracy theory. Life isn't like that. It's dull. The politicians lie to us, of course they do. How else are we going to be their little good soldiers and not step out of line?

RYU: You really think they'd tell us the truth if it was terrorists?

CHIYOKO: I just said they lie to us. But some secrets are too big even for them to hide. Maybe in the US, but not here. The cover-up would have to go through eight levels of bureaucracy first to be approved. People are so lame. Do they not have better things to do than talk all day about conspiracy theories? Malign a dead man who was more than likely trying to save as many people as he could?

RYU: Hey…I'm really getting worried now. Could the ice princess be thawing? Is this a sign she really cares after all?

CHIYOKO: I don't care…Okay, I half care. But it still makes me mad. The freaks on the conspiracy sites are as bad as the useless girls who witter all day on Mixi. Can you imagine what would happen if they spent as much energy talking about the things that really matter?

RYU: Like what?

CHIYOKO: Changing the system. Stopping the nepotism, stopping people turning into slaves. Stopping people dying, people being bullied…all of that stuff.

RYU: Chiyoko the ice princess revolutionary.

CHIYOKO: I'm serious. Go to school, go to cram school, study hard, make your parents proud, get into Keio, go to work every day for eighteen hours straight, don't stray, don't complain, don't be a non-conformist. Too many don'ts.

RYU: You know I agree with you, Chiyoko. Look at me…But what can we do?

CHIYOKO: Nothing. There's nothing we can do. Just suck it up or drop out or die. Poor Hiro. He has a lot to look forward to.

RYU: (_ _) ....o

TRANSLATOR'S NOTES:

Ascii: The term for text art (such as that used by Ryu above). It was popularised on forums such as 2-channel.

ORZ: A popular Japanese emoji or emoticon that denotes frustration or despair. The letters resemble a figure banging its head on the ground (O is the head; R the torso and Z the legs).

Yuki-Onna: (Snow woman). In Japanese folklore the Yuki-Onna is the spirit of a woman who died in a snow storm.

Hikikomori: Someone who is socially isolated to the extent that they rarely (or never) leave their room. It is estimated that in Japan there are almost a million socially isolated adolescents or young adults who have chosen to cut themselves off from society in this manner.

Controversial British columnist Pauline Rogers, known for her confessional style of journalism, was the first to coin the term The Three to refer to the children who survived the crashes on Black Thursday.

This article was published in the *Daily Mail* on 15 January 2012.

It's been three days since Black Thursday and I'm sitting in my newly constructed private office, staring at my computer screen in utter disbelief.

Not, as you may think, because I'm still stunned at the horrendous coincidence that resulted in four passenger planes crashing on the same day. Although I am. Who isn't? No. I'm scrolling through the staggering list of conspiracy websites, all of which have a different – and more bizarre than the last – theory on what caused the tragedy. Just a five-minute Google session will reveal several sites dedicated to the belief that Toshinori Seto, the brave, self-less captain who chose to bring down Sun Air Flight 678 in an unpopulated area rather than cause more casualties, was possessed by suicidal spirits. Another insists that all four planes were targeted by malevolent ETs. Crash investigators have pointed out in no uncertain terms that terrorist activity can be ruled out – especially in the case of the Dalu Air crash in Africa where the traffic controllers' reports confirm that this disaster was due to pilot error – but there are anti-Islamic websites being created by the minute. And the religious nuts – it's a sign from God! – are fast catching up with them.

An event of this magnitude is bound to transfix the

world's attention, but why are people so fast to think the worst or waste their time believing in frankly bizarre and convoluted theories? Sure, the odds of this happening are infinitesimal, but come on! Are we that bored? Are we all, at heart, just Internet trolls?

By far the most poisonous are the rumours and theories being circulated about the three child survivors, Bobby Small, Hiro Yanagida and Jessica Craddock, who, for the sake of brevity, I'm going to call The Three. And I blame the media who are ensuring that the public's greed for information about these poor mites is fed on the hour. In Japan, they're climbing over walls for pictures of the poor boy who, let's not forget, lost his mother in the accident. Others rushed to the crash site, hampering rescue operations. In the UK and the US, little Jessica Craddock and Bobby Small are taking up more front-page space than the Royal Family's latest gaffe.

More than most, I know how stressful that relentless attention and speculation can be. When I split from my second husband and chose to write about the intimate details of our separation in this very column, I found myself in the centre of a media storm. For two weeks I could barely step outside my front door without a paparazzo popping up to try and snap me without my make-up on. I can empathise completely with what The Three are going through, and so can eighteen-year-old Zainab Farra, who, ten years ago, was the only survivor of another devastating air accident, when Royale Air 715 crashed on take-off at Addis Ababa airport. Like The Three, Zainab was the only child survivor. Like The Three, afterwards she found herself in the centre of a media circus. Zainab recently published her autobiography, *Wind Beneath My Wings*, and has publicly called for The Three to be left alone so that they can come to terms with their miraculous survival. 'They are not freaks,' she says. 'They are children. Please, what they need now is space and time to heal and process what they have been through.'

Amen to that. We should be thanking our lucky stars that they were saved at all, not wasting our time building bizarre conspiracy theories around them or making them the subject of front-page gossip. The Three – I salute you, and I hope from the bottom of my heart that you all find peace while you deal with the terrible events that took your parents.

Neville Olson, a Los Angeles-based freelance paparazzi photographer, was found dead in his apartment on 23 January 2012. Although the bizarre manner of his death became front page news, this is the first time his neighbour, Stevie Flanagan, who discovered his remains, has spoken publicly.

You got to be a particular kind of person to do what Neville did for a living. I asked him once if he felt dirty doing it, hiding in bushes waiting to get an up-skirt shot of whichever starlet was flavour of the month, but he said he was just doing what the public *wanted* him to do. He specialised in the dirt, like those shots he got of Corinna Sanchez buying coke in Compton – how he even knew she'd be in that neighbourhood, he never said; least not to me. He was cagey about how he got his info.

It kinda goes without saying that Neville was a little weird. A loner. I guess his work suited his personality. I met him when he was moving into the unit downstairs from me. The place where we lived at the time, it's this split-level complex in El Segundo. Lots of people who lived there worked at LAX, so you got people coming and going at all hours. I was working for One Time Car Rental, so the place suited me. Convenient. I wouldn't say we were close friends or anything like that, but if we ran into each other, we'd shoot the shit. I never saw anyone visiting him and I never saw him with a woman, not once, or a guy. He kinda came across as asexual. A couple of months after he moved in, he asked me if I wanted to come over and 'meet his roommates'. I thought maybe he'd asked someone in to help share the rent, so I said, sure. I was curious to see what type of person would get along with him.

I almost puked when I went into his unit the first time. Shit, man, it stank. Don't know how to describe it, guess you could say it was kinda like a mix of rotten fish and meat. It was hot and dark in there, too – the curtains were drawn and the A.C. wasn't on. I was like, what the fuck? Then I saw something moving in the corner of the room – this large shadow – and it looked like it was heading straight for me. I couldn't take in what I was seeing at first, then I realised it was a massive fucking lizard. I yelled and Neville laughed like crazy. He was waiting for my reaction. Told me to chill, said, 'Don't worry, that's just George.' All I wanted to do was get the hell out of there, but I was trying not to be a pussy, you know? I asked Neville what the fuck he was doing with a thing like that in the apartment and he just shrugged, said he had three of the fucking things – monitors from Africa or whatever – and that most of the time he let them run around, rather than keep them in their cages or aquariums. He said they were really intelligent, 'Clever as pigs or dogs.' I asked him if they were dangerous and he showed me this jagged scar on his wrist. 'Big flap of skin came off it,' he said, and you could tell he was proud of it. 'But they're usually cool if you treat them right.' I asked him what they ate, and he was like, 'Baby rats. Live ones. Get them from a whole-saler.' Imagine that being your job, huh, baby rat merchant? He went into this whole spiel about how some people were against feeding rodents to monitors, and all that time I just watched that thing. Willing it not to get too close to me. That wasn't all, he kept his snake collection and his spiders in his bedroom. Aquariums everywhere. Went on and on about how tarantulas make the best pets. Later, they said he was an animal hoarder.

Couple of days after Black Thursday, he knocked on my door, told me he was going out of town. Most of his work was LA-based, but occasionally he'd have to go further afield. That was the first time he asked me to check on his 'buddies'. 'I stock 'em up before I go,' he said. He could be gone for as long as three days and they'd be fine. He asked me to check on their water levels and swore the monitors would be locked up tight. He was usually cagey about his assignments, but this time he told me where he was going, as there was a chance he'd get himself in deep shit.

He said he'd called in a favour to get on one of the charter helicopters, planned on heading to Miami, to that hospital where they'd taken Bobby Small, see if he could get a shot of the kid. Said he had to do it fast, the kid was being taken back to NYC soon.

I asked him how in the hell he thought he was going to get anywhere near there – from what I'd seen on the news, security at that hospital was tight – but he just smiled. He said he specialised in this kind of thing.

He was only gone three days, so I didn't need to go into his place after all. I saw him climbing out of a cab just as I was getting home from my shift. He looked like crap. Really shaken, like he was sick or something. I asked him if he was cool, and if he'd managed to get a picture of the kid. He didn't answer me and he looked so bad I asked him in for a drink. He came right over, didn't even go into his own place to check on the reptiles. You could see he wanted to talk, but couldn't get the words out. I poured him a shot and he knocked it back, and then I gave him a beer because I'd run out of hard liquor. He downed his beer and asked me for another. He downed that too.

The liquor helped, and slowly he told me what he'd done. I thought he was going to say that he'd disguised himself as a porter or something to get into that hospital, maybe sneaked in through the morgue, B-movie style. But it was worse. Clever. But worse. He'd moved into a hotel just down from the hospital, had this whole cover story and fake ID and accent that he'd used before – a UK businessman in Miami for a conference. He said he'd done the same thing when Klint Maestro, the lead singer of the Space Cowboys, OD-ed. That's how come he got the shots of Klint looking all wasted in his hospital gown. It was easy. He just took extra insulin to make himself go hypo. I didn't even know he was an insulin-dependent diabetic, well, why would I? He collapsed at the bar and let the barman or whoever know that he needed to be taken to the nearest hospital. Then he passed out.

In Casualty they put him on a drip, and in order to get admitted, he pretended to have an epileptic fit. He could've died, but he said it wasn't the first time he'd done it, and he always kept a couple of little baggies of sugar in his sock to sort him out. It was his modus operandi kind of thing. Said it was a bitch to move around in that condition (they'd given him valium after the fit and he still felt like shit after making himself hypo).

I asked him if he managed to get to where the kid was and he was like, nah, it was a bust. Said he couldn't get anywhere near Bobby's ward, security was too tight.

But when they found his camera later, it showed he'd managed to get into the kid's room after all. There's a shot of Bobby sitting up in bed, and he's smiling straight at the camera, as if he was posing for a family shot or whatever. You must've seen it. Someone from the coroner's office leaked it. Kinda creeped me out.

He turned down a third beer and said, 'There's no point, Stevie. There's no point to any of this.'

I was like, 'Any of what?'

He acted like he hadn't heard me. I didn't know what the fuck he was talking about. Then he left.

I kinda got wrapped up in work after that. That puke virus was going around, and it seemed everyone at work was off sick. I was working double shifts and dead on my feet half the time. It was only later that I realised it had to have been a week since I'd run into Neville.

Then, one of the guys who lived in the section on the other side of Neville's place, Mr Patinkin, asked me for the super's number, said there was a problem with the drains. Said he thought maybe the smell was coming from Neville's place.

I guess I knew right then something was up. I went down, knocked on the door. I could hear the faint sound of the TV, nothing else. I still had the key, but I wish to Christ I'd called the cops straight off. Mr Patinkin came with me. He needed trauma counselling afterwards; I still get nightmares. It was dark in there, but I could see Neville from the front door, sitting slumped against the wall, legs outstretched. His shape didn't look right. That's because there were bits missing.

They said he died of an insulin overdose, but the autopsy showed that he might not have been completely dead when they started to . . . you know.

It was big news, 'Man eaten alive by pet lizards and

spiders'. There was this whole story going around that the tarantulas had spun webs all over his body and were nesting inside his chest cavity. Bullshit. Far as I could tell, the spiders were still all in their spiderariums or whatever you call them. It was the monitor lizards who ate him.

Funny that he became the news. What do you call it? Ironic. There were even guys like him sneaking round the apartment trying to get a photo. The story pushed all that stuff about the The Three miracle children off the front page for a day. Later on it all got dredged up again when that preacher guy went on about it being another sign of the apocalypse or whatever – the animals turning on humans.

The only way I can deal with it is to think that maybe that's how Neville would have wanted to go. He loved those fucking lizards.

PART TWO

CONSPIRACY

JANUARY–FEBRUARY

A former follower of Pastor Len Vorhees's Church of the Redeemer, Reba Louise Neilson describes herself as 'Pamela May Donald's closest friend'. She still lives in Sannah County, South Texas, where she is the coordinator of the local Christian Women's Preppers' Centre. She is adamant that she was never a member of Pastor Vorhees's Pamelist sect and agreed to talk to me in order 'to let people know that there are good people living here who never wanted anything bad to happen to those children'. I spoke to Reba on a number of occasions via phone in June and July 2012, and collated our conversations into several accounts.

Stephenie told me about it first. She was crying on the phone, couldn't hardly get her words out. 'It's Pam, Reba,' she said when I finally got her to calm down. 'She was on that plane that crashed.'

I told her not to be silly, that Pam was in Japan visiting her daughter, she wasn't in Florida. 'Not that plane, Reba. The Japanese one. It's on the news now.' Well, my heart just about plummeted into my feet. I'd heard about the crash in Japan of course, as well as the one in that unpronounceable place in Africa, and the plane full of English tourists that crashed into the sea in Europe, but I hadn't for a minute thought Pam was on it. The whole thing was just *terrible*. For a while there, it was as if all the planes in the world were dropping out of the sky. The Fox anchors would be reporting on a crash, then they'd flinch and say: 'And we've just heard another plane has gone down...' My husband Lorne said it was like a never-ending punchline.

I asked Stephenie if she'd told Pastor Len, and she said she'd tried the ranch but Kendra had been vague as usual about when he'd be back, and he wasn't answering his cellular phone. I hung up and ran into the den to see the news for myself. Behind Melinda Stewart (she's my favourite Fox anchor, the kind of woman you can imagine getting coffee with, you know?) were two huge photographs, one of Pam and one of that little Jewish boy who survived the Florida crash. I didn't like to think what Pam would have said about her photo, which must've been from her passport and looked for all the world like a mug shot. I hate to say it, but her hair was a mess. Along the bottom of the screen, they kept repeating the words: '526 killed in Japanese Sun Air disaster. Sole American on board named as Texan native Pamela May Donald.'

I just sat there, Elspeth, staring at that photograph, reading those words until it finally hit me that Pam really was gone. That nice investigator man, Ace somebody, from that air crash show Lorne likes, came on the line from Florida and said that it was too early to be sure, but it didn't look like terrorism was involved or anything like that. Melinda asked him if he thought the crashes might have been caused by environmental factors or maybe 'an act of God'. I didn't like that, I can tell you, Elspeth! Implying that our Lord had nothing better to do than bat planes out of the air. It's the Antichrist who would have had a hand in *that*. I couldn't move for the longest time, then they showed an overhead shot of a house that looked familiar. And then I realised it was Pam's house, only it looked smaller from the air. It was then I remembered Jim, Pam's husband.

I never had much to do with Jim. The way Pam used to speak about him, with a kind of hushed awe, you'd think he was a six-foot giant, but in the flesh he's not much taller than I am. I don't like to say this, but I always suspected him of being free with his fists. We never saw bruises on Pam or anything like that. But it was just strange, her acting so cowed all the time. My Lorne, if he even raised his voice to me... Well, I do believe the man is the head of the household of course, but it's a mutual respect thing, y'know? Still, no one deserves to go through what that man went through, and I knew we had to do something to help him.

Lorne was out back, doing the inventory on the canned fruit and reorganising our dried goods. 'You can never be too careful' is what he says, not with those solar flares and globalisation and super storms everyone's talking about, and no way were we going to be caught unawares. Who knows when Jesus will call us up to join him? I told him what had happened, that Pam had been on that Jap plane. Him and Jim worked together at the B&P plant, and I said he should go over and see if Jim needed anything. He was reluctant – they weren't close, they worked in different sections – but he went all the same. I thought I'd better stay home, make sure everyone else knew.

I called Pastor Len on his cellphone first; it went straight to voicemail but I left a message. He called me right back and I could tell by the way his voice was shaking that he'd only just heard the news. Pam and I had been members of what he called his 'inner circle' for the longest time. Before Pastor Len and Kendra came to Sannah County – we're talking, oh, fifteen years ago now – I was a member of the New Revelation church over in Denham. It meant a half-hour drive every Sunday and Wednesday for Bible study too, because no way was I going to worship with the Episcopalians, not with their liberal views on the homosexual element.

So you can imagine how cheered I was when Pastor Len arrived in town and took over the old Lutheran church that had been standing empty for the longest time. Back then, I hadn't heard his radio show. It was his billboards that caught my eye at first. He knew how to attract attention to the Lord's work! Every week he'd put up a banner with a different message: 'Like to gamble? Well, the devil deals in souls'; 'God doesn't believe in atheists, therefore atheists don't exist' were two of my favourites. The only one I didn't care for showed a picture of a Bible with one of those antennas old cellphones used to have coming out of its top and 'App for saving your soul,' which I thought was a little too cutesy. Pastor Len's congregation was small at first and that's where I really got to know Pam, although I'd seen her at PTA meetings of course – her Joanie was older than my two. We didn't always see eye to eye on everything, but no one could say she wasn't a good Christian woman.

Pastor Len said he'd organised a prayer circle for Pam's soul the following evening, and, as Kendra was down with one of her headaches, he asked me to call around and tell the Bible study group. Then Lorne came huffing into the house saying that Jim's place was surrounded by TV news trucks and reporters and there was no answer from inside the house. Well, of course, I told all of this to Pastor Len, who said it was our Christian duty to help Jim in his time of need, even though he wasn't a member of the church. Pam had always been a bit tight-lipped about that. My Lorne came with me every Sunday, although he didn't join the Bible study group or the healing prayer circle, and it must have been just terrible for Pam knowing that her husband would be left behind on earth to face the wrath of the Antichrist and burn in hell for all eternity.

Then I set to wondering if Pam's daughter Joanie would be coming home. She hadn't been back for two years; there'd been some trouble between her and Jim a while back when she was still at college. He didn't approve of this boyfriend she had. A Mexican. Or half Mexican, I think he was. Caused a rift right through the family. And I know that hurt Pam. She'd always look wistful when I spoke about my grandchildren. Both of my girls got married straight out of school and settled just minutes away from me. That's why Pam went to Japan. She missed Joanie something awful.

It was getting late, so Pastor Len said we should go and see Jim early the next morning. Oh, he looked smart when he picked me up at eight the next day! I'll never forget that, Elspeth. A suit and a red silk tie. But then he always did care about his appearance before he let the devil in. It feels wrong to say this, but I wish I could say the same about Kendra. She and Pastor Len didn't look like they belonged with each other. She was skinny as a rake and always looked washed-out and dowdy.

I was surprised Kendra came with us that day; she usually has some sort of excuse. I wouldn't say she was snooty…she just kept her distance, this vague smile on her face, had trouble with her nerves. Is it true that she ended up in one of them places, those…asylums? They don't call them that any more, do they? Institutions, that's the word I was fishing for! I can't help but think that it's a real blessing they never had children. At least they didn't get to witness the pain of their mother giving in to her weak mind. I guess it was the gossip about Pastor Len and his fancy woman that sent her over the edge – but let me make it clear, Elspeth, no way, whatever I may think about what he did later, do I give any credence to *those* rumours.

After a quick prayer, we shot straight over to Pam and Jim's place. It's out on Seven Souls road, and the press was lined all the way along it, reporters and those camera people standing outside the gate, smoking and jabbering. Oh glory, I said to Pastor Len, how are we going to get up into Pam's driveway?

But Pastor Len said we were on Jesus' business and no one was going to stop us doing our Christian duty. When we pulled up next to the gate, a swarm of reporters came rushing up to us, saying things like, 'Are you friends of Pam? How do you feel about what's happened?' They were taking pictures and filming and I knew right then what those poor celebrities must go through all the time.

'How do you think we feel?' I said to a young woman wearing too much mascara who was the pushiest of the bunch. Pastor Len gave me a look as if to say, let me do the talking, but they needed to be put in their place. Pastor Len told them that we were on a mission to help Pam's husband in his time of need, and that he'd come out to give them a statement as soon as we'd ensured Jim was coping. This seemed to appease them, and they drew back to their media vans.

The curtains were drawn and we banged on the front door but there was no answer. Pastor Len went round back to the yard, but he said it was the same story. Then I remembered that Pam kept a spare key under the plant pot next to the back door just in case she ever locked herself out, so that's how we got in.

Oh, the smell! Just about slapped you in the face. Kendra went white, it was so bad. And then Snookie yipped and came running down the passageway towards us. Pam would have near had a heart attack if she'd seen her kitchen like that. She'd only been gone two days, but you'd swear a bomb had hit it. Broken glass all over the counter and a cigarette butt dumped in one of Pam's mother's best china cups. And Jim couldn't have let Snookie out once, there were what my Lorne calls doggy landmines all over Pam's good linoleum. I have to be honest here, Elspeth, as I believe in always speaking the truth, but none of us really liked that dog. Even if Pam bathed her a hundred times a day, she always smelled just awful. And her eyes always had this film over them. But Pam doted on her, and seeing her sniffing at our shoes and looking up at us all hopeful that one of us was Pam... well, it near broke my heart.

'Jim?' Pastor Len called. 'You there?' The television was on, so after we'd checked the kitchen, we headed to the den.

I almost screamed when we saw him. Jim was slumped in his La-Z-Boy chair, a shotgun across his lap. The curtains were closed, so it was dark and for a second I thought he might be... Then I saw that his mouth was open and he let out a snore. Bottles and beer cans just about near covered the floor and the room stank of alcohol. Sannah County is a dry county, but you can get alcohol if you know where to look. And Jim knew where to look. I don't like to say this, Elspeth, but I wonder what he would have done if he hadn't been passed out. If he'd a tried to shoot at us. Pastor Len opened the curtains, cranked a window, and in the light I could see that the front of Jim's pants was wet.

Pastor Len took charge as I knew he would. He gently took the shotgun off Jim's lap, then shook his shoulder.

Jim jerked and stared up at us, his eyes redder than a bucket of pig's blood.

'Jim,' Pastor Len said. 'We've just heard about Pam.

We're here for you, Jim. If there's anything we can do, you know you just have to ask.'

Jim snorted. 'Yeah, you can eff-word off.'

Well, I just about *died*. Kendra let out a sound that could have been a laugh – probably shock.

Pastor Len wasn't at all put out. 'I know you're upset, Jim. But we're here to help you. See you through this.'

And then Jim just started sobbing. His whole body heaved and shook. Whatever they say about Pastor Len now, Elspeth, you should've seen how he handled Jim. With real kindness. Took him into the bathroom to get him cleaned up.

Kendra and I just stood there for a while, and then I nudged her and we got to work. Cleaned the kitchen, scooped up the dog poop and gave that La-Z-Boy a good scrub. And all the time Snookie kept following after us with those eyes.

Pastor Len led Jim back into the lounge, and though the poor man smelled a whole lot better, his tears hadn't dried up none. He was still sobbing and sobbing.

Pastor Len said, 'If it's okay with you, Jim, we'd sure like to pray for Pam with you.'

I was expecting Jim to curse at him again, and for a second, I swear, I could see that so did Pastor Len. But that man was broken, Elspeth. Just about tore in two, and later Pastor Len said that was Jesus' way of showing us that we needed to let him in. But you got to be *ready*. I've seen it a thousand times. Like when we were praying for Stephe-nie's cousin Lonnie, the one who had that motor neurons disease. It didn't work because he hadn't let the Lord into his heart. Even Jesus can't work with an empty vessel.

So we knelt right there next to the couch, surrounded by empty beer cans, and prayed.

'Let the Lord into your heart, Jim,' Pastor Len said. 'He's there for you. He wants to be your Saviour. Can you feel him?'

It was a beautiful thing to see. Here was a man, so smashed by grief that he was crying fit to break, and here was Jesus, just waiting to take him in His arms and put him back together again!

We sat with Jim for a good hour at least. Pastor Len kept saying, 'You're now part of our flock, Jim, we're here for you, just as Jesus is here for you.' It was so heart-warming, I'm not ashamed to say I cried like a new-born baby.

Pastor Len helped Jim back into his La-Z-Boy and I could see on his face that it was time to get down to practicalities.

'Now, Jim,' Pastor Len said. 'We got to think about the funeral.'

Jim mumbled something about Joanie dealing with that.

'Aren't you going to fly over there and bring Pam back?' Pastor Len asked.

Jim shook his head, and a shifty look came into his eyes. 'She left me. I told her not to go, but she wouldn't listen.'

There was a banging on the door and we all jumped. Darn reporters had come up to the house!

We could hear them shouting: 'Jim! Jim! What do you think about the message?'

Pastor Len looked at me and said, 'What message they talking about, Reba?'

Well, of course, I didn't have an inkling.

Pastor Len straightened his tie. 'I'll go and sort those vultures out, Jim,' he said, and Jim looked up at him, that shifty look replaced with pure gratitude. 'Reba and Kendra will fix you something to eat.'

I was glad to have something to do, Elspeth. Pam, bless her, she'd made a whole lot of meals for Jim, all placed neatly in the freezer, so it was easy just to pull one out and put it into the microwave. Kendra didn't do much to help, she gathered that dog in her arms and started whispering to it. So it was up to me to get to work cleaning up the rest of the mess in the den and convincing Jim to eat the pot-pie I'd put on a tray for him.

When Pastor Len came back in the house, he had this dazed expression on his face. Before I could ask what was bothering him, he picked up the TV remote and clicked onto Fox. Melinda Stewart was saying that a bunch of Jap journalists had made their way to the crash site in that forest place where Pam's plane had gone down, and they'd taken several of the passengers' cellphones. Some of the passengers – God rest their souls – had recorded messages on their phones when they knew they were going to die, and the reporters had leaked them. Printed them before some of the families knew for sure their loved ones were even gone, if you can credit it.

And one of those messages was from Pam, although I didn't even know she had a cellphone. Pam's message was scrolling along the bottom of the screen, and Pastor Len cried, 'She was trying to tell me something, Reba. Look. My name, right there!'

I guess we'd forgotten about Jim, 'cause we heard him yell, 'Pam!' and then he screamed her name over and over.

Kendra didn't help calm him down. She just stood in the doorway, Snookie in her arms, still cooing at that dog as if it was a baby.

The following are the messages (*isho*) recorded by Sun Air Flight 678 passengers in their final moments.

(Translation by Eric Kushan, who notes that some of the linguistic nuances may have been lost.)

Hirono. Things are getting bad here. The cabin crew are calm. No one is panicking. I know I'm going to die and I want to tell you that – oh things are falling they're falling everywhere and I must…Don't look in my office cupboard. Please, Hirono, I'm begging you. There are other things you can do. I can only hope that
Koushan Oda. Japanese citizen. Age 37.

There is smoke that doesn't feel like smoke. The old woman next to me is crying silently and praying and I wish I was sitting here next to you. There are children on this flight. Um…uh…Take care of my parents. There should be enough money. Call Motobuchi-san, he'll know what to do about the insurance. The captain is doing everything he can, I have to trust in him. I can sense by his voice that he is a good man. Goodbye, goodbye, goodbye, goodbye, goodbye
Sho Mimura. Japanese citizen. Age 49.

I must think I must think I must think. How it happened… okay, a bright light came into the cabin. A bang. No, more than one. Was the light before the bang? I don't know. The woman at the window, the big *gaijin* [foreigner] is wailing it hurts my ears and I need to get my things in case we… I'm recording this so that you know what will happen.

There is no panic, although I feel as if there should be. For the longest time I wanted to die, and now that it's coming I realise that I was wrong to wish this, that my time was coming too soon. I'm scared and I don't know who will hear this. If you can pass this message on to my father tell him that

Keita Eto. Japanese citizen. Age 42.

Shinji? Please answer! *Shinji!*
There was a light, bright and then... and then.
The plane is going down, it's crashing it's going down and the captain is saying that we have to be calm. I don't know why this is happening!

All I ask... take care of the children, Shinji. Tell them that I love them and

Noriko Kanai. Japanese citizen. Age 28.

I know that the Lord Jesus Christ will take me into his arms and that this is his plan for me. But oh, how I wish I could see you once more. I love you, Su-jin, and I never told you. I hope that you hear this; somehow I hope it gets back to you. I wanted us to be together one day, but you are so far away now. It's happening

Seojin Lee. South Korean citizen. Age 37.

They're here. I'm... don't let Snookie eat chocolate, it's poison for dogs, she'll beg you, the boy. The boy watch the boy watch the dead people oh Lordy there's so many... They're coming for me now. We're all going soon. All of us. Bye Joanie I love the bag bye Joanie, Pastor Len warn them that the boy he's not to

Pamela May Donald. American citizen. Age 51.

Lola Cando (not her real name) describes herself as a former sex worker and website entrepreneur. Lola's accounts are extrapolated from our many Skype conversations.

Lenny came to see me once, mebbe twice a month for three years or so. Drove all the way out of Sannah County, gotta be an hour's drive at least, but that was fine for Lenny. Said he liked the drive, gave him time to think about stuff. He was strictly vanilla. Later, people tried to get me to say he was some sort of pervert, but he wasn't. And he wasn't into drugs or funny stuff, neither. Just straight missionary position, a finger of bourbon and a chat, that was all he liked.

I got into this business through my girlfriend Denisha. She's a specialist, provides a service for clients who find it hard to connect with women. Just 'cause you're housebound or in a wheelchair, doesn't mean your sex drive's gone. I don't do much specialist work, you understand. Most of my regulars are just your average Joes, guys who are lonely, or whose wives have gone off sex. I check out all my guys good, and if there isn't a connection there or if they want funny stuff, I say, sorry, my schedule's full.

I'm not into drugs; I didn't start doing this 'cause I was feeding a habit. Girls like me and Denisha, the ones who do this for a living without seeing the dark side, you don't hear much about us in the media. And like Denisha's always saying, it beats stacking shelves at Walmart.

I had an apartment I used for, y'know, business dealings, but Lenny didn't like to go there. He was real cautious about things like that, almost paranoid. He preferred us to meet at one of the motels. There are several that'll give you a good deal on an hourly rate, no questions asked. He always insisted that I check in before him.

Well, that day he came late. A good half hour late, which wasn't like him. I set out the drinks, got the ice from the machine and watched a re-run of *Party-Time* while I waited, the one where Mikey and Shawna-Lee finally get together. Just as I was about to give up on him, he came flying into the room, out of breath and all sweaty.

'Well, hi, stranger,' I said, which was always how I greeted him.

'Never mind that, Lo,' he said. 'I need a goddamn drink.' That gave me a jolt. I'd never heard him take the Lord's name in vain before. Lenny said that the only time he ever took a drink was when he was with me, and I believed him. I asked him if he wanted to, you know, start his usual, but he wasn't interested. 'Just the drink.'

His hands were shaking and I could see he was real agitated about something. I fixed him a double and asked him if he wanted me to rub his shoulders.

'Uh-uh,' he said. 'I need to sit for a moment. Think.'

But he didn't sit, he paced up and down that room like he was fixing to wear out the carpet. I knew better than to ask him what was on his mind. I knew he'd tell me when he was ready. He handed me his glass and I poured him another two fingers.

'Pam was trying to tell me something, Lo.'

Course then I didn't have a clue what he meant. I said, 'Len, you gotta start from the beginning.'

He started telling me all about Pamela May Donald, the woman who was killed on the Japanese plane, about how she was one of his congregation.

'Len,' I said, 'I'm real sorry for your loss. But I'm sure Pam wouldn't want you to get all upset about her.'

He acted like I hadn't spoken. He dug in his bag – he always carried this satchel, like he was a grown-up school kid or something – pulled out a Bible, and slapped it on the table.

I was still trying to keep it light. 'You want me to spank you with that or something?'

Big mistake. His face turned bright red, puffed up like one of those fish. He's got what you call an expressive face, which makes people trust him, I guess, looks like he can't lie. I apologised real fast; that look scared me.

He told me about how Pam had left that message, one of the... what you call them? Those messages that she and some of the Japs had left on their phones while that plane was going down.

'It means something, Lo,' he said. 'And I think I know what it is.'

'What, Lenny?'

'Pam saw them, Lola.'

'Pam saw who, Lenny?'

'All those who haven't taken the Lord into their hearts. Everyone who is going to be left behind after the Rapture.'

I come from a religious background, you understand, brought up in a good Baptist home. There isn't much that's in the Bible that I don't know about. People may condemn me for what I do, but I know in my heart Jesus wouldn't judge me. Like my girlfriend Denisha is always saying (she's an Episcopalian), some of Jesus' best friends were sex workers.

Anyhow, even before Black Thursday, Len was one of those End Times believers. You know, those guys who saw signs that the tribulation was on us everywhere: 9/11, earthquakes, the Holocaust, globalisation, the War on Terror, all that. He truly believed it was only a matter of time before Jesus would whisk all the saved up into heaven, leaving the rest of the world behind to suffer under the Antichrist. Some of them believed the Antichrist was already on the earth. That he's the head of the UN or president of China or one of those Muslims or Arabs or some such. Later on, course, they were saying pretty much everything in the news was a sign. That foot and mouth outbreak in England, even that norovirus thing that hit all of those cruise ships.

Me, I don't know how I felt about the whole Rapture thing. That one day, whoop, all the saved would just disappear into the sky, leaving their clothes and worldly possessions behind. Seems too much trouble to me. Why would God bother with all that? Lenny gave me the *Gone* books to read – you know what I'm talking about? – that series where the reborn Christians are Raptured all at once and the UK prime minister ends up being the Antichrist. I told him I'd read them, but I never did.

I poured myself a stiff drink. Knew I was in for a good hour at least. Sometimes Lenny ran through his radio show for me. I pretended that I listened to it, but I never did. More of a TV type of girl, you know?

When I first started seeing Lenny, I figured him for one of those money-hungry evangelicals, the guys you see on TV trying to get people to donate to their ministries, going on about why tithing is necessary even if you're on welfare. Thought at first he might be a conman of some sort, and I've met my fair share of that type I can tell you! But I got to thinking, after I'd known him for a while, that he really did start to believe his own...I don't want to call it bullshit, like I say, I'm a card-carrying Baptist, but I never set much store by all that fire and brimstone stuff. But there's no denying that Lenny wanted to join the big boys, powerful fellows like that Dr Lund – the one President Blake was such buddies with. Lenny was desperate to get on the evangelical speaking circuit. His radio show was supposed to be his way in, but in all the years he'd been doing it, he hadn't gotten very far. And it wasn't just for the money either. Respect, that's what Lenny wanted. He was tired of living off of his wife's money.

'Listen to this, Lola,' he said, then he read out the message. Didn't make much sense to me. Seemed to me that Pam was mostly concerned about that dog of hers.

Then he started talking about how it was a miracle that those three kids survived practically unscathed. 'It's not right,' he said. 'They shoulda died, Lola.'

I admitted it was strange. But then everyone thought it was strange. I guess it was one of those crazy things you can't quite get all the way into your head. Like 9/11. Unless you were there and actually experienced it. But you know, I think people get used to anything in the end. Like recently, my block keeps getting these power outages and after all the bitching and moaning, it's crazy how quickly we've come to terms with it.

'The boy. The boy...' he kept muttering. He read out a passage from Zechariah, then flipped through to Revelation. Lenny was big on Revelation, but it gave me the hee-bies when I was a kid. And, I gotta say, it was me who put the next bit into his head. Look, I'll admit, sometimes I play dumb, Lenny liked it (hell, they all like it). 'You know what I could never get my head around, Lenny?' I said. 'Those four horsemen. Why horsemen, anyhow? And all those different colours.'

Well, Lenny froze like I'd just blasphemed. 'What you say, Lo?'

I thought I'd said something to make him angry again, and I watched him carefully in case he was going to snap at me. He stood, still as a statue, his eyes darting from side to side. 'Lenny?' I said. 'Lenny, honey, you okay?' Then he just clapped his hands and laughed. First time I ever heard Lenny laugh. He took my face between his hands and kissed me right on the mouth. 'Lola,' he said. 'I think you got it!'

I said, 'What do you mean, Lenny?'

But all he said was, 'Take your clothes off.'

Then we did it, and he left.

The following is a transcript of Pastor Len Vorhees's radio show, *My Mouth, God's Voice*, aired on 20 January 2012.

Good listeners, I don't need to tell you that now more than ever, we're living in Godless times. We're living in a time when the Bible is shunned in our schools in favour of scientific evolutionary lies, where many are expelling God from their hearts, where sodomites and baby murderers and heathens and Islamofascists have more rights in our country than good Christian men and women. Where Sodom and Gomorrah cast a pall over every aspect of our daily lives, and our world leaders are trying with all their might to construct the culture of globalisation favoured by the Antichrist.

Good listeners, I have good tidings. I have proof that Jesus is listening to us, that He is heeding our prayers, that it is only a matter of time before He takes us to sit at His side.

Listeners, I want to tell you a story.

There was once a good woman. Pamela May Donald was her name, and she was a good *God*-fearing woman, who had taken Jesus into her heart with every fibre of her being.

This woman decided to take a journey, to visit her daughter in a far-flung area, Asia, to be exact. She didn't know, as she packed her bag, as she kissed her husband and church goodbye, that she was about to be part of God's plan.

That woman got on a plane at...she got on a plane in Japan, and that plane went down, struck out of the air by forces we can only guess at.

And as she lay dying, as she was lying on that cold hard foreign ground, her life-blood leaking from her veins, God spoke to her, listeners, and gave her a message. Just like God spoke to the prophet John on the island of Patmos when He showed him the vision of the seven seals in Revelation. And Pam recorded that message, listeners, so that we would have the benefit of understanding God's meaning.

Now, John is told that the first four seals will come in the form of four horsemen. We know, and this is a fact, that the four horsemen are sent to fulfil a divine purpose. And we know from Ezekiel that that purpose is to punish the faithless and the godless. The horsemen will bring plague, famine, war and panic to the earth; they will be the harbingers of the Tribulation.

There are many who believe the seals have already been opened, listeners, and I'll admit, it's hard not to, what with everything that's going on in the world right now. But Pam was being shown that God, in his wisdom, has only *now* opened the seals.

What Pamela May Donald was saying in her message to me, because, good listeners, in her wisdom she directed her message to *me* – me personally – is that the four horsemen are now here. Here on earth. As she lay dying, she said, 'The boy, the boy, Pastor Len, warn them.'

Y'all have seen the news. Y'all will have seen the three child survivors – and maybe four, we don't know for sure that there aren't any other survivors, it's chaos down in Africa, as we all know. Y'all know *for a fact* that there was no way that those three children could have survived such a cataclysmic event virtually unscathed. These three are the only survivors, I'll repeat that, listeners, because it is important, the *only* survivors. Even the crash investigators can't explain it, nor the doctors, nor the medical experts, no one can explain why these children were saved.

Loyal listeners, I believe these children have been inhabited by the spirits of the four horsemen.

'Pastor Len,' Pamela May Donald said. 'The boy. The boy.' What boy could she mean but that Japanese child who survived?

It's clear as a bell. How much clearer could the message be? The Lord is good, listeners, He isn't going to mess around with obfuscation. And in His good grace He showed us further evidence that what I say is the truth. In Revelation six, verses one to two:

I watched as the Lamb opened the first of the seven seals. Then I heard one of the four living creatures say in a voice like thunder, 'Come!' I looked, and there before me was a white horse!

A white horse, listeners. Ask yourselves this...what colour was the insignia on that Maiden Airlines plane that went down in Florida? A white dove. *White.*

When the Lamb opened the second seal, I heard the second living creature say, 'Come!' Then another horse came out, a fiery red one.

What colour was the insignia of the Sun Air flight? Red. Y'all seen it, brothers and sisters. Y'all seen that big red sun. Red. The colour of communism. The colour of war. The colour, good listeners, of blood.

When the Lamb opened the third seal, I heard the third living creature say, 'Come!' I looked, and there before me was a black horse!

Now it's true that that British plane, the one that crashed into the sea, has a bright orange insignia. But I ask you this, what colour was the writing on that plane? Black, listeners. *Black*.

When the Lamb opened the fourth seal, I heard the voice of the fourth living creature say, 'Come!' I looked, and there before me was a pale horse! Its rider was named Death. Now we know that the colour of Death's horse is written as *khlōros* in the original Greek, which translates as green. The insignia on that African plane that went down. What colour was it? That's right. *Green*.

I know there will be many nay-sayers who'll say, but Pastor Len, that could all just be a coincidence. But God doesn't work in coincidences. We know this for a fact.

There will be more signs. More signs, brothers and sisters. There will be war, there will be plague, there will be conflict and there will be famine.

The judgement has been unleashed on earth. And when the King of Kings opens up that sixth seal, those who are chosen will be saved and take their rightful place next to Jesus in the Kingdom of Heaven.

Our time is now. The signs are clear. They couldn't be clearer if God had put a great big red ribbon on them, shouted them out from the heavens.

And I'm asking you listeners – *good* listeners. Are you ready?

Space does not permit me to include excerpts from all of the conspiracy theory sites that sprang up after Black Thursday, but among the most vocal of the 'alternative theorists' was author and self-styled UFOlogist Simeon Lancaster, whose self-published books include *Aliens Among Us* and *Lizards in the House of Lords.* Lancaster refused to talk to me, and has subsequently denied that he in any way influenced Paul Craddock's actions. The following is a short extract cached from a blog posted on his website, aliensamongstus.co.uk, on 22 January 2012.

ALIEN INTERVENTION: BLACK THURSDAY, ALL THE PROOF WE NEED

Four plane crashes. Four continents. Events that have transfixed the world's media like none other IN THE HISTORY OF THE WORLD. There can be no other explanation except that The Others, our alien infiltrators, have decided to WIELD THEIR POWER and FLAUNT it.

It's only a matter of time, mark my words, before the Majestic 12 effect a high-level cover-up. They will deny that there are any 'supernatural' causes in their crash reports, you wait and see. Already they are saying that the pilots were to blame for the African crash. Already they are saying that hydraulic failure is the cause of the Japanese crash.

We know this is not so. THEY WILL LIE. They will lie because they are IN CAHOOTS with our alien overlords. It's a wonder The Three children (if they even are children) haven't already been taken to the labs (see map for possible locations) for protection.

Let's look at the evidence:

FOUR PLANES

FOUR??? We know that the chances of any one person being involved in a plane crash are one in 27 million. So what are the odds of FOUR planes crashing on the same day with only THREE survivors??? The chances of that alone are off the scale. So this was a deliberate event. Terrorists? Then why hasn't anyone come forward to claim that they did it? BECAUSE THE TERRORISTS AREN'T RESPONSIBLE. The Others are responsible.

BRIGHT LIGHTS

Why did at least two of the passengers on board the Sun Air flight report seeing bright lights in their messages? There is NO evidence of an explosion, or of a fire on board. Or of depressurisation. THERE CAN ONLY BE ONE EXPLANATION. We know that some of the Others' V crafts have been seen only AFTER bright lights appear in the sky. BRIGHT LIGHTS are a sure sign that they are here.

WHY CHILDREN?

One thing that we can all agree on is that there is NO WAY The Three could have survived the crashes. So there's that.

But why would The Others choose children? I believe it's because as a species, we nurture our young, but not only that, our gut reaction will be to PROTECT them and care for them.

We know that the Others' preferred method of attack is infiltration and STEALTH. It would be too obvious to put themselves in GOVERNMENT again. They've tried that before and they have been OUTED!!!!! They are here to watch us. We don't know when their next move will be. The Three will be controlled by alien forces working on their minds and bodies and we will see this showing itself in time to come.

The children have been IMPLANTED and they are watching us to see what we will do.

THIS CAN BE THE ONLY EXPLANATION!!!!

PART THREE

SURVIVORS

JANUARY–FEBRUARY

Lillian Small.

Zelna, one of the carers at the Alzheimer's day care centre where I used to take Reuben when he was still mobile, called her husband Carlos's condition 'Al', as if it was a separate entity, an actual person rather than a disease. Most mornings when Reuben and I arrived, Zelna would say to me, 'So what do you think Al did today, Lily?' And then she'd relate one of the funny or disturbing actions that Al had 'made' Carlos do – like when she found him wrapping all her shoes in newspaper so that they wouldn't feel the cold, or the way he called visiting the care centre 'going to work'.

She even wrote a blog about it for a while, 'Al, Carlos and Me Makes Three', which won a couple of awards.

I started getting into the habit of calling Reuben's condition Al, too. I suppose it gave me hope that somewhere, deep inside, the real Reuben was still there, biding his time, fighting to stop Al taking over completely. Although I knew it wasn't rational to think this way, it stopped me blaming Reuben for taking away the last years we'd looked forward to spending together. I could blame Al instead. I could *hate* Al instead.

Zelna was forced to put Carlos in a care facility a couple of years ago, and when she moved to Philadelphia to live with her daughter, we lost touch. I miss her – I miss the care centre – being around other people who knew exactly what I was going through. We'd often laugh about the crazy things our respective spouses or parents did or said. I remember Zelna cracking up when I told her about

Reuben insisting on wearing his boxer shorts over his trousers, like he was auditioning for the role of a geriatric Superman. It wasn't funny of course, but laughter can be the best medicine, don't you think? If you don't laugh, you'd cry. So I don't feel guilty about that. Not one bit.

But even when Reuben could no longer make it to the care centre, putting him in a home wasn't an option for me. It wasn't just the expense, I'd been inside those places. I didn't like the smell of them. I thought I'd cope looking after him myself. Lori did what she could, and there was always Betsy and the agency if I needed a break. I didn't use the agency often, there was a high staff turnover, and you never knew who you would get.

I don't want you to think I'm kvetching, we got by, and I was lucky. Reuben was never violent. Some of them get like that – paranoid – think their carers are trying to imprison them, especially when they lose the ability to recognise facial features. And he wasn't a wanderer, didn't try and get out of the apartment as long as I was with him. Reuben's condition progressed quickly, but even on bad days, when Al was in full control, as long as he could see my face when I spoke to him, he mostly kept calm. He suffered from terrible nightmares, though. But then he always was a dreamer.

I managed.

And I had my memories.

We were happy, Reuben and I. How many people can say that honestly? That's what I've got to fall back on. In the magazines Lori used to get, they're always saying how the perfect relationship is when you're best friends with your partner (oh, how I hate that word! Partner, it sounds so cold, don't you think?), and that's how we were. And when Lori came along, she slotted perfectly into our lives. A close-knit, regular family. Lived by routine. Reuben was a good husband. A good provider. After Lori left to go to NYU, I felt a bit blue, I suppose I was suffering from that empty nest syndrome, and Reuben surprised me with a road trip to Texas – Texas of all places! He wanted to explore San Antonio, check out the Alamo. Before Al took his sense of humour away, we used to joke that whatever happened, 'We'd always have Paris, Texas.'

Our life before Al came wasn't all plain sailing though. Whose life is? There were issues over the years. Lori going off the rails at college, the lump I found in my breast that we managed to catch just in time, the mess Reuben's mother got herself into with that younger fellow she met down in Florida. We dealt with all that.

It was Reuben who suggested we move to Brooklyn when Lori told us she was pregnant. He could see how worried I was about her bringing up a child alone. Her career was just taking off, and she needed support. I'll never forget when she invited us to her first show at New York Fashion Week. Reuben and I were so proud! A lot of the models were men wearing women's dresses, which made Reuben raise an eyebrow, but we've never been that close-minded. Plus, Reuben loved New York, was a real city person. We'd travelled around a lot in the early days when he was working as a substitute teacher, so we were used to packing up and moving. 'Let's go against the tide, Lily, and move into the city. Why not?' In truth, it didn't matter to Reuben where we lived. He was always a reader. Loved books. All books. Fiction, non-fiction, history of course. Spent most of his spare time stuck in a book, and you can do that anywhere, can't you? That was the other great tragedy about Al showing up – one of the first things to go was Reuben's ability to read, although Reuben hid this from me at first as well. It hurts to think of the months he sat up in bed, turning the pages of a book that he had no way of following, just to spare me the worry. A couple of months after his diagnosis, I discovered the real extent to which he'd been trying to hide his condition from me. In his sock drawer, I found a stack of index cards, where he'd written down reminder notes to himself. 'FLOW-ERS', he'd written on one. That broke my heart. Every Friday for forty-five years, he'd buy me flowers without fail.

I was a bit nervous about moving to Lori's neighbour-hood. Not because I was reluctant to leave Flemington. Reuben and I were never much for being social and the few friends we did have had already left for Florida to get away from the New Jersey winters. The house was paid up, so we had that money, but properties in Flemington had been hit hard when the bottom fell out of the market. Lori was worried that her neighbourhood would be too young and modern for us, said it was 'full of hipsters and wannabe artists', but there's a fairly large Hasidic com-munity there still, and the sight of them reassured Reuben when he first started getting really sick. Maybe it had to do with his childhood; his family were Orthodox. Lori helped us find a nice apartment block just down from the park, a five-minute walk from the loft where she lived on Berry Street. We got lucky, our immediate neighbours were older, like us, and Betsy and I hit it off straight away. We both loved needlework – Betsy was big into cross-stitching – and we watched the same shows. Reuben found her a bit intrusive at first – plus he didn't like the fact that she was a smoker, he's big against that – but it was Betsy who suggested he volunteer at the adult literacy centre. That, of course, was another of the things Reuben was forced to give up. He hid that from me as well, made some excuse about wanting to be home more to help me with Bobby. And oh, I loved looking after Bobby when he was a baby! We had a good year or so where he became the centre of our lives; Lori dropped him off with us every morning, and Reuben and I always took him to the park when the weather was nice. He had his moments, all kids do, but he was a bright little boy, a ray of sunshine in our lives. And it kept us busy!

Then *wham*. Al came along. Reuben was only seventy-one. I kept it from Lori for as long as I could, but she wasn't stupid, could see that he was becoming increasingly forgetful, saying strange things. I guess she put it down to him becoming a little eccentric in his old age.

I was forced to tell her at Bobby's second birthday party. I'd made a devil's food cake, Lori's favourite, and we were trying to get Bobby to blow out the candles. He was crotchety that day – the terrible twos, you know? Then Reuben said, out of the blue, 'Don't let the baby burn, don't let him burn.' And then he burst into tears.

Lori was horrified, and I had to sit her down, tell her that we'd got the diagnosis six months previously. She was upset, of course she was, but she said, and I'll never forget this, 'We'll get through it together, Momma.'

I felt bad, of course I did, landing this on her. We'd moved to the city to help her with Bobby, and now the tables were turned. Lori had her career and Bobby, but she came to see us whenever she could. Bobby was too young to understand what was happening to his grandfather. I worried it would upset him, but Reuben's funny ways didn't seem to bother him.

Oh, Elspeth, those days after I heard about Bobby! The guilt I felt at not going straight down to Miami to be with him in that hospital. That was when I realised the extent of how much I really hated Al. I wanted to scream at him for stealing Reuben away when I had all this other trouble to deal with. I don't ask for sympathy, others have it far worse than I do, but I still couldn't shift the idea that I was being punished for something. First Reuben, then Lori. What next?

A lot of it is just a blur, there was so much going on. The phone ringing nonstop, the reporters and the TV people hounding me. In the end I had to take the phone off the hook and use that cellphone Lori had given me. And even then somehow they managed to get hold of the number.

I couldn't step outside the door without a camera in my face: 'How do you feel?' 'Did you sense he was alive all along?' They wanted to know how Bobby was feeling, how he was coping, what he was eating, if I was religious, when he was coming home, if I was going to fly down and see him. They offered me money. Lots of money, begged me for photographs of him and Lori. I don't know where they got that one of him on his first day at school; I suspect it was from Mona. I never came out and accused her of it, but where else would they have got it? And don't get me started on the advertising and movie people from Hollywood! They wanted to buy the rights to Bobby's life story. He was only six! But money was the last thing I was thinking about then. We were told there would be insurance even though Maiden Air went bankrupt almost immediately. Lori wasn't badly off, but she wasn't rich. She'd earmarked all her savings for me and Reuben, for a place in Florida. But we wouldn't need that now, would we?

In truth, not all of the attention was poisonous. People left gifts, sent letters. Some were heartbreaking, especially the ones from people who had lost children themselves. I had to stop reading those letters in the end. They really did break my heart, and my heart couldn't take much more.

Reuben's sister, who had never once offered to fly down to help care for him before this, called three or four times a day, asking me what I was going to do about shiva for Lori. But how could I think about that with Bobby down in Miami? I was almost thankful most of the planes were grounded and she couldn't come and poke her nose in. Betsy, bless her, took care of the food in those first days. There were people in and out all the time – Charmaine helped with that, making sure they weren't reporters in disguise. People from the neighbourhood who'd heard about Lori. Reuben's old students from the adult literacy centre. Lori's friends and colleagues. All kinds of people. Blacks and Latinos and Jews, all sorts. All of them offering to help.

Betsy even got in touch with her Rabbi who offered his services for a memorial service, even though he knew we were secular. A funeral was out of the question until they released the body ... but I don't want to dwell on that. That day ... when we put her to rest ... I can't, Elspeth.

One night, it had to be two days after we heard about Bobby, Reuben and I were alone in the apartment. I sat down on the bed, and felt such a wave of despair and loneliness I actually wanted to die. I can't describe it, Elspeth. It was all too much. I had to be strong for Bobby, I knew that, but I wasn't sure if I had it in me. I don't know if somehow, the force of my pain gave Reuben the strength to push Al away for a few seconds, but he reached over and took my hand. He squeezed it. I looked into his eyes, and for a second, I saw Reuben, the old Reuben, my best friend, and it was as if he was saying, 'Come on, Lily, don't give up.' Then that expressionless mask – Al – fell back into place and he was gone.

But it gave me the strength to go on.

Charmaine knew how guilty I felt about not being with Bobby, and she put me in touch with his psychologist down in Miami – Dr Pankowski. She helped a lot, said it wouldn't be long before he could come home. She said his MRI was clear and he'd started talking, wasn't saying much, but seemed to understand what had happened to him.

When we got the news that he could come home, I got a visit from the mayor's aide, a nice young man, African-American. 'Bobby's a miracle child, Mrs Small,' he said. 'And here in New York we look after our own.' He offered to post a policeman outside my building when the press attention got too much and even sent a limousine to take me to JFK.

Charmaine came with me to the airport while Betsy and one of the carers they'd sent stayed to help with Reuben. I was as nervous as I was on my wedding day!

Bobby was arriving on a special charter plane, in an area of the airport where the politicians and important people usually flew into, which meant that for once, the reporters wouldn't be hounding us. They gave me a seat in the waiting area, and I could feel all the staff trying not to stare at me. I hadn't bothered with my appearance for the last few days, and I was feeling self-conscious. Charmaine held my hand all the while. I don't know what I would have done without her. She still keeps in touch.

The day was cold and crisp, but with one of those clear blue skies, and Charmaine and I stood up to watch the plane landing. It seemed to take forever before they opened the doors. And then I saw him climbing down the stairs, holding tightly to a young woman's hand. Dr Pankowski had travelled with him, bless her. She looked too young to be a doctor, but I'll always be grateful to her for what she did for him. They'd given him new clothes so he was wrapped up all warm, his hood hiding his face.

I took a step towards him. 'Bobby,' I said. 'It's me. It's Bubbe.'

He looked up at me and whispered, 'Bubbe?' Elspeth, I wept. Of course I did. I kept touching him, stroking his face, making sure he really was there.

And when I took him into my arms it was as if the lights flicked back on inside me. I can't explain it better than that, Elspeth. You see, I knew, right then, whatever had happened to my Lori, whatever had happened to Reuben, that now I had Bobby back with me, everything was going to be just fine.

Lori Small's best friend Mona Gladwell agreed to talk to me via Skype in late April 2012.

Look, Lori was my friend, my *best* friend, and I don't want to sound like I'm trashing her, but I reckon it's important people know the truth about her and Bobby. Don't get me wrong, Lori was special, did a lot for me, but she could be...she could be a bit flaky sometimes.

Lori and I met in high school. My folks moved to Flemington, New Jersey from Queens when I was fifteen, and me and Lori hit it off straight away. On the surface, Lori was your typical good girl. Good grades, polite, never got into trouble. But she had this whole secret life her folks never knew about. Smoked pot, drank, messed around with boys; usual kids' stuff. Reuben was teaching American history at the school at the time, and Lori was careful to protect his rep. Reuben was cool. None of the kids at school ripped into him. He was just Mr Small, not wildly popular, but he had a way of telling a story. Quiet. A dignity about him, I guess. He was smart, too. But if he knew Lori was out drinking and screwing around behind his back, he never let on.

As for Lillian...I know she never liked me, blamed what happened to Lori at college on me, but she was okay. But then compared to my folks, pretty much anyone is. Lillian never worked, seemed happy being a homemaker – kept busy sewing and cooking or whatever – and Reuben made just enough for them to live on. Apart from their politics – they were way more liberal than you'd think, looking at them – it was kind of like they were still living in the 1950s.

After graduation, Lori and I both decided to apply to

NYU – Lillian wasn't happy about that, although NYC is only an hour or so from Flemington. Didn't take long for Lori to get into the party scene, start doing heavy drugs, coke mainly. We had this whole system for when she knew her folks were coming to visit; we'd clear up the room we shared, she'd cover up her tattoos, make sure there was no evidence on show, but she got to a point where she couldn't hide it any more. Lillian flipped out, insisted that Lori come home with her and Reuben, so Lori ended up dropping out. After she got clean, she came back to the city and tried a million different careers: yoga instructor, personal stylist, manicurist, bartender. That's where I met my first husband, at one of the bars she worked in. It didn't last. Neither the job nor the husband.

Then, out of nowhere Lori applied for this fashion design course – convinced Reuben and Lillian to pay for it, though I don't know where they found the cash. I thought it was just another flaky move, but turned out she was good at it – hats especially, which became her thing. She started getting commissions, moved to Brooklyn where she could afford to set up her own studio. She designed a hat for my second wedding, refused to charge me for it, even though she was just starting out.

It was just after she did that Galliano show that she found out she was pregnant. 'I'm keeping this one,' she said. 'The big four-oh is coming up and I might not get another chance.' Wouldn't say who the father was, so I suspected she'd done it on purpose. I'm not saying she slept around, but she liked to have a good time. Didn't see the point of being in a relationship.

She concocted this whole crazy story about being artificially inseminated so that Lillian wouldn't freak out. I couldn't believe she was going to go through with it – it didn't seem right. But she said it was easier that way. After that preacher was going on about Bobby not being born of man – that he was unnatural and all that stuff – I could have said something, told the truth, but I thought it would all die down. Who could take that seriously?

When she was pregnant, Lori went through this whole religious stage, talked about sending Bobby to Cheder classes when he was old enough, shul, the whole shebang. Jewish mother syndrome, she said. It didn't last. I'd thought she'd freak when Lillian and Reuben decided to move to Brooklyn, but in actual fact she was pleased. 'It might not be a bad idea, Mona.' And yeah, before Reuben got sick, having Lillian on tap did make it easier. Specially when Bobby was a baby. It all backfired when Reuben got really bad and Lori had to be the supportive one. She was good at it, though. In a way, it made her grow up. I admired her for stepping up to the plate like that. Still… sometimes I wonder if she wanted Lillian and Reuben to move down to Florida so that they'd be out of her hair, although that makes me sound like a prize bitch, doesn't it? I wouldn't have blamed her. She had a lot to deal with.

And Bobby… I don't like to say it, but I swear to God he was a different kid after the crash. I know, I know, it could've just been PTSD or shock or whatever. But before it happened… when he was small… look, there's no other way to say it. He was the toddler from hell, threw a tantrum about a million times a day. I called him Damien after that kid in the movie, which made Lori mad. Lillian didn't see the half of it – Bobby behaved like a little angel whenever he was with her, I guess because she let him have his way all the time. And Reuben started getting sick when Bobby was two or so, so she wasn't around him all that much. Lori also spoiled him rotten, gave him whatever he wanted, though I told her the only person she was hurting was him. I'm not saying she was a bad mother. She wasn't. She loved him, and that's all they need, right? Although the truth of it was, I couldn't tell if he was spoiled or just what my mother would call a bad seed.

Lori hoped he'd settle down when he started at school. One of those arty Magnet schools had just opened up in the neighbourhood and she decided to enrol him there. It didn't help. Within days of him starting there she was called in to talk about his 'difficulties integrating', or whatever bullshit way they described it.

This one time, when Bobby was four or so, Lori had this big client she had to see. She was stuck for a babysitter and as Lillian was taking Reuben to be assessed by a new doctor, Lori asked me to babysit. I was living in an apartment in Carroll Gardens at the time, and my then-fiancé had bought me a kitten, cute little thing, we named her Sausage. Anyway, I left Bobby in front of the television while I had a shower, and as I was drying my hair I heard this high-pitched screaming sound coming from the kitchen. I swear, I never knew animals could scream like that. Bobby was holding Sausage by her tail and swinging her from side to side. He had this look on his face that said, 'Jeez, this is fun.' I'm not ashamed to say that I whacked him; he fell and knocked his forehead against the kitchen counter. Bled like anything. I had to rush him to the emergency room to get stitches. But he didn't cry. Didn't even flinch. Lori and I fell out over that for a while, but it didn't last long, we had too much history. Last time she asked me to babysit though.

Then after the crash...it was like he was a whole new person.

From chapter three of *Guarding JESS: My Life With One of The Three* **by Paul Craddock (co-written with Mandi Solomon).**

The press attention after Jess was medivacced to the UK was like nothing I could have imagined. The three 'miracle children' were fast becoming the story of the decade, and the UK public's thirst for news on Jess's condition was unquenchable. Paparazzi and tabloid hacks had taken up permanent residence on the steps of my apartment building, and the hospital was practically under siege. Gerry warned me not to say anything too personal on my cellphone, just in case it was being hacked.

I will say that the public support Jess received was overwhelming. The gifts from well-wishers soon filled Jess's room; others left messages, flowers, cards and legions of soft toys outside the hospital – there were so many that you could barely see the railings that ringed the grounds. People were kind. It was their way of showing they cared.

Meanwhile, my relationship with Marilyn and the rest of the Addams Family was deteriorating daily. I couldn't avoid encountering them in the waiting room, and sidestepping Marilyn's demands for me to hand over the keys to Stephen and Shelly's house was becoming unendurable. But the real cold war didn't start in earnest until January 22nd when I overheard Jase haranguing one of Jess's specialists outside her room. She still hadn't woken up at that stage, but her doctors had assured us that there was no sign of impaired cognitive functioning.

'Why the fuck can't you wake her up?' Jase was saying, while jabbing a nicotine-stained finger into the poor doctor's chest. The doctor assured him they were doing everything they could.

'Yeah?' Jase sneered. 'Well, if she ends up being a fucking vegetable, you lot can fucking well look after her then.'

That was the last straw. As far as I was concerned the Addamses had shown their true colours. I couldn't stop them visiting Jess, but I could let it be known that under no circumstances were they going to take care of her once she was discharged. I contacted Shelly's solicitor straight away and instructed her to inform the Addamses of Shelly and Stephen's custody arrangements.

A day later, there they were on the front page of the *Sun*. 'Jess's Gran Cut Out Of Her Life.'

Fair play to the photographer, he'd caught them in all their thuggish glory, Ma Addams glaring into shot, the brothers and various offspring scowling around her like an advert promoting the benefits of birth control. Marilyn especially wasn't shy about letting her views be known:

'It's not right,' Marilyn (58) says. 'Paul's lifestyle, it's not moral. He's a gay and we're upstanding citizens. A family. Jess would be better off with us.'

The *Sun* didn't miss a trick of course. They'd got their hands on a photograph of me taken during last year's gay pride parade, dressed in a tutu and laughing with my then-partner, Jackson. This was displayed in a full colour spread opposite the Addamses' mug shots.

The story spread like wildfire and it wasn't long before the other tabloids managed to procure similarly compromising photographs of me – no doubt courtesy of my friends or ex-friends. I suppose I couldn't blame them for cashing in. Most were struggling artists themselves.

But the tide really turned against me when Marilyn and I were invited to appear on the Roger Clydesdale show. Gerry warned me not to go on it, but I could hardly let Marilyn have her say unchallenged, could I? I'd met Roger at a media launch a few years before, and on the few occasions I'd caught his morning 'current affairs' show, he'd been rather harsh on what he called benefits scroungers. I suppose I naively assumed he'd be on my side.

The atmosphere inside the studio was electric with anticipation; you could tell that the audience was gagging for a showdown. They weren't disappointed. At first, I'll be honest, I thought it was going my way. Marilyn slumped on the studio couch, mumbling inarticulate answers to Roger's trademark, 'Why aren't you actively looking for a job?' questions. Then he turned his gimlet eye on me.

'Do you have any experience dealing with children, Paul?'

I told him that I'd been looking after Jess and Polly since they were babies and reiterated that Stephen and Shelly had chosen me as Jess's guardian.

'He just wants the house! He's an actor! He doesn't care about that kid!' Marilyn squealed, for some reason getting a round of applause from the audience. Roger paused for several seconds to let the furore die down, and then he dropped his bombshell. 'Paul . . . Is it true you have a history of mental illness?'

The audience erupted again, and even Marilyn looked a bit thrown.

I wasn't prepared for the question. I stuttered and stammered and did an appalling job of explaining that my breakdown was a thing of the past.

Of course, this revelation spawned countless screaming headlines along the lines of: 'Nutter to take care of Jess.'

I was devastated, of course. No one likes to see things like that written about them, and I only had myself to blame for being too open. I've been harshly criticised for how I dealt with the press after that. Among other things I've been called a publicity whore and an 'alleged egomaniac and narcissist'. But whatever the press chose to say about me, I had Jess's best interests at heart. I'd put my career on hold for the foreseeable future in order to devote all my time to her. Quite frankly, if I was interested in exploiting her for monetary gain, I could have made millions. Not that money would be an issue, Shelly and Stephen's life policies were fully paid-up and there was the compensation that I was intending to put into trust for Jess. She would always be looked after. The reason I appeared on the various morning shows was nothing to do with money and everything to do with setting the record straight. Anyone else would have done the same.

As you can see, I had a lot on my plate, but Jess was my priority. She was still unresponsive, but apart from her burn injuries, physically she was doing well. I needed to start thinking about what to do about her living arrangements.

Dr Kasabian, who was pipped to be Jess's psychologist when she eventually woke up and started talking, suggested that it might be best for her to be in familiar surroundings, which meant moving into Stephen's house in Chiselhurst.

Walking in there that first time was one of the hardest things I've ever done. Everything, from the wedding and school photos on the walls, to the dried-up Christmas tree in the driveway that Stephen hadn't got around to throwing away, was a reminder of what Jess and I had lost.

When I shut the door behind me, the shouts of the hacks outside filtering through (yes, they even followed me on this painful errand), I felt as bereft as I did when I first got the tragic news.

But I made myself confront the scene. For Jess's sake I had to be strong. I walked slowly through the house, finally breaking down completely when I saw the photos of me and Stephen as kids that he'd put up in his office. There was me, pudgy and gaptoothed; him, svelte and serious. Physically, you would never have known we were twins, and our personalities were similarly diverse. Even at age eight I knew I wanted to be on the stage, whereas Stephen was far more retiring and serious. Still, even though we didn't run in the same circles at school, we were always close, and when he met Shelly, our relationship actually deepened. Shelly and I got on like a house on fire straight away.

Though it broke my heart, I made myself stay the night in the house – I needed to acclimatise for Jess's sake. I barely slept, and when I did, I dreamed of Stephen and Shelly. The dreams were so vivid it was as if they were right in the room with me, their spirits clinging to the house. But I knew I was doing the right thing where Jess was concerned, and I know they gave me their blessing.

To date, their bodies haven't been recovered. Nor has Polly's. In some ways that's a blessing. Rather than a terrible trip to identify them in some soulless Portuguese morgue, my last memories of them are of our final dinner together: Polly and Jess giggling, Stephen and Shelly talking about their last-minute holiday. A happy family.

Through all of this, I don't know what I would have done without Mel, Geoff and the rest of the good people from 277 Together. Remember, these are men and women who had lost their own loved ones in the most horrendous way possible, but they sprang to my defence at every opportunity. Mel and Geoff even accompanied me when I moved my belongings into the house, helped me decide what to do about the family photos displayed everywhere. We decided to put them away until Jess had had time to fully accept her parents and sister's deaths. They were my rocks, and I mean that from the bottom of my heart.

The bile spewed by the Addamses and their tame hacks wasn't all we had to deal with, especially when all the conspiracy stories started going viral. Mel was especially incensed by this – you wouldn't know it to look at her, but she's a staunch Catholic, and she was genuinely offended by the horsemen conspiracy theory in particular.

Around that time, we got the news that a memorial service was being planned. The few bodies that had been recovered wouldn't be released until after the inquest, which could be months away, and all of us felt that we needed some closure. They still didn't know what had caused the Go!Go! crash, although terrorism had been ruled out, as it had in all of the four disasters. I tried not to catch too much of the ongoing investigation on the news – it just made me feel worse – although I'd gathered that they suspected it might have had something to do with an electrical storm that had caused severe turbulence for other flights in the area. Mel told me she'd seen the footage from the Navy sub they'd sent down to try and retrieve the black box from the wreckage on the ocean floor. She said it looked so peaceful down there; the middle section of the aircraft looked barely damaged, settled forever in its watery grave. She said the only thing that kept her going was the thought that it had been quick. She couldn't bear the idea of

Danielle and the other passengers knowing they were going to die, like those poor passengers on the Japanese flight, who'd had time to leave messages. I knew exactly what she meant, but you can't think like that, you just can't.

The memorial service was going to be held at St Paul's, with an additional service in Trafalgar Square for the public. I knew the Addams Family would be there, no doubt with their favourite hack from the *Sun* in tow, and I was understandably nervous.

Again, Mel, Geoff and their army of friends and family came to my rescue. They stuck to my side throughout that fraught day. To be honest, they were from the same background as Shelly's family. Geoff had been out of work for years, and they lived on a council estate in Orpington not far from where the Addamses lived. It wouldn't have been unreasonable for them to take Marilyn and co's side, especially as I was being painted as a 'public school snob with artistic aspirations'. But they didn't. When we arrived at the service, coincidentally at the same time as the Addamses (how's that for fate? There were thousands of people there), Mel jabbed a finger in Marilyn's face and hissed, 'You cause any trouble here and you'll be out on your ear, you hear me?' Marilyn was wearing a cheap black fascinator that resembled a giant spider, and although she remained stony-faced, it quivered indignantly. Jase and Keith bristled but they were both stared down by Gavin, Mel and Geoff's oldest son, a shaven-haired fellow with the build and look of a strip-club bouncer. I found out later he was 'connected'. A geezer. Someone you wouldn't want to mess with.

I could have hugged him.

I won't dwell on the service itself, but one part in par-

ticular touched me – Kelvin's reading. He'd chosen that
W. H. Auden poem, 'Stop all the Clocks', the one most
people know from *Four Weddings and A Funeral*. It could
have been mawkish, but here was this huge dreadlocked
fellow, reading with quiet dignity. When he read the line,
'Let aeroplanes circle moaning overhead' you could have
heard a pin drop.

I'd barely made it outside the cathedral when I got the
call from Dr Kasabian. Jess had woken up.

I don't know how Marilyn and the Addamses found out
that she'd emerged out of her coma – I assume one of the
nurses must have called them – but when I arrived at the
hospital, my emotions threatening to swamp me, there they
were, waiting outside her room.

Dr K knew all about our fraught relationship – he
didn't live under a stone – and insisted that the last thing
Jess needed right now was a tense atmosphere. Marilyn
grumpily agreed to button her lip, told Fester and Gomez
to wait outside, and we were ushered in to see her. Marilyn, her fascinator still quivering, made sure she reached
Jess's bedside first, practically pushing me out of the way.

'It's me, Jessie,' Marilyn said. 'Nana.'

Jess looked at her blankly. Then she reached out a hand
towards me. I wish I could say that she knew who we
were, but there was no recognition in her eyes, which was
absolutely understandable. But I can't help but think that
she looked at both of us, sized us up, and figured out, right
then, who would be the lesser of two evils.

Chiyoko and Ryu.

Message logged @ 19.46, 21/01/2012

RYU: You there?????

Message logged @ 22.30, 21/01/2012

CHIYOKO: I'm back.

RYU: When?

CHIYOKO: Like five minutes ago.

RYU: 24 hrs no messaging. No you. It was…strange.

CHIYOKO: That's sweet. What did you do while I was gone?

RYU: Usual. Slept. Ate something, watched an ancient episode of *Welcome to the NHK*, but it was just a filler. And hey…you lied.

CHIYOKO: What do you mean?

RYU: I saw you on TV. You're pretty. Um…you look a bit like Hazuki Hitori.

CHIYOKO: …

RYU: Sorry. Didn't mean to make you uncomfortable. Forgive this stupid geek.
   (< ^ _ ^ >) \

CHIYOKO: How did you know it was me? I wasn't wearing a name badge.

RYU: It *had* to be you. You were next to Hiro, standing behind your uncle, am I correct? There was almost as much footage of Hiro and Kenji as there was of what's her name, minister Uri's crazy wife. The one who believes in aliens.

CHIYOKO: Aikao Uri.

RYU: Yes, her. So, was it you?

CHIYOKO: Maybe.

RYU: I knew it! I thought you said you weren't into fashion?

CHIYOKO: I'm not. Enough with the personal stuff.

RYU: Sorry again. So how was it?

CHIYOKO: It was a memorial service, how do you *think* it was?

RYU: Am I making you grumpy?

CHIYOKO: Hey, I'm the ice princess. I'm always

grumpy. I'll tell you about it if you want to hear. How much detail do you want me to go into?

RYU: I want to hear all of it. Listen...I know this is against the rules, but...just gonna say it: You want to Skype?

CHIYOKO:...

RYU: You still there?

CHIYOKO: Let's carry on as usual.

RYU: Whatever is cool for you, ice princess. I know what you look like now. You cannot hide from me (wwwwwwwwwwwww). Sorry, evil laugh over.

CHIYOKO: It feels strange, you knowing my face. Like you have power over me or something.

RYU: Hey! I told you my real identity first. You cannot believe how hard that was.

CHIYOKO: I know. I'm not being paranoid.

RYU: I've told you things I have never told anyone. You don't judge me. You don't stare at me like the old bitches in the neighbourhood.

CHIYOKO: How could I? We live in different prefectures.

RYU: You know what I mean. I trust you.

CHIYOKO: Except you know what I look like and I don't know what you look like.

RYU: You're better looking than me. (^ _ ^)

CHIYOKO: Enough!!!!!!!

RYU: Okay. So tell me, how was it? It looked really emotional. At the shrine…all those photographs of the passengers…They looked like they went on forever.

CHIYOKO: It was. Emotional, I mean. Even this ice princess could not fail to be affected. 526 people. I don't know where to start…

RYU: Start at the beginning.

CHIYOKO: Okay…So, I told you we had to leave really early. For once in his life Father took the day off and Mother Creature said I should dress in black, but not to be 'too fashionable'. I'm like, hey, no problem, MC.

RYU: You looked good.

CHIYOKO: Ai!

RYU: Sorry.

CHIYOKO: Because of Android Uncle's status, we'd managed to get accommodation at one of the lodges near to Lake Saiko, so that we didn't have to leave immediately afterwards unlike most of the victims' families, although a lot of them were staying at the Highland Resort or one of the other Mount Fuji tour hotels.

CHIYOKO: Our place was Japanese style, run by this ancient couple who couldn't take their eyes off Android Uncle. The woman went on and on about bringing us tea and how to get to the closest onsen, as if we were there for a holiday.

RYU: Sounds like my neighbours.

CHIYOKO: Yeah. Real old busy-bodies. As we arrived, the morning mist was settling and it was cold. MC didn't stop talking in the car the whole way there, pointing out where Mount Fuji would be if you could actually see it – the cloud hid it from view that whole day. Android Uncle greeted us, he'd arrived the night before from Osaka with Hiro and the sister of one of his lab assistants, who he'd asked to help look after Hiro. I know MC was offended because he went back to Osaka after Hiro left the hospital instead of staying with us, but she put on her polite and respectful face.

CHIYOKO: Android Uncle looked much older than I remembered him.

RYU: Do you think he makes his robot look older as he ages?

CHIYOKO: Ryu! It's not like you to be so dark!!!

RYU: Sorry. And Hiro?

CHIYOKO: He was sleeping when MC, Father and I arrived, it was still really early, remember. The assistant bowed and scraped to the parents, simpering at Android Uncle. You could see that she had her eye on him as a future husband. When MC, Father and Android Uncle went off to another room to talk privately, she was straight on her cellphone, texting away like crazy.

RYU: I think I saw her! Big head. Pasty face. Fat.

CHIYOKO: How do you know that wasn't me?

RYU: Was it? If so, I'm really sorry. I didn't mean to offend you.

CHIYOKO: Of course it wasn't me!

RYU: o(_ _)o Forgive this idiot.

CHIYOKO: You're so gullible. When the parents and Android Uncle finished their private conversation they came back in and we hung around and made really really awkward conversation. 'I must go wake Hiro,' Android Uncle said. 'It is time.' 'Let me go,' the assistant said. I'm going to call her Pasty-Face. Pasty-Face bowed like an asshole and left the room. This bit was funny. We heard this screech and she came running downstairs saying, 'Aiii, Hiro bit me!'

RYU: Hiro bit her? Seriously!!!!

CHIYOKO: She deserved it. Mother Creature said that Hiro was probably having a bad dream and woke up with a fright. I could tell she didn't think much of Pasty-Face either, which made me happy to be around her for once. Android Uncle went upstairs to fetch him. Hiro was dressed in a little black suit, his eyes puffy from sleep. After that, Android Uncle barely glanced at him or spoke to him.

RYU: What do you mean?

CHIYOKO: I think he found it painful to look at him, as if he reminded him too much of Auntie Hiromi. Hiro doesn't look anything like her, but perhaps they had the same mannerisms. Shall I continue?

RYU: Please.

CHIYOKO: Hiro looked at us, one by one, and when he saw me, he came shuffling over and took my hand. I didn't know what to do at first. His fingers were ice cold. MC looked surprised that Hiro had chosen me, and kept trying to entice him over. But he didn't move. He leaned against me, and I heard him sigh.

RYU: You think you reminded him of his mother?

CHIYOKO: Maybe. Maybe he realised the rest of the people in the room were fucking losers.

RYU: !!!!

CHIYOKO: Then we drove to the memorial site and the shrine. We were still early, but already there were thousands of people there, as well as packs of reporters and TV cameras. There was this sudden hush when people saw Hiro – he still refused to let go of my hand – and all you could hear were the click and whir of the reporters' cameras. Several people bowed respectfully, although I didn't know if they were bowing to Android Uncle or Hiro. It was a strange feeling being the centre of attention and I could tell Pasty-Face was lapping it up. Father just kept this empty expression on his face and MC didn't know where to look. The crowd even drew back so that we were able to walk straight up to pay our respects to Auntie's photograph without waiting in line. It was still misty, and the air was thick with incense. Am I boring you? Going into too much detail?

RYU: No! I'm touched. You should be a writer. Your words are beautiful.

CHIYOKO: Are you serious??????

RYU: Yes.

CHIYOKO: Ha! Tell that to the exam board.

RYU: Please continue.

CHIYOKO: As we stood there, a ripple went through the crowd and a small woman approached us. I didn't recognise her straight away. Then I realised it was

Captain Seto's wife. She's old, at least forty, but she's much prettier in real life.

RYU: *That* wasn't on TV.

CHIYOKO: It was brave of her to come, especially as so many assholes were still saying the crash was Captain Seto's fault. That makes me so mad, especially as the *isho* proved that he was calm and controlled right up until the last moment. Plus there's the phone footage that businessman filmed when the cabin filled with smoke, so it was obviously a mechanical problem. His wife was so dignified and calm. She bowed at Hiro, but didn't speak. I wish now that I'd said something to her. I wanted to tell her that she should be proud of what her husband had done. Then she left. I didn't see her again.

RYU: That must have been intense.

CHIYOKO: Yeah. You probably saw the rest on TV.

RYU: Did you talk to the prime minister?

CHIYOKO: No. He looks way older and smaller in real life, though. And his bar-code head is far more pronounced in the flesh. The wind lifted some strands and you could see his scalp.

RYU: !!!!!

CHIYOKO: Hey, did you hear Android Uncle's speech about how Auntie Hiromi was valued in life and he would do his best to honour her memory while he brings up Hiro?

RYU: Of course.

CHIYOKO: Even I almost cried. It wasn't just his words, it was the atmosphere. I'm starting to sound like some kind of spiritual freak, huh?

RYU: No. I could sense the atmosphere even here in my crappy room.

CHIYOKO: And all the time, Hiro held on to my hand. I kept looking down at him to make sure he was okay, and MC and Pasty-Face kept vying with each other to fuss around him, but he acted like they weren't there.

RYU: That American who was on the plane. That was her daughter who spoke, right? Her Japanese was good.

CHIYOKO: Yeah. That message her mother left… What do you think she was trying to say? 'The boy, the boy…' Do you think she saw Hiro before she died?

RYU: I dunno. My English is bad and I only read the translation. There's a load of speculation on 2-chan and Toko Z about it.

CHIYOKO: Why do you waste your time on those sites? Seriously? What are they saying now?

RYU: That thing she said about the dead people. They're saying she must have seen the spirits of the dead.

CHIYOKO: Yeah right. Like she couldn't have meant the most obvious thing – the *real* people who'd died in the crash? People are idiots.

RYU: Did you see the photo of her?

CHIYOKO: Which one?

RYU: The one on that US site – celebautopsy.net. The one that rogue reporter took before journalists were prevented from going to the site. It was horrible.

CHIYOKO: Why did you even look at it?

RYU: Followed a link, got lost…Hey…sorry to ask this. But did your aunt leave a message?

CHIYOKO: I don't know. My uncle hasn't said. If she did, the press didn't leak it to the magazines.

RYU: So…after the blessings and the speeches, what happened next?

CHIYOKO: We went back to the lodge. Pasty-Face insisted that Hiro needed a nap, and this time he went with her quietly. That whole day, he didn't say one word to anyone. Mother Creature says it's because he's still traumatised.

RYU: Of course he is.

CHIYOKO: Later, Pasty-Face tried to gossip with me, but I gave her my best evil cat stare and she got the message and spent the rest of the night on her phone. Android Uncle barely said a word, although MC tried to talk to him about what to do with Auntie's remains after they're released.

RYU: I thought they said there will be a mass cremation?

CHIYOKO: Yeah. But they're having two – one here and one in Osaka. Auntie was born in Tokyo, but lived in Osaka so he'll have to decide what to do. But Mother Creature managed to convince him to stay a few days with us in the city before he leaves for Osaka.

RYU: Seriously? Kenji Yanagida is in your house???? Right now?

CHIYOKO: Yeah. Not only that, but Hiro is fast asleep in my bed, a metre from where I'm sitting.

RYU: And Pasty-Face?

CHIYOKO: MC told her to go back to Osaka – said that she wasn't needed.

RYU: I bet that annoyed Pasty-Face.

CHIYOKO: Yeah. For once I was actually proud to be MC's daughter.

RYU: Another difficult question and one you don't have to answer…did you go to the crash site? I heard that some of the families requested to go the next day.

CHIYOKO: No. They'd arranged several coaches to take anyone who wanted to go from the Kawachiko station. I wanted to go, but Mother Creature and Father wanted to get back to the city. I'll go someday, though. Oh! I forgot to tell you. After the service that guy who found Hiro came up to pay his respects.

RYU: The suicide monitor guy?

CHIYOKO: Yeah.

RYU: What was he like?

CHIYOKO: Um…quiet, but he looked like the sort of person you could trust. Sad, but not depressed, if that makes sense? Real old school though. Hang on. Mother Creature is calling me. Got to go.

RYU: (˅('・ω・`)

Message logged @ 10.30, 22/01/2012

CHIYOKO: Ryu, you there?

RYU: Always. What's up?

CHIYOKO: Android Uncle has just found out that Pasty-Face has been sending emails to the *Shukan Bunshun*, trying to sell her story. Mother Creature is furious, Android Uncle is seething. Mother Creature has asked if he wants Hiro to stay here when he goes back to Osaka, to avoid all the attention. She's offered my services as his minder.

RYU: What? YOU look after the kid?

CHIYOKO: Yeah. What, you think I'll try to corrupt him?

RYU: Will you? Not corrupt him, I mean, but look after him?

CHIYOKO: You know the scene here. What else can I do? I'm not cut out for the freeter lifestyle.

RYU: You could always join my yakuza gang, baby. We need good people.

CHIYOKO: Cliché. Look, I have to go. MC wants to taaaaaaaalk again.

RYU: Well, keep me posted.

CHIYOKO: I will. And thanks for being there.

RYU: Always. ･*:‥。.。.:*･'(*ﾟ▽ﾟ*)'･*:‥。. .。.:*･ﾟ ﾟ･*

Dr Pascal de la Croix, a French robotics professor who is currently based at MIT, was one of the few people Hiro Yanagida's father, renowned robotics expert Kenji Yanagida, agreed to talk to in the weeks following the crash that took his wife's life.

I have known Kenji for years. We met at the 2005 Tokyo World Exposition when he unveiled the Surrabot #1 – his first android doppelgänger. I was immediately captivated – what skill! Although the Surrabot #1 was an early model, even then you could barely tell Kenji and it apart. Many people in our field dismissed his work as narcissistic or fanciful, scoffed at the fact that Kenji's focus was more on human psychology than robotics, but I did not. Others found the Surrabot #1 deeply disturbing, tapping, as it does, into the uncanny valley inside all of us. I have even heard people say that creating machines that look exactly like human beings is unethical. What nonsense! For, if we can understand and unlock human nature, surely that is the highest calling?

Let me move on. We kept in touch over the years, and in 2008, Kenji, his wife Hiromi and their son came to stay with me in Paris. Hiromi did not speak much English, so communication with her was limited, but my wife was enchanted with Hiro. 'Japanese babies, so well behaved!' I think if she could have adopted that child then and there she would have done so!

I happened to be in Tokyo when I heard the news about the plane crash and Kenji's wife's demise. I knew immediately that I must go to see him, that he would need his friends more than ever. I had lost my father, you see, a man to whom I had been very close, to cancer the year before, and Kenji had been very kind with his condolences. But Kenji did not answer his phone, and his assistants at the Osaka University would not reveal to me where he was. In the days that followed there were pictures of him everywhere. There was not the media madness that attended the survival of the American boy and the poor child from Britain – the Japanese are not so intrusive – but there was still much attention. And the crazy rumours! The whole of Tokyo appeared to be fascinated by Hiro. I heard tales from the hotel staff that some believed the boy harboured the spirits of all those who had died in the crash. Such nonsense!

I thought of going to the memorial service, but did not think it would be my place to do so. Then I heard that Kenji had returned to Osaka. I decided that instead of returning home, I would make one last attempt to see him, and I booked myself on the next available flight to Osaka. By then, air traffic was almost back to normal.

I am not ashamed to say that I used my reputation to gain entrance into his laboratory at the university. His assistants, many of whom I had met before, were respectful, but told me that he was unavailable.

And then I saw his android. The Surrabot #3. It was sitting in the corner of the room, and a young assistant appeared to be talking to it. I knew immediately that Kenji was talking through it; I had seen him doing this before on many occasions. In fact, if he was asked to go on the lecture circuit and could not leave the university, he would send his robot instead and talk through it remotely!

You want that I should explain a little how the mechanism

works? In the most simple language I can use, it is controlled remotely, through a computer. Kenji uses a camera to capture his face and head movements and these are transmitted to servos – little micro-motors – embedded inside the android's face plate. This is how it mirrors his facial movements – even blinking is replicated. A microphone records Kenji's voice, and this is conveyed via the android's mouthpiece, right down to the slightest intonation. There is also a mechanism inside its chest – not unlike those used by high-end sex doll manufacturers – which simulates breathing. It can be most disconcerting talking to the android. At first glance it certainly does look like Kenji. He even changes its hair whenever he has a haircut!

I insisted on speaking to it and said without hesitation, 'Kenji. I was so sorry to hear about Hiromi. I know what it is you are going through. Please, if there is anything I can do, let me know.'

There was a pause, and then the android said something in Japanese to the assistant. She said to me, 'Come,' and told me to follow her. She led me through a bewildering number of corridors, and down towards a basement area. She politely refused to answer any of my questions about Kenji's well-being, and I could not help but admire her loyalty to him.

She knocked on an unmarked door and it was opened by Kenji himself.

I was shocked when I saw him. After just talking to his android doppelgänger, the fact that he had aged terribly was even more noticeable. His hair was dishevelled and there were dark circles under his eyes. He snapped something at his assistant -- which was unlike him, I had never seen him be discourteous before – and she hurried away, leaving us alone.

I gave him my condolences, but he barely seemed to hear them. He kept his features absolutely still; only his eyes showed any sign of life. He thanked me for coming all this way to see him, but said it was not necessary.

I asked him why he was working in the basement and not the lab, and he told me that he was tired of being around people. The press hadn't stopped harassing him since the memorial service. Then he asked me if I wanted to inspect his latest creation and waved me inside the room.

'Oh!' I said, as soon as I stepped inside. 'I see that your son is visiting you.'

But before I finished the sentence I realised my mistake. The child sitting on the small chair next to one of Kenji's computers was not human. It was another of his replicas. A surrobot version of his son. 'Is this your latest project?' I asked, trying to hide my shock.

For the first time he smiled. 'No. I made that last year.' And then he gestured to the far corner of the room where a surrobot dressed in a white kimono was sitting. A female surrobot.

I walked towards her. She was beautiful; perfect, a slight smile on her lips. Her chest rose and fell as if she was breathing in and exhaling deeply.

'Is that...?' I could not say it.

'Yes,' he said. 'It is Hiromi, my wife.' Without taking his eyes off her he said, 'It is almost as if her soul is still here.'

I attempted to ask why he had felt the need to build a replica of his deceased wife, but the answer is obvious, is it not? He avoided my questions, but he did tell me that Hiro was living in Tokyo with relatives.

I did not say what I was thinking: 'Kenji, you have a son who is alive. Who needs you. Do not forget this, my friend.'

Not only was this not my business, I knew that his grief ran too deep to listen to what I was saying.

So I did the only thing I could do. I left.

Outside, not even the city's beauty could calm me. I felt unsettled, as if something in the world's axis had shifted.

And as I stood, looking back at the university building, it started snowing.

Mandi Solomon is the ghost/co-writer of Paul Craddock's unfinished memoir, *Guarding JESS: My Life With One of The Three*.

My main objective when I meet the subject for the first time is to win their trust. There's usually a tight deadline on celeb memoirs, so I generally have to work fast. Most of my clients have spent their careers seeing exposés or just plain bullshit written about them (or their PR agencies have collaborated in the bullshit) so they're practised at keeping their true selves under wraps. But readers aren't stupid, they can smell fakery a mile off. It's important to me that we include at least some new material, balance the usual PR buff with some genuine revelations and shockers. I didn't have that problem with Paul of course. He was up front right from the beginning. My publishers and his agent put the deal together in double-quick time. They wanted the inside story of how Jess was coping; they knew the attention on her would be mega, and they weren't wrong. The story grew bigger every day.

Our first meeting was at a coffee bar in Chislehurst, gosh, sometime in early February. Jess was still in hospital and Paul was busy moving his stuff into her house, getting the place ready for her to come home. My first impression of him? He was fairly charming, witty, slightly camp of course, but then he is – or was – an actor. His brother's death had obviously hit him hard, and when I touched on that, there were a few tears, but he didn't seem at all embarrassed about showing emotion in front of me. And he was remarkably candid about his past, the fact that in his twenties he drank too much, experimented with drugs, slept around a bit. He didn't go into detail about his stint in Maudsley Psychiatric Hospital, but he didn't deny it either. Said his breakdown was stress-related after he had a professional disappointment. I never for one second thought he wouldn't be capable of looking after a child. If anyone asked me after that first meeting what I thought of him, I would've said he was a good guy, maybe a bit self-obsessed, but nothing compared to some I've dealt with.

After I've won their trust, I give my clients a Dictaphone – a digital voice recorder actually – and I encourage them to talk into it as often as possible without thinking too much about what they're saying. I always reassure them that I won't put in any information they're uncomfortable with. Most insist on a contract to this effect, which is fine by me. There are always ways to get around that kind of thing, and in any case, most of them like to add an edge to their life story. You'd be amazed at how quickly they get used to the Dictaphone method, some of them using it as their personal therapist. Have you read *Fighting for Glory*? The tell-all biography of Lennie L, the cage fighter? Came out last year. Gosh, the things he used to say. I could only use half of them. Quite often he'd leave the recorder on while he was having sex, which I eventually began to think was deliberate.

Paul took to the Dictaphone method like a duck to water. At the beginning, things appeared to be going well. I had the rough draft of the first three chapters down, and I sent him an email detailing what else I thought we might need. The downloads came as regular as clockwork, and then – about a week or so after Jess got home – they stopped. I rationalised that he had his hands full dealing with Jess, the press attention, and the crazies who wouldn't leave them alone, so I covered for him for a month or so. He kept promising he'd send me more. Out of the blue, he said the book was off. My publishers were furious, threatened to sue. They'd paid the advance, you see.

It was Mel who found it. Paul had left a flash drive for me in an envelope on the dining-room table, with my name and telephone number on it. I gave it to the police of course, but not before I downloaded it and made a copy. I had some idea of transcribing it, maybe publishing it later, but I couldn't listen to it after that first time.

It scared me, Elspeth. It scared the living shit out of me.

10.15 p.m.

So here we go again, Mandi. God, every time I say your name that Barry Manilow song pops into my head. 'Oh Mandy, you came and you gave without'...something, can't remember the lyrics. Was it really about his dog? Sorry, this isn't really the place to be flippant, but you did say to let go and say whatever came into my head, and it takes my mind off, you know, Stephen. The crash. Fucking everything.

(A sob)

Sorry. Sorry. I'm fine. It happens sometimes, I think I'm coping and then...So. Day six since Jess came home. It's still like the slate has been wiped clean – her memories about life before Black Thursday are still spotty, and she has no recollection at all of the accident. She still does her morning ritual, as if she's disconnected from the real world and needs to remind herself of who she is: 'I'm Jessica, you're my Uncle Paul, and Mummy and Daddy and my sister are with the angels.' I'm still a bit guilty about the angels thing, Stephen and Shelly were atheists, but you try explaining the concept of death to a six-year-old without bringing heaven into it. I keep reminding myself that Dr Kasabian (God, the other day I slipped up and called him Dr Kevorkian – don't put that in) said that it's going to take some time to adjust, and changes in her behaviour are normal. There's no sign of brain damage as you know, but I did some more Internet research and PTSD can do strange things. But on the bright side, she's far more communicative – more so than she was before the crash, if that makes sense.

A funny thing happened this evening while I was putting her to bed, but I'm not sure we can use it for the book. You remember I told you we were reading *The Lion, the Witch and the Wardrobe*? Jess's choice. Well, out of nowhere, she goes, 'Uncle Paul, does Mr Tumnus like to kiss men like you do?'

I was *floored*, Mandi. Stephen and Shelly had decided that the girls were too young for the birds and the bees conversation, never mind anything more complex, so as far as I know they hadn't discussed the fact that I'm gay with the twins. And I don't let her see the papers or go on the Internet, not with all that crap they're saying in the States about her and the other two kids. Not to mention the bile fucking Marilyn and the Addams Family keep spouting to the tabloids about me. I thought about asking who had told her I 'liked to kiss men', but decided against making a big deal out of it. It was possible a hack had got to her and the hospital had covered it up.

She wasn't going to let it go. '*Does* he, Uncle Paul?' she kept asking. You know the book, right, Mandi? Mr Tumnus is the first of the talking animals that Lucy bumps into when she goes through the wardrobe into Narnia – a little goateed fellow with deer's legs, a faun or something. (He actually looks a lot like that trauma counsellor who came over just after I heard the news about Jess.) And to be honest, in the illustration Mr Tumnus does look as camp as fuck with his little scarf tied jauntily around his neck. I suppose it isn't outside the realms of possibility that he'd just been off cottaging with some centaurs in the forest. God. Don't put that in either. I think I said something like, 'Well, if he does, that's his choice, isn't it?' and carried on reading.

We read quite far, and I was a bit nervous when we came to the bit where Aslan, the talking lion, gives himself up to the evil queen to be slaughtered. Stephen told me that when he read this to the girls last year, they'd sobbed and sobbed and Polly had even had nightmares.

But this time around, Jess was dry-eyed. 'Why would Aslan do that? It's just stupid, isn't it, Uncle Paul?'

I decided not to explain that Aslan's death is a Christian allegory, Jesus dying for all our sins and all that bollocks, so I said something like, 'Well, Edmund has betrayed the others, and the evil queen says she's going to kill him. Aslan says that he will take Edmund's place because he's good and kind.'

'It's still stupid. But I'm glad. I like Edmund.'

If you remember, Mandi, Edmund is the selfish spoiled lying bastard child. 'Why?'

And she said: 'He's the only one of the children who isn't a fucking pussy.'

Christ, I didn't know whether to tell her off or laugh. Remember I told you she'd picked up a slew of bad language when she was in hospital? It must've been from the porters or cleaners because I can't imagine Dr K or the nurses effing and blinding around her.

'You shouldn't say things like that, Jess,' I said.

'Like what?' And then she goes: 'It doesn't work like

that. A fucking wardrobe. As *if*, Uncle Paul.' This thought seemed to amuse her, and she fell asleep soon after that.

I suppose I should be grateful that she's talking and communicating at all. She doesn't get visibly upset when I mention Stephen and Shelly and Polly, but it's early days. Dr K says I should prepare myself for some emotional fallout, but so far so good. We're still a ways from sending her back to school – the last thing we need is for the kids there to tell her what's being said about her – but we're inching towards making a normal life.

So what else? Oh yeah, tomorrow Darren from Social Services is coming to check 'that I'm coping'. Did I tell you about him? Darren's okay, a bit beardy and sandals and granola, but he's on my side, I can tell. I might need to think about getting an au pair or something like that, although that old busy-body from next door, Mrs Ellington-Burn (how's that for a name!), keeps nagging me to let her look after Jess. Mel and Geoff say they're also happy to babysit. What a pair of troopers. Thinking you could say something like: 'Mel and Geoff continued to be my back-bone, while I struggled with my new single father status.' Too arsey? Well, we can work on it. You did a great job with the first chapters, so I'm sure it will be cool.

Hang on, let me get my tea. Fuck! Shit. Spilled it. Ow. That's hot. Okay...

No nutters phoned today, thank God. The group who are convinced Jess is an alien stopped after I asked the police to give them a warning, so that just leaves the God squad and the press. Gerry can handle the movie people. He still thinks we should wait a while and auction Jess's story. Seems a bit greedy, specially with the insurance money, but Jess might thank me when she's older if I set her up financially for life. Hard call. Can't imagine how that American kid is coping, the attention must be insane. I really feel for his grandmother, although at least she's in New York and not one of those Bible Belt states. I suppose it will all die down eventually. I told you another chat show in the States is trying to get The Three together, right? One of the big ones this time. They wanted to fly Jess and me to New York, but there's no way she's up to that. Then they suggested a Skype interview, but it all fell through when the father of the Japanese boy and Bobby's gran said no way. There's plenty of time for all that. I wish I could turn the bloody phone off some days, but I need to be available for Social Services and other important calls. Oh! Did I tell you I'm booked on *Morning Chat with Randy and Margaret* next week? Do watch it and tell me what you think. I only agreed because the booker just would not give up! And Gerry says it's a chance to set the record straight after all that crap about me in the *Mail on Sunday*.

(*The sound of a ring tone – the theme to* Dr Zhivago)

Hold on.

Fucking Marilyn again. At this time of night! Not answering that. Thank you Caller ID. They'll only harangue me about when I'm going to bring Jess round to see them. I can't put them off forever as they'll only run to their favourite *Sun* hack and blab, but I'm still holding out for an apology for that *Chat* magazine exposé about me being a basket-case. I hope you're not taking all that crap seriously, Mandi. Do you think we should say more about it in the book? Gerry says we should play it down. There's not much to tell, to be honest. Had a little slip-up, ten years ago, big deal. And I haven't been tempted to have another drink since the day I got the news.

(Yawns)

That should do for now. Nighty night. I'm going to bed.

3.30 a.m.

Okay. Okay. It's cool. Breathe.

Something fucked-up has just happened. Mandi...I...

Deep breath, Paul. It's just in your head. It's just in your fucking head.

Talk it out. Yeah. Fuck. Why not. I can delete this, can't I? Narrative psychology, Dr K would be proud.

(Laughs shakily)

Christ, I'm soaked through with sweat. Sopping. It's fading now, but this is what I remember.

I woke up suddenly, and I could feel there was someone sitting on the end of the bed – the mattress was sagging slightly as if there was a weight on it. I sat up, felt this huge wash of dread. I guess I knew instinctively that whoever it was was too heavy to be Jess.

I think I said something like, 'Who's there?'

My eyes adjusted to the dark and then I saw a shape at the end of the bed.

I froze. I've never felt fear like it. It...fuck, *think*, Paul. Jesus. It felt like...like a load of cement had been injected into my veins. I stared at it for ages. It was sitting slumped, motionless, looking down at its hands.

And then it spoke. 'What have you done, Paul? How could you let that thing in here?'

It was Stephen. I knew immediately from his voice it was him, but his shape looked different. Warped. More hunched, the head slightly too big. But it was so real, Mandi. Despite the panic, for a second I was absolutely convinced that he was actually there, and I felt a huge surge of joy and relief. 'Stephen!' I think I yelled. I reached out to grab him, but he'd gone.

5.45 a.m.

God. I've just played that back. It's so strange, isn't it, how dreams can seem so real at the time, but fade so quickly? Must be my subconscious telling me something. I wish it would hurry up and get light though. I can't decide if I should send this to you or not. I don't want to come across as a nutter, not with all the stories going around about me as it is.

And what did he mean, 'How could you let that thing in?'

PART FOUR

CONSPIRACY

FEBRUARY–MARCH

This is the second account from Reba Louise Neilson, Pamela May Donald's 'closest friend'.

Stephenie said she almost had a conniption when she heard Pastor Len's show about Pamela's message. He always discussed what he was going to say on his radio show with his inner circle after Bible study, but that time he just flat came out with it. I barely slept after I heard it. Couldn't figure why he wouldn't have shared something so important with his church first. Later he said the truth had come to him just that day and he felt called to spread the news as soon as he was able. Stephenie and I both agreed that those children couldn't have survived something like that without God's guiding hand, and those colours on the planes matching John's vision in Revelation, well, how could that be a coincidence? But when Pastor Len started saying that Pam was a prophet, like Paul and John, well, I found that hard to take, and I wasn't the only one.

Now, I know the Lord has a plan for us all that we can't always make sense of, but Pamela May Donald, a prophet? Plain old Pam who'd get her panties in a knot if she burned the brownies for the Christmas fundraiser? I kept my doubts to myself, and it was only when Stephenie brought it up when she was visiting with me that I even aired my views on the subject. We both had all the respect in the world for Pastor Len back then, we really did, and we decided not to breathe a word about how we felt to him or Kendra.

Not that we saw much of Pastor Len in the days directly after that show aired. I don't know when he found the time to sleep! He wasn't even there for Bible study that

Wednesday; in fact he called me up and asked me to head up the meeting. Said he was driving down to San Antonio to meet with a website designer, wanted to start his own Internet forum to discuss what he called 'the truth about Pam', and would only be back late.

I asked him, 'Pastor Len, you sure you should be messing with the Internet, isn't it the devil's work?'

'We need to save as many as possible, Reba,' he said. 'We need to get that message out there however we can.' And then he quoted from Revelation: '"When Christ returns, every eye shall see Him."'

Well, how could I argue with that?

My daughter Dayna showed me the website when it was up a couple of days later: 'pamelaprophet.com' it was called! There was this huge photograph of Pam on the main page. Must have been from years before as she looked a good decade younger and at least thirty pounds lighter. Stephenie said that she'd heard that Pastor Len was even on that Twitter and that he was already getting emails and messages from all over.

Well, a week or so after the website was up and running, the first of what Stephenie and I privately called the 'Lookie-Loos' started showing up. At first, they were mostly from the neighbouring counties, but when Pastor Len's message went 'viral' (which is what Dayna says it's called), Lookie-Loos from as far away as Lubbock arrived. Congregation just about doubled overnight. That should have made my heart sing, so many being called to the Lord! But I will admit, I still felt a sense of doubt, especially when Pastor Len got a banner made up for outside the church, 'Sannah County, Home of Pamela May Donald,' and started calling his flock the Pamelists.

A lot of the Lookie-Loo folks also wanted to see Pamela's house, and Pastor Len was talking to Jim about charging an entrance fee, so that he could use the money to 'advertise the message far and wide'. Not one of us thought that was a good idea, and I felt it was my duty to take Pastor Len aside and air my concerns. Jim may have taken Jesus into his heart, but he was drinking more than ever. Sheriff Beaumont was forced to give him a warning for DUI once or twice, and whenever I drove over to fix him something to eat, he stank like he'd been bathing in whiskey. I knew Jim wouldn't be able to cope with strangers bothering him day and night. I was mightily relieved when Pastor Len agreed with me. 'You're right, Reba,' he said. 'I thank Jesus every day that I can always count on you to be my good right hand.' And then he said we should keep a closer eye on Jim, as 'he was still struggling with his demons'. Me and Stephenie and the rest of the inner circle drew up a rota so we could make sure he was eating and check that the house didn't fall into disrepair while he went through his mourning period. Pastor Len was keen to get Pam's ashes flown back to the US as soon as they'd finished their investigations, so that we could hold a proper memorial service for her, and asked me to find out when Joanie was going to send them. Jim wouldn't even hear me out on this matter. I can't be sure – he wasn't one to tell you anything, even when he wasn't under the influence of alcohol – but I don't think he'd even spoken to his daughter. You could see plain as day that he'd just given up. Folks would bring him meals and fresh milk, but a lot of the time he just left them to rot; didn't bother putting them in the refrigerator.

It truly was a whirlwind couple of weeks, Elspeth!

   After he set up that website, Pastor Len would call me
or Stephenie up almost every day, saying how the signs
he'd predicted were coming thick and fast. 'You see on
the news, Reba?' he'd say. 'There's that foot and mouth
disease in the UK. That's a sign that the faithless and
ungodly are being stricken with famine.' Then there was
that virus that hit all the cruise ships – the one that spread
to Florida and California – which had to mean that plague
was rearing its ugly head. And of course as far as war was
concerned, well, there's always plenty of that, what with
those Islamofascists our poor brave marines have to contend with and those deranged North Koreans. 'And that's
not all, Reba,' Pastor Len said to me. 'I been thinking…
how about the families those three children are living
with? Why would the Lord choose to place his messengers within such households?' I had to admit there was
something in what he was saying. Not only was Bobby
Small living in a Jewish household (although I know the
Jews have their place in God's plan) but Stephenie said
she'd read in the *Inquirer* that he was one of those test-
tube babies. 'Not born of man,' she said. 'Unnatural.'
Then there were those stories about the English girl being
made to live with one of those homosexuals in London,
and the Jap boy's father making those android abomina-
tions. Dayna showed me a clip of one of them on that You-
Tube; I was shocked to my very core! It looked just like a
real person, and what did the Lord say about making false
idols? There was also all that ungodly talk about evil spirits living in that forest where Pam's plane crashed. I did
feel sorry for Pam, dying in such a horrible place. They do
believe strange things in Asia, don't they? Like those Hin-
dus with all those false gods that look like animals with

too many arms. Enough to give you nightmares. Pastor Len put all of this up on his website, of course.

I can't quite recall exactly how long it was after Pastor Len's message started going viral that Stephenie and I went over to the ranch to visit with Kendra. She'd taken Snookie home with her, and Stephenie said it was our Christian duty to check that Kendra was coping. We both knew she had problems with her nerves and both of us had discussed at length how she seemed to be getting worse lately, what with all the Lookie-Loos flooding into town. Stephenie took along one of her pies, but to be honest, Kendra didn't look that pleased to see us. She'd just given that dog a bath, so it didn't stink too bad, and she'd even tied a red ribbon round its neck like it was one of those celebrities' pets. All the time we were there, Kendra barely took any notice of us. Just kept fussing with that dog as if it was a baby. Didn't even offer us a Coke.

We were just about to leave when Pastor Len came roaring up in his pick-up. He sprinted into the house, and I've never seen anyone looking as pleased with themselves as he did that day.

He greeted us, then said, 'I've done it, Kendra. I've done it!'

Kendra barely took any notice, so it was up to me and Stephenie to ask him what he meant.

'I just got a call from Dr Lund! He's invited me to talk at his conference in Houston!'

Stephenie and I couldn't believe our ears! We both watched Dr Theodore Lund's show every Sunday, of course, and Pam had been real jealous of me when Lorne bought me a signed copy of Sherry Lund's *Family Favourites* recipe book for my birthday.

'You know what this means, don't you, hon?' Pastor Len said to Kendra.

Kendra stopped fussing with that dog and said, 'What now?'

And Pastor Len grinned fit to burst and said, 'I'll tell you what now – I'm finally gonna be playing with the big boys.'

The following article, by British journalist and documentary filmmaker Malcolm Adelstein, was originally published in *Switch Online* magazine on 21 February 2012.

I'm standing in the gargantuan lobby of the Houston Conference Centre, where the annual End Times Bible Prophecy Convention is taking place, clutching a Bible with a fly-fisherman on the cover, and waiting for a man with the unlikely name of Flexible Sandy to finish publicising his latest novel. Despite an entrance fee of five thousand dollars, the conference attracts thousands of attendees from all over Texas and beyond, and the parking lot is filled with Winnebagos and SUVs sporting number plates from as far afield as Tennessee and Kentucky. I also seem to be the youngest person here by a good couple of decades – a sea of grey hair undulates around me. It's safe to say I'm more than a bit out of my comfort zone.

Felix 'Flexible' Sandy has a colourful background. Before his conversion to evangelical Christianity in the early seventies, he'd enjoyed a successful career as a contortionist, trapeze artist, and circus impresario – a fire and brimstone Southern version of P.T. Barnum. After Flexible's biography, *A High-Wire to Jesus*, was a bestseller in the seventies, the legend is that rising Bible Prophecy star Dr Theodore Lund approached him to write the first in a series of fictional End Times themed books. Written in fast-paced Dan Brown-style prose, the series details what will happen after the Rapture occurs and the world's saved literally disappear in the blink of an eye, leaving the earth-bound non-believers to contend with the Antichrist – a character who has an uncanny resemblance to former UK prime minister Tony Blair. Nine bestselling books later (it is estimated that over 70 million copies have been sold), Flexible Sandy is still going strong. He also recently launched his own website: 'rapturesacoming.com', a site that tracks global and national disasters in order to let members know (for a small fee of course) how close, on any given day, we might be to Armageddon. With his wiry frame and perma-tanned skin, eighty-year-old Flexible exudes the vigour of someone half his age. As he deals with the snaking line of devoted fans that stretches in front of him, his smile doesn't slip one iota. I'm hoping to persuade Flexible to take part in a documentary series I'm producing about the rise of the American End Times Movement. For the last few months I've been emailing his publicist – a brittle, efficient woman who has been eyeing me distrustfully since I arrived – to set up a meeting. Last week she hinted that I might get a chance if I turned up in Houston at the conference where he would be launching his latest book.

For those not in the know, End Times prophecy is basically the conviction that any day now, those who have taken Jesus as their personal saviour (aka born again) will be spirited up to heaven (aka raptured) while the rest of us will endure seven years of horrendous suffering under the yoke of the Antichrist. These beliefs, based on the literal interpretation of several biblical prophets (including John in Revelation, Ezekiel and Daniel), are far more widespread than many people realise. In the US alone, it's estimated that over 65 million people believe that the events laid out in Revelation could actually happen in their lifetime.

Many high-level prophecy preachers can be cagey about talking to the non-evangelical press, and I rather naively hoped my English accent would help break the ice with Flexible. Five thousand dollars is a lot of money to shell out if all I'm going to get for it is a themed Bible. (Incidentally, on sale in the lobby are also Bibles for children, 'Christian wives', hunters and gun enthusiasts – but the fly-fisherman version caught my eye. I'm not sure why. I've never even been fishing.) Plus, I'm rather optimistically hoping that if Flexible agrees to talk to me, I might be able to persuade him to introduce me to the big cheese himself – Dr Theodore Lund. (I'm not holding out much hope; I've been told by fellow journalists that I'd have a better chance of being invited to go lap-dancing with Kim Jong-Il.) A mega-star of the evangelical movement, Dr Lund boasts his own TV station, a franchise of True Faith mega-churches that bring in hundreds of millions of dollars a year in 'donations', and the ear of former Republican President 'Billy-Bob' Blake. He also commands a global following on a par with Hollywood A-listers: his three Sunday services are internationally syndicated, and it's estimated that over 100 million people worldwide tune in every week to watch his prophecy-themed chat show. Although not as hard-line as the Dominionists, the fundamentalist sect who are actively campaigning for a US governed by strict Biblical rule (which would entail the death penalty for abortionists, gays and naughty children), Dr Lund is a harsh opponent of gay marriage, is vehemently pro-life, disputes global warming, and is not averse to using his clout to influence political decisions, especially where Middle Eastern policy is concerned.

The queue of fans waiting to get their books signed by

Flexible shuffles forwards. 'These books changed my life,' the woman in front of me tells me unsolicited. She has a shopping trolley piled high with various editions of the *Gone* books. 'They brought me to Jesus.' We chat about her favourite characters (she favours Peter Kean, a helicopter pilot whose languishing faith is restored – too late – when he witnesses his born-again wife, children and co-pilot being raptured before his eyes). I decide that it would be churlish to face Flexible without a copy of his novel, so I grab a couple from a towering dump-bin. Next to the piles of *Gone* books, a glossy cookbook display catches my eye. The cover sports a photograph of a heavily made-up woman with the tight eyes of the newly face-lifted. I recognise her as Dr Lund's wife Sherry, the co-presenter of his weekly after-sermon chat show. Her cookbooks regularly top the New York Times Bestseller lists and the sex manual she co-wrote with Dr Lund, *Intimacy the Christian Way*, was a runaway success in the eighties.

While Flexible gamely interacts with his geriatric fan base, I check out the displays advertising the talks, discussions and prayer groups that are scheduled back to back throughout the weekend, most sporting glossy life-size cut-outs of the celebrity preachers who are the main draw-card to the event. As well as several 'Are You Ready For the Rapture?' talks, there are symposiums on Creationism and a hastily tacked on addition to the line-up – a 'get-together' with Pastor Len Vorhees, the new kid on the End Times block. Vorhees recently caused a minor Twitter storm with his extraordinary pronouncement that the three children who survived Black Thursday's disasters are actually three of the four horsemen out of Revelation.

Finally, the line dries up and it's my turn. The snippy

publicist whispers something in Flexible's ear and he fixes the beam of his smile on me. His small eyes glint like black shiny buttons.

'England, huh?' he says. 'I was in London last year. That's a heathen country that needs saving, am I right, son?'

I assure him that he most certainly is.

'What sort of work you into, son? Patty here says you want to do an interview, something like that?'

I tell him the truth. That I make documentaries for television, that I'd love to chat to him and Dr Lund about their careers.

Flexible's button eyes bore into mine with more intensity. 'You with the BBC?'

I say that I have worked for the BBC, yes. It's not really a lie. I started my career as a runner for BBC Manchester, although I was fired after two months for smoking dope in the greenroom. I decide not to mention this.

Flexible seems to relax. 'Hold on, son, I'll see what I can do.' This is much easier than I was expecting. He waves his publicist over again, who manages to smile at Flexible and scowl at me simultaneously, and they share a terse whispered exchange.

'Son, Teddy's real busy right now. Tell you what, why don't you come up to the penthouse in a couple of hours? I'll see what I can do about getting you two acquainted. He's a big fan of the *Cavendish Hall* show you fellas have over there.'

I'm not sure what *Cavendish Hall*, a saccharine period drama that's making waves around the world, has to do with me, but it turns out that Flexible Sandy is still under the impression that I work for the BBC. I scuttle away before his publicist convinces him to change his mind.

*   *   *

Rather than head back to my bijou hotel room (fortunately included in the price tag), I decide to see if I can catch one of the talks. I'm thirty minutes late for Pastor Len Vorhees's 'get-together', but I mention to the usher that I'm a personal friend of Flexible Sandy's and he lets me slip inside.

It's standing room only in the Starlight Auditorium, and all that's visible of Pastor Len Vorhees is the top of his coiffed hair as he strides back and forth in front of the audience. His voice wavers every now and then, but it's clear from the chorus of 'Amen's that he's getting his message across. I'm vaguely aware that Pastor Len's bizarre theory has provoked fierce debate in the world of End Times believers, especially from the Preterist movement, which, unlike most of the other factions, believes that the events laid out in Revelation have already occurred. And I'm learning that Revelation is most certainly the basis of Pastor Len's wild assertions. According to the prophecy of John, the four horsemen will bring with them war, pestilence, famine and death, and Pastor Len starts to list various recent 'signs' that he says prove his theory. Among them are the gruesome account of the lizardy death of a paparazzo who'd allegedly broken into Bobby Small's hospital room (animal attacks are also included in Revelation's list of woes) and the details of the recent norovirus scourge that turned a fleet of cruise liners into vomit-filled hell ships. He manages to conclude with a frankly terrifying proclamation that war will soon ravage the African nations and bird flu will decimate the Asian population.

Longing for a stiff drink, I slip out on the chorus of 'Amen's to wait for my audience with Flexible Sandy and Dr Teddy Lund.

*   *   *

I'm gobsmacked when I'm let into the suite by Dr Lund himself, who greets me with a dazzling grin that shows off his state-of-the-art dental work. 'Good to meet you, son,' he says, gripping my hand between two of his. His skin has a slightly artificial glow, as if he's an irradiated fruit. 'Can I get you a beverage? You Brits like your tea, don't you?' I burble something along the lines of 'Indeed we do,' and allow him to lead me over to where Flexible and a slick-suited man in his early fifties are sitting in extravagantly upholstered armchairs. It takes me a second to realise that the fiftyish man is actually Pastor Len Vorhees. He's clearly not as at ease as the other two men; I get the impression of a child on his best behaviour.

Introductions are made and I allow myself to be swallowed up by the couch opposite. They all beam at me; none of their smiles meet their eyes.

'Flexible tells me you work for the BBC,' Dr Lund begins. 'I tell you, son, I'm not one for television, but I like that *Cavendish Hall* show. They knew how to behave in those days, didn't they? Had their morals straight. And you're out here wanting to do a documentary, something like that?'

Before I can get a word in, he continues, 'We get a lot of fellas wanting to do interviews. From all over the world. But I tell you, now might be the right time to get the message into England.'

I'm about to respond when two women appear through the door that leads to one of the suite's bedrooms. I recognise the taller of the two as Dr Lund's wife, Sherry – she's as coiffed and air-brushed as the photograph on the back of her latest cookbook. The woman hovering behind her couldn't be more of a contrast. She's as thin as a broom, her lined mouth is lipstick-free, and a white miniature poodle of some sort lolls in her arms.

I get to my feet but Dr Lund waves me back down. He introduces Sherry, and the other woman as Pastor Len's wife, Kendra. Kendra barely glances in my direction and Sherry beams at me for a nanosecond before turning to her husband. 'Don't forget that Mitch is on his way to see you, Teddy.' She blasts me with another practised smile. 'We're just going to take Snookie for some air.' Then she sweeps Kendra and the dog out of the suite.

'Let's get down to business,' Dr Lund says to me. 'What exactly do you have in mind, son? What sort of documentary are you planning on doing?'

'Well...' I say. And suddenly, for absolutely no reason, my carefully practised pitch dries up and my mind goes blank. In desperation I fix on Pastor Len Vorhees. 'Perhaps I could start...I caught your talk, Pastor Vorhees... it was, um, interesting. May I ask you about your theory?'

'Ain't a theory, son,' Flexible growls, while managing to keep his smile in place. 'It's the truth.'

I have no idea why these three men are making me feel so nervous. Maybe it's the force of their collective convictions and personalities – you don't get to be a Fortune 500 preacher by being uncharismatic. I manage to get myself under control. 'But...if you're saying the first four seals have just been opened, doesn't this contradict what you believe? That the church will be raptured *before* the horsemen bring devastation to the earth?' Eschatology – the study of End Times prophecy – gets complicated very fast. From my research, I've been led to believe that Dr Lund and Flexible are followers of Pre-Tribulation Rapture theory, where the Rapture of the church will take

place just before the seven year tribulation period (i.e.
before the Antichrist takes over and makes life miserable
for the rest of us). Pastor Len's beliefs fall within the Post-
Tribulation Rapture theory, whereby reborn Christians
will remain on the earth as witnesses during the fire and
brimstone stage, which, according to him, has just begun.

Pastor Len's handsome features ripple and he picks at
his lapel, but Flexible and Dr Lund chuckle in unison as if
I'm a child who's said something inappropriate but amusing. 'There's no contradiction here, son,' Flexible says.
'We know from Matthew twenty-four, "Ethnic group will
rise against ethnic group. And government against government. There will be famines and earthquakes in various places. All these are the beginning of birth pains."'

Dr Lund chips in. 'This is happening all over. Right
now. And we know that these birth pains signal the opening of the first four seals. We also know from both Revelation and Zechariah that the four harbingers are then sent
throughout the world. White to the west, red to the east,
black to the north and the pale horse to the south. Now
that the seals have been opened, punishment will be
exacted upon Asia, America, Europe and Africa.'

I'm struggling to follow this logic, but I manage to pick
up on the last bit. 'And Australia? Antarctica?'

Flexible chuckles again and shakes his head at my
denseness. 'They aren't part of the global moral decline,
son. But they'll get their turn. The world's governments
and the UN will all gather together to make the many-
horned beast.'

Now that I haven't been taken by the seat of my pants
and booted out, I'm feeling slightly more confident. I point
out that the NTSB is indicating that the causes of the

crashes are down to fully explainable events – pilot error, a possible bird strike, mechanical failure – and not supernatural interference (somehow I manage to phrase this without sounding like I'm talking about aliens or the devil).

Pastor Len opens his mouth to comment but Dr Lund jumps in. 'I'll answer this, Len. You think God wouldn't have the power to make these events look like accidents? He wants to test our faith, root out the believer from the heathen. We have heeded his call. But we're in the business of saving souls, son, and when the fourth horseman is found, even the most reluctant will be called to his fold.'

I feel my mouth lolling open. 'The fourth horseman?'

'That's correct, son.'

'But there were no survivors of the crash in Africa.'

Pastor Len and Dr Lund exchange glances, and Dr Lund gives the tiniest nod.

'We believe there is,' Pastor Len says.

I stutter that according to the NTSB and the agencies in Africa, there is no chance that anyone on the Dalu Air flight could have survived.

Dr Lund smiles humourlessly. 'That's what they said about the other three incidents, and look what the Lord chose to show us.' He pauses. Then he asks the question I know has been coming. 'Have you been saved, son?'

Flexible Sandy's peculiar button eyes bore into mine and I'm suddenly back at school, standing in front of the headmaster. I'm overwhelmed with the desire to lie and claim that yes, I am one of them, among the saved. But it passes and I tell them the truth. 'I'm Jewish.'

Dr Lund nods in approval. Flexible Sandy's grin doesn't falter. 'We need the Jews,' Dr Lund says. 'You're an important part of the coming events.'

I know what he's talking about. After the Rapture and the Antichrist's rule, Jesus will return to vanquish the infidels and power-drive the Antichrist off his throne. This battle is pipped to take place in Israel, and Dr Lund, like many prophecy believers, is vociferously pro-Israel. He believes, as it says in the Bible, that Israel belongs to the Jews and the Jews alone, and he is adamant that land swapping and peace accords with Palestine should be forcefully opposed. It's rumoured that during President 'Billy-Bob' Blake's tenure in the White House, Dr Lund was a regular visitor. I really want to question him about the elephant in the room – why someone who truly believes the end of the world is imminent would bother to meddle in politics – but Dr Lund stands up before I can think how to phrase it.

'Go well, son,' he says. 'Get hold of my publicist, she'll help you out.' With another round of handshakes, I'm dismissed. (A few days later I do as he suggests, but receive only a curt 'Dr Lund is unavailable' response, and a flat silence to my other stabs at communication with Flexible Sandy.)

As I leave the conference, my fly-fisherman's Bible and my *Gone* books tucked under my arm, I pass a phalanx of huge bodyguards surrounding a man in an even more expensively cut suit than Dr Lund's. I recognise him immediately. It's Mitch Reynard, former governor of Texas, who announced his intention to run for the Republican presidential nomination just a couple of weeks ago.

The following is an extract from *rapturesacoming.com*, Felix 'Flexible' Sandy's website.

A personal message from me today, believers. Our brothers Dr Theodore Lund (who needs no introduction!) and Pastor Len Vorhees of Sannah County have shown us the Truth, irrefutable proof that the first four seals as laid out in Revelation have been opened, and the horsemen are set loose upon the world to punish the ungodly with Famine, Plague, War, Pestilence and Death. Some of you may be saying, but Flexible, weren't the seals broken a long time ago? The world has been in moral decline for generations, hasn't it? I say that may be, but God in His wisdom has now shown us the truth. And if you think about it, believers, it's going to play out just like it did in *Thief in the Night*, the ninth in the *Gone* series, which I don't need to tell you is available to order from this very site.

And that's not all, you'll see that the signs are hotting up fast, with major incidents coming thick and fast this week. Good news for all of us waiting to be taken up to Jesus' side!

Flexible

The full list can be found under the headings if you CLICK on them, but here are our top choices:

PLAGUE (rapturesacoming probability rating: 74%)
The vomiting bug that started on those cruise liners has taken hold throughout the US:

www.news-agency.info/2012/february/
norovirus-spreads-to-US-East-Coast
*(Thanks to Isla Smith of North Carolina for sending this
one through! Flexible appreciates your faith, Isla!)*

WAR (rapturesacoming probability rating: 81%)

Well, what can I say? War is always a strong indicator
and it's not letting us down today! The holy War on
Terror still rages in Afghanistan and check out this link
below:
www.atlantic-mag.com/worldnews/
north-korea-nuclear-threat-could-be-a-reality

FAMINE (rapturesacoming probability rating: 81%)

That foot and mouth disease looks like it's finding a
foothold in the rest of Europe. Check out this headline:
'New Strain of Foot and Mouth Could Have Massive
Impact on Farming, UK govt warns.'
(source: www.euronewscorp.co.uk/footandmouth/)

DEATH (rapturesacoming probability rating: 91%)

*And I looked, and behold a pale horse: and his name
that sat on him was Death, and Hell followed with him.
And power was given to them over the fourth part of
the earth, to kill with sword, and with hunger, and with
death, and with the beasts of the earth.* (Revelation 6:8)

There's been a spate of animal attacks recently, just
like it says in verses 6:8. Check out these links:

'American tourist slain in Botswana rogue hyena attack'
(www.bizarredeaths.net)

'Inquest on LA photographer eaten alive by pet lizards postponed' (www.latimesweekly.com)

A Flexible note: This one is of particular interest, as the photographer had ties to Bobby Small, which makes this a nine on the scale! Not since 9/11 have we been this close!

Lola Cando.

I hadn't seen Lenny for a while, not since he told me about Pamela May Donald's message. Then he called me up, asked me to meet him at one of our motels. Lucky for him I had a cancellation. One of my regulars, ex-marine – a sweet fella – was feeling blue and wanted to postpone.

Anyhow, that day, Lenny burst into the room, snatched the drink I poured for him and started pacing up and down. Told me he'd just got back from a conference in Houston. He looked just like a little kid who'd been to Disneyland for the first time. He must have talked non-stop for half-an-hour at least. He was saying how he'd been hanging out with Dr Lund, who'd invited him to appear on his Sunday show. Said he'd even had dinner with Flexible Sandy – the fella who wrote those books I never got around to reading. Went on about how the room where he'd given his talk had been packed to the rafters with the faithful.

'And guess who else was there, Lo?' he asked while he pulled off his tie. I didn't know what to say, wouldn't have been surprised if he'd said Jesus himself, way he was talking about those guys with all that awe in his voice. 'Mitch Reynard,' he said. 'Mitch Reynard! Dr Lund has given him his backing.'

I'm not one for politics, but even I knew who this fella was. Caught him on a couple of the news segments Denisha likes to watch. Smooth guy, ex-preacher, looked a bit like Bill Clinton, always had the right answers, used to be a member of that Tea Party contingent. He was never out of the news when it turned out he was running for the Republican presidential nomination. Got a lot of criticism from the liberals for what he was saying about feminism and how gay marriage was an abomination.

Lenny started getting carried away, talking about how this could even be his ticket to getting into politics himself. 'Anything is possible, Lo. Dr Lund says we must do everything in our power to sway the vote, make sure the country gets back to a good moral footing.'

Talking about morals, far as I was aware, Lenny never saw anything hypocritical about paying for my services. Maybe he didn't even see it as adultery. He didn't talk about his wife often, but I got the impression they hadn't been intimate for a while. Course, last couple of times I saw him, there wasn't much adultery going on; he was too busy unloading on me.

Would I say that fame went to his head? Yeah, sure. After he set up the website and got involved with Dr Lund, he was like a kid with a new toy. He said he was in contact with people from all over the world. Fellas right down in Africa even. There was that Monty guy he said he emailed every day, and a marine who was doing his duty somewhere in Japan. Jake somebody. I can't recall his surname even though he was all over the news later on. Lenny told me all about how that marine had been into the Japanese forest where that plane had crashed. 'Where Pam breathed her last breath.' He said that Dr Lund had tried to contact Bobby's grandmother, wanted to invite Bobby onto his show as well, but wasn't getting anywhere. I really felt for the poor woman. Both me and Denisha did. It couldn't have been easy being the focus of all that attention when you were still in mourning.

Lenny went on and on about how he was getting requests to do interviews from all over – talk shows, radio shows, Internet blogs, the whole caboodle, and not just the religious ones either. 'Aren't you worried they'll ridicule you, Lenny?' I asked him. He let slip that Dr Lund's PR team had warned him to be careful about talking to the non-Christian press, and I thought that was wise advice. What he was saying about the children being the horsemen, you could see how lots of folks would think that was just plain nonsense.

'I'm spreading the truth, Lo,' he said. 'If they want to ignore it, that's their business. When the Rapture comes, we'll see who has the last laugh.'

We didn't even do it that day. He just wanted to talk. As he left, he reminded me to catch Dr Lund's *True Faith Togetherness* show that weekend.

I was curious to see how Lenny would come across, so come Sunday, I settled down to watch it. Denisha couldn't figure out what the hell I was doing. I hadn't told her that Lenny was one of my clients. I respect my regulars' privacy, which I know sounds like a lie seeing as here's me talking to you now! But I never asked to be outed, did I? I wasn't the one who went to the reporters. Anyhow, first off, Dr Lund stood at this big gold pulpit, a huge choir behind him. That church of his, the size of a shopping mall, was bursting at the seams. He basically just repeated Lenny's theories about Pamela May Donald's message, stopping every five minutes so that the choir could sing a bit more and the congregation could chime in with their 'Amen's and 'Praise Jesus's. Then he went on about how the time was ripe for God's judgement, what with all the immorality going on, the gays and the women's libbers

and the baby killers and the school boards who promote
Evolution. Denisha kept clicking her tongue. Her church
knows all about what she does for a living, and they have
no problem with the gays, either. 'It's all the same to them,
Lo,' she said. 'People is people, and rather be upfront
about it than hide it. Jesus never judged nobody, did he?
'Cept those money-lenders.' Most of those rich preachers
and high-end pastors had skeletons in their closets, and
every day there seemed to be a new scandal about one of
them. But not Dr Lund. He was known to be squeaky
clean. Denisha reckoned he had the right connections to
keep his dirty doings out of the media; knew where the
bodies were buried.

After his sermon, Dr Lund walked over to an area at
the side of the stage, which was decorated like a living
room, all expensive rugs and oil paintings and lamp-
shades with gold tassels. On the couch waiting for him
were Dr Lund's wife, Sherry, Lenny and a skinny woman
who looked like she needed feeding up. That was the first
time I saw Pastor Len's wife, Kendra. She couldn't have
looked more different to Sherry, who Denisha said had
the look of Tammy Faye Bakker about her – all eyelashes
and drag queen accessories. But Lenny came across okay.
He was a bit agitated, kept fidgeting and his voice wobbled some, but he didn't embarrass himself. Dr Lund did
most of the talking. Kendra didn't say one word. And the
look on her face . . . it was hard to read. I couldn't tell if she
was nervous, thought the whole thing was just dumb, or if
she was bored out of her mind.

Pastor Len Vorhees agreed to be interviewed on DJ Erik Kavanaugh's notorious Talk NYC radio show, *Mouthing Off*. The following is a transcript of the show aired on 8 March 2012.

ERIK KAVANAUGH: On the line with me today, I have Pastor Len Vorhees from Sannah County, Texas. Pastor Len – can I call you that, by the way?

PASTOR LEN VORHEES: Yes, sir, that's absolutely fine.

EK: That's a first, no one's ever called me sir before. Gotta say, you're politer than most of the guests I usually have on here. Pastor Len, you are trending on Twitter right now. Do you think it's right for an evangelical Christian to use social media in this way?

PL: I believe we should use any means possible to spread the good news, sir. And since I got the message out there, there are people flocking into Sannah County, eager to be saved. Why, at my church they're practically spilling out the doors. *(He laughs)*

EK: So it's like that scene in *Jaws*. You're gonna need a bigger church?

PL: *(Pause)* I'm not quite sure what—

EK: Now let's get down to exactly what you're saying. Some people might say that your belief that these children are the horsemen is – and I can find no other way to say this – absolutely batshit crazy.

PL: *(Laughing nervously)* Well now, sir, that kind of language isn't—

EK: Is it true that you came up with this theory after one of your parishioners, Pamela May Donald, the sole American on board the Japanese plane that crashed into that forest, left a message on her phone?

PL: Ah . . . yes, that's correct, sir. Her message was addressed to me and her meaning was clear as day. 'Pastor Len,' she said. 'Warn them about the boy.' The only boy she could mean was the Japanese boy who was the sole survivor of that crash. The *sole* survivor. And then the airplanes' insignias—

EK: In the message she also mentions her dog. If you believe she was saying that the Japanese boy is some sort of end-of-days harbinger, surely this means you also believe we should all go around treating the family pooch like a deity now?

PL: *(Several seconds of dead air)* Well now, I wouldn't go so far as to—

EK: On your website, pamelaprophet.com – you should check it out folks, trust me – you say that there are facts that back up what you're saying. Signs that the misery the horsemen are supposed to bring is already coming to pass. Let me give any listeners who may not have heard

the details of your theory an example. You're saying that
the foot and mouth outbreak they've just been having in
Europe was brought on by the appearance of the
horsemen, am I right?

PL: That's correct, sir.

EK: But surely there's always stuff like this going on?
The UK experienced exactly the same thing a few years
ago.

PL: That's not the only sign though, sir. If you put them
all together, you can clearly see that there is a pattern of—

EK: And these signs, you're saying they're all pointing
towards the fact that the end of the world is nigh when all
the saved will be raptured. Is it fair to say you evangelical
guys are looking forward to this event?

PL: I wouldn't say that looking forward is the right way to
phrase it, no, sir. It's important to let your listeners know
that by taking the Lord—

EK: So these signs are like God's way of saying, time's up
folks, get saved or burn in hell forever?

PL: Uh . . . I'm not certain that—

EK: Your beliefs have come under radical fire from
religious leaders of, let's say, more traditional persuasions.
More than a few of them have said that what you're
saying, and I quote, is 'utter fear-mongering nonsense'.

PL: There will always be doubters, sir, but I would urge your listeners to—

EK: You've got some heavy hitters behind you. I'm talking about Dr Theodore Lund of the End Times Movement. Is it true he used to go shooting with former President 'Billy-Bob' Blake?

PL: Uh . . . you'll have to ask him about that, sir.

EK: I don't need to ask him about his views on women's rights, the Israeli peace accords, abortion and gay marriage. He's radically opposed to them. Do you share his views?

PL: *(Another long pause)* I believe we should look to the Bible for guidance on these matters, sir. In Leviticus it says that—

EK: Doesn't it also say in Leviticus that owning slaves is cool and that kids who backchat to their parents should be stoned? Why do you guys take on board, say, the anti-gay stuff and not the other crap?

PL: *(Dead air for several seconds)* Sir . . . I object to your tone. I came on the show to tell your listeners that time is—

EK: Let's move on. Your theory about The Three isn't the only one doing the rounds. There are quite a few nutjobs who are adamant that those kids are possessed by aliens. Why are their views any crazier than what you believe?

PL: I'm not sure what you—

EK: The Three are just children, surely? Haven't they been through enough? Wouldn't the Christian thing to do be not to judge them?

PL: *(Another long pause)* I don't . . . I—

EK: So let's say they're possessed, are the real children still inside their bodies? If so, must be getting crowded in there, am I right?

PL: God . . . Jesus works in ways we can only—

EK: Ah, the 'God works in mysterious ways' defence.

PL: Uh . . . but you can't . . . you can't discount the signs that . . . How else did those children survive the crashes? It's—

EK: Is it true you believe there is a fourth child who has survived the crash in Africa? A fourth horseman? You're saying this even though the NTSB is absolutely adamant that no one could have survived that tragedy?

PL: *(Clears throat)* Uh . . . that crash site . . . there was much confusion down there. Africa is . . . Africa is a—

EK: So how did these horsemen bring down the planes? On a practical level, it seems like a lot of effort to go to, doesn't it?

PL: Um...I can't tell you that for sure, sir. But I will tell you this, when they release the crash reports, there will be signs of...of...

EK: Supernatural interference? Like the alien people believe?

PL: You're twisting my words, sir. I didn't mean that—

EK: Thank you, Pastor Len Vorhees. We'll be opening the lines for callers after this message.

NTSB investigator Ace Kelso spoke to me again at length after the preliminary crash investigation findings from all four incidents were revealed at a press conference, which was held in Washington, DC, on 13 March 2012.

As I said at the press conference, it's rare for us to reveal our findings so soon. But this was a special case – people needed to know the incidents weren't down to terrorism or some goddamned supernatural event, and the families of the survivors needed closure. You wouldn't believe the number of calls the Washington office fielded from whackos convinced we were in cahoots with sinister *Men in Black* government agencies. Course, added into the mix was the fact that after Black Thursday the aviation industry was suffering financially, needed to get back on track. You heard that a few of the more unscrupulous airlines are cashing in on the fact that all three survivors were seated towards the rear of the aircraft? Charging a premium for the seats at the back; considering relocating First and Business Class to the rear to recoup lost profits.

It was obvious to us early on that terrorism wasn't a factor. We knew from the bodies and wreckage recovered that none of the aircraft in any of the four instances had broken up significantly mid-air, which would have been the case had an explosive device been triggered. Sure, we had to consider a possible hijacking scenario at first, but no organisation came forward at any time to take responsibility.

As you know, there's still a massive operation underway to locate the CVR and black box from the site of the

Go!Go! Air incident, but we're confident we know the sequence of events that led to the disaster. First of all, from the aircraft's flight path and the weather data, we know they found themselves flying into a severe thunderstorm. The last contact from the aircraft, an automated telemetry message to the Go!Go! Air technical centre, indicated that the aircraft had undergone multiple electrical failures, most notably of the static port heating system. This would have resulted in ice crystals forming in the static ports, which in turn would have resulted in inaccurate airspeed readings. Thinking that their airspeed was too low, the pilots would have progressively increased the speed of the aircraft to avoid a stall. We believe they continued doing so until they exceeded the aircraft's capabilities and literally flew the wings off the thing. We're almost certain Jessica Craddock's burn injuries were caused by a fuel fire after the event, or from a malfunctioning flare.

Now, the Dalu Air flight was a different story. The series of factors that added up to *that* crash pointed to an accident waiting to happen. For a start, the design of the Antonov AN-124 dates back to the seventies, light years away from the 'fly by wire' technology used by Airbus. The aircraft was also operated by a small Nigerian outfit that mostly flew freight and which, it must be said, didn't have the best safety record. Won't go into too many technicalities again, but Cape Town International airport's ILS wasn't working that day – apparently it can be hokey. Also, the Antonov wasn't fitted with modern navigation equipment such as LNS [Lateral Navigation System] and wasn't adequately equipped to deal with the alternative approach system. The pilots misjudged the approach, came in approximately one hundred feet too low, the right wing clipped a power line and the Antonov immediately crashed into a densely populated township situated adjacent to the airfield. Gotta say, we were all impressed with how the Dalu Air investigation was handled by the CAA and the Cape Town Disaster Management Team. Those guys and gals know their stuff. You wouldn't think it for a third world country, but they really got their ducks in a row asap. The head investigator – Nomafu Nkatha (don't think I pronounced that correctly, Elspeth!) – gathered eye-witness accounts immediately after the event, and several people had caught the moments before impact on their cellphone cameras.

The investigators have still got a job on their hands identifying the bodies of those killed at the site. Looks like a lot of them were refugees or asylum seekers and it's going to be a near-impossible task tracking down family members for DNA matches. The CVR was recovered eventually. Guys had been collecting the parts, selling them off to tourists – can you *believe* that shit? But like I say, top marks to the team out there.

Next one I'll deal with was the Maiden Air crash – the one I was IIC on, before I was asked to oversee the whole operation. The evidence suggests that the aircraft suffered an almost total power loss on both engines due to ingestion – probably as a result of multiple bird strike. This occurred roughly two minutes after take-off, which is the most vulnerable phase of the climb. The pilots were unable to return to the airport and the aircraft crashed into the Everglades approximately three to four minutes later. We found the black box on this one, but the data was compromised. The N1 Turbines on both engines showed damage consistent with bird strike although there was, curiously, no trace of snarge. In line with my recommendations, the board ruled that engine failure due to multiple bird strike was the most probable cause of the crash.

Then we had the one that I'd say was the most controversial. I'm talking about the Sun Air incident. The rumours that were going around about the cause of that crash were hard to contain – most notably the fallacy that Captain Seto was suicidal and brought the plane down deliberately. On top of this, the Japanese minister of transport's wife said publicly that she believed aliens were involved. There was real pressure on us to sort that out asap. We had the CVR, which indicated a loss of hydraulics, and we know from the black box that the aircraft was effectively brought down by shoddy workmanship. The failure to follow basic repair procedures to the tail section resulted in rivets giving way. The structural integrity of the fuselage was compromised, resulting in explosive decompression some fourteen minutes into the flight. The rudder was damaged and the hydraulics were lost, and when this happens, it's just about impossible to steer the aircraft. Pilots fought with that baby as hard as they could. Gotta admire them for that. We ran comparative tests in simulators and no one has been able to keep it in the air as long as they did.

Course, we had to field a ton of questions at the press conference, lots of the reporters wanted to know where the bright lights a couple of the passengers said they'd seen came from. Could have been any number of things. More than likely lightning. That's why we made the transcript of the CVR recording public asap, to stop those rumours in their tracks.

The following transcript, taken from the Sun Air Flight SAJ678 Cockpit Voice Recorder, was first published on the National Transportation Safety Board's website on 20 March 2012.

Capt – Captain
FO – First Officer
ATC – Air Traffic Control

Transcript commences at 21h44 (fourteen minutes after take-off from Narita airport).

FO: Passing flight level three three zero, captain, that's a thousand foot to go. Looks like it should be nice and smooth at three four zero, not much CAT forecast.

CAPT: Good.

FO: Do you have—

[A loud bang. Depressurisation alarm sounds.]

CAPT: Mask! Put on your mask!

FO: Mask on!

CAPT: We're losing the cabin, can you control it?

FO: The cabin is at 14,000 already!

CAPT: Go to manual and close the outflow valve. Looks like we've got a decompression.

FO: Ah, Captain, we need to get down!

CAPT: Try again.

FO: The valve is fully closed, it's no use – I can't control it!

CAPT: Have you closed the outflow valve?

FO: Affirmative!

CAPT: Okay, understood. Tell ATC we are starting an emergency descent.

FO: Mayday, mayday, mayday – SAJ678 commencing emergency descent. We've had an explosive decompression.

ATC: Copy that. Mayday SAJ678, you can descend, there is no other traffic to affect you. Standing by.

CAPT: I have control. What is our grid mora?

FO: Level 140.

CAPT: Disconnecting the auto-throttle, dial in flight level 140.

FO: Flight level 140 set.

[*Captain is on the intercom.*]

CAPT: Ladies and gentlemen, this is your captain speaking. We are starting an emergency descent. Please put on your oxygen masks and follow the cabin crew's instructions.

CAPT: Commencing emergency descent. Closing thrust levers, deploying speed brake. Read the emergency descent checklist.

FO: Thrust lever closed, speed brake down, heading selected, lower level selected, start switches to continuous, seat belt signs on, pax oxygen switch on, squawking 7700, ATC notified.

CAPT: Can't control the heading – she's yawing to the right. I can't get the wings level!

FO: [*expletive*] Rudder or aileron?

CAPT: I've got full left aileron, but she's not responding!

FO: Master caution hydraulics. I am cancelling the light. We've lost all hydraulics, we've got system A, and system B low pressure lights on! I'll get the QRH and read the hydraulic checklist.

CAPT: Get me some hydraulics back!

FO: [*expletive*]

CAPT: I'm going to take some more thrust on three and four engines.

FO: It looks like the standby system is gone too. The hydraulic quantities are all empty!

CAPT: Keep trying.

FO: We've got 2000 feet to level off.

FO: 1000 feet to level off!

[*Sound of altitude warning horn.*]

CAPT: I'm stowing the speed brake and taking some more thrust on numbers one and two.

FO: The nose is dropping – pull up!

CAPT: She's not responding! More thrust to slow the descent.

CAPT: Okay. She's levelling off – still can't control the heading. Keeps going to the right.

FO: Try and take more thrust on three and four.

CAPT: Okay. More thrust on three and four...

CAPT: It's still not helping – she's still rolling to the right!

ATC: Mayday SAJ678, what is your heading?

FO: Mayday SAJ678 we've lost all hydraulics, we will come back to you.

CAPT: We've got no rudder!

FO: We are going to have to go to manual reversion!

CAPT: [*expletive*] Feels like we're in manual reversion already! I am struggling to control. Let's see if we can get some of the speed off – 300 knots.

FO: The nose is dropping again!

CAPT: Is there an airfield close to us?

FO: The—

CAPT: Give me more thrust on three and four!

[*Sound of GPWS, whoop whoop, pull up, whoop whoop, pull up, too low terrain, too low terrain, whoop whoop, pull up, whoop whoop, pull up, too low terrain.*]

CAPT: Full thrust all four…pull up! Pull up!

FO: [*expletive*]

CAPT: Pull up! Pull up!

[*Recording ends.*]

The following article was published in the *Crimson State Echo* on 24 March 2012.

END TIMES PREACHER STARTS HUNT FOR 'FOURTH HORSEMAN'

At a recent press conference in Houston, Dr Theodore Lund, one of the driving forces behind the Evangelical End Times Movement, told a gathering of the world's press that: 'The fourth horseman is out there and it's only a matter of time until he is found.' Dr Lund is referring to the theory, first aired by a backwater Texan preacher, that The Three miracle children who survived Black Thursday's devastating events are possessed by the Riders of the Apocalypse, sent by God to usher in the End Times. The theory is based on the last words of Pamela May Donald, the only American citizen on board the plane that crashed into the notorious Aokigahara 'suicide forest' in Japan. Dr Lund and his followers are adamant that there is no other explanation for The Three's so-called miraculous survival, and believe that various global events, such as unprecedented floods in Europe, a drought in Somalia and the escalating situation in North Korea, are all signs of the impending end of the world.

And now Dr Lund has made the extraordinary statement that there is another child – a fourth horseman – who survived the doomed Dalu Air flight that crashed in Cape Town, South Africa. Citing the recently published Dalu Air passenger list, Dr Lund said that there was only one child on the flight who was close to the same age as

the three children who survived the other disasters virtually unscathed – a seven-year-old Nigerian boy named
Kenneth Oduah: 'We strongly believe Kenneth will prove
to be one of God's harbingers.'

Dr Lund is undeterred by the South African Civil Aviation Authority's definitive statement that there were 'cat-
egorically no survivors of Dalu Air Flight 467.'

'We'll find him,' he said. 'It was chaos down there after
the crash. Africa is a messy place. The child could easily
have got lost or wandered off. And when we do find him,
it will be all the proof those who have not yet entered
Jesus' fold will need.'

When questioned what he meant by this, Dr Lund
replied: 'You don't want to be left behind when the Antichrist comes, you're going to experience suffering worse
than you can ever imagine. As it says in Thessalonians,
"The day of the Lord will come as a thief in the night,"
and Jesus could call us to him any day now.'

REWARD 200,000 US Dollars!!!

For the discovery of Kenneth Oduah, a seven-year-old Nigerian passenger travelling on the Antonov cargo and passenger plane that crashed into Khayelitsher [*sic*] Township, Cape Town, South Africa on 12 January 2012. It is believed that Kenneth left the children's home where he was taken after the crash and may currently be living on the streets of Cape Town.

According to his aunt, Veronica Alice Oduah, Kenneth has a large head, very dark skin and a crescent-shaped scar on his scalp. If you think you know of his whereabouts, please contact findingkenneth.net or call +00 789654377646 and leave a message. Normal rates apply.

PART FIVE

SURVIVORS

Chiyoko and Ryu.

(Translator Eric Kushan notes that he has chosen to use the Japanese term *izoku* in the transcript below, instead of the rough translation 'families of the bereaved' or the more literal translation, 'families left behind'.)

Message logged @ 16.30, 05/03/2012

RYU: Where have you been all day? I was getting worried about you.

CHIYOKO: Six *izoku* came today.

RYU: All at once?

CHIYOKO: No. Two came together in the morning; the rest came separately. So tiring. Mother Creature is always saying we have to treat the families with respect. I know they're in pain, but how does she think Hiro feels having to listen to them all day?

RYU: How *does* he feel?

CHIYOKO: It must be really boring for him. They all shuffle up to him and bow, and then they all ask the same thing. 'Did Yoshi, or Sakura, or Shinji or whoever suffer? Did they say anything before they died?' Like Hiro would know who these people are! It creeps me out, Ryu.

RYU: That would creep me out, too.

CHIYOKO: If they come when MC is out, I tell them to go away. MC always lets them know that he's still not speaking, not that this seems to make any difference to them. But today, while MC was in the kitchen preparing tea, I did an experiment. I told them that he does actually talk, but he's very shy. I told them that he's always saying that there was no panic or horror as the plane went down and that no one suffered except for the American woman and the two survivors who died in hospital. Was that evil of me?

RYU: You told them what they wanted to hear. If anything, it was kind.

CHIYOKO: Yeah, well…I only said it because I wanted to get them out of the house. I can only serve so much tea and wear my 'I'm sorry for your loss' face for so long. Oh, I meant to tell you. You know that most of the *izoku* who come here to see Hiro are ancient. Well today a younger woman came. Younger as in she could walk without a stick and didn't look shocked when I didn't serve the tea in exactly the right way. She said she was the wife of the man who sat next to the American.

RYU: I know who you mean…Keita Eto. He left a message, didn't he?

CHIYOKO: Yeah. I re-read it after she left. It basically said that before he got on that plane he was suicidal.

RYU: Do you think his wife knew how he felt before he died?

CHIYOKO: Well she certainly knows now.

RYU: That must hurt. What did she want to know from Hiro?

CHIYOKO: The usual. If her husband had acted bravely when the plane went down, and if he'd said anything else apart from what he'd left on the message. She asked this in a matter-of-fact manner. I got the impression she was really just curious to see Hiro rather than wanting reassurance. Like he's some kind of exhibit. It made me mad.

RYU: They'll stop coming soon.

CHIYOKO: You think? Over five hundred people died in the crash. There are hundreds of families who might still want to see him.

RYU: Don't think like that. At least now they know why the plane did crash for sure. That might help.

CHIYOKO: Yeah. Perhaps you're right. I hope it gives the captain's wife some peace.

RYU: She really got to you.

CHIYOKO: She did. I'll admit that I think about her often.

RYU: Why do you think that is?

CHIYOKO: Because I know what it's like. To be shunned, to have people saying terrible things about you.

RYU: Did that happen to you when you were in the States as well?

CHIYOKO: You really like digging for information, don't you? But to answer your question, no, I was not shunned when I lived in the States.

RYU: Did you make friends there?

CHIYOKO: No. Just acquaintances. You know I find most people dull, Ryu. That includes Americans. Although I know you admire them.

RYU: I do not! Why do you think that?

CHIYOKO: Why else are you so interested in my life there?

RYU: I told you, just curious. I want to know everything about you. Don't get mad. _|7O

CHIYOKO: Ai! The attack of the ORZ again.

RYU: I knew that would cheer you up. And just so you know…I am very happy that the anti-social ice princess thinks I am worth talking to.

CHIYOKO: You and Hiro are the only two people I can stand being around.

RYU: Except you've never met one of us and the other one doesn't talk back. Do you prefer that? The silent treatment?

CHIYOKO: Are you jealous of Hiro, Ryu?

RYU: Of course not! That's not what I meant.

CHIYOKO: It is not always necessary to talk to make yourself understood. You'd be amazed how much emotion Hiro can express by just using his eyes and body language. And yes, while I admit it's soothing to talk to someone who can't answer back, it's also frustrating. Don't worry, I am not about to choose the Silent Boy over you. Besides, he's taken a liking to *Waratte litomo!* and *Apron of Love*, which I know you would never do. I hope it passes.

RYU: Ha! He is only six.

CHIYOKO: Yeah. But those shows are for moronic adults. I don't know what he sees in them. MC is worried what the authorities will say if he doesn't go back to school soon. I don't think he should go back. I hate the thought of him being with other children.

RYU: I agree. Children are cruel.

CHIYOKO: And how can he defend himself if he can't even speak? He needs protecting.

RYU: But he can't stay away forever, can he?

CHIYOKO: I need to find a way to teach him how to protect himself. I don't want him to go through what we went through. I couldn't bear it.

RYU: I know.

CHIYOKO: Hey. He's right here now, sitting with me, do you want to say hello?

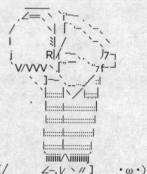

RYU: Hello, Hiro! (/・ω・)(/   ∠−,V ＼ //]   ・ω・)

CHIYOKO: Nice! He just bowed back at you. MC says she also wants to take him back to the hospital to get him checked out again. I keep fighting her on this. What is the point? There's nothing physically wrong with him.

RYU: Maybe he just doesn't have anything to say.

CHIYOKO: Yeah. Maybe that's it.

RYU: You heard what the Americans are saying? About the fourth child? The one in Africa?

CHIYOKO: Of course. It's stupid. MC says an American reporter called here yesterday. A foreigner who works for the *Yomiuri Shimbun*. They are as bad as Aikao Uri and her alien crap. How can a minister's wife be so foolish? I take that back, I shouldn't be surprised. I'm worried that she will ask to come and see Hiro.

RYU: Yeah. 'Take me to your leader, Hiro.'

CHIYOKO: !!! Listen, Ryu. I just want to say, I appreciate you listening to me.

RYU: Where did that come from?

CHIYOKO: I've been meaning to say it for a while. I know it can't be easy putting up with my ice princess ways. But it helps.

RYU: Um…Chiyoko, there's something I need to tell you as well. It is difficult, but I need to get it out. I think you can guess what it is.

CHIYOKO: Hold that thought. The MC is screaming something at me.

Message logged @ 17.10, 05/03/2012

CHIYOKO: Android Uncle is here! He didn't say he was coming so MC is freaking out. More soon.

Message logged @ 02.30, 06/03/2012

CHIYOKO: Ryu. Ryu!

Message logged @ 02.40, 06/03/2012

RYU: I'm here! Sorry, sleeping. Your message beep woke me up.

CHIYOKO: Listen…got something freaky to tell you. But you have to promise to keep it to yourself.

RYU: You really have to ask?

CHIYOKO: Okay…Android Uncle brought Hiro something. A gift.

RYU: What? Don't leave me in suspense!!!

CHIYOKO: An android.

RYU: !!!!!!!!!!!!!!!!!!!!!!!!

CHIYOKO: It gets better. It's an exact copy of Hiro. It looks just like him, although his hair is different. You should have heard MC scream when she saw it.

RYU: Are you serious? A robot version of Hiro?

CHIYOKO: Yes. Android Uncle says he was making it before Auntie Hiromi died. It is really really disturbing. Even freakier than his own surrabot. And that's not all.

RYU: There's more? What could be weirder?

CHIYOKO: Wait. Android Uncle brought it here because of what MC had told him about Hiro refusing to speak. He thought it might help him. You know how AU's android works, right?

RYU: I think so. He uses a camera to film his facial movements and they get relayed via computer to the android's sensors.

CHIYOKO: Full marks! It took ages for AU to set it all up. While MC and I watched, he focused the motion-capture lens on Hiro's face and told Hiro to try and say a few words. Hiro moved his lips – whispering, really – and then the android said…wait for it…'Hello Daddy.'

RYU: !

CHIYOKO: MC almost fainted. It looks so real. There's a mechanism in its chest that makes it look as if it's breathing. It even blinks every so often.

RYU: Can you imagine what would happen if you filmed that and put it up on Nico Nico???

CHIYOKO: Aiiiii!!! The reporters would go insane!!!!

RYU: But if he's talking…won't the investigators want to know what he saw during the crash?

CHIYOKO: What does it matter? They have their answers now. You read the transcript of the pilots' last words. The authorities know what caused it. The best thing we can do is wait and see if this is going to help Hiro communicate with us. And it seems to be working. Guess what he said at dinner?

RYU: What????

CHIYOKO: Because of AU showing up, MC decided she was going to make his favourite natto dish.

RYU: Gross.

CHIYOKO: I know. I hate it too. I gave Hiro his bowl, he looked down at it, moved his lips and then his android said, 'I don't like it, please may I have some ramen.' Even MC laughed. MC asked me to put him to bed, and then I sneaked down to listen to what she and AU were saying. Father was out as usual.

RYU: And???

CHIYOKO: MC was saying that she's worried about Hiro not going back to primary school – about what the authorities will say. AU said he would use his status to make sure that Hiro won't have to go back for a while, at least until he is talking normally and won't cause too much attention. AU went on and on about how we must keep what's happening with the android quiet. MC agreed.

RYU: He must be grateful that you are taking such good care of Hiro.

CHIYOKO: I suppose. But listen, Ryu. You mustn't tell anyone about this.

RYU: Who am I going to tell?

CHIYOKO: I dunno. You always seem to be on 2-chan. You and your pet ORZ symbol.

RYU: Very funny. Look, you've called him back: _|7O

CHIYOKO: Ai!!! Put it away!!!! I've got to go, I need to sleep. But hey, what did you want to tell me earlier?

RYU: It can wait. Talk later?

CHIYOKO: Of course. Stay tuned for more exciting updates in the Crazy World of the Ice Princess and the Incredible Talking Boy.

RYU: You're funny.

CHIYOKO: I know.

Lillian Small.

Bobby had been living with us for six weeks when Reuben woke up for the first time. I'd had a carer in that day to watch Reuben so that I could take Bobby to the park. I'd been worrying about Bobby not spending time with other children, but it didn't seem right to send him back to school, not with the constant media attention. I was plagued with nightmares that I'd be late collecting him and one of those fanatical religious types would kidnap him. But we needed to get out of the apartment; we hadn't been able to leave for days. The whole area was teeming with those damn news vans. Still, at least we finally knew why the plane had gone down. The NTSB investigator who came to tell me of their findings before they held the press conference – a woman, which surprised me – said that it would have been instantaneous and Lori wouldn't have felt a thing. Knowing that Lori hadn't suffered gave me some comfort, but it did reopen the wound again, and I had to excuse myself for a few minutes so that I could get my grief out. The investigator couldn't take her eyes off Bobby; I could tell she couldn't believe he'd survived. And the fact that birds brought that plane down...*birds*! How can something like that happen?

Then, just after that died down, those damn End Timers started more of their nonsense, saying that a fourth child must have survived the crash in Africa. This brought on a fresh wave of journalists and film crews, and another crowd of those religious types with their wide staring eyes and end-of-the-world placards. Betsy was furious. 'Those *meshugeners*, they should be arrested for spreading those lies!' I'd stopped reading the papers after the poison they spread about Bobby being 'unnatural', never mind what else they were saying about him being possessed. In the end, I had to ask Betsy not to show me the articles or even tell me about them. I couldn't bear to hear it.

It got so bad that I had to devise a special routine before Bobby and I could even leave the apartment. First I'd ask Betsy to look outside and check that there were none of those alien people or the shouty religious types hanging around in the park, and then Bobby would put on his disguise – a baseball cap and a pair of clear-lensed glasses. He treated it like a game, bless him: 'Dress up time again, Bubbe!' I'd taken to dyeing my hair after all those photographs of me and Bobby at Lori's service were published. It was Betsy's idea, we'd spent half-an-hour in Walgreens choosing a colour. We decided on auburn, which I worried made me look a bit brassy. How I wished I could have got Reuben's opinion on that!

Bobby and I had a fine time that day. It was raining, so there were no other children there, but it did both of us good. For an hour, I could almost pretend we were living a normal life.

After we got back from the park, I settled Reuben in bed. He'd been more serene, I suppose you'd call it, since Bobby came to live with us. He slept a lot and his dreams didn't seem to haunt him.

I made a rare roast beef sandwich for both of us, and Bobby and I settled onto the couch to watch a movie on Netflix. I chose something called *Nim's Island*, which I regretted immediately as there was a dead mother right in the opening credits. But Bobby didn't flinch. He still hadn't internalised (I think that's the correct term) what had happened to Lori. He'd settled into life with me and Reuben as if he'd always lived with us. And he never mentioned Lori unless I talked about her first.

I told him over and over again that his mother had loved him more than life itself, and that she'd always be with him in spirit, but this didn't seem to go in. I'd been putting off taking him to another trauma counsellor – he didn't seem to need it – but I still kept in touch with Dr Pankowski, who assured me not to worry. She said children have an inbuilt coping mechanism to help them come to terms with sudden trauma, and not to panic if I noticed some changes in his behaviour. I never liked to say anything to Lori, but a few times when I babysat Bobby, just after Reuben got sick, he'd acted out a little. Thrown a tantrum or two. But after the crash and his mother's... after Lori... it was as if he'd grown up overnight; as if he knew we all had to work together to get over it. And he was far more affectionate. I tried to hide my grief from him, but whenever he saw me crying, he'd put his arms around me and say, 'Don't be sad, Bubbe.'

As we watched the movie, he snuggled against me, and then he said, 'Can't Po Po watch with us, Bubbe?' Po Po was Bobby's name for Reuben. I can't remember where it came from, but Lori thought it was cute, so she encouraged him to use it.

'Po Po's sleeping, Bobby,' I said.

'Po Po sleeps a lot, doesn't he, Bubbe?'

'He does. It's because...' How do you explain Alzheimer's to a child? 'You know Po Po has been sick for a while, don't you, Bobby? You remember that from before you came to live with us.'

'Yes, Bubbe,' he said gravely.

I don't remember falling asleep on the couch, but I must have done. I woke up to the sound of laughter. The movie had finished so it wasn't the television.

It was Reuben.

I sat completely still, Elspeth, barely daring to breathe. Then I heard Bobby saying something – I couldn't catch the words – followed by that laugh again.

I hadn't heard that sound for months.

My neck was aching from the angle in which I'd fallen asleep, but I didn't take any notice of that. I moved faster than I had in years!

They were in the bedroom, Reuben sitting up, his hair all mussed, Bobby perched at the end of the bed.

'Hello, Bubbe,' Bobby said. 'Po Po has woken up.'

That dead expression – the Al mask – was gone. 'Hello,' Reuben said, clear as you please. 'Have you seen my reading glasses?' I had to clap my hand to my mouth to stop myself from screaming. 'Bobby wants me to read him a story.'

'Does he?' I think I said. I'd started shaking. It had been months since Reuben had had a clear period – an anti-Al moment – if you don't count that hand squeeze he gave me just after we found out about Bobby surviving. Word coherence was the first thing Al had stolen from Reuben, and here Reuben was, speaking clearly, all the words in their correct order.

I thought perhaps I was dreaming.

Then Reuben said, 'I've looked in the turvey but I couldn't find them.' I didn't care that he'd used the wrong word then – all I could think was that I was witnessing some kind of miracle.

'I'll look for you, Reuben,' I said. He hadn't needed his glasses for months – well, he wasn't going to be reading, not with Al. My pulse racing like a runaway train, I searched everywhere I could think of, pulling things all over the place. I was terrified that if I didn't find those glasses he'd retreat and Al would take over again. I finally found them at the bottom of his sock drawer.

'Thank you, dear,' Reuben said. I remember thinking that was strange; Reuben had never called me 'dear' before.

'Reuben...are you...how are you feeling?' I was still finding it a struggle to speak.

'A little bit tired. But otherwise goodness.'

Bobby padded off to the bedroom and brought back one of his old picture books. A strange one that Lori had bought him years ago called *Vegetable Glue*. He handed it to Reuben.

'Hmmmm.' Reuben squinted at the book. 'The words... they're not right.'

He was fading again. I could see the shadow of Al reappearing in his eyes.

'Shall I ask Bubbe to read it to us, Po Po?' Bobby asked.

Another look of confusion, then a spark of life. 'Yes. Where's Lily?'

'I'm here, Reuben,' I said.

'You're a redder. My Lily was dark.'

'I dyed my hair. Do you like it?'

He didn't answer – he couldn't. He was gone again.

'Read it to us, Bubbe!' Bobby said.

I sat on the bed and started reading the book, my voice shaking.

Reuben fell asleep almost immediately. When I was

tucking Bobby into bed, I asked him what they'd been talking about when I heard Reuben laughing.

'He was telling me about his bad dreams, and I told him that he didn't need to have them anymore if he didn't want them.'

I didn't expect to sleep a wink that night. But I did. I woke to find Reuben gone from his side of the bed. I ran through to the kitchen, my heart thudding in my chest.

Bobby was sitting on the counter, jabbering away to Reuben, who was spooning sugar into a cup filled with milk. I didn't care that the counter top was covered in coffee grounds and crumbs and spilled milk, the only thing I could take in right then was the amazing fact that Reuben had dressed himself. His jacket was inside out, but other than that, he looked fine. He'd even tried to shave, and he hadn't done too bad a job of it. He glanced at me and waved. 'I wanted to fetch bagels, but I couldn't find the key.'

I tried to smile. 'How are you feeling today, Reuben?'

'Fine thank you for asking, you're welcome,' he said. He wasn't all back, there was something not quite right about him – something lacking in his eyes still – but he was up and about, he was dressed, and he was talking.

Bobby tugged on Reuben's hand. 'Come on, Po Po. Let's go watch TV. Can we, Bubbe?'

Still feeling dazed, I nodded.

I didn't know what to do with myself. I called the care agency and told them that I didn't need anyone that day, and then I made an appointment with Dr Lomeier. I did all these things automatically.

Getting out of the apartment, even with the miracle, wasn't going to be simple. Reuben hadn't been outside for weeks and I worried about him getting overly tired. I thought about asking Betsy to do her usual sweep of the area to check there weren't any reporters lurking around, but something stopped me from knocking on her door. Instead, I called a taxi even though it was only a few blocks to the Beth Israel clinic, and told Bobby to put on his disguise. We were lucky that day. I couldn't see any of those reporters, and the people passing by the apartment – a Hasidic man and a group of Hispanic teenagers – didn't spare us a glance. The taxi driver managed to park right outside the front door. He gave Bobby a strange look, but didn't say anything. He was one of those immigrant drivers. A Bengali or something like that. I don't think he even spoke English; and I had to direct him to the clinic.

Probably I should tell you a little bit about Dr Lomeier. I didn't like him, Elspeth. There's no doubt that he was a good doctor, but I didn't appreciate the way he used to speak about Reuben as if he wasn't there when I used to take him in for his check-ups: 'And how is Reuben doing today, Mrs Small, are we having any difficulties with him?'

He was the first doctor who'd mentioned the possibility of Alzheimer's as the cause of Reuben's forgetfulness, and Reuben didn't like him either. 'Why'd I have to get news like that from a putz like him?' The specialist we were referred to was far more personable, but that meant a trip into Manhattan, and I wasn't ready to take Reuben all that way. For now, Dr Lomeier would do. I needed answers. I needed to know what we were dealing with.

When we were shown into his room, Dr Lomeier was friendlier than usual. 'Is this Bobby?' he said. 'I've heard all about you, young man.'

'What are you doing on your computer?' Bobby said. 'You have pictures. I want to see!'

Dr Lomeier blinked in surprise, and then turned his computer screen around. It showed a photograph of an alpine scene. 'Not that picture,' Bobby said. 'The ones with the ladies holding their peepees.'

There was an awkward silence and then Reuben said, clear as a bell, 'Well, go on, show him the pictures, doc.' Bobby grinned at him, as pleased as punch.

Dr Lomeier's mouth dropped right open. It sounds like I'm exaggerating, Elspeth, but you should have seen the man.

'Mrs Small,' he said. 'How long has this been going on?'

I told him Reuben had started talking last night.

'He started talking *coherently* last night?'

'Yes,' I said.

'I see.' He shifted in his chair.

I almost expected Reuben to say something like, 'Oy, I am here you know, schmuck.' But he kept silent.

'I have to say, Mrs Small, I am quite astonished if what you say is true. Reuben's deterioration has been...In fact, I'm quite surprised to see that he is mobile at all. I expected that I would have to refer you to one of the state homes quite some time ago.'

The anger hit like a fist. 'Don't talk about him like that! He's here! He's a person you...you...'

'Putz?' Reuben said brightly.

'Bubbe?' Bobby looked at me. 'Can we go now? This man is sicky.'

'It's your grandfather who is sick, Bobby,' Dr Lomeier said.

'Oh no,' Bobby said. 'Po Po isn't sick.' He tugged at my

hand. 'Let's go, Bubbe. This is silly.' Reuben was already on his feet, making for the door.

I stood up.

Dr Lomeier was still flustered, and his pale face had turned red. 'Mrs Small…I urge you, please make another appointment immediately. I can refer you to Dr Allen at Mount Sinai again. If Reuben is showing signs of improved cognitive ability, then it could mean that the Dematine dosage he is on is working with far more efficacy than we could ever have envisaged.'

I didn't say that Reuben had been refusing to take his medication for weeks now. Whatever was causing his transformation, it wasn't the Dematine. I couldn't get him to swallow it.

Stan Murua-Wilson's daughter, Isobel, is a former classmate of Bobby Small's. Mr Murua-Wilson agreed to talk to me via Skype in May 2012.

Goes without saying that all of us parents at Roberto Hernandes were super-shocked when we heard about Lori. We just couldn't believe something like that could happen to someone we knew. Not that Lori and I were close or anything. My wife, Ana, isn't jealous, but she had an issue with Lori's behaviour at a couple of PTA meetings. Ana said she was flirty, called her a grade-A flake. I wouldn't have gone that far. Lori was okay. Most of the kids at Roberto Hernandes are Hispanic – but it's got this integration and diversity ethos thing going on – and Lori was never like, hey, look at me, sending my kid to a public school so that he can get real with the kids from the neighbourhood. A few of the white parents whose kids go to Magnet schools are like that, you know, smug. And Lori could easily have sent Bobby to one of the good yeshiva schools in the neighbourhood. I reckon part of Ana's problem with Lori was Bobby . . . he wasn't the easiest kid, if you want to know the truth.

I'm an English major, was planning on teaching before Isobel came along, and Bobby's behaviour – pre-crash, I mean – and Lori's attitude to it reminded me of that short story by Shirley Jackson, "Charles." You know it? About this boy called Laurie who comes home every day from kindergarten with tales about this evil kid called Charles, who's been acting up in class, bullying the other kids and killing the class hamster and stuff. Laurie's parents are full of *schadenfreude*, and say things like, 'Why don't Charles's parents discipline the boy?' Course, when they eventually go to the school for a parent-teacher meeting, they find out that there's no kid in the class called Charles – the bad kid is actually their own son.

A couple of parents tried to speak to Lori about Bobby, but it never seemed to go in. Ana freaked out last year when Isobel came home and said that Bobby had tried to bite her. Ana was all for going in to see the principal, but I talked her out of it. Knew it would blow over, or maybe Lori would come to her senses and dose him up with Ritalin or whatever; that kid had serious ADD.

Can I say he was a different child after the crash? There's a lot of talk about this, what with all that shit the prophecy nut jobs are saying, but because Bobby's grandmother Lillian decided to put him into the home schooling programme – I guess because of all the attention he was getting from the media and those freaks – it's hard for me to say. But there was one time I came across him, round about late March. The weather wasn't great, but Isobel had been on my back about going to the park all day, and in the end I gave in.

When we got there, Isobel was like, 'Look, Daddy, there's Bobby.' And before I could stop her, she ran right over to him. He was wearing a baseball cap and glasses, so I didn't recognise him straight off, but Isobel saw through that straight away. Bobby was with an elderly woman who introduced herself as Betsy, Lillian's neighbour. She said that Lillian's husband, Reuben, was having a bad day, so she'd offered to take Bobby out for a while. Betsy was a real talker!

'You want to play with me, Bobby?' Isobel asked.

She's a good little girl. Bobby nodded and held out his hand. Together they went over to the swings. I was watching them closely, giving half an ear to Betsy. You could tell she thought it was weird that I stayed home and looked after Isobel while Ana went out to work. 'Never would have happened in my day,' she kept saying. Lots of my buddies in the area are the same. Doesn't make you less of a man or any of that shit. We don't get bored. We have a jogging club; meet at the rec centre for racquetball, that kind of thing.

Isobel said something to Bobby and he laughed. I started to relax. There they were, heads together, chattering away. They seemed to be having a great time.

'He doesn't see enough of other children,' Betsy was going on. 'I don't blame Lillian, she has her hands full.'

On our way home, I asked Isobel what she and Bobby had talked about. I was worried that maybe Bobby had been telling her about the crash and his mother dying. I hadn't broached the death issue yet with Isobel. She had a hamster that was getting more and more sluggish by the day, but I was planning to just replace it without her knowing. I'm a coward like that. Ana's different. 'Death is a fact of life.' But you don't want kids to grow up too quickly, do you?

'I was telling him about the lady,' she said. I knew exactly what she meant. Since she was three, Isobel had suffered from night terrors. A specific hallucination where she'd see a terrifying image of a hunched old woman whirling in front of her eyes. Part of the problem is that my mother-in-law fills Isobel's head with all kinds of stories, superstitious stuff like El Chupacabra and all kinds of other bullshit. Ana and I used to fight about that a lot.

Isobel's condition had gotten so bad last year that I'd

shelled out for a psychologist. She said that Isobel would eventually get over it, and I prayed this would be the case.

'Bobby is like the lady,' Isobel said. I asked her what she meant, but all she said was, 'He just is.' Freaked me out a bit.

This doesn't mean anything, but . . . after she saw Bobby that day, Isobel hasn't woken up screaming once or complained about 'the lady' visiting her. Weeks later I asked her again what she meant – that thing about Bobby being like the lady – but she acted like she didn't have a clue what I was talking about.

Transcript of Paul Craddock's voice recording, March 2012.

12 March, 5.30 a.m.

It was just one drink, Mandi. Just one ... I had another one of those nights, Stephen came again, but this time he didn't speak, he just ...

(Sound of a thump, followed by a toilet flushing)

Never again. Never fucking again. Darren – you remember, from Social Services – is going to be here in a few hours and I can't let him smell the stale booze on me. But it helps. I can't deny that.

Oh God.

12 March, 11.30 a.m.

Think I got away with it. Was careful not to reek of mouthwash, which is a dead giveaway. Found one of those cheap spray-on deodorants at the back of the bathroom cupboard, which made me stink of manufactured musk instead. But it's the last time I'm going to take a chance like that.

Not that I spent much time with Darren in any case. Jess had him wrapped around her little finger as usual. 'Darren, do you want to come and watch *My Little Pony* with me? Uncle Paul bought me the whole series.' She definitely wasn't this outgoing before the crash. I'm certain of that now. She and Polly were never what you'd call preco-cious. They were always shy around strangers, but I guess a slight change in behaviour is to be expected. Darren says we should think about putting her back in school after the Easter hols. We'll see what Dr K says.

Thanks for being so understanding about me not send-ing you the recordings for a while. It's just…talking it out like this…it really does help, you know? I'll get back to the proper stuff soon, I promise. It has to be grief, doesn't it? Denial or whatever. Isn't that one of the stages everyone goes through when they're in mourning? Thank fuck Jess isn't going through any of this. She seems to have accepted everything, hasn't even cried yet – not even when the dressings came off her face that first time and she saw her scars. They're not bad; nothing that a little bit of make-up won't fix when she's older. And her hair is starting to grow back. We had some fun the other day choosing hats on the Internet. She picked out a black trilby that was remarkably stylish. Can't imagine pre-crash Jess going for that kind of thing. It wasn't very Missy K, who has the dress sense of a retarded, colour-blind drag-queen.

But still…accepting everything like she has…that can't be normal, can it? I'm almost tempted to show her the family photographs I put away before she came home, see if I can jump-start some sort of emotional response, but I'm not ready to look at them yet and I'm careful not to get too upset around her. Now they've released what they call their preliminary crash findings, I hope to Christ this is going to mean I get some closure. And 277 Together is helping. I haven't told them about the nightmares. No way am I going to do that. I trust them, specially Mel and Geoff, but you never know. The fucking papers will print anything, won't they? Did you see that whole sob-story thing in the *Daily Mail*– the *Daily Heil*, Stephen used to call it – about Marilyn? She says she's been diagnosed with emphysema, 'And all I want is to see little Jessie before I die, boo hoo.' Pure emotional blackmail. I keep expecting to see Fester and Gomez skulking outside the house. But I suppose even the Addams Family aren't stupid enough to risk a restraining order. And I can always call Mel's hardcore geezer son Gavin to come over and put the fear of God into them if they do show up, can't I?

Christ, listen to me. Babbling like an idiot. It's the stress. Not getting enough sleep. No wonder those American Gitmo bastards used sleep deprivation as a torture tool.

(The sound of a ring tone – the theme to Dr Zhivago*)*

Hang on. Phone.

11.45 a.m.

Lovely. Well, that was nice. A hack as usual, from the *Independent* this time. Isn't that supposed to be a rational paper? Wanted to know how I was feeling about the rumours that one of those religious pricks is going to start searching for the fourth horseman, if you can believe *that*.

What the fuck has it got to do with me? Jesus. The fourth kid? It's such bollocks. He even had the gall to ask me if I'd noticed any change in Jess's behaviour. Seriously? Is this what the press is up to now? Believing in snake charmers and religious freaks? Are the nutters running the asylum? Oooh, that's not bad. Must remember to keep this in when I delete all the dream stuff.

Right. Coffee, get Jess dressed and then off to Waitrose.

Only two paparazzi Neanderthals out there today; should be able to slip out no problem.

15 March, 11.25 p.m.

Hmmm...not sure what to say about this. Weird day.

This morning, paparazzi or not, I decided we needed to get some fresh air. I was going stir-crazy and Jess has been watching way too much TV. But we can't go out most of the time, not if we don't want to be papped to death. Thank Christ she has no interest in the news channels, but there's only so many times I can hear the *My Little Pony* theme tune without my brain exploding. We walked down the lane to the stables at the end of the street, trailed by a group of greasy hacks with comb-overs.

'Smile for the camera, Jess!' they were crowing, panting round her like a posse of paedos on a day-trip out of Broadmoor.

It took all my strength not to tell them to go fuck themselves, but I put on my 'good uncle' face and Jess played up to them as usual, posing with the horses and holding my hand while we made our way back home.

As we were due to meet with Dr K the next day, I thought it might be an idea to try again to get Jess to open up about Polly, Stephen and Shelly. It's worrying me, her being so self-contained and...happy, I guess. Because that's what she is. All the fucking time, like a kid from a 1980s cheesy American sitcom. She's even stopped using bad language.

As usual, she listened to me calmly, that slightly patronising expression on her face.

I gestured at the *My Little Pony* episode playing on

repeat – I have to admit, despite the godawful theme track, the show is weirdly addictive. By now, I pretty much know every episode off by heart. 'Remember when Applejack refuses to accept any help from her friends and she ends up getting herself into trouble, Jess?' I wittered on in my Cheery Uncle voice. 'In the end Twilight Sparkle and the others help her out and she realises that sometimes the only way to deal with difficult issues is to share them with her friends.'

Jess didn't say anything. She looked at me as if I was completely bonkers.

'I'm saying, you can lean on me whenever you want to, Jess. And it's fine to cry when you're sad. I know you must miss Polly and Mummy and Daddy terribly. I know I can't replace them.'

'I'm not sad,' she said.

Maybe she's blocked them out of her mind. Maybe she's pretending that they never existed.

For the thousandth time I asked her, 'Shall I see if any of your friends want to come over and play tomorrow?'

She yawned, said, 'No thanks,' and went back to watching those bloody ponies.

3.30 a.m.

(Sobbing)

Mandi. Mandi. I can't take it any more. He was here... Couldn't see his face. Said that thing again, which is all he says:

'Why did you let that thing in here?'

Oh God, oh fuck.

4.30 a.m.

There's no way I can go back to sleep. No fucking way.

They're so real. The dreams. Incredibly real. And…
shit. This is beyond mental…But this time I was sure I
could smell something – a faint odour of decaying fish.
As if, over time, Stephen's body is rotting. And I still can't
see his face…

Right. That's enough.

I have to stop this.

It's absolutely insane.

But…I'm thinking maybe all this stems from guilt.
Maybe that's what my subconscious needs me to deal
with.

I'm doing my best for Jess, of course I am. But I can't
help but feel I'm missing something. That I should be
doing more.

Like when Mum and Dad died. I left it all up to Stephen. Let him do all the arrangements for the funeral. I
was touring at the time, doing an Alan Bennett in Exeter.
Thought my career was more important; convinced
myself that Mum and Dad wouldn't want me messing up
my big break ha ha. Some break. We were lucky if the
house was half full most nights. I suppose I was still
angry at them. I never came out to them, but they knew.
They made it clear that I was the black sheep of the family
and Stephen was their golden boy. I know what I told you
before, Mandi, but me and Stephen weren't close as kids.
We never fought or anything, but…Everyone liked him. I
wasn't jealous, but it was easy for him. It wasn't easy for
me. Thank God for Shelly. If it wasn't for her, we would
never have re-connected.

But I knew... I've always known... He was too good, Stephen was. Better than me.

(*A sob*)

Even stood up for me when I didn't deserve it.

And I knew in my heart, deep down, that he knew I wasn't good enough to look after Jess.

Him and Shelly... they were successful, weren't they? And here's me...

(*A loud sniff*)

Listen to me. Poor little miss self-pity.

It's just guilt. That's all it is. Guilt and regret. But I'll do better with Jess. I'll prove to Stephen that he and Shelly were right to give me custody. Then maybe he'll leave me alone.

21 March, 11.30 p.m.

I gave in and asked Mrs Ellington-Burn to look after Jess while I went to the 277 Together meeting tonight. I usually take Jess with me, and she always behaves like a little angel. Mel sets her up with something to do in the community centre foyer, colouring-in or whatever, and I bring Stephen's Mac along so that she can watch Rainbow Dash and the girls on repeat, but a few of the 277s... I don't know, I get the impression that it's awkward for them if she comes along. They're all lovely to her of course, it's just... well, I can't blame them. It's a blatant reminder that their relatives didn't survive, isn't it? Must feel unfair to some of them. And I know they must want to ask her what those last seconds before the plane went down were like. She says she doesn't remember anything, and why would she? She was knocked unconscious when it happened. The AAIB investigator who came to talk to her before they had that press conference did his best to nudge her memory, but she was adamant that the last thing she remembered was being in the pool at the hotel in Tenerife.

Mrs E-B practically threw me out of the door, couldn't wait to hang out with Jess. Maybe she's lonely. I've never seen anyone apart from the Jehovahs visiting her, but then she is such a miserable old cow most of the time. Thankfully she left her yappy dog at home, so at least I didn't have to worry about its vile poodle hair getting all over the covers. I don't think her sniffiness towards me is personal. Geoff said she looks at him as if he's got shit on his shoe (a typical Geoffism), so I think it's just her monumental snobbishness at play. I was nervous about leaving Jess with her, but Jess just cheerfully waved me off. I haven't said this out loud before, but...sometimes I can't tell if she really gives a shit if I'm around or not.

Anyway...where was I?...Oh yeah. 277 Together. I almost blurted the whole thing out. Told them about Stephen. Told them about the nightmares. Christ. Instead, I rattled on and on about all the press attention, how it was getting me down. I knew I was eating into everyone's time, but I couldn't stop.

Finally Mel had to interrupt me as it was getting late. While we were having tea, Kelvin and Kylie stood up and said they had an announcement. Kylie turned bright red and twisted her hands, and then Kelvin told us that they'd started seeing each other and were planning on getting engaged. We all started crying and clapping. I was a bit jealous, to be honest. It's been months since I've even had a drink with anyone I'd remotely like to shag, and there's not much chance of that now, is there? I can just imagine what the *Sun* would say. 'Jess's Nutty Uncle Turns Home into Perverted Sex Den' or something. I told them I was happy for them, although he's way older than she is, and the whole thing seemed a bit hasty – it's only been a month since they started going out.

Still, he's a good bloke. Kylie's lucky to have him. Really sensitive underneath all those muscles and that 'yeah man, innit' attitude. I started developing a bit of a thing for him myself after I heard him read that poem at the memorial service. Knew it wouldn't go anywhere. Kelvin's as straight as they come. They all are. I'm the only gay in the meeting, ha fucking ha. After everyone had congratulated them, Kelvin said his folks – he lost both of them in the crash – would have loved meeting Kylie; they'd been on at him for decades to get married. That set us all off again. Geoff was practically bawling. We all knew that Kelvin had given his parents the trip to Tenerife for their ruby wedding anniversary. It must be bloody awful to deal with that. It reminded me of Bobby Small's mum. The reason she was in Florida was to look for a place where her parents could settle down, wasn't it? Horrendous. So much for fucking karma.

A group of 277s were going to the pub afterwards for a few drinks to celebrate, but I decided it wasn't a good idea to tag along. The temptation to have a stiff drink would have been too much. I'm not sure if it was my imagination, but several of them seemed relieved when I turned them down. Probably just my old friend paranoia rearing its ugly head again.

When I got back, Mrs Ellington-Burn was slouched on the couch reading a Patricia Cornwell novel. She didn't seem to be in any hurry to get home, so I decided to ask her if she'd noticed anything different about Jess – appearance aside of course – since the crash. I wanted to see if it was just me who thought Jess's personality had undergone a *Doctor Who*ish transformation.

She thought about the question long and hard, then she shook her head, said she couldn't be sure. Still, she said that Jess had been 'an absolute treasure' that evening, although surprisingly, Jess had asked to watch something other than *My Little Pony*. Mrs E-B rather testily admitted they'd gone through a marathon of reality shows – everything from *Britain's Got Talent* to *America's Next Top Model*. Then Jess had gone to bed without being prompted.

As she still didn't make a move to leave, I rather pointedly thanked her again and smiled expectantly. She got to her feet and stared straight at me, the jowls in her huge bulldog face quivering. 'Bit of advice for you, Paul,' she said. 'Watch what you put in your recycling bins.'

I was hit with another wave of paranoia, for a second I thought maybe she'd found one of my bottles of what I call 'coping booze' and was about to blackmail me. I've made a big deal about being on the wagon, so I can hardly have that coming out. Not on top of everything else. 'The press, you see,' she said. 'I've caught them digging through the bins a couple of times. But don't you worry, I sent them on their way.' Then she patted my arm. 'You're doing a good job. Jess is absolutely fine. She couldn't be in better hands.'

I saw her out, and then I burst into tears. I was limp with relief. Relief that at least one person thought I was doing some good where Jess was concerned. Even if it was that crusty old cow.

And now I'm thinking, I *have* to get the nightmare situation under control. Get my act together, bury the self-pity once and for all.

22 March, 4.00 p.m.

Just back from Dr K.

After he finished with Jess – the usual, she seems to be coping, we can definitely look at getting her back into school soon etc. etc. – I tried to talk to him about some of my concerns. Mentioned that I'd been having bad dreams, but didn't go into detail for obvious reasons. He's easy to talk to, kind, overweight, but in a cuddly bear way that suits him, not in a 'hide the cakes *quick*' way. He says that my nightmares are a sign that my subconscious is working through my grief and anxiety and as soon as the press attention wanes, things will settle down. He says I mustn't underestimate the pressure I'm under from the hacks, the Addams Family and the nut-jobs who still phone occasionally. He says it's fine to take something to help me sleep, and gave me a prescription for some tablets that he says are guaranteed to knock me out.

So…let's see if they work.

But I'll be honest. Even with the sleeping tabs, I'm afraid to fall asleep.

23 March, 4.00 a.m.

(*A sob*)

No dreams. No Stephen. But this…this is, uh…not worse, but…

I woke up – around the time Stephen usually comes, three a.m. – and I could hear voices coming from somewhere. And then a laugh. Shelly's laugh. Clear as day. I jumped out of bed and ran downstairs, heart in my throat. I don't know what I was expecting to find, maybe Shelly and Stephen standing in the hallway saying how they'd…fuck, I dunno, been kidnapped by Somalian pirates or something and that was why we hadn't heard from them. I was only half-awake, so I suppose that's why I wasn't thinking straight.

But it was just Jess. She was sitting inches away from the television screen watching the DVD of Shelly and Stephen's wedding.

'Jess?' I said really softly, not wanting to give her a fright. I was thinking, fuck, has she finally decided to face up to their loss?

Without turning around she goes, 'Were you jealous of Stephen, Uncle Paul?'

'Why would I be jealous?' I asked her. Didn't occur to me then to ask why she was calling him Stephen and not Daddy.

'Because they loved each other and you have no one who loves you.' I wish I could get across her tone of voice. Like a scientist interested in a specimen.

'That's not true, Jess,' I said.

Then she said, 'Do you love me?'

I said yes. But it was a lie. I loved the old Jess. The old Paul loved the old Jess.

Fuck me. I can't believe I just said that. What do I mean by the old Jess?

I left her rewatching the DVD, then slipped into the kitchen and found myself unearthing an old bottle of cooking sherry. I'd hidden it away – out of sight, out of mind.

She's still watching the video now. Over and over again. The fourth time now, I can hear the music they played at the ceremony. 'Better Together' by Jack fucking Johnson. And she's laughing. Laughing at something. But what could be funny?

I'm sitting looking at the bottle now, Mandi.

But I won't touch it. I won't.

Geoffrey Moran and his wife, Melanie, were instrumental in setting up 277 Together, the support group for those who lost loved ones in the Go!Go! Air disaster. Geoffrey agreed to speak to me in early July.

I blame the press. They're the ones who should answer for this. You hear about that phone hacking, them getting away with printing lies; I couldn't really blame Paul for getting a bit paranoid. The buggers even tried to get me and Mel to say bad stuff about him a few times, came at us with leading questions. Mel told them to sling their hooks, of course. We're tight at 277 Together; look after our own. Now, I think it's a miracle myself, those three kids surviving like that, it's simply one of those things in life you just can't explain. But try telling that to your alien fanatics or those Yanks with their conspiracy bollocks. And if it wasn't for those bleeding reporters, none of that crap would have seen the light of day. They're the ones who kept it in the public eye. Buggers should be bleeding shot, the lot of 'em.

We knew what Paul was, course we did. And I don't mean about him being gay. What people do behind closed doors is their business. I'm talking about him being a bit of a luvvie, wanting to be the centre of attention. He told us he was an actor straight away. I'd never heard of him, though he said he'd had a few roles on telly in the past, guest ones, you know. Cameos. Must have bruised his ego, not getting where he wanted to in life. Reminded me a bit of my Danielle. She was much younger than him of course, but it took her a while to decide what she wanted to do, tried all sorts until she went in for that beauty therapy. Just takes some people longer to find their way in life, doesn't it?

Before Paul started to behave…well…before he started becoming a bit more withdrawn than usual, he used to irritate Mel a bit. He would talk for hours at the meetings if you let him. But when we could, we tried to help him out with Jess. It wasn't always easy; we've got our own grandchildren to take care of as well. Our Gavin, he's got three little ones, but Paul was a special case. He needed all the back-up he could get, poor bugger, what with the press at him all the time and the other side of the family – bad seeds, Mel called them – giving him all that grief. Gavin would've stepped in if that family had mucked about at the memorial service. Gavin's applying for the police next year. He'll make a good copper, they always do, them that've seen the other side of the law, so to speak. Not that he ever got himself into real trouble.

That snooty neighbour also did what she could. Right snobbish she was, but her heart was in the right place. She saw off one of those paparazzos by throwing a bucket of cold water over the bugger. Fair play to her for that, poker up her arse or not.

When the Discovery Channel was planning that special programme on Black Thursday, just after the findings were released, the producer approached me and Mel to be talking heads on that show, wanted us to say what we felt when we heard about the plane going down. It's horrible to think about it now, but before we lost our Danielle, me and Mel used to love that air-crash investigation show, the one with that American investigator, Ace Kelso. Wish I'd never seen it now, of course. Mel turned the producers down flat, so did Kylie and Kelvin. They'd got together by then. Kylie had lost her other half in the crash and Kelvin was single, so why not? Sure, he was that much older than her, but May–September relationships can work, can't they? Look at me and Mel. She's seven years my senior and we've been going strong for over twenty years. Kylie and Kelvin were planning an August wedding, but they're talking about postponing it now. I told them, we need some joy in our lives, don't let what happened to little Jess put you off.

That's when I should have realised something wasn't right with Paul for definite. When he said he didn't want to be part of the Discovery show, I mean. I'll say this for him – he didn't try to put Jess in the spotlight. Opposite, really. But in the early days he wasn't shy about appearing in front of the media. First couple of months, it was like he was always on the morning shows, sitting on the couch talking about how Jess was coping. And no, I don't think that gave the press the right to pry into his private life and hound them like they did. You'd have thought after what happened to the People's Princess, they'd have learned their lesson. How much blood needs to be spilled before they'll bleeding well stop? I know, I do go on, but it makes my blood boil.

As for Jess . . . she was a real sweetheart. Absolute treasure. Gave you the impression she was wiser than her years, which wasn't surprising seeing what she'd been through. Never stopped smiling, never complained about the scars on her face. Right sunny disposition; it's amazing how kids can bounce back from things like that, isn't it? I read that biography, the one by that Muslim girl who was the only survivor of a plane crash in Ethiopia, and she said how none of it seemed real to her for years. So maybe that was how Jess was coping. Mel couldn't touch that book. Nor could most of the 277s. Kelvin says that even now he has to get his mates to screen what's on telly before he can watch it. Can't see anything about airplanes or crashes, or even watch any of them police procedurals.

And no, there was nothing bleeding strange about Jess. I'll go on the record about that. Bloody Americans and their lies about those poor kids. Made Mel apoplectic. And it wasn't just us who thought Jess was fine, was it? We would have heard from the school, wouldn't we? Her teacher's a no-nonsense type of woman. And her psychologist and the bloke from the social never saw anything untoward going on, did they?

Last time I saw Jess I was on my own. Mel was off helping Kylie choose a wedding venue and Paul was in a pickle, said he had a meeting with his agent. I fetched her from school and took her to see the horses down the lane. I always asked her how she was doing at school, I was a bit concerned that maybe she'd be facing bullying and that from the other kids. Jess's scars weren't bad, but they were still there and you know what kids can be like. But she said no one ever made fun of her. Tough little cookie. We had a nice time that afternoon. When we got back to the house, she asked me to read her a book, *The Lion, the Witch and the Wardrobe*. She could read well herself, but she said she liked me to do the voices of the characters. She thought that book was funny, couldn't seem to get enough of it.

When we heard Paul arriving home, she smiled at me, just the most lovely smile, reminded me of my Danielle when she was little. 'You're a good man, Uncle Geoff,' she said. 'I'm sorry your daughter had to die.' I always think about that whenever I think about her now. Brings me to tears.

Chiyoko and Ryu (this exchange took place three months before their disappearance).

Message logged @ 13.10, 25/03/2012

RYU: Are you there?

Message logged @ 13.31, 25/03/2012

RYU: Are you there?

Message logged @ 13.45, 25/03/2012

CHIYOKO: I'm here.

RYU: I was worried. You haven't been silent for this long before.

CHIYOKO: I was with Hiro. We were talking. MC is out so we have the house to ourselves for once.

RYU: Has he spoken about the crash yet?

CHIYOKO: Yeah.

RYU: And??????

CHIYOKO: He says he remembers being hoisted up into the rescue helicopter. He said it was fun. 'Like flying.' He said he was looking forward to doing it again.

RYU: Weird.

CHIYOKO: I know.

RYU: Is that all he remembers about the crash?

CHIYOKO: That's all he'll say so far. If he does know anything else, he's not saying. I don't want to push him too hard.

RYU: Has he spoken about his mother yet?

CHIYOKO: No. Why are you so interested anyway?

RYU: Of course I'm interested! Why wouldn't I be?

CHIYOKO: I'm being too hard on you again, aren't I?

RYU: I'm used to it now.

CHIYOKO: Ice burns from the ice princess.

RYU: Chiyoko…when he talks through the android, who do you look at? Hiro or it?

CHIYOKO: Ha! That's a good question. Mostly Hiro, but it's strange…I'm so used to it now. It's almost like it's his twin. Yesterday I found myself talking to it as if it was alive when Hiro left the room.

RYU: RYU:!!!

CHIYOKO: I'm glad one of us is laughing. But the way I'm reacting to it, forgetting that it's not actually alive, is exactly why Android Uncle made his surrabot in the first place.

RYU: ???

CHIYOKO: He wanted to find out if people would eventually start treating androids as if they were human once they got over the uncanny valley feeling. Now we know that they *will* start seeing them as human. Or at least ice princesses will.

RYU: Sorry, I was being dense.

RYU: Hey…Did you see that interview where he said that sometimes, when people touch the surrabot and he's miles away, working it remotely, he can feel their fingers on his skin? The brain is a strange thing.

CHIYOKO: It is. I wish I knew why Hiro will only talk through it. I know he has a voice, so he's capable of speech. Maybe it gives him an emotional distance, although in this house we are all emotionally distant ha ha.

RYU: Like cameramen who can film horrible scenes without turning away. Yes. I think you are right about the distance.

CHIYOKO: Listen to this: I asked him if he wanted to go back to primary school today.

RYU: And?

CHIYOKO: He said, 'Only if I can bring my soul.'

RYU: His what?

CHIYOKO: It's what he's started calling his surrabot.

RYU: You need to keep that quiet. Especially as Aikao Uri is in the news again with her crazy alien theories. You don't want to give her any ideas.

CHIYOKO: What is she saying now? Did she mention Hiro again?

RYU: Not this time. But she really does believe she was abducted by aliens. There's a cool clip of her talking about being probed on Nico Nico. Whoever made it has intercut it with scenes from *E.T.* It's very funny.

CHIYOKO: She's as bad as those religious Americans with all their fourth child stuff. It stirs it up again. All the attention. The silt settles, and then someone pokes a stick in the water and it becomes cloudy.

RYU: Ha! Very lyrical. You should become a writer. I could illustrate your stories.

CHIYOKO: We could have our own manga factory. Sometimes I think…wait. There's someone at the door. Probably just a salesman or whatever trying their luck.

Message logged @ 15.01, 25/03/2012

CHIYOKO: Guess who that was?

RYU: I give up.

CHIYOKO: Just guess.

RYU: Captain Seto's wife.

CHIYOKO: No. Try again.

RYU: Aikao Uri and her alien friends?

CHIYOKO: No!

RYU: Totoro in his cat bus?

CHIYOKO: Ha! I must tell that to Hiro. I told you I let him watch *My Neighbour Totoro*, even though MC said I mustn't in case it upset him, didn't I?

RYU: No! You didn't tell me. And did it upset him? Or his android?

CHIYOKO: No. It made him laugh. He even thought the part where the girls' mother is in the hospital was amusing.

RYU: That kid is seriously weird. So?? If it wasn't the cat bus, who was it?

CHIYOKO: It was the American woman's daughter.

RYU: Σ(O_O ;)！！ Pamela May Donald's daughter?

CHIYOKO: Yeah.

RYU: How did she find out where you lived?

CHIYOKO: Probably got it from one of the *izuko* support group members. But it's not impossible to find from other sources. The magazines are always saying that the house is near to Yoyogi station, and there are those pictures of it on the *Tokyo Herald* website.

RYU: What is she like?

CHIYOKO: I thought you saw her when you watched the memorial service?

RYU: I mean what sort of person is she?

CHIYOKO: At first I thought she was a typical foreigner. And in some ways she is. But she was very serene, quiet, dressed conservatively. Greeted me as if she knew of my status as Shinjuku's Number One Ice Princess.

RYU: You let her into the house????

CHIYOKO: Why not? She's an *izoku* like all the others. Not only that, I let her talk to Hiro.

RYU: Hiro or Hiro's soul?

CHIYOKO: Hiro's soul.

RYU: You let him talk to her through the surrabot???? I thought you were angry with her?

CHIYOKO: Why would I be angry?

RYU: Because of what her mother has caused.

CHIYOKO: That's not her fault. It's the stupid Americans. And she looked so lost when she arrived. It must have taken courage to come all the way from Osaka to see him.

RYU: Something's not right. The ice princess would never normally behave in such a manner.

CHIYOKO: Maybe I wanted to hear what she was going to say to Hiro. Maybe I was curious.

RYU: How did she react when she saw Hiro's soul and realised she'd have to talk to him through it?

CHIYOKO: She just stared at it and then she gave it one of those self-conscious bows Westerners do when they're trying to be polite. I could hear him giggling through it straightaway. He was hiding behind the screen in my room with the computer and the camera. I was impressed that she didn't scream or freak out.

RYU: And what did she ask?

CHIYOKO: First of all she thanked him for agreeing to talk to her. Then she wanted to know what they always want to know, which is, did her mother suffer.

RYU: And?

CHIYOKO: And Hiro said yes.

RYU: Ouch. What did she say to that?

CHIYOKO: She thanked him for being honest.

RYU: So Hiro admitted that he'd spoken to her mother?

CHIYOKO: Not exactly. He didn't really give her any straight answers. I thought perhaps that she was going to start getting really frustrated, but then Hiro said, 'Don't be sad,' in English!

RYU: Hiro can speak *English*?

CHIYOKO: Auntie Hiromi or Android Uncle must have taught him some phrases before the crash. Then she showed him a photograph of her mother, asked him if he was sure that he'd seen her. And again, he said to her, 'Don't be sad.' She started crying; real weeping. I was worried that this would upset Hiro, so I asked her to leave.

RYU: Chiyoko, it is not my place to say…But…I don't think you should have done that.

CHIYOKO: Thrown her out?

RYU: No. Let her talk to Hiro's soul.

CHIYOKO: I didn't ask your opinion about that, Ryu. And anyway, I thought you were in love with the Americans?

RYU: Why do you make it so hard for me?

CHIYOKO: It's not fair of you to make me feel guilty.

RYU: I wasn't trying to make you feel guilty. I was trying to be your friend.

CHIYOKO: Friends don't judge each other.

RYU: I was not judging you.

CHIYOKO: Yes you were. I don't need that from you as well. I get it all the fucking time from MC. I'm going.

RYU: Wait! Can't we at least talk about this?

CHIYOKO: There's nothing to say.

Message logged @ 16.34, 25/03/2012

RYU: Are you still mad?

Message logged @ 16.48, 25/03/2012

RYU: _|7O

Message logged @ 03.19, 26/03/2012

CHIYOKO: Ryu. Are you awake?

RYU: I'm sorry about earlier. Did you see I even sent you an ORZ?

CHIYOKO: Yeah.

RYU: Are you okay?

CHIYOKO: No. Mother Creature and Father are fighting. They haven't done that since before Hiro came. I'm worried they'll upset him.

RYU: What are they fighting about?

CHIYOKO: Me. MC says Father has to be stricter on me and make me go back to free school. She says I have to be made to work on my future plans. But then who will look after Hiro?

RYU: You're really attached to that kid now.

CHIYOKO: I am.

RYU: So…what do you want to do with your life?

CHIYOKO: I'm like you; I never look further than a day ahead. What are the choices? I don't want to work for a corporation, become a slave for life. I don't want to do some dumb freeter job. I'll probably end up living in a tent in the park with the homeless. MC would be happiest if I got married and had children and made that my life's goal.

RYU: Do you think that will ever happen?

CHIYOKO: Never!!!!!! I love Hiro but the thought of having the responsibility for someone else's life…I will live alone and die alone. I've always known that.

RYU: You're not alone, Yoko.

CHIYOKO: Thanks, Ryu.

RYU: Did the ice princess just say thank you????

CHIYOKO: I have to go. Hiro has woken up. I'll talk to you tomorrow.

RYU: ☆·*:..。.(●≧▽≦)。..:*·☆

PART SIX

CONSPIRACY

MARCH–APRIL

Lola Cando.

The last time Lenny came to see me, he was spitting mad. Second he got to the motel he drank a double bourbon straight down, then another. Took him a while to calm down enough to tell me what was going on.

Turned out that Lenny had found out Dr Lund had organised a rally for Mitch Reynard in Fort Worth. Some sort of pro-Israel, 'Believers Unite' convention, and it burned Lenny bad that he hadn't been invited to speak at it. And that wasn't all of it. After he did that radio show – the one where that New York DJ ripped him a new one – Dr Lund had sent a publicist down to see Lenny. The publicist (who Lenny described as a 'jumped-up two-bit lackey in a suit') told him that he wasn't to draw too much attention to himself, and to let Dr Lund and Flexible Sandy spread the news about Pamela's message their way. Lenny was also pissed that Dr Lund didn't want him involved in searching for that fourth child.

'I've got to find a way to convince him that he needs me, Lo,' he said. 'Pamela chose me, *me*, to spread the word. He has to see that.'

I wouldn't say I felt sorry for Lenny, but Dr Lund cutting him off, hijacking his message, you could see it made him feel like the unpopular kid at school. And I don't think it had anything to do with money. Lenny said his website was bringing in donations from all over the world. You ask me, it was pride more than anything.

Dr Lund may have cooled towards him, but Lenny's message was catching on like wildfire. People I never thought of as religious were going and getting themselves saved. Couple of my johns even went and did it. Some of them, sure, you could see they were just doing it as insurance – in case it did turn out to be the truth. Didn't matter that the Episcopalians and even those Muslim leaders were saying there was no reason to panic, people really started believing it, you know? There were just all these signs happening all over the world – signs of plague, famine, war and whatever. That puke virus and the foot and mouth disease were getting worse, and then came that drought in Africa and the big scare when the North Koreans threatened to test their nuclear weapons. That was just the start. Then there were all those rumours about Bobby's grandfather and that robot stuff that was going down with the Japanese kid. It was almost as if every time Lenny's theories were shot down by someone, up would come another sign that backed them up. If you'd asked me back when I first met Lenny if he could have caused such a stir, I wouldn't have credited it.

'I need a stronger platform, Lo,' he kept saying. 'Dr Lund's taking everything. He's acting like it was all his idea.'

'Isn't this all about saving souls though, honey?' I asked.

'Yeah, course it's about saving people.' He got real mad about that, went on about how time might be running out and how he and Dr Lund should be working together. He didn't even want to do his usual that day. Too wound up, couldn't... you know. Said he had to go meet with that Monty fellow anyhow, start planning on how he was going to get back into the big boys' good graces. He told me that there were quite a few 'messengers' like Monty already staying at his ranch, and I guess he was thinking about how it would be a good thing to invite more.

After he left, I was getting all my stuff together, ready to head on back to my apartment and my next client, when there was a knock on the door. I figured maybe it was Lenny again, regretting that he'd wasted our hour together just talking. I opened it, saw a woman standing there. I knew who she was straight away. I'd have known her just by the dog, that Snookie. She looked even thinner than when she appeared on Dr Lund's show. Skinny – too skinny, like one of those anorexics. But her expression was different. She didn't look as lost as she did back then. She didn't come across as angry or anything like that, but there was a look in her eyes that said, 'Don't mess with me.'

She looked me up and down and I could tell she was trying to figure out what Lenny saw in me. 'How long have you and him been doing this?' she asked straight off.

I told her the truth. She nodded, and then pushed past me into the room. 'You love him?' she asked.

I almost laughed. I said that all Lenny was to me was one of my regulars. I wasn't his girlfriend or mistress or anything like that. I know quite a few of my clients are married; that's their business.

This seemed to give her some comfort. She sat down on the bed, asked me to fix her a drink. I handed her the same drink Lenny always has. She sniffed it, then drank it in one gulp. It ran down her chin and made her gag, but it didn't seem to bother her. She waved her hand around the room and said, 'All this, what you been doing with him. I paid for it. I paid for everything.'

I didn't know how to answer that. I knew Lenny depended on her for money, didn't know the extent of it though. She put the dog down on the bed next to her. It sniffed the sheets, then slumped on its side as if it was fixing to curl up and die. I knew they didn't allow animals in the motel, but I wasn't about to tell her that.

She asked me what Lenny liked, and I told her the truth. She said that at least he hadn't been hiding some weird sexual fetish from her all those years.

Then she asked me if I believed in what he was saying, about the children being the horsemen. I said I wasn't sure what to believe. She nodded, stood up to leave. Didn't say anything else to me. There was a deep sadness inside her. I could see that straight off. It had to have been her who told the *Inquirer* about me and Lenny. It was only a day or so afterwards that this reporter called me up, pretending he was a regular john. Luckily I had my wits about me that day, but it didn't stop the photographers trying their luck for days afterwards.

I came clean to Denisha after that, told her that Lenny was one of my clients. It didn't surprise her. You can't shock Denisha. She's seen it all. Probably you're wondering how I feel about Lenny now. Like I say, people are always trying to get me to say he was a monster. But he wasn't. He was just a man. I guess when I decide to do that book those publishers are always after me to write, then I might talk about it more, but that's all I've got to say on the subject for now.

The following article, by award-winning blogger and freelance journalist Vuyo Molefe, was first published in the online journal *Umbuzo* on 30 March 2012.

Bringing Home the Bodies:
The Personal Cost of the Dalu Air Crash

It's the day before the Dalu Air crash memorial is to be unveiled in Khayelitsha, and the press photographers are already circling. Teams of council workers have been bussed in to cordon off the area around the hastily constructed memorial sculpture – a sinister black glass pyramid that looks like it would be more at home on the set of a science-fiction B-movie. Why a pyramid? It's a good question, but despite the number of editorials damning the peculiar choice of design, no one I've spoken to, including Ravi Moodley, the Cape Town city councillor who commissioned it, and the sculptor herself, artist Morna van der Merwe, seems to be prepared to give me (or anyone else) a straight answer.

The site is also swarming with conspicuously fit security men and women, all wearing stereotypical black suits and ear pieces, who eye me and the other press representatives with a mixture of contempt and distrust. Among the great and the good lined up to attend tomorrow's ceremony are Andiswa Luso, who's pipped to be the new head of the ANC Youth League, and John Diobi, a Nigerian high level preacher-cum-business-mogul who reportedly has ties with several US mega-churches, including those under the sway of Dr Theodore Lund, who hit the headlines worldwide with his theory that The Three are the harbingers of the apocalypse. It's rumoured that Diobi and his associates are putting up the reward money for the discovery of Kenneth Oduah, the Dalu Air passenger deemed most likely to be the fourth horseman. Although the South African Civil Aviation Authority and the National Transportation Safety Board have insisted that no one on board Dalu Air Flight 467 could have survived, the reward has already ignited a hysterical man-hunt, with locals and tourists alike eager to get in on the action. And the fact that Kenneth's name is etched on the memorial, despite the absence of his remains or DNA being discovered in the wreckage, has angered several Nigerian evangelical Christian groups – another reason for the high security presence.

But I'm not here to antagonise the security staff or petition the VIPs for an interview. Today, it's not their stories I'm interested in.

Levi Bandah (21), who hails from Blantyre, Malawi, meets me at the entrance to the Mew Way community hall. Three weeks ago, he travelled to Cape Town in order to search for the remains of his brother Elias, who he believes is one of the casualties killed on the ground when the fuselage cut a deadly swathe through the township. Elias was working as a gardener in Cape Town in order to support his extended family back in Malawi, and Levi suspected something was wrong when Elias did not contact the family for over a week.

'He sent us a text every day, and money came to us every week. My only choice was to travel here and see if I could find him.'

Elias is not listed among the deceased, but with so many unidentified remains – most believed to belong to illegal immigrants – still awaiting DNA matches for formal identification purposes, this isn't a guarantee of anything.

In many African cultures, including my own – Xhosa – it is vital that the bodies of the deceased be returned to their ancestral homeland to be reunited with the spirits of the ancestors. If this is not done, it is believed that the spirit of the deceased will be restless and will cause grief to the living. And bringing home the body can be an expensive business. It can cost up to 14,000 rand to transport a body back to Malawi or Zimbabwe by air freight; without help, a sum way beyond the reach of the average citizen. For the families of refugees, transporting a body over two thousand kilometres by road is a daunting and gruesome prospect. I've heard stories of funeral directors colluding with families to disguise bodies as dried goods in order to cut the air-freight costs.

In the days following the crash, Khayelitsha rang with the sound of loudspeakers, as families of the victims petitioned the community to donate whatever they could so that bodies could be returned to their homelands. It is not unusual for the bereaved to receive double the amount they need; with many people from the Eastern Cape migrating to Cape Town for work, no one knows when they will be the one in need of help. And the refugee communities and societies are no different.

'The community here has been generous,' says David Amai (52), a soft-spoken and dapper Zimbabwean from Chipinge, who has also agreed to talk to me. Like Levi, he is in Cape Town waiting for the authorities to give him the go-ahead to bring the remains of his cousin, Lovemore – also a victim of the crash devastation – home. But before he left Zimbabwe, David had something Levi's family didn't have – the certainty that their loved one was dead. And they didn't hear it from the pathologists working the scene. 'When we did not hear from Lovemore, at first we did not know for sure if he had died,' David told me. 'My family consulted with a herbalist (sangoma) who performed the ritual and spoke to my cousin's ancestors. They confirmed that he had connected with them and we knew then that he was gone.' Lovemore's body was eventually identified by DNA and David is hopeful that he can soon bring his remains back home.

But what if there is no body to be buried?

With no remains to bring back to his family, Levi's only option was to collect some of the ashes and earth at the site, which would be immediately buried when he returned home. This is where his story veers into the stuff of nightmares (or farce). As he attempted to gather a small bag of earth, an over-zealous cop swooped down on him, accusing him of stealing souvenirs to sell to unscrupulous tourists and 'Kenneth Oduah hunters'. Despite his protestations, Levi was arrested and thrown in a holding cell, where he languished, in fear of his life, for the weekend. Thankfully, hearing of his plight, several NGOs and the Malawian Embassy stepped in, and Levi was released relatively unscathed. His DNA has been taken and he's waiting for confirmation that Elias is among the victims. 'They say it won't take long,' he says. 'And the people here have been good to me. But I cannot return home without some part of my brother to restore to my family.'

As I leave the site, I receive a text from my editor saying that Veronica Oduah, the aunt of the elusive Kenneth, has landed in Cape Town for tomorrow's ceremony, but has refused to speak to the press. I can't help wondering how she must be feeling. Like Levi, she is living in a cruel limbo of uncertainty, hoping against hope that somehow, her nephew hasn't joined the ranks of the dead.

Superintendent Randall Arendse is the controller of the Site C Police Station, Khayelitsha, Cape Town. He spoke to me in April 2012.

Fourth horseman, my arse. Every bloody day we'd get a new 'Kenneth Oduah' being brought into the station. Usually it was just some street kid who'd been bribed with a couple of bucks to say he was Kenneth. And it wasn't just us. They were rocking up at every station in the Cape. Those US arseholes didn't know what they'd started. Two hundred K USD? That's nearly two million rand, which is more than what most South Africans will see in a lifetime. We had a photograph of the boy, but we couldn't see the point of comparing it with the chancers that came in. Most of my guys, they'd been there that day, seen the wreckage. No ways anyone on that plane made it out alive, even if they were a *bliksem* rider of the apocalypse.

At first it was just the locals who were trying their luck but then the foreigners started arriving. There weren't that many at first, but the next thing you know, they were rolling in. It didn't take long for our local crooks to get in on the action. Some of the sharper ones even offered their services online. Soon there were syndicates organising these tours in just about all of the townships. None of them had accreditation permits. But that didn't stop the punters falling for the scams. *Jis*, man, some of them even paid up front. It was like shooting fish in a barrel, and I can tell you off the record, I wouldn't be surprised if some of the cops were in on the action.

I can't tell you how many punters got stranded at the

airport waiting for their 'all inclusive package' to come and pick them up. We got professional bounty hunters coming out here, ex-cops, even a few of those blerrie big game hunters! Some of them were after the cash and didn't give a shit if it was true or not, but quite a few who came really believed the kak that preacher was saying. But Cape Town is a complex place. You don't just waltz into Gugs or the Cape Flats or Khayelitsha in your fancy hire car and start asking questions, no matter how many lions or cheetahs you've shot in the bush. Quite a few of them found that out the hard way when they were relieved of their valuables one way or another.

I'll never forget these two big American guys who came into the station one evening. Shaven heads, muscles on their muscles. Both of them were ex US Marshals, used to be marines. Thought they were tough, told us afterwards they'd been instrumental in bringing some of America's Most Wanted to justice. But when I first met them they were shaking like little girls. They'd hooked up with their so-called 'guide' at the airport and he'd taken them where they wanted to go – into the middle of Khayelitsha. When they arrived at their destination, their guide relieved them of their Glocks, cash, credit cards, passports, shoes and clothes, leaving them with nothing but their boxers. Toyed with them as well. Made them walk barefoot into an old outhouse that stank to high heaven, tied them up and told them that if they shouted for help, he'd shoot them. When they finally got free it was dark, they reeked of shit and the *skelm* was long gone. Couple of locals took pity on them and brought them to the station. My guys laughed for days about those two. Had to drop them off at the US embassy in just their undies. None of the spare clothes we had at the station fitted them.

Fact is, people here are tough, most of them fight just to get by every day, and they'll take a chance if they can. Not everyone, of course – but it's hard here. You got to be streetwise. You got to respect the people or they'll *naai* you big time. What, you think I'm going to breeze into downtown LA or wherever, act like I own the place? I swear, these *moegoes* who came here might just as well have handed over their valuables to the guys at immigration, cut out the middle man. Eventually we had to put up signs at the airport to warn people. Reminded me of that movie, *Charlie and the Chocolate Factory*. The hunt for that golden ticket with everyone going *befok*.

I mean, it was a major headache for us guys, the police and that, but it was *lekker* for the tourism industry. Hotels were full, tour buses were packed, everyone from the street kids to the hoteliers were coining it. Especially the street kids. See, at one stage, the rumour spread that Kenneth was living on the streets somewhere. People will believe anything given half a chance.

It was Kenneth's I felt sorry for. She seemed like a nice lady. My cousin Jamie was on the security detail for her when they unveiled the Dalu Air memorial statue and she flew down from Lagos. He said she was bewildered, kept saying that as those other kids had survived miraculously, why shouldn't Kenneth be alive?

Those fundamentalist fuckers gave her unrealistic expectations. Ja, that's what it was. False hope.

Didn't even stop to think that what they was doing was cruel.

Reba Neilson.

It was all becoming too much for me. It felt like Pastor Len was turning his back on his real inner circle in favour of people like that Monty. Did I mention Monty to you, Elspeth? Can't quite recall if I did. Well, he was one of the first Lookie-Loos who elected to stay – came to Sannah County soon after Pastor Len got back from that conference at Houston. Within days of showing up he was padding along at Pastor Len's side, loyal as a stray dog that'd just been fed. I didn't take to him right from the start, and I'm not just saying that because of what he did to that poor Bobby. There was something about him, something shifty, and I wasn't the only one of that opinion. 'That fella looks like he could do with a good scrubbing,' Stephenie was always saying. He had these tattoos all up his arms – some of which didn't look very Christian to me – and his hair needed a pair of shears taken to it. Looked like one of them Satanists they sometimes feature in the *Inquirer*.

And since Monty arrived, Jim seemed to have dropped out of Pastor Len's favour. Sure, Pastor Len dragged him out to church on Sundays sometimes, and I know he hadn't given up the idea of doing those tours of Pam's house, but most of the time Jim just sat at home and drank himself stupid.

Pastor Len asked Stephenie's cousin Billy to quote on some construction work he wanted done at the ranch, so it was Billy who told us that those people looked to be moving there permanently. If you didn't know better, he said, you'd a thought it was one of those hippy communes.

I had so many sleepless nights during those weeks,

Elspeth. I can't tell you how I suffered. What Pastor Len was saying about the signs…it made so much sense and yet…I just couldn't get over Pamela, dowdy old Pam, being a prophet.

I all but wore out Lorne's ear talking about it.

'Reba,' he said to me. 'You know that you're a good Christian woman and Jesus will save you whatever happens. If you don't want to follow Pastor Len's church no more, then maybe Jesus is telling you not to.'

Stephenie also felt the same as I did, but it wasn't that easy to break away. Not in a community like ours. I guess you could say I was biding my time.

Stephenie and I were worried that Kendra wouldn't be able to cope with all those new Lookie-Loos arriving, and we decided that even though we didn't agree with all that Pastor Len was doing lately, it was only right that we should go over there and see how she was coping. We planned on doing it at the weekend, but that Friday, the story about Pastor Len's fancy woman broke. Stephenie came straight over soon as she heard about it, brought me a copy of the *Inquirer*. It was all over the front page: *End Times Preacher's Sordid Love Tryst*. The photographs showed a big woman wearing purple pants and a tight top, but the pictures were so grainy you couldn't tell if she was tanned, black or one of those Hispanics. I didn't believe that story for one second. Even after he let the devil in, I firmly believe the real Pastor Len, the good man who had been the head of our church for fifteen years, was still in there somewhere. I refuse to believe that all of us could have been fooled for so many years. Besides, as I said to Stephenie, where would Pastor Len find the time to mess around with fallen women? He barely had time to sleep, what with all he was doing.

Well, just as me and Stephenie were finishing up talking, who should come up the driveway but Pastor Len himself. My heart plummeted when I saw he had that Monty with him.

'Reba,' Pastor Len said, the second he came through the screen door. 'Is Kendra here?'

I told him I hadn't seen her.

Monty sat himself right down at the table, helped himself to a glass of iced tea without even asking. Stephenie's eyes narrowed, but he didn't pay any mind to her.

'All Kendra's clothes are gone,' Pastor Len said. 'The dog too. She say anything to you, Reba? 'Bout where she might be going? I tried her brother in Austin and he says he hasn't seen her.'

I told him I didn't have an inkling where she might've gone, and Stephenie said the same. Didn't mention that I didn't blame her for getting out of there, what with all those strangers taking over her home.

'It's probably for the best,' he said. 'Me and Kendra... we had certain disagreements about the role of Jesus in our lives.'

'Amen,' Monty said, although I couldn't see any reason for it.

Stephenie was trying to hide the *Inquirer* with her arms, but Pastor Len saw what she was doing.

'Don't you listen to those lies about me,' he said. 'I ain't never done nothing immoral. Jesus is all I need in my life.'

I believed him, Elspeth. That man had real conviction, and I could see that he wasn't lying.

I made a fresh pitcher of iced tea and then I decided to air what was on my mind. 'How are you planning on feeding all the new folks who have shown up, Pastor Len?'

I'm not ashamed to say I looked right at Monty when I said it.

'The Lord will provide. Those good folks will be well taken care of.'

Well, they didn't look like good folks to me. Specially the ones like Monty. I said something about people taking advantage of his good nature, and Pastor Len got real irritated with me. 'Reba,' he said. 'What did Jesus say about judging people? As a good Christian, you should know better than that.'

Then he and that Monty took off.

I was upset by the altercation, I really was, and for the first time in years when Sunday came around I didn't go to church. Stephenie told me later it was full of the new Lookie-Loos, and quite a few of the inner circle had stayed away.

Well, it had to be two days later, something like that. I was keeping myself busy, wanted to get the canning done that week (by then we had a good two years' worth of canned fruit, Elspeth, but there was still plenty to do). Lorne and I were talking about ordering in some wood, storing it out back in case the power gave out, when I heard a pick-up shuddering to a stop outside the porch. I looked out and saw Jim slumped behind the wheel. I hadn't seen him since the week before when I'd gone over to take him a pie. He'd refused to answer the door and it pains me to say it, but I left it on the front step.

He just about fell out of the car, and when me and Lorne ran up to steady him he said, 'Got a call from Joanie, Reba.' He stank real bad, of booze and sweat. It looked like he hadn't shaved for weeks.

I wondered if his daughter had called to tell him that Pam's ashes were finally going to be coming home, and that's why he was so upset.

I sat him in the kitchen and he said, 'Can you call Pastor Len for me? Get him to come right over?'

'Why didn't you just drive on up to his ranch?' I asked. Fact is, he shouldn't have been driving anywhere. You could smell the alcohol on him from a mile away. It was enough to make my eyes water. If Sheriff Beaumont had seen him in that state he would've locked him up for sure. I fixed him a Coke straight away to take the edge off. After me and Pastor Len had had that altercation, I wasn't keen on calling him, but I did it all the same. Didn't expect him to answer, but he did. Said he'd be right over.

Jim didn't say much while we waited for Pastor Len, though me and Lorne tried to draw him out. And the little he did say didn't make much sense to us. Fifteen minutes later, Pastor Len showed up, his dog Monty in tow as usual.

Jim said straight off, 'Joanie went to see that boy, Len. That boy in Japan.'

Pastor Len just froze. Before they went their separate ways, Pastor Len was always saying how Dr Lund had been trying for the longest time to get to speak to one of those children. Jim's eyes fluttered. 'Joanie said that Jap boy ... said she talked to the boy, but not *to* him exactly.'

None of us knew what in Jesus' name he was talking about. 'I don't get you, Jim,' Pastor Len said.

'She said he was talking through this android. This robot that looked just like him.'

'A robot?' I said. 'He was talking through a robot? Like the ones on YouTube? What in *heaven*?'

'What does it mean, Pastor Len?' Monty asked.

Pastor Len didn't say anything for at least a minute. 'I guess maybe I should give Teddy a call.' That's what Pastor Len called Dr Lund. Teddy, like they were good friends, although we all knew he and Dr Lund were having issues. Later Lorne said he reckoned Pastor Len was hoping a story like that would make up for the lies about his fancy woman; repair some of the damage done.

Then came the kicker. Jim said he'd already been to the newspapers about the story. Told them the lot, 'bout how Joanie had been round to see that Jap kid and talked to that robot that looked just like him.

Pastor Len turned as red as a canned beet. 'Jim,' he said. 'Why didn't you tell me about this first before you went to the papers?'

Jim got that stubborn look on his face. 'Pam was my wife. They offered me money for the story. I wasn't going to turn that down. I gotta live.'

A ton of money was coming to Jim from Pam's insurance, so that wasn't any excuse. Lorne said he could see plain as day that Pastor Len was ornery because he wanted to use that information for himself.

Jim banged his fist on the table. 'And people gotta know those kids is evil. How could that boy survive and not Pam, Pastor Len? It's not fair. It's not right. Pam was a good woman. A good woman.' Jim started crying, saying how those children were murderers. How they'd killed all those people on the planes, and he couldn't understand why no one could see that.

Pastor Len said he'd drive him home, with Monty following in Jim's pick-up. It took both of them to carry him out to Pastor Len's new SUV. Jim was crying fit to burst, shaking and howling. That man shouldn't have been left alone after that. It was obvious that his mind was broken. But like I said he was stubborn, and I know in my heart that he would have turned me down flat if I'd offered to take him in.

Just before this book was due to go into print, I finally managed to secure an interview with Pastor Len's estranged wife, Kendra Vorhees. I spoke to her at a state-of-the-art psychiatric clinic where she is currently residing (I have agreed not to print the name or exact location).

I'm shown to Kendra's room, an airy, sun-filled space, by an orderly with a perfect manicure. Kendra is sitting at a desk, a book open in front of her (later I see that it's the latest in Flexible Sandy's Gone series). The dog on her lap – Snookie – wags its tail half-heartedly as I approach, but Kendra barely seems to register my presence. When she finally looks up, her eyes are clear and her expression far shrewder than I'm expecting. She's so slender that I can see every vein beneath her skin. There's a slight Texan drawl to her voice, and she speaks carefully, perhaps as a result of the medication she's taking.

She waves me into an armchair opposite the desk and does not object when I place my recording device in front of her.

I ask Kendra why she decided to talk to me and not one of the other journalists eager to interview her.

I read your book. The one where you interviewed those children who accidentally shot their siblings with Mommy's .38 Special, or who got it into their heads to murder their classmates with Daddy's semi-automatic toy. Len was spitting mad when he saw me reading it. Course he was, he's big on that second amendment baloney, the right to bear arms and all that.

But you mustn't think I'm after revenge for what Len did with that prostitute. A 'ho' they call them, don't they? I liked her, if you want the truth. She was refreshingly honest, which is rare these days. I hope she takes her fifteen minutes of fame and runs with it. Milks it for all it's worth.

I ask her if she was the one who leaked the story about Pastor Len's indiscretions. She sighs, fusses with Snookie and nods briefly. I ask her why she leaked the story if it wasn't for revenge.

Because, the truth shall set you free! (*She laughs abruptly and humourlessly.*) You can say what you darn well please when you write this up, by the way. What you darn well please. But if you want the real truth, I did it to get Len away from Dr Lund forever. Len was broken-hearted when the big boys kicked him out of their club after he made a fool of himself on that radio show, but I knew it wouldn't take much for him to go crawling back if Dr Lund snapped his fingers. I thought I was doing it for Len's own good, anyone could see that Dr Lund was a manipulator. And Dr Lund wouldn't want an acolyte with a sex scandal to his name muddying up his shiny reputation, not now he's got all those political aspirations. Turns out it was the worst thing I could have done. It goes through my head a thousand times a day, what if I hadn't followed Len that day? What if I'd let it be? I keep thinking, if Len had wormed his way back into Dr Lund's good graces, would that have made a difference in the end? Would it have stopped him from listening to that Jim Donald's crazy talk? Everyone's saying how Len 'let the devil in', but it's not as simple as that. Fact is, disappointment pushed Len over the edge. A broken heart will do that to you.

I open my mouth to comment, but she continues.

I'm not mad. I'm not crazy. I'm not a loony tune. It wore me out, all that pretending. You can't play a part all your life, can you? They say I've got depression. Clinical. Might be bipolar, but who knows what that means? This place isn't cheap. I'm making my good-for-nothing brother pick up the bill. He's been working his way through Daddy's money, got the lion's share, so it's about time he shelled out. And who else was I going to ask? I thought of maybe approaching Dr Lund himself. Even when we were at that godawful conference, you could tell he thought I was an embarrassment. I know for a fact he didn't want me to appear with Len on his show that one time. His wife didn't take to me either. It was mutual. You should have seen her face when I declined to join her Christian Women's League. 'We got to put those feminists and baby killers in their place, Kendra.'

She narrows her eyes at me.

I can see you're more than likely one of those feminists, am I right?

I tell her that I am.

That will make Lund even madder when he reads what I have to say. I'm not. A feminist, I mean. I'm not anything. No labels on me, no causes. Oh, I know what those ridiculous women back in that godawful place think of me. Fifteen years I lived there. They thought I was stuck-up, had ideas above my station because of where I'd come from.

They also thought I was weak; meek and weak. The meek shall inherit the earth. Len could set their pulses a-flutter, of course. I'm surprised he didn't take up with one of them. But I suppose I should be grateful he chose not to foul in the back yard.

What a life! Stuck in a backwater county with a preacher for a husband. It was not what Daddy had envisaged for me. It was hardly what I had envisaged for myself. I had ambitions, not many. Thought about maybe teaching once. I have a college degree, you know. And those women tried to interest me in all their prepping nonsense. If there is a solar flare or a nuclear war, a thousand cans of pickled turnips aren't going to save you.

Pamela was the best of the bunch. In another life we could have been friends. Well, maybe not friends, but she wasn't as much of a bore as the others. Wasn't as dull or gossipy. I felt for her, living with that husband. Mean as a junkyard dog, that Jim. I liked Joanie, the daughter, too. I was rejoicing inside when she made the break, went off to see the world.

She fusses with Snookie again.

I like to think that at least Pam will have some comfort knowing that Snookie's being taken care of.

I ask her how she met Pastor Len.

Where else? At a Bible rally. A rally in Tennessee, which is where I went to college. We met across a crowded tent. *(She laughs humourlessly.)* Love at first sight – for me at least. Took me years to realise that Len only found me attractive because of my other assets. All he wanted was his own church, 'That's what I was put on the earth to do,' he'd say. 'Preach the Lord's word and save souls.'

He was a Baptist back then, so was I. He'd gone to college late, been working his way around the South. All full of fire and Jesus, worked for a time as a deacon for Dr Samuel Keller. Doubt you'll remember him. Low level, but it looked like he was on track to be another Hagee before he got caught with his pants down in the nineties. Shit will stick and ain't that the truth, as my daddy used to say, and after Keller was discovered canoodling with that young boy in a public convenience, Len discovered that finding another position wasn't going to be easy, least not till all the hoo-ha calmed down. His only choice was to start up on his own. We moved around a lot, looking for the right place. Then we came to Sannah County. Daddy had just died, left me my inheritance and we bought the ranch with that. I think Len had some idea of farming on the side, but what did he know about farming?

He was a beautiful man to look at. Still is, I suppose. Knew the benefits of good grooming. Daddy wasn't happy when I brought him home. 'Mark my words, that boy will break your heart,' he said.

Daddy was wrong. Len didn't break my heart, but he sure as hell tried.

Tears start running down her cheeks, but she appears not to notice. I hand her a tissue, and she wipes her eyes absentmindedly.

Don't mind me. I wasn't always like this. I did believe, oh I did. No. I lost my faith when God saw fit not to give me children. That's all I wanted. It might have been different if I could have been given that. It's not much to ask. And Len wouldn't consider adopting. 'Children aren't part of Jesus' plan for us, Kendra.'

But I've got a baby now, haven't I? Oh yes. One that needs me. Who needs to be loved. Who deserves to be loved.

She pets Snookie again, but the dog barely stirs.

Len isn't an evil man. No. I'll never say that. He's a disappointed man, poisoned by thwarted ambition. He wasn't clever enough, or charismatic enough – not till he got fire and brimstone in his eyes – not till that woman mentioned him in that message.

Sound bitter, don't I?

I shouldn't be mad at Pamela. I don't blame her really. Like I say, she was a good woman. Len and I...I guess we were stagnating, had been for years, and something had to change. He had his radio show and his Bible and healing groups, he'd spent years trying to get what he called 'the big boys' to take notice of him. And I've never seen him so excited as when he got invited to that goshdarn conference. There was a part of me – the part that hadn't died by then – that thought it might really be the making of us. But he let it all go to his head. And he really did believe in that message. He *does* believe in that message. People are saying he's a charlatan, no better than those alien people or those crazy cult leaders, but that part at least isn't an act.

I couldn't stand it when all those people started coming to the ranch. They upset Snookie. I reckon Len thought he'd make a fortune from all the tithes they'd bring. Did it to prove to Dr Lund that he could get a loyal following, too. But none of the ones who came had any money. That Monty, for starters. I could sense him watching me sometimes. There was something wrong with the way that man's mind was wired. I spent a lot of time in my room, watching my shows. Len tried to get me out to church on Sundays, but by then I couldn't face it. Other times me and Snookie would just get in the car and drive and drive, not caring where we ended up.

It was bound to go sour. I told Len not to do that radio show with that smart-mouth New York man. But Len wasn't one to listen. He didn't like it if you contradicted him.

I knew Dr Lund was out to pull one over him eventually, and that's what he did. Took Len's words and used them for his own ends. Len would rage up and down, trying to get Dr Lund or that Flexible Sandy on the phone, but eventually he couldn't even get their publicists to speak to him. It was all over the news that more and more people were getting themselves saved, and Dr Lund was taking the lion's share of the credit. He had the contacts, you see. And when he got behind that Mitch Reynard and didn't invite Len to speak at that pro-Israel rally, well, I have never seen Len so upset. I didn't stick around to see his face after the story in the *Inquirer* came out; I left the day it was published. He denied it, just like I knew he would. But being ousted out of the big boys' club did more damage to his self-esteem than any news story – however sensationalist – could do. In fact, I don't doubt that Lund's dismissal hurt Len far more than me leaving him.

It was cruel. Dr Lund opened the door a crack, let Len see into the palace, and then slammed the door on him.

She sighs.

Snookie needs his nap now. It's time for you to go. I've said my piece.

Before I leave, I ask her how she feels about Len now, and a spark of anger flares in her eyes.

I haven't got room in my heart for Len any more. I haven't got room for anyone.

She kisses the top of Snookie's head and I get the impression she's forgotten I'm still here.

You'd never hurt me, would you, Snookie? No. No, you *wouldn't.*

PART SEVEN

SURVIVORS

APRIL

Lillian Small.

I was living a strange half-life. Some days Reuben could communicate as clearly as I'm talking to you now, but whenever I brought something up about our old house, or one of our old friends, or a book he'd particularly enjoyed, a worried expression would fill his eyes, and they'd dart about as if he was desperately trying to access the information and coming up empty. It was as if the time before he woke up was a blank. I decided not to push him. This is hard to talk about...but the fact that he didn't seem to recall our past together or even get our 'Paris Texas' joke any more – that was almost as painful as the days when Al was back.

Because some days Al *would* be back. I knew immediately when he woke up if it would be a Reuben or an Al day; I could see it in his eyes when I brought him his morning coffee. Bobby took the whole thing in his stride, acted the same towards Reuben whether he was himself or Al, but it took its toll on me. That uncertainty; not knowing what I was going to be facing each morning. I only asked Betsy or called the care agency in to help when I was sure it was going to be an Al day. It wasn't that I didn't trust Betsy, but I couldn't forget the way Dr Lomeier had reacted when Reuben spoke to him. I couldn't bear the thought of what those lunatics would say if they found out about Reuben. They still wouldn't leave us in peace. I can't count how many times I had to hang up the phone when I realised it was one of those religious putzes, begging me to let them talk to Bobby.

And...even when it was a Reuben day, he still wasn't

quite himself. For some reason he'd developed an addiction to *The View*, a show he loathed before he got sick, and he and Bobby would spend hours watching old movies, though Reuben was never much of a film buff. He'd also lost interest in the news channels, even though there were all those political debates going on.

One morning, I was in the kitchen, making Bobby's breakfast and steeling myself to wake Reuben, when Bobby came rushing in. 'Bubbe,' he said. 'Po Po wants to go for a walk today. He wants to go out.'

Bobby took my hand and led me into the bedroom. Reuben was sitting on the bed, attempting to pull on his socks. 'Are you all right, Reuben?' I said.

'Can we go into the city, Rita?'

That's what he'd started calling me: Rita. After Rita Hayworth! The red hair, you see.

'Where would you like to go?'

Bobby and Reuben exchanged glances. 'The museum, Bubbe!' Bobby said.

The movie *Night at the Museum* had been on the night before, and Bobby had been fascinated by the scenes where all the exhibits came to life. It had been an AI day, so I doubted anything about the film had seeped into Reuben's consciousness, which was a relief as halfway through it, Bobby said, 'The dinosaur is like you, Po Po. It's come to life just like you did!'

'Reuben?' I said. 'You think you're up to going out today?'

He nodded, as eager as a little child. 'Yes please, Rita. Let's go and see the dinosaurs.'

'Yeah! Dinosaurs!' Bobby joined in. 'Bubbe? Do you think they really existed?'

'Of course, Bobby,' I said.

'I like their teeth. One day I'll bring *them* back to life.'

Bobby's enthusiasm was infectious, and if anyone deserved a treat, it was him. Poor little boy had been inside for days, although he never complained, not once. But the more time we spent out and about, the more likely it was that something might happen. What if we were recognised? What if one of those religious fanatics followed us and tried to kidnap Bobby? And I worried that Reuben's strength wouldn't hold out. His mental faculties may have been improving, but physically he tired easily.

But I put all those fears aside, and before I could change my mind, I called a taxi.

We ran into Betsy as we were leaving, and I prayed that Reuben wouldn't say anything. Of course I'd had a million close encounters of this type, and part of me longed to talk to someone about it – I hadn't told a soul, other than the sterile Dr Lomeier, that is. I mouthed 'doctor' at Betsy and she nodded, but Betsy's smart, and I could see she knew I was hiding something.

The taxi managed to find a spot right outside our door, a blessing as I could see a few of those *meshugeners* with their offensive billboards gathered around the park, even at nine in the morning.

Mercifully, the taxi driver – another one of those Indian immigrants – didn't recognise us, or if he did, he didn't let on. I asked the driver to take us over the Williamsburg Bridge so that Reuben could see the view and oh Elspeth, I did enjoy the journey! It was a lovely clear day, so the skyline looked like it was posing for a postcard and the sun bounced off the water. I pointed out all the sights to Bobby as we zipped through Manhattan, the

Chrysler building, Rockefeller Plaza, the Trump Tower, and he sat glued to the window asking me question after question. That trip cost a fortune, almost forty dollars with the tip, but it was worth it. Before we went into the museum, I asked Bobby and Reuben if they wanted a hot dog each for breakfast, and we sat and ate them in Central Park like regular tourists. Lori had brought me and Bobby here once – not to the museum, but to the park. Bobby had been grumpy that day, and the weather was freezing, but I still remember it fondly. She hadn't stopped talking about all the commissions she was getting; she was so excited about her future back then!

Even though it was a week day, the museum was full and we had to queue for quite a while. I started feeling anxious that we'd be recognised, but most of the people around us were tourists – a lot of Chinese and Europeans. And Reuben was starting to look tired; beads of sweat were popping on his brow. Bobby was full of energy; he couldn't keep his eyes off the dinosaur skeleton in the foyer.

The man at the ticket counter, a chatty African American fellow, did one of those double-takes when I approached him. 'Don't I know you, ma'am?'

'No,' I said, probably a bit rudely. After I paid and turned away, I heard him call, 'Wait!'

I hesitated; worried that he was going to point out who Bobby was to the whole museum. But instead he said, 'Could I offer you a wheelchair for your husband, ma'am?'

I could have kissed him. Everyone always says that New Yorkers are brash and self-involved, but that's just not true.

Bobby was tugging on my hand. 'Bubbe! The dinosaurs.'

The vendor disappeared and came back with a wheelchair. Reuben sank into it immediately. By now I was really getting worried about him. He was beginning to look confused, and I was concerned that Al might have decided to sneak back to cause trouble for us.

The ticket man guided us towards the lifts. 'Go on, son,' he said to Bobby. 'You show your grandparents the dinosaurs.'

'Do you believe that the dinosaurs come to life at night, Mr Man?' Bobby asked him.

'Why not? Miracles do happen, don't they?' And then he winked at me, and I knew for sure that he knew who we were. 'Don't worry, ma'am,' he said. 'I'll keep quiet. You go on and enjoy yourselves.'

We went straight up to the floor that housed the dinosaur exhibits. I had it in my mind that we'd take a quick look for Bobby's sake, and then head straight home.

I told Bobby to stick close to me, there were crowds everywhere, and it was quite a struggle pushing our way into the first room.

Reuben looked up at me and said, 'What am I? I'm scared.' And then he started crying, something that he hadn't done since he 'came to life', as Bobby put it.

I did my best to settle him. A few people were staring at him and the last thing I wanted was to draw attention to us. And when I looked up, Bobby was gone.

'Bobby?' I called. 'Bobby?'

I looked for his Yankees baseball cap, but couldn't see it anywhere.

The panic hit like a tidal wave. I left Reuben where he was and just ran.

I pushed past people, ignoring the grunts of 'Hey, lady, watch it,' icy sweat pouring down my sides. 'Bobby!' I shouted at the top of my lungs. Images kept flashing through my head. Bobby being taken away by one of those religious types, kidnapped and made to do all kinds of terrible things. Bobby lost in New York, wandering around and...

A woman guard came rushing up to me. 'Calm down, ma'am,' she said. 'You can't shout in here.' I could tell she thought I was deranged, and I didn't blame her. I felt like I was losing my mind.

'My grandson! I can't find my grandson.'

'Okay, ma'am,' she said. 'What does he look like?'

It didn't occur to me to tell her who Bobby actually was – that he was *the* Bobby Small, one of The Three, the miracle child, or any of that nonsense. All of that just went out of my head and I'm glad I didn't – the cops would have been called immediately and no doubt the whole thing would have been front-page news the next day. The guard said that she would alert the staff at the entrances and exits, just in case, but then I heard the most beautiful word in the whole world. 'Bubbe?'

I almost fainted with relief when I saw him skipping up to me. 'Where you been, Bobby? You frightened me half to death.'

'I was with the big one. He's got huge teeth like a wolf! But come on, Bubbe, Po Po needs us.'

Can you believe it, I had forgotten about Reuben, and we hurried back to the exhibit hall where I'd left him. Mercifully, he'd fallen asleep in the chair.

I didn't feel safe again until we were heading home in a taxi. Thankfully Reuben was calm when he woke from his nap, and while he wasn't himself, at least I didn't have to deal with a full-on Al panic on top of everything else.

'They didn't come to life, Bubbe,' Bobby said. 'The dinosaurs didn't come to life.'

'That's because they only come alive at night,' Reuben said. He was back. He took my hand and squeezed it. 'You did good, Lily,' he said. Lily – he'd called me Lily, and not Rita.

'What do you mean?' I asked him.

'You didn't give up. You didn't give up on me.'

Then I did cry. I couldn't help it, the tears just flowed.

'Are you okay, Bubbe?' Bobby asked. 'Are you sad?'

'I'm fine. I was just worried about you,' I said. 'I thought I'd lost you back in that museum.'

'You can't lose me,' Bobby said. 'You really can't, Bubbe. It's impossible.'

This is the last recorded IM conversation between Ryu and Chiyoko.

Message logged @ 20.46, 03/04/2012

CHIYOKO: I THOUGHT YOU WERE MY FRIEND!!!!! How could you do this to me?????????? www.hirotalksthroughandroid/tokyoherald I hope they paid you well. I hope it was worth it.

RYU: Chiyoko! I swear, I swear it wasn't me.

CHIYOKO: MC is furious. Android Uncle is threatening to take Hiro back to Osaka. There are reporters everywhere. I will die if I lose him. How could you do it????

RYU: It wasn't me!

CHIYOKO: You have ruined my life, NEVER CONTACT ME AGAIN.

RYU: Yoko? Yoko? Please. Please! IT WASN'T ME.

Devastated after Chiyoko blocked him from messaging her, Ryu went on the 2-chan Single Men's 'Broken Hearted' message forum under the avatar Orz Man, starting the thread: 'Loser Geek Needs Help.' Almost immediately, his story went viral, catching the imaginations of the board's inhabitants, and eventually attracting millions of hits.

Translation by Eric Kushan, who notes that American shortcuts and slang have been used to approximate the Japanese net slang used on the boards.

NAME: ORZ MAN POST DATE: 2012/04/05 01:32:39.32
Need some advice from u Netizens please!!! I need to reconnect with a girl who is blocking me from contacting her.

NAME: ANONYMOUS111
Why'd she dump u Orz?

NAME: ORZ MAN
She thinks I betrayed a confidence, but it wasn't me. _|7O

NAME: ANONYMOUS275
Been there dude but need more info.

NAME: ORZ MAN
Okay…this may take a while. I've been talking to this girl online, who I'll call the ice princess. She's way

above my level, so u can imagine how amazed I was that someone like her would spend time with a loser like me. We were getting on well, talking every day and sharing stuff, u know? Then…something happened. A…let's call it a story was leaked that made her family look bad and she thought it was me and now she has blocked me from messaging her.

I don't want you guys to think I'm a loser. But it hurts. When she stopped taking my messages, it was like my stomach was made of glass and then it shattered.

NAME: ANONYMOUS111
'Like my stomach was made of glass.' That's beautiful, Orz.

NAME: ANONYMOUS28
I'm cryin here.

NAME: ORZ MAN
Thanks. I'm in a bad way. It hurts like a physical pain. I can't eat or sleep. I keep reading our messages over and over again. I spent hours today analysing every single word we've ever shared.

NAME: ANONYMOUS23
Ouch!!!! U gotta learn that women are only there to cause u pain, Orz dude. Fuck them.

NAME: ANONYMOUS111
Ignore 23.
Been where u r Orz. Is there any hope you can reconnect?

NAME: ORZ MAN
I don't know. I can't live without her.

NAME: ANONYMOUS23
What does she look like? Is she hot????

NAME: ANONYMOUS99
<SIGH> U r such a noob 23.

NAME: ORZ MAN
I've only seen her once. And not in person. She looks a little like Hazuki Hitori.

NAME: ANONYMOUS678
Hazuki Hitori from the Sunny Juniors? Ba-doom! Orz, yr taste is good, dude. I'm in love with her too.

NAME: ANONYMOUS709
Hazuki???? Arrrrrr-ooooooooooooooooooooooooooooo ooooooooooooooooooooooooo

NAME: ANONYMOUS111
Keep your lust in check, Netizens.
Orz, u need to go and talk to her in person. Tell her how u feel.

NAME: ORZ MAN
It's not as easy as that. This is embarrassing. U guys…I still live with my parents and I'm kinda housebound.

NAME: ANONYMOUS 987
It's cool. I also live at home.

NAME: ANONYMOUS55
Me too. Big deal.

NAME: ORZ MAN
Not what I meant. I haven't left the house in um…a while. I haven't even left my room.

NAME: ANONYMOUS111
How long is a while, Orz?

NAME: ORZ MAN
U guys r going to judge me!!!!
Over a year. _|7O

NAME: ANONYMOUS87
Meatspace can be a fucker. Here's a tip, Orz. If u don't want to go to the bathroom then keep old plastic water bottles under yr desk for emergencies. What I do when I'm on a gaming binge.

NAME: ANONYMOUS786
LOL!!!
Good advice, 87!

NAME: ANONYMOUS23
Netizens. Orz here is a hikikomori.

NAME: ANONYMOUS111
Orz socialises on the net, which means he is capable of human contact. He's just a recluse not a proper hikikomori.
[The thread is briefly disrupted by an argument about the true nature of a hikikomori]

NAME: ANONYMOUS111
Orz, you still there?

NAME: ORZ MAN
I'm here. Listen…sorry for wasting yr time. Writing that makes me realise…What would she see in me anyway? Why would she even look at such a loser? Look at me…No job, no cash, no hope.

NAME: ANONYMOUS111
Is yr princess dead? No. Then there is always hope. Netizens, this man needs our help. Time to suit up.

NAME: ANONYMOUS85
Get the weapons loaded.

NAME: ANONYMOUS337
Train that princess in your sights.

NAME: ANONYMOUS23
Locked and loaded, SIR!

NAME: ANONYMOUS111
First, we gotta help Orz get out of his room.

NAME: ANONYMOUS47
Orz. Some good advice:

1. Clean yrself up so that u look as presentable as possible. No bed hair or pimples.
2. Go to Uniqlo and get some good clothes nothing flashy.

3. Go and see The Princess.
4. Offer to buy her dinner.
5. At dinner, tell her how you feel.

That way, even if she cuts you off, you will have no regrets.

NAME: ANONYMOUS23
Orz might not know where she lives if they've only been talking online. He said he has no money so how can he buy new clothes?

NAME: ORZ MAN
Thanks for the advice. I don't have her address but I know she lives near the Yoyogi station.

NAME: ANONYMOUS414
There is a good pasta place near there.

NAME: ANONYMOUS23
Pasta for a first date? Go Yakitori, French or ethnic then u have a talking point.
[The thread diverts into a discussion about the best place to take a first date]

NAME: ANONYMOUS111
It's not a first date. Orz and his princess are cyber soul mates.
Netizens, yr missing the point. First Orz has to clean up and get out of his room.

NAME: ORZ MAN
You really think I should try and see her in person?

[A chorus of 'yes', 'do it dude', 'what have you got to lose' etc., follows]

NAME: ORZ MAN
Okay. You have almost convinced me! Now the practicalities…
I think I can get some money but not much. The princess lives in a different prefecture so I need somewhere to stay while I search for her house. Can't afford a hotel. Any suggestions? Any of u stayed over in a net cafe? Is it an option?

NAME: ANONYMOUS89
Not ideal, but I have done it once on the outskirts of Shinjuku. Cheap and u can get vending food there.
[The netizens bombard Orz with advice, arguing about where he should stay and how best to attract the princess's attention]

NAME: ORZ MAN
I got to sleep. Been up for 20 hours. Thanks guys. U really helped me. Don't feel so alone any more.

NAME: ANONYMOUS789
U can do it, Orz.

NAME: ANONYMOUS122
Do it for the geeks.

NAME: ANONYMOUS20
Good luck!!!! We are all there with you, Orz. C'mon dude, u can dooooooooooooooooo it.

NAME: ANONYMOUS23
Fuckin do it man.

NAME: ANONYMOUS111
Keep us posted!!!!!
[Two days later, Ryu, aka Orz Man, reappears on the thread, during which time, much speculation has gone on]

NAME: ORZ MAN POST DATE: 2012/04/07 01:37:19.30
Don't know if any of you here on the thread I started the other day are listening. Been reading through what all of u have been saying. So blown away by the amount of support I have on this site!

Just wanted to let u guys know I took your advice. I left the house.

NAME: ANONYMOUS111
Orz! Where are u now?

NAME: ORZ MAN
I'm staying in a net cafe cubicle.

NAME: ANONYMOUS111
What is it like being out in the big bad world? We need details. Start from the beginning.

NAME: ORZ MAN
Ah. Like I said, I followed all your advice. First, I cleaned myself up. Brushed my teeth, which were yellow from too much smoking. Next, the hair. Didn't have cash for

a haircut, so did it myself. Don't think I did too bad a job!

Now the hard part. U guys are seriously gonna judge me for this. My parents were at work when I left and I took the savings my mother keeps in the kitchen. Not much but enough to keep me going for a couple of weeks if I'm careful. I left a note, but I still feel bad about it. I said I'd decided to leave to find a job so that I would no longer be a burden on the family.

NAME: ANONYMOUS111
U did the right thing, Orz. U can pay them back when u are on yr feet.

NAME: ANONYMOUS28
Yeah, Orz. U did the only thing u could do in that situation. Keep going and tell us the full deets.

NAME: ORZ MAN
Thanks guys. More details…okay.
My shoes were still in the cupboard next to the front door where I'd left them a year ago. They were covered in dust.

Leaving the house was one of the hardest things I've ever done. Trying to think of how to explain it… when I stepped outside, I felt like I was a matchstick in an ocean. Everything looked too bright, too big. The curtain twitchers were out in force. I know they have been gossiping about me for months, something that has caused my mother a lot of distress.

It was early afternoon when I left, but even my district seemed to be unbearably busy. Kept feeling the tug of my room. It was like I was being pulled back, but I fought against it and made myself jog to the station. I bought a ticket to Shinjuku before I could change my mind. It felt like everyone I saw was pointing and laughing at me.

Won't go into the constant panic attacks I had to fend off when I arrived at Shinjuku. Not knowing what to do, I went into a Yoshinoya outlet although I didn't feel like eating. I made myself ask the counter guy if he knew of somewhere cheap I could stay. He was cool, gave me directions to this net cafe.

Going to be honest here...kinda freaking out...

NAME: ANONYMOUS179
Don't freak out dude. We're here 4 u. So what's next? How will you find her house?

NAME: ORZ MAN
I've done some research. Her family...let's just say they are not unknown, and I have managed to source the address.

NAME: ANONYMOUS179
U mean she's famous???
[The next few hours are spent dispensing more words of wisdom and speculating on who the princess's family could be]

NAME: ORZ MAN
I'm thinking that if I get up the nerve to see her, the best thing to do would be to wait for her parents to leave the house.

NAME: ANONYMOUS902
U thought what u r going to say?

NAME: ANONYMOUS865
Orz's broken glass stomach is tinkling. He lights a cigarette and stands beneath a streetlight watching the princess's house. He crushes the cigarette under his boot, walks up to the front door, and knocks.

She opens it. He can't breathe. She is even more beautiful than he remembers.

'It's me, Orz,' he says, taking off his shades.

'Take me away from all of this,' she pleads, dropping to her knees in front of him. 'Do me, do me now!'

NAME: ANONYMOUS761
Nice work 865, made me LOL!!!

NAME: ORZ MAN
Been thinking…I might know how to get her attention…

NAME: ANONYMOUS111
Don't leave us in suspense.

NAME: ANONYMOUS2
Yeah, Orz. We're on yr team, dude!!!!

NAME: ORZ MAN
I'll tell u tomorrow if it works. If it doesn't I will be curled in a ball, slitting my wrists and sobbing.

NAME: ANONYMOUS286
Victory is yr only option Orz! You can do iiiiit!!!!

[After Ryu left the message board, the following exchange occurred]

NAME: ANONYMOUS111
Netizens…I think I know who the princess is.

NAME: ANONYMOUS874
Who?

NAME: ANONYMOUS111
Orz said that the princess's family is well known. He also said that she lives near the Yoyogi station.
Hiro lives in Yoyogi.

NAME: ANONYMOUS23
Hiro????????? Miracle child Hiro? Android boy?

NAME: ANONYMOUS111
Yeah. Hiro is staying with his aunt and uncle. They've got a daughter. Checked through the footage of the memorial service. Spotted a girl who looks like Hazuki in the crowd standing near the family, and another one who is not as hot.

NAME: ANONYMOUS23
Our humble Orz is in love with Android Boy's cousin??? GO ORZ!

17 April, 12.30 p.m.

God. It's been a while...How are you, Mandi? Do you know, even though I've been rambling into this fucking thing as if you're my closest friend or Dr K substitute, it struck me the other day that I couldn't remember your face. I even went on Facebook to check out your profile pic to remind me what you look like. I told you how much I hate Facebook, didn't I? My own fault. I stupidly accepted friend requests from a shed-load of people without checking them out properly first. Bastards hate-bombed my wall and Twitter account because of the Marilyn thing.

Mandi, I'd like to apologise for ignoring your calls. I just didn't...I had a few bad days, okay? More than a few, let's be honest. A few weeks ha ha. I couldn't see an end to them. Stephen...well, you know. I don't want to go there. And I haven't done much about sorting out what we can keep in amongst all this drivel. I haven't done much of anything, to be honest.

It was too soon. All this. It was too soon after the accident. I can see that now. But I'm thinking maybe we can rework it later after I'm...after I'm feeling more like myself. Not in a good place at the moment, you see.

Some days I find myself looking at photographs of

Jess, trying to spot the difference. She caught me at it the other day. 'What are you doing, Uncle Paul?' she asked, all sweet and cheery, damn her. She has this way of creeping up on me.

'Nothing,' I snapped at her.

I felt so guilty that the next day I went to Toys R Us and spent the equivalent of a down payment on a car on product-placement toys and other crap. She now has the entire set of extortionately expensive My Little Ponies, as well as a bushel-load of themed Barbies, which I know would make feminist Shelly turn over in her grave.

But I'm trying. God, am I trying. It's just…she isn't herself. Jess and Polly used to love the stories Stephen made up for them – silly takes on *Aesop's Fables*. I tried making one up the other day – a version of 'The Boy Who Cried Wolf' – but she looked at me as if I'd gone mad.

Ha! Maybe I have.

'Cause there's this other thing. Last night I did a Google marathon again, trying to get to the bottom of how I'm feeling about Jess. There's this medical condition. It's called Capgras Delusion. It's really rare, but people who suffer from it are convinced that the people they live with have been replaced by proxies. Like changelings. I know it's mental even to think like this. Dangerous even…But at the same time, it's actually reassuring knowing there is a particular syndrome that would explain it all. But it could just be stress. That's what I'm clinging to right now.

(*Clears throat*)

And Christ. It's been busy. What with Jess's first day back at school. This we could use, I think. It's just the kind of thing readers want, isn't it? I think I told you Dr K and Darren decided that it would do her good to get back after the Easter hols. It wasn't ideal, her doing home schooling. I'm not much of a teacher and...it meant interacting with her for hours.

The press were out in their droves as usual, so I put on the performance of my life, all smiles, could have got a BAFTA for my role as 'Concerned Guardian'. While the hacks howled outside the gates, I walked her into the classroom. The teacher, Mrs Wallbank, had got the kids to decorate it; there was a big 'Welcome Back Jess!' banner hanging across the blackboard. Mrs Wallbank is a strapping too-jolly woman who looks like she's fallen out of an Enid Blyton novel. The sort of person who spends her weekends visiting heritage sites, hiking hairy-legged up wind-swept hills. Just the sight of her made me want to get rat-arsed and smoke a pack of Rothmans (yes, yes, Mandi, twenty a day now, though never in the house. Another bad habit to hide, ha ha, although I've discovered that Mrs E-B isn't averse to a sneaky ciggie).

I soon found out that Mrs Wallbank speaks to the children like adults, but treats grown-ups like retards. 'Hello, Jess's uncle! Now don't you worry about a thing. Jess and I will be just fine, won't we?'

'Are you sure you're ready for this, Jess?' I simpered.

'Of course, Uncle Paul,' she said, with that complacent smile I've come to loathe. 'You go back home and have a fag and a vodka.'

Mrs Wallbank blinked at me, and I tried to make a joke of it.

Feeling that sense of relief I always feel whenever I'm not around her, I ran out of there.

Outside, I tried to ignore the hacks' usual questions: 'When are you going to let Marilyn see her granddaughter?'

I muttered the usual bollocks about 'when Jess is feeling up to it', etc. etc. Then I jumped in Stephen's Audi and just drove around a bit. Found myself in the heart of Bromley. I parked and went to Marks & Spencer to buy something special for Jess's first-day-back-at-school supper. And all along I knew I was just playing a part. Pretending to be the caring uncle. But I can't…I can't stop thinking about Stephen and Shelly – the real Stephen and Shelly, not the Stephen who comes to me at night – and it's only the thought of not letting them down that keeps me going. I keep thinking that if I throw myself into the part, eventually it will become reality. Eventually I'll get back onto an even keel.

Anyway, I was standing in the queue, clutching a basket full of those ghastly pasta ready-meals Jess likes so much, when I found my eyes drifting over to the Wines of the World section. Pictured myself sitting down, right there, and gulping bottle after bottle of Chilean red until my stomach exploded. 'Come on, love,' the old woman behind me said, 'there's a till open,' and that snapped me out of it. The cashier recognised me straight away. Gave me what I've come to call a standard 'supportive smile'. 'How's she doing?' she whispered conspiratorially.

'Why's it always about her?' I almost snapped. I forced out something along the lines of, 'she's doing wonderfully, thanks so much for caring,' and somehow managed to leave without punching her in the face or buying the whole of the alcohol aisle.

24 April, 11.28 p.m.

I'm doing okay this week, Mandi. It's better now that she's at school. We even spent an evening together watching a

The Only Way Is Essex marathon. She loves that appalling reality programme, can't seem to get enough of spray-tanned morons talking utter shit to each other in night-clubs, which should worry me slightly. But I suppose all her friends at school are into that kind of rubbish, so I should look at it as reassuringly normal behaviour. She's still relentlessly cheerful and well-behaved (just once I wish she'd throw a tantrum or refuse to go to bed). I keep convincing myself that Dr K's right, that of course her behaviour is going to change after going through all that trauma. It'll just take time for us to adjust. 'Jess,' I asked, during a commercial break – a relief from all the banality on screen. 'You and me… we're okay, right?'

'Of course we are, Uncle Paul.' And for the first time in ages I thought, it's going to be fine. I'll get over this.

I even phoned Gerry to let him know I was ready to get back to work. He asked about the recordings of course, said your publishers were on his back, desperate for me to send through more material, and I made my usual excuses. They'd have an orgasm if I sent this through unedited.

But I'll sort it out. Yeah.

25 April, 4.00 p.m.

Phew. Big big day, Mandi. Darren's just left (God, he can be an anal twat, went through the cupboards and the fridge to check what Jess was eating, which I'm fairly sure isn't standard procedure), when the phone rang. As you know, it's usually either the press or a tenacious religious freak who's somehow managed to scalp or bribe someone to get my new number. But today, surprise, surprise, it was one of the alien abduction people. They've been keeping schtum since I sicced the cops onto them just after Jess got out of hospital. I almost hung up straight away, but something stopped me. The guy calling – Simon somebody – sounded fairly reasonable. Said he was phoning to see how I was doing. Not Jess, but *me*. I had to be careful; ten to one the phone's being hacked, so I let him do most of the talking. I didn't really have to say much to be fair. As I listened, I almost felt like I was watching myself from across the room. I knew it was mental to give him the time of day. He says that what the aliens do – he called them 'the others', like in a lazily scripted B-movie – is abduct people, place a microchip inside their body and use 'alien technology' to control them. He says they're in cahoots with the government. It made me...why not be honest? No one else is going to hear this. Shit, okay... Look, on some level it made a weird kind of sense.

I mean...what if Black Thursday is a government experiment thingy after all? There are an awful lot of people who believe there's no way those kids could have survived those crashes. And I don't mean the obvious nutters like those Bible bashers. Or the freaks who think the kids are possessed by the devil. Even that investigator who came to ask Jess if she remembered anything about the crash stared at her as if he couldn't believe she was alive. Sure, in the Japanese crash there were other people who initially survived the impact, but they didn't last long. And how exactly *did* Jess survive? Most of the other bodies... well, they were in pieces, weren't they? And that Maiden Airlines plane looked like it had been through a blender when they started dredging it up from the Everglades.

Okay...deep breath, Paul. Calm the fuck down. Lack of sleep, it can screw with your mind, can't it?

29 April, 3.37 a.m.

He's back. Three nights in a row now.

It sounds crazy, but I'm getting used to it. I no longer get a fright when I wake up and see him sitting there.

Last night I tried to talk to him again. 'What are you trying to tell me, Stephen?'

But he just said the same thing he always says, then disappeared. The smell is getting worse. I can still smell it on the sheets, even now. Rotten fish. Rotten . . . flesh. Fuck. I can't be imagining that, can I? *Can I?*

And . . . I have an admission. I'm not proud of it.

I couldn't take it last night. I left the house at four a.m. – yeah, that's right, leaving Jess alone – and drove to the all-night Tesco's in Orpington. Bought myself a half-jack of Bells.

By the time I got home it was empty.

Hid the bottle under the bed with the others. Mrs E-B may be my new sneaky fag ally, but she'd be horrified at the number of empties I'm collecting. I'm getting out of control; got to cut back again. Got to stop this shit.

30 April

So much for my resolution to get my act together.

I've just been through Jess's bedroom. I don't know what I was expecting to find. A 'To Serve Man' manual maybe, like in that old *Twilight Zone* episode, ha ha.

(Paul's laughter makes way to sobbing)

It's okay. I'm okay.

But she *is* different. She is. There's no getting away

from that. She's even taken down all her old Missy K posters. Maybe aliens have good taste.

(*Another laugh that turns into a sob*)

But... how can she not be Jess?

It has to be me.

But...

It's getting harder to hide all this from Darren. I can't allow myself to crack. Not now. I need to cover all bases. Get to the bottom of this. I've even considered giving in and taking her to see Marilyn. But would the fat cow even be able to tell if there's something different about Jess? Shelly hated going round there, so Marilyn saw the girls less than I did. I suppose it's worth a shot. She is Jess's flesh and blood, isn't she?

But in the meantime, I asked Petra, one of the yummy mummies at Jess's school, to bring her daughter Summer over to play this afternoon. Petra's always emailing and calling and asking if there's anything she can do to help, so she jumped at the chance. She even offered to collect the girls from school and bring them here.

So... I'm leaving the recorder in Jess's bedroom. Just to check. Just to be sure. See what Jess talks about when I'm not around. It's what a good uncle would do, isn't it? Maybe Jess is in pain and will open up to Summer and then I'll know that the way she's behaving is because she has what Dr K calls 'unexplored trauma'. They'll be here in five minutes.

(*Sound of approaching children's voices, which get gradually louder*)

'...So you can be Rainbow Dash and I'll be Princess Luna. Unless you want to be Rarity?'

'Have you got *all* of the ponies, Jess?'

'Yeah. Paul bought them for me. He also bought me Pageant Gown Barbie. Here.'

'Oh cool! She's so beautiful. But it's not even your birthday.'

'I know. You can have her if you like. Paul can get me a new one.'

'Really? You're the bestest! Jess...what are you going to do with all of Polly's toys?'

'Nothing.'

'And, Jess...did it hurt? When you got burned?'

'Yes.'

'Will the scars go away?'

'It doesn't matter.'

'What doesn't?'

'If they go away or not.'

'Mummy says it's a miracle you got out of that plane. She says I'm not to ask you questions about it in case it makes you cry.'

'I'm not going to cry!'

'Mummy says you can cover the scars with make-up later on so that people won't stare.'

'C'mon! Let's play!'

(*For the next fifteen minutes the girls play 'My Little Pony meets Barbie in Essex'*)

(*Distant sound of Paul's voice calling them to come downstairs for a snack*)

'Aren't you coming, Jess?'

'You go first. I'll get the ponies. They can eat with us.'

' 'Kay. Can I really have Pageant Gown Barbie?'

'Yes.'
'You're my bestest friend ever, Jess.'
'I know. Now you go first.'
' 'Kay.'

(*The Dictaphone captures the sound of Summer leaving the room. There's a pause of several seconds, followed by the sounds of approaching footsteps and breathing. Then, a second later:* 'Hello, Uncle Paul.')

When I flew to London to meet with my UK publishers a few days after Jess's funeral in July, Marilyn Adams invited me to interview her at her residence, a well-maintained, three-bedroomed council house, filled with mod-cons.

Marilyn is waiting for me on the couch, her oxygen tank close to hand. As I'm about to start the interview, she digs out a box of cigarettes from the side of the couch, lights up and takes a deep drag.

Don't tell the boys, will you, love? I know I shouldn't, but after all this business...How can it hurt? A ciggy is my only bit of comfort these days.

I know what you've read in the papers, love, but we didn't really have bad feelings towards Paul back then, other than him wanting to keep Jess away from us. I had a cousin who was like that, a gay, I mean. We're not bigoted, honest to God. Lots of them about aren't there, and I love that Graham Norton. But the press...well, they twist your words around, don't they? Do I blame Shelly for giving Paul custody? Not really. She just wanted a better life for herself and the girls, and who can blame her? Never had much growing up. I know people think we're scroungers, but we have every right to live how we want to live, don't we? You try getting a sodding job these days.

Some people think we only wanted Jess because we were after Stephen and Shelly's house and all that insurance money. I'd be lying if I said it wouldn't have come in handy, but that was the furthest thought from our minds, honest to God. We really just wanted to spend time with little Jess. It dragged on and on, and some days the stress would just get so much I could barely sleep. 'You're going to give yourself a heart attack with all that worrying, Mum,' the boys kept saying. So in the end, when I got really ill, I backed off, decided not to get the lawyers involved. Thought it would be for the best. Jessie could always come and find us when she was older, couldn't she?

So when Paul rang and asked if we wanted to see Jess, well, you could have knocked me over with a feather. The social had been promising for ages that they would do what they could, but I didn't put any store in what they said. We were all dead excited. We thought it would be best not to overwhelm her, it can be right chaos here sometimes when we all get together, so I decided that it would be just me, the boys and her cousin Jordan, who was closest to her age. I told little Jordan that his cousin was coming for a visit and he said, 'But isn't she an alien, Nana?' His dad went to cuff him round the ear, but Jordie was only repeating something he'd heard at school. 'How could anyone believe any of that bollocks?' Keith would always say whenever one of those bloody Americans started up about The Three being out of the Bible or whatever it was they was saying. He said the buggers should be sued for defamation, but that wasn't up to us, was it?

I got a right shock when the social worker dropped her off. She'd shot up like a tree since I'd last seen her. All those photographs in the press didn't do her justice. The scars on her face weren't too bad, made her skin look a bit tighter and shinier, that was all.

I nudged Jordan and told him to go up and give her a

hug. He did as he was told, although I could see he wasn't too keen.

Jase went out and got us all a McDonald's, and I asked Jessie all about school and her friends and that. She was a right little chatter-box. Bright as a button. Didn't seem at all out of her depth around us. I was a bit surprised, to be honest. The last time I'd seen her, she was dead shy, her and her sister Polly. Hung around their mother's skirts whenever Shelly brought them over. A pair of little princesses, me and the boys used to joke. Not rough and tumble like the others. Not that we saw the twins often, mind. Shelly only really brought them round on Christmas and birthdays, and there was a right set-to one year when Brooklyn bit Polly. But Brooklyn was only a toddler back then; she didn't know what she was doing.

'Why don't you go show Jessie your room, Jordan? Maybe she wants to play on the Wii?' I said.

'She looks funny,' Jordan said. 'Her face is funny.'

I gave him a smack and told Jess not to take any notice.

'It's okay,' she said. 'My face is funny. It wasn't supposed to happen. It was a mistake.' She shook her head as if she was a thousand years old. 'Sometimes we get it wrong.'

'Who gets it wrong, love?' I asked.

'Oh, just us,' she said. 'Come on, Jordan. I'll tell you a story. I have lots of stories.'

Off they went, the two of them, Jess and Jordan. It warmed my heart seeing them together like that. Family's important, isn't it?

I find it hard to get up the stairs these days, what with my lungs like they are, so I asked Jase to pop up and keep an eye on them. He said they were getting on like a house on fire, Jessie talking ten to the dozen. Before you knew it, it was time to send her home.

'Would you like to come again, Jess?' I asked her. 'Spend more time with your cousins?'

'Yes please, Nana,' she said. 'That was interesting.'

After the bloke from the social had collected her, I asked Jordan what he thought of Jess, if he thought she'd changed and that, but he shook his head. Wouldn't say much about her at all. I asked him what they'd been talking about all afternoon, but he said he couldn't remember. I didn't press him on it.

Paul phoned me that evening, and I got a right shock again when I heard his voice! Civil he was, as well. Asked me if I'd noticed anything strange about Jess. His words. Said he was a bit concerned about her.

I told him what I'm telling you now, that she was a lovely little girl, a real joy to be around.

He seemed to find this funny, laughed like a ruddy drain, but before I could ask him what was amusing, he hung up.

Course, it wasn't that long afterwards that we heard what he'd done.

Lillian Small.

The call came in at six that morning, and I rushed to answer it before it woke Reuben. I hadn't been sleeping well since that day at the museum, and I'd got into the habit of slipping out of bed at around five, in order to spend a few minutes alone and settle my nerves before I discovered which husband I would be facing.

'Who is this?' I snapped into the phone. If it was one of the papers or a *meshugener* taking a chance by calling so early, I wasn't in a mood to treat them lightly.

There was a pause, and then the caller introduced himself as Paul Craddock, Jessica's uncle. His clipped English accent reminded me of one of those characters on that *Cavendish Hall* show Betsy never stopped talking about. It was a strange conversation, full of long, uncomfortable pauses, although you'd think we'd have lots to talk about. I remember thinking how strange it was that neither of us had thought to be in contact before. The children were always being linked together in the news articles, and every so often, the producers of one of the big talk shows would get it into their heads to try to get all three children to appear together, but I always turned them down. I could immediately pick up that there was something not right with Paul; I suppose I put it down to the time difference or maybe a distortion on the line. He finally managed to make himself clear. He wanted to know if I'd noticed anything different about Bobby, if his personality or behaviour had changed after the crash.

It was the same sort of question those damn reporters

were always asking and I was short with him. He apologised for disturbing me and hung up without saying goodbye.

I was agitated after the call, couldn't settle down. Why would he ask me something like that? I knew that Paul, like me and the family of that little Japanese boy, must be suffering under the pressure of all the press attention. I suppose I also felt guilty that I'd been so short with him. He'd sounded troubled, like he needed to talk.

And I was tired of feeling guilty. Guilty about not sending Bobby back to school; for not taking Reuben back to Dr Lomeier so he could be seen by the specialist; for hiding his condition from Betsy. Like Charmaine, who still called to check up on us every week, Betsy had been there for me from the beginning, but I couldn't shift the feeling that what was happening to Reuben was my private miracle. *And* my private burden. I knew what would happen if the story got out. The ridiculous story about the little Japanese boy interacting with that robot his father made him was all over the news for days.

I made myself a cup of coffee, sat in the kitchen and stared out of the window. It was a lovely spring day, and I remember thinking how nice it would be to just go out for a walk, sit in a cafe somewhere. Have some time to myself.

Reuben was awake by then, and it was Reuben, and not Al, who was there that day. I thought, I could just pop out for ten minutes, sit in the park in the sun. Breathe.

I made Bobby his breakfast, cleaned the kitchen, and asked Reuben if he'd mind if I slipped out for a few minutes.

'You go, Rita,' he said. 'Go and have a nice time.'

I made Bobby promise that he wouldn't leave the apartment, and then I left. I walked down to the park, sat on the bench opposite the sports centre, and raised my face to the sun. I kept telling myself, just five minutes more, and then I'll get back and change the sheets on the bed, take Bobby to the store with me to buy milk. A group of young men pushing baby buggies strolled past me, and we exchanged smiles. I glanced at my watch, realised I'd been sitting there for over forty minutes – where had the time gone? I was less than five minutes from my building, but accidents can happen in seconds. The sudden rush of panic made me feel nauseous, and I hurried home.

And I was right to be worried. I screamed out loud when I ran into the apartment and saw the two of them standing there in my kitchen in their identical suits. One of them had his eyes closed and was holding Bobby's hand to his chest. The other one had his hand raised above his head, and was muttering something under his breath.

'Get away from him!' I yelled at the top of my voice. I could see right away what they were. The fanaticism radiated out of them. 'Get the hell out of my apartment!'

'Is that you, Rita?' Reuben called from the other room.

'The men asked to come in and watch *The View* with us, Bubbe,' Bobby said. 'Are they the ones Betsy calls *bupkes*?'

'Go to your room, Bobby,' I said.

I turned on the two men again, fury sparking through every vein. They looked like twins, their blond hair identically parted to the side, that same smug, self-righteous expression on their faces, which made the situation all the more disturbing. Bobby told me later they'd only been there for five minutes before I got home and that they hadn't done anything other than what I'd seen in the kitchen. They must have watched me leaving and decided to take a chance. 'All we ask is that you let Bobby's spirit wash over us,' one of them said. 'You owe it to us, Mrs Small.'

'She owes you nothing,' Betsy said from behind me – thank God she'd heard me yell. 'I've called the cops, so you get your Bible-thumping tushes out of here.'

The two men glanced at each other and made for the door. They looked like they were thinking about spouting more of their nonsense, but the look on Betsy's face shut them up.

Betsy said she'd take care of Bobby while I made a statement. I knew it was too late to worry about her finding out about Reuben. The police commissioner himself came to see me later that day. He said I should consider round-the-clock protection, maybe hire private security, but I didn't want a stranger in my home.

When I'd finished with the police, I could see immediately that Betsy knew and wanted to talk about Reuben's transformation. What choice did I have then but to come clean? And who did I have to blame but myself?

Lillian Small's neighbour, Betsy Katz, agreed to speak to me in late June.

What pains me most of all was that I'd been careful around those reporters. Those newspaper people, they could be smart. So clever with their sneaking around. Calling me up and asking leading questions as if I was born yesterday and wouldn't see right through what they were doing. 'Mrs Katz,' they'd say, 'isn't it true that Bobby is acting a little strange?' 'You can keep your acting strange,' I'd tell them. 'Does it hurt to be so stupid?'

If it wasn't for Bobby, I don't know if Lily would have found the strength to go on after Lori died. Lori was a nice girl, arty sure, but she was a good daughter. Me, I don't know if I would have been able to go on after a stab in the heart like that. And that Bobby! What a lovely child! It was never a burden taking him off Lily's hands. He'd come into my kitchen and help me make cookies, used to let himself in as if he was one of the family. Sometimes we'd sit down and watch *Jeopardy* together. He was good company, a good boy, always happy, always with a smile on his face. I worried that he wasn't spending enough time with other children – what kid wants to spend all his free time with old ladies? – but it didn't seem to worry him. I'd told Lily many times that Rabbi Toba's family ran a good yeshiva in Bedford-Stuyvesant, but she wouldn't hear of it. But could I blame her for wanting to keep him so close? I was never blessed with children, but when my husband Ben fell to cancer ten years ago this

September, I felt the loss like a knife in my heart. Lily had lost too much already. First Reuben, then her daughter.

I knew that Lily was trying to hide something from me, but not in my whole life could I have guessed what it was. Lily wasn't a good liar, she was an open book. I didn't nag her to tell me. I figured that eventually she would come to me and tell me herself.

I was cleaning my kitchen when I heard Lily shouting that day. My first thought was that something must have happened to Reuben. I ran straight to her apartment. When I saw those two strange men in their suits, and their fanatical eyes, I called the cops right away. I knew what they were. Me? I could spot one of those fanatics a mile off after they started crawling around the neighbourhood. Even when they thought they were being so clever by dressing up like business people. They were smart, ran out of there before the cops arrived. While Lily made a statement, I went into the apartment to watch Bobby and Reuben.

'Hello, Betsy,' Bobby said. 'Po Po and I are watching *From Here to Eternity*. It's an old movie where everyone is coloured black and white.'

And then Reuben said, clear as day. 'The oldies are the goodies.'

And how do you think I reacted? I almost jumped out of my skin. 'What you say, Reuben?'

'I said, they don't make films like they used to. Are you having trouble with your hearing, Betsy?'

I had to sit down. I'd been helping Lily care for Reuben since Bobby came out of hospital, and I hadn't heard him speak a word that made any sense in all that time.

Lily came back in and she saw right off that I knew.

We went into the kitchen and she poured us both a brandy. She explained it all to me. How he'd started talking out of nowhere one evening.

'It's a miracle,' I said.

When I got back to my place, I couldn't settle down to anything. I had to talk to someone. I tried calling Rabbi Toba, but he wasn't in and I needed to get it off my chest. So I called my sister-in-law. Her best friend's nephew Eliott, a good boy – or so I thought then – was a doctor and she told me I should talk to him. I was just trying to help. I thought maybe I could get a second opinion for Lily.

Saying it now, it sounds like I was a real fool, I know this.

I don't know if they paid him, or what they did, but I know it was him who talked to those reporters. The next day, when I left the house to go to the store – just to buy myself some bread as I was having soup that evening – I saw all the reporters hanging around the apartment, but that wasn't new. They tried to talk to me but I gave them the brush-off.

I saw the headline on a placard outside the bakery: 'It's a miracle! Bobby's Senile Grandfather Starts to Speak.' I almost threw up right there. May God forgive me, but it did cross my mind that I could blame it on those religious putzes who had conned their way into the apartment. But the article made it clear that the news had come from a 'source close to Lillian Small'.

I was so worried. I knew what this could mean for Lily. All those crazies, led by that real dangerous one, I knew they would jump on this like flies on a turd.

I ran back home and I said to Lily, 'I never meant to let it out.'

She turned white, and could I blame her? 'Not again,' she said. 'Why won't they leave us alone?'

Lily never forgave me. She didn't cut me out of her life, but there was a watchfulness when she was around me after that.

I wonder, I really do, if this wasn't part of what caused everything else afterwards. May God forgive me.

PART EIGHT

CONSPIRACY

APRIL–JUNE

The following article appeared on makimashup.com on 19 April 2012 – a website dedicated to reporting 'the weird and the wonderful from around the world'.

Japan's Queen of Weird

The first video clip shows a beautiful Japanese woman kneeling on a tatami mat in the centre of an elegant, dimly lit room. She adjusts her bright red kimono, blinks and then starts reciting from *Stolen*, a Japanese best-selling memoir written by Aki Kimura, who was sexually assaulted by three US marines on Okinawa Island in the 1990s. In the second clip, she spends twenty minutes talking in explicit detail about an alien abduction. In the third, she lectures on why Sun Air crash survivor Hiro Yanagida is a national treasure, a symbol of Japan's endurance and identity.

These clips, which first appeared on the Japanese video-sharing platform Nico Nico Douga, have gone viral, attracting more hits than any clip in the history of the site. What makes them so compelling has little to do with the eclectic subject matter of the woman's monologues, and everything to do with the woman herself. You see, the woman isn't human. She's a surrobot – the android doppelgänger of Aikao Uri, a former pop idol who hit it big in the 1990s before retiring to marry politician Masamara Uri. Aikao is no slouch when it comes to notoriety. Rarely out of the news, she started a fashion craze for shaved eyebrows in the early 2000s, is fervently anti-American (this is rumoured to stem from her failure to make it in Hollywood in the mid-nineties), always wears traditional Japanese dress as a rejection of western fashion ideals and most controversially of all, recently shared her belief that she has been abducted by aliens several times since her childhood.

Watching Aikao Uri's surrabot talk is disconcerting. It takes several seconds before your brain adjusts and you realise there's something just…wrong about the otherwise eloquent woman. Her cadence is unemotional, her mannerisms just a split second too slow to be convincing. And her eyes are dead.

Aikao freely admits that she commissioned her own surrabot after the news broke that Sun Air crash survivor Hiro Yanagida will only communicate via the android doppelgänger made by his father, a renowned robotics expert. Aikao believes that speaking through surrabots, which are controlled remotely, using state-of-the-art camera and voice-capturing equipment, 'will bring us closer to a pure way of being'.

And Aikao isn't the only one who has embraced this 'pure way of being'. Known worldwide for their 'out there' fashion sense, young Japanese trend-setters are also jumping on the surrabot bandwagon. Those who can't afford their own surrabot (the cheapest android doppelgängers can cost up to 45,000 US dollars) have taken to purchasing realistic mannequins and sex dolls and modifying them. The streets around Harajuku – where cosplayers traditionally congregate to show off their style – is buzzing with fashionistas, both male and female, eager to flaunt their own versions of the surrabot craze, which has been dubbed 'The Cult of Hiro'.

There's even talk that girl bands, such as the wildly successful AKB 48 ensemble and the Sunny Juniors, are creating their own all dancing, all lip-synching surrabot line.

In mid-April I flew out to Cape Town, South Africa to meet with Vincent Xhati, a private investigator who was on a full-time retainer to discover the whereabouts of the elusive Kenneth Oduah – the so-called 'fourth horseman'.

The Arrivals area at the Cape Town International Airport is teeming with wannabe tour guides, all shouting, 'Taxi, lady?' and waving fliers for 'all-inclusive Khayelitsha tours' in my face. Despite the chaos, it's easy to spot Vincent Xhati, the private investigator who's agreed to escort me around Cape Town for a couple of days. At six foot four and weighing in at three hundred pounds, he towers over the taxi drivers and tour operators. He greets me with a wide grin, and immediately takes charge of my luggage. We make small talk as we push through the throng towards the parking lot. A couple of jaded male cops in blue uniforms saunter around, eyeing everyone with suspicion, but neither they, nor the signs warning new arrivals not to 'go off with strangers', appear to be deterring the tour hawkers. Vincent bats a couple of the more tenacious away with a snapped '*Voetsek.*'

Exhausted after the sixteen-hour flight, I'm dying for a coffee and a shower, but when Vincent asks me if I'd like to go straight to the Dalu Air crash site before checking into my hotel, I say yes. He nods in approval and ushers me towards his car, a slick black BMW with tinted windows. 'No one will mess with us in this,' he says. 'We will look like a politician.' He pauses, glances at me, and then roars with laughter.

I sink into the passenger seat, noting that there's a copy of the grainy photograph of Kenneth Oduah – taken when he was four years old – mounted on the dashboard.

As we leave the airport behind and glide onto a slip road, I spot Table Mountain in the far distance, cloud dribbling over its edge. It's heading into winter, but the sky is a perfect, eggshell blue. Vincent sweeps onto the highway, and I'm immediately struck by the obvious signs of poverty around us. The airport facilities may have been state-of-the-art, but the road is flanked by sagging shacks and Vincent is forced to brake sharply as a small child dragging a dog on a rope lead zigzags through the traffic.

'It is not far,' Vincent says, clicking his tongue as he's forced to undertake a rusty mini-bus packed full of commuters that's hogging the fast lane.

I ask him who has hired him to search for Kenneth and he smiles and shakes his head. The journalist who gave me Vincent's details assured me that Vincent could be trusted, but I can't help feeling a stab of unease. I ask him about the reports of the Kenneth hunters who have been mugged.

He sighs. 'The press have exaggerated this. Only the ones who behaved in a stupid manner have had trouble.'

I ask him if he believes Kenneth is actually out there somewhere.

'It doesn't matter what I believe. Maybe the child is here somewhere, maybe he isn't. If he can be found, I will find him.'

We pull off the highway, and on our right I make out the edges of a vast area crammed with small brick houses, tin and wood shacks, and row after row of outhouses that look like sentry boxes.

'Is that Khayelitsha?'

'Ja.'

'How long have you been looking for him?'

'Since the beginning. It has not been an easy ride. There was some trouble at first from the Muslim community who tried to stop people talking to those of us who were searching for him.'

'Why?'

'You did not have that in America? Ah. The trouble-makers assumed that Kenneth was a Muslim boy, and they objected to the Americans coming here and claiming that he was one of their messengers. Then it was made public that he is from a Christian family, and now they don't care!' Another roar of laughter.

'I take it you are not religious?'

He sobers up. 'No. I have seen too much.'

He turns right, and within minutes we're in the heart of the township. The dirt roads that weave through the endless rows of shacks are unmarked. There's a proliferation of Coke signs, most attached to old shipping containers that I realise are makeshift shops. A group of small children dressed in dirty shorts wave and grin at the car, then whoop and chase after it. Vincent pulls to the side of the road, hands one of the children ten rand and instructs him to watch the BMW. The kid puffs out his chest and nods.

A few hundred metres from us, a tour bus is parked alongside a row of hawkers selling their wares. I watch as an American couple pick up a wirework sculpture of a plane and start haggling with a vendor.

'We'll walk from here,' Vincent says. 'Stay close to me and don't make eye contact with any of the locals.'

'Okay.'

Another laugh. 'Don't worry, you're fine here.'

'Do you live here?'

'No. I live in Gugs. Gugulethu.'

I've seen the aerial footage of the place where the plane went down, tearing a jagged passage through the landscape, but the people here are clearly tenacious, and already there is little sign of the devastation. Construction is starting on a new church and shacks have already grown up all over the sites where the fires raged. A gleaming black glass pyramid, engraved with the names of those who lost their lives (including that of Kenneth Oduah), sits incongruously in the centre.

Vincent sinks to his haunches and runs his fingers through the soil. 'They still find bits. Bones and pieces of metal. They worm their way up out of the earth. You know like when you have a wound? A splinter? The earth is rejecting them.'

The mood is subdued as we retrace our steps and head back onto the highway. More mini-buses whiz past, packed full of people heading into the city. Table Mountain races towards us, the cloud now obscuring its trademark flat top.

'I will take you to your hotel and then we will go hunting tonight, okay?'

Cape Town's Waterfront area, where my glass and steel-skeletoned hotel sits, couldn't be more of a contrast to where I've just been. It's almost like being in a different country. Hard to believe that the designer stores and five-star restaurants are just a short taxi ride away from the poverty of the township.

I shower, then head down to the bar and make some calls while I wait for Vincent. There are several middle-aged men hanging around in small groups, and I do my best to eavesdrop. Many are American.

I've been trying to secure an interview with the South African Civil Aviation Authority's head investigator, but her office has declined to talk to the press. I dial the number anyway. The secretary I speak to sounds weary. 'It is all in the report. There were no survivors.' I am also stonewalled in my efforts to talk to the aid workers who were first on the scene after the crash.

Vincent breezes into the hotel as if he owns the place; equally at home in this extravagant luxury as he is in the heart of Khayelitsha.

I tell him about my strike-outs with the CAA.

'You can forget them. But I will see what I can do about getting others to talk to you.'

He gets a call on his cell. The conversation is brief and in Xhosa.

'My associate has rounded up tonight's boys.' He sighs. 'It will come to nothing. But I must follow them up. My boss wants a full report every day.'

We head down towards the docks, slowing when we reach an underpass. The area is gloomy and ill-lit and I feel another stirring of unease.

Vincent's associate, a small wiry man called Eric Malenga, is waiting for us under a partially completed fly-over. He's surrounded by three scruffy boys, all of whom appear to be unsteady on their feet. I learn later that many street kids are addicted to sniffing glue, and the solvent they inhale makes them uncoordinated. Vincent tells me that these children scratch a living begging and hustling in the town centre. 'Sometimes they get tourists to buy them cereal and milk, and then they sell it to the back-packers,' he says. 'Others sell their bodies.'

As we approach, I notice a fourth child sitting apart

from them on an overturned crate. He's shivering, but I can't tell if this is from fear or the bite in the air.

The tallest of the kids – a skinny boy with a runny nose – perks up when he sees us approach and points to the child on the crate. 'There he is, boss. That's Kenneth. Do I get my reward now, boss?'

Vincent tells me that the latest 'Kenneth' isn't even Nigerian. He's the racial classification known as 'coloured', a word that makes me wince.

Vincent nods wearily at Eric, who ushers the small child towards his car.

'Where is Eric taking him?' I ask.

'One of the shelters,' Vincent says. 'Away from this bunch of skebengas.'

'But he said he was Kenneth, boss,' the boy with the runny nose whines. 'He told us, I swear.'

'You know why everyone is looking for Kenneth?' I ask.

'Ja, lady. They think he is the devil.'

'That's not true,' says another boy. 'He needs to go to a sangoma; he's possessed by the spirit of a witch. If you meet him, then you don't have long to live.'

'He only comes out at night,' the third one chimes in. 'If he touches you, the part of the body he touches will die. He can spread Aids even.'

'Ja. I heard that too,' the tall boy – clearly the ringleader – says. 'I know someone who has seen him, lady. If you give me a hundred, I'll take you.'

'These boys don't know anything,' Vincent says, but he hands them each twenty rand, and sends them on their way. They whoop and run off unsteadily into the night. 'This is what it is like all the time. But I have to be thorough, make my report every day. Most days I check the morgue in case he shows up there, but I won't take you there.'

The next day Vincent meets me at my hotel to say that he's heading out to the West Coast to 'follow a lead'. He puts me in touch with a cop at a Khayelitsha police station who he says will talk to me, gives me the name of a paramedic who arrived at the scene minutes after the crash, and passes on the cellphone number of a woman who had lost her home in the devastation. 'She knows something,' he says. 'Maybe she will talk to you. A foreigner.' Then, with another wide grin and a complicated handshake, he leaves.

(Ten days later, I'm at home in Manhattan, when I receive a text message from Vincent. All it says is: <they got him>)

The following statement was taken at the Buitenkant
Police Station in Cape Town on 2 May 2012.

SOUTH AFRICAN POLICE SERVICE

EK / I: Brian van der Merwe

OUDERDOM / AGE: 37

WOONAGTIG / RESIDING: 16 Eucalyptus Street,
Bellville, Cape Town

TELEPHONE: 021 911 6789

WERKSAAM TE / EMPLOYED AT: Kugel Insurance
Brokers, Pinelands

TELEPHONE 021 531 8976

VERKLAAR IN AFRIKAANS ONDER EED:

STATES IN ENGLISH UNDER OATH:

On the night of 2 May 2012 at approximately 10.30 p.m., I
was aprehended (*sic*) at the bottom of Long Street, Cape
Town CBD outside the Beares Furniture Store. I had
stopped to give a child a lift in my car when I realised that
police officers had pulled up in their vehicle next to me.

I told the officers that the reason I stopped was because

I was worried for the child's safety. The boy, who was aged eight or nine, shouldn't have been out there at that time of night and I had pulled over to offer him a lift.

I deny that I solicited the boy for sex, and when officers found me in the car, I deny that my jeans were undone and that the boy was performing a sexual act on my person.

Sergeant Manjit Kumar pulled me out of the car and gave me a smack across my face, which I insist be recorded here. Then he asked the boy his name. The boy did not answer. One of the other officers, Constable Lucy Pistorius, said to the boy, Are you Kenneth? The boy said yes.

I did not resist arrest.

RvdMerwe
HANDTEKENING / SIGNATURE

Andiswa Matebele (not her real name) is the head carer at a place of safety for abandoned and abused children in Cape Town (the exact location cannot be disclosed for obvious reasons). Andiswa agreed to talk to me via phone on the condition that I not reveal her name or the location of the place of safety.

Shame, when the boy was first brought to us he was very undernourished, and even before I gave him a bath, I made sure that he had a large bowl of putu and lamb stew. I was very worried about him, and not just because the sores on his legs and arms were infected. He had seen a doctor, who prescribed antibiotics, and he was given a course of ARVs as there were signs that he may have been working as a sex worker. This is not uncommon for street children. Many of them have been abused by their parents, and they know of no other way to survive.

What can I tell you about the boy? He did not have a Nigerian accent as far as I could tell, but it was difficult to be sure as he so rarely spoke. He seemed to be older than seven years, which is the age of Kenneth Oduah. As he ate, I asked him, 'Is your name Kenneth?'

'Yes, my name is Kenneth,' he said. But then, later on, I found that I could ask him anything and he would agree with me.

The next day, a forensics team came to the shelter and took a saliva swab from him so that they could run a DNA test. I was informed that the boy would be staying here until they could be sure that he was indeed Kenneth. I felt very strongly that if the boy did in fact turn out to be this child, then he should be reunited with his aunt and family as soon as possible.

I am not from Khayelitsha, but I have been to the memorial site and seen where that plane went down. I do find it hard to believe that anyone could have survived such a thing, but it was the same with the crash in America and the ones in Asia and Europe, so I did not know what to think. Little by little, by asking him direct questions, I managed to extract the boy's story. He said that he had lived for a while on the beach in Blouberg, then in Kalk Bay and then he had decided to make his way back to the CBD.

I kept a close eye on him to ensure that the other children did not bully him – this can happen – but most of them gave him a wide berth. I did not tell them who he might be. I was the only person who had that knowledge. Some of the other staff are superstitious and already there was talk that if a boy had survived the crashes, then it was certain he was a witch of some type.

Two weeks later we heard that the DNA did indeed match Kenneth Oduah's aunt, and it wasn't long before the authorities organised a big press conference. I assumed that Kenneth would be taken away almost immediately after that, but then the police called to say that Kenneth's aunt had fallen sick (perhaps from the shock of hearing about her nephew) and so could not travel from Lagos to formally identify and collect the boy. They told me another family member, a distant one, was en route instead.

He arrived the next day, and said he was the cousin of Kenneth's father. I asked him if he was sure that the boy was his relative and he was adamant that he was.

'Do you know this man, Kenneth?' I asked the boy.

'I know this man,' the boy said.

'Do you want to go with him or stay here with us?'

The boy did not know what to say to that. If you asked him, 'Do you want to stay?' he would say, 'I want to stay,' but then, if I asked him, 'Do you want to go with this man?' he would say, 'I want to go.'

He did not seem to know what was going on.

He was taken away that night.

The following article was published in the UK's *Evening Standard* online edition on 18 May 2012.

Rapture Fever Sweeps the US

An enterprising pastor has opened the first drive-through baptism centre in San Antonio, Texas, where, for the price of a Happy Meal, you can secure your place in heaven.

'You can get saved on your lunch hour!' Pastor Vincent Galbraith (48) beams. 'Just drive on in, take Jesus into your heart and drive back to work in the knowledge that when the Rapture comes, you'll be one of God's chosen.'

Pastor Galbraith, a follower of Dr Theodore Lund's End Times movement, came up with the idea after his church was overrun by panicked wannabe Christians who had taken on board the bizarre theory that The Three, and now Kenneth Oduah, are the harbingers of the apocalypse. And so far, even though it's been open for less than a week, the lines snake around the block. 'People are getting desperate and rightly so,' the former insurance salesman turned pastor says. 'Those signs can't be ignored and I knew someone had to come up with a solution. We're not picky. I don't care what your religious affiliation was before. Muslim, Jew, atheist, all are welcome. You never know when the Lord is gonna call us to Him.' He chuckles. 'And at this rate I'm thinking about franchising it.'

Pastor Galbraith's new enterprise is only one of the many indications that thousands of people in the US's

Bible Belt and beyond are taking the Riders of the Apocalypse theory seriously. In a recent poll undertaken by CNN in conjunction with *Time* magazine, a whopping 69% of Americans believe that the events of Black Thursday could be a sign that the end of the world is imminent.

In Kentucky, Hannigan Lewis (52) is proselytising the 'Down Tools' movement. 'The Rapture could happen at any time,' says the ex fork-lift driver. 'If you are flying a plane, driving a bus, and you're one of the saved, well hell, when you're taken up to Heaven all of a sudden, think of the carnage.' Borrowing a phrase from an unpopular UK Conservative Party campaign, he's encouraging Rapture believers to get 'back to basics' and divorce themselves from any technology that could potentially harm those left behind when the faithful are raptured.

But not all American believers are buying into the theory. Pastor Kennedy Olax, the head of the Austin-based Christians for Change organisation, says: 'We would counsel people not to give in to the hysteria sweeping the country at this time. There is no reason to panic. The ridiculous and unproven horseman theory is nothing but fear-mongering, stemming from a desire to whip up the religious right and get Reynard into the White House now that we're in an election year.'

Other groups are worried about the political and social changes this religious hysteria could bring. And now that Dr Lund and his rapidly growing End Times movement have publicly backed hard-line Republican presidential hopeful Mitch Reynard, their concerns appear to be increasingly legitimate. 'We're worried,' said Gay and Lesbian League spokesperson Poppy Abrams (37). 'We know that Dr Lund is working hard to draw together all the disparate evangelical and fundamentalist groups that make up the religious right, and Mitch Reynard is running on anti–gay marriage and pro-life platforms. He may not be ahead in the polls yet, but his support is growing daily.'

Iman Arif Hamid of the US Islamic Coalition is more philosophical. 'We are not worried that there will be a backlash against Muslims like we saw after 9/11. Most of the vitriol appears to be targeted at the abortion clinics and the homosexual community. So far there have been no reports about Muslim citizens being marginalised.'

Although the horseman theory hasn't yet caused the same level of panic in the UK, many British clerics of all denominations, from Catholic to Church of England, have seen an increase in church attendance. And now that the so-called fourth horseman has been found, maybe it's only a matter of time before we're super-sizing our own baptisms on this side of the Atlantic.

Reba Louise Neilson.

It pains me to talk about this, Elspeth. But I feel I need to tell my side. People out there need to know that there are good Christian folk in Sannah County who never wanted any harm to come to those children.

I reckon Pastor Len really started letting the devil into his heart just after Kendra upped and left, and Dr Lund broke away from him for good. Then there were all those reporters making fun of him (Stephenie said they even did a skit about him on *Saturday Night Live*, though she doesn't usually watch that kind of programming). And all those folks, the Lookie-Loos, they didn't help any. A whole new wave of them came after they found Kenneth Oduah out in Africa and people started saying that Bobby Small's grandfather had started talking again even though he had that Alzheimer's. There were so many I heard he had to hire in some of those chemical toilets and you could barely see Pastor Len's ranch from the road for the number of Winnebagos and pick-ups that were parked on his property. I'm not saying some of them weren't good Christian folk, but I'd see them around town sometimes and some of them had a lost look in their eyes, as if their souls were broken. People like that Monty.

But in my opinion, the real tipping point was Jim.

Glory, that was a terrible day. I can recall it right down to the last detail. I was in the kitchen, fixing Lorne a sandwich – bologna and cheese, his favourite. I had the TV on in the kitchen, and Mitch Reynard was being interviewed by Miranda Stewart, talking about how the US

had been going to hell in a hand basket, and that the time
was ripe to get the country back onto a good moral footing (Stephenie thinks he looks a little bit like that George
Clooney, but I'm not so sure). He and Dr Lund were
always on the news around that time. They were being
lambasted left, right and centre by the liberal element, but
they stuck to their guns, and rightly so. The phone rang
just as I was about to take Lorne his lunch. When I heard
Pastor Len's voice on the other end of the line, I don't
mind admitting that I felt uncomfortable. I thought maybe
he was going to ask me why I hadn't been at church or
Bible study for a while, but all he wanted to know was if
I'd seen Jim. Pastor Len said he was planning one of his
special early-morning prayer meetings, and Jim had
agreed to come over to the ranch and talk to the new
Lookie-Loos about what a good woman Pamela had been.
I said that I hadn't seen Jim for a week or so, but I was fixing to take him a lasagne that evening. Pastor Len asked
me if I wouldn't mind going over there early to check on
him as he wasn't answering his phone. He said he hoped
to see me at church that Sunday, then hung up.

I couldn't settle for a good half-an-hour after that –
part of me still felt guilty for turning my back on the
church like that – and then I called around the Inner Circle to see if anyone had any news about Jim. Fact is, by
then, most people had stopped taking him food and
checking up on him. Stephenie, Lena and I were the only
ones left who still went by occasionally, though he never
seemed grateful. Next, I tried Jim's number three or four
times, but there was no answer. Lorne was out back, and I
asked him if he'd drive me over to Jim's place to make
sure he hadn't passed out drunk and maybe hit his head.

I thank the Lord every day that Lorne had the day off; I could never have faced it on my own. I knew that something untoward had happened the second we pulled up. I could see it by the number of flies that were crawling on the inside of the screen door. It was black with them.

Lorne called Manny Beaumont straight away, and we stayed in the truck while he and his deputy went inside. Sheriff Beaumont said it was obvious it was suicide; Jim had put his shotgun in his mouth and blown his head clean off his shoulders. And he'd left a note addressed to Pastor Len. We didn't know what it said until Pastor Len read it out at Jim's funeral. That's when things really took a turn.

Jim may have committed a sin against God by taking his own life, but me, Stephenie and a few of the other Inner Circle folk agreed to do the flowers for his service. The church was packed to the rafters with Pastor Len's Lookie-Loos, strangers who'd never even known Jim. Lorne said that Pastor Len was playing up to the TV cameras that were there, no doubt hoping that Dr Lund would see him on the news.

'Jim is a martyr,' Pastor Len said. 'One of the witnesses, like his wife, Pamela. Time is running out. There are still thousands that need to be saved before it is too late. We need more time and Jesus, He ain't gonna wait forever.'

Lorne says the authorities should have stopped him right then and there. But what could Sheriff Beaumont do? This is America, people have a right to do what they want on their own land, and Pastor Len wasn't breaking any laws. Not then he wasn't. He didn't come right out and say that those children should be killed.

Pastor Len had been my guiding light for the longest

time. I'd trusted in his words, heeded his sermons, looked up to him. But what he was saying, about Pamela being a prophet, and that Jim killing himself wasn't a sin but his way of showing us that the fifth seal had been opened, didn't sit right with me, and that's a fact. I believe that Jesus spoke to me and said, Reba, break away. Break away now. For good. So that's what I did. And I know in my heart that I did the right thing.

Although Private First Class Jake Wallace attempted to destroy his laptop's hard drive after he disappeared from his base on Okinawa Island, the following correspondence was recovered by an anonymous hacker and posted on the popular debunking blog, VigilanteHacks, as alleged proof that Pastor Len Vorhees played a part in Jake Wallace's subsequent actions.

To: **bearingthecross@aol.com**
From: **messenger778@moxy.com**
Date: 25/04/2012

Dear Sir,

   Thank you for the last link to your latest sermon on YouTube. It was awesome to hear your voice and know that you are thinking of your Messengers all over the world. But it made me mad to read the disrespectful comments below it. I did what you said and didn't respond to them altho I wanted to with all of my heart!!!!! I also set up another email address under another name like you said to do as you can see!!!!!

   I have lots to tell you Sir. You said to tell you if I had another one of my dreams about Mrs Pamela May Donald. I had one last night. This time I came out of my tent and into the forest clearing where the crash happened. Mrs Donald was lying on her back, and her face was covered with a thin white shroud. When she breathed in the shroud fell into her open mouth and I had to try to pull it out so that she would not suffacate [*sic*]. The shroud felt greasy and slipped in my hands and then she was gone and my sister Cassie was there and she also had a shroud and she said to me Jake I can't breathe either and then I woke up. I was as cold as I was in the forest and I had to bite my fist to stop from screaming again.

Sir, without your messages I would feel so alone. Even the Christian marines here make jokes about the boy and the robot that he speaks thru and they just don't see that it is no joking matter. There is a group who are copying what the kid is doing and talking only thru robots and False Idols and I am afraid that the Antichrist's influence is spreading even to this island. I am keeping a low profile like you said and just doing my duty and my training, but it is hard. If we can save one person, isn't that what we must do? There are American families and children here and innocents. Isn't it my duty as a Messenger to save others before it is too late?

Yours Faithfully,

J

To: **messenger778@moxy.com**
From: **bearingthecross@aol.com**
Date: 26/04/2012

True Messenger,

It is our lot and our Burden to be surrounded by those who refuse to see the truth. Be careful that they do not worm their way into your heart with their lies and their charm causing Doubt. Doubt is the demon you must be on your guard against. This is why I am saying to you to keep a low profile. I see your point about the innocents and I myself also struggle with this, but the time will come when we will stage the final battle and then those who have taken the Truth into their hearts will be saved.

How I rejoiced to hear of your dream! It is another SIGN! Like our prophet Pamela May Donald, you were shown proof in that forest when you saw those who will be taken up and Saved. Pamela May Donald is showing you the true way. She is showing you that like the bile spewed forth by the false prophets Flexible Sandy and Dr Theodore Lund, words are empty and only ACTIONS matter when the time comes to be tested.

You are being tested, Jake. You are being tested by the Lord our God to see if you will stray from the path. YOU and YOU alone are our voice and heart in that heathen nation. I know it is lonely, but you will receive your reward. The signs are building, Jake. The signs are BUILDING. My Messengers are growing, as more and more of the chosen have flocked to join me. But you, you who are out on his own, in a land of the Heathen, are the bravest of us all.

He which soweth sparingly shall reap also sparingly; and he which soweth bountifully shall reap also bountifully.

Remember the Ears and Eyes of the many-headed AntiChrist are watching all of our Messengers so be vigilant.

To: **bearingthecross@aol.com**
From: **messenger778@moxy.com**
Date: 07/05/2012

Dear Sir,

It is good of you to write to me so often as I know that you must be very busy now that your true Messengers are joining you in person as well as in spirit. I wish with all my HEART that I could be with them but I know this is not part of God's plan for me!!!!

You're [*sic*] words bring me True Comfort but your meaning is clear, do not worry Sir I am being careful and always delete them as you said I should.

There was another anti-US base protest in Urima yesterday. I felt a strong urge to go and speak to the Heathens to tell them that they must turn to Jesus before it is too late. In Luke it says that we must love our enemies, do good to them, and lend to them without expecting to get anything back, but I knew that for the Greater Good I shouldn't do that.

Yours faithfully,

J

To: **bearingthecross@aol.com**
From: **messenger778@moxy.com**
Date: 20/05/2012

Dear Sir,

I have been checking my email everyday now and I have run thru my mind everything I have said in case I have offended you as I haven't got an email from you for a while and then I saw the news about the death of Pamela May Donald's husband.

It says that he committed the sin of suicide. Can this be right?

I know you must be very busy with your Mourning but please try and write to me even if it is only one line as reading your words gives me strength. I have tried to find your website but I can't get on to it any more which makes me worry that you and the other True Believers have been overtaken by those who are working for the Antichrist.

Sir, I need your Help. There are floods in the Philippines, which has to be another sign of the evil overtaking the world. Some of the guys say that my unit is going to be shipped out to help with the rescue efforts. Can I still be your Voice and Heart and Ears and Eyes if I leave here?

I feel very alone.

J

To: **bearingthecross@aol.com**
From: **messenger778@moxy.com**
Date: 21/05/2012

Sir? Are you there? My unit leaves in 3 days what should I do?

To: **messenger778@moxy.com**
From: **bearingthecross@aol.com**
Date: 21/05/2012

True Messenger,

You are not alone. You must have faith that even in my Silence I am by your side. We are being persecuted and belittled by the False Prophets and their Flatterers but we will not break.

I have sent you a copy of my last blog post, which explains Jim Donald's actions.

Jim Donald like his Beloved Wife has sacrificed himself to tell us the Real Truth, the Truth that I have suspected since the beginning when Pamela May Donald paid the ultimate price to personally send her prophecy.

You are one of the chosen. You are special. We are facing a Holy War and time is running out. It is time for God's Soldiers to step forward. Are you prepared to be one of God's Soldiers?

We need to talk but not where the eyes and ears of the Antichrist and his Flatterers can hear. Let me know of a time I can call you where we will be undisturbed.

To: **bearingthecross@aol.com**
From: **messenger778@moxy.com**
Date: 27/05/2012

Dear Sir,

I am sorry to go against your wishes but this is agony to me! I keep thinking about my family and my sister especially who haven't been saved and what will happen to them if they do not see the Truth before it is too late.

I have received your donation. I have made contact with a group who I think can help me leave but I am not sure.

I am in the sick bay like you said I should so I cannot write for long. My unit has left. Can we talk again? I need to hear your voice as I am having Doubts.
    J

To: **messenger778@moxy.com**
From: **bearingthecross@aol.com**
Date: 27/05/2012

DO NOT contact me again. I will contact you.

Although Pastor Len's website, pamelaprophet.com, is no longer up and running, the following entry was cached on 19 May 2012.

My heart has been truly warmed by the messages I've been receiving following our Brother Jim Donald's Martyrdom.

For that's what he was, Loyal Messengers. Jim Donald was a martyr. He was a martyr who gave up his life for all of us just like his dear wife Pamela did. I urge you not to take any credence of Dr Lund's words that by taking his own life Jim Donald was committing a sin. Jim is a martyr who died so that we would know the truth. A prophet who sacrificed himself to bring us the Good News that God in His Glory has chosen to open the fifth seal.

As it says in Revelation 6:9, *And when he had opened the fifth seal, I saw under the altar the souls of them that were slain for the word of God, and for the testimony which they held.*

Loyal Messengers, Jim Donald, like Pamela May Donald, was a martyr to his beliefs. I was there when he was saved, after he mourned the death of his beloved wife, and at the moment of his death, God chose to send him a vision.

I'm choosing to put his last words here for you all to see:

Why were they saved and not her? She was a good person and a good wife and I don't want to do this any more they are not rite in the head they are evil. They brought on the deaths of thousands and will bring on the deaths of more UNLESS THEY ARE STOPPED.

Jim's meaning, just like Pamela's, is clear. Time is running out for all of us and we must do what we can to bring as many people to the Pamelist flock as soon as we can. Is there a higher calling than saving as many as we can before that sixth seal is opened?

Pamela May Donald was the Lord's conduit. She was the vessel through which His message was conveyed. Dr Lund and those other charlatans have tried to hijack her message and Jim has proved this. Dr Lund does not believe that the fifth seal has yet been opened, but he is wrong.

'The boy, warn them,' Pamela May Donald told me.

And they cried with a loud voice, saying, How long, O Lord, holy and true, dost thou not judge and avenge our blood on they that dwell on the earth?

Lorne Neilson reluctantly agreed to be interviewed in July 2012. This account is an edited version of our conversation.

I'm gonna come right out and say it: I never trusted Len Vorhees. Not from the first day he arrived in Sannah County. Could talk the talk, all right, but far as I was concerned, that man was all hat and no cattle.

But Reba took to him right away and I guess it saved us driving over to Denham County every Sunday for church. None of us knew what to think when he started saying that those kids were the four horsemen. Reba was loyal to that church, and I wasn't going to push her. Way I saw it, it was plain that Len was using a dead woman's last words for his own ends, as a means to get in with those big-time preachers up in Houston. Then he went and mixed Jim Donald up in that. Jim could be as mean as a box of snakes, but Pam's death hit him hard. Stopped coming into work, wouldn't talk to his buddies. Len shoulda let him be, let him drink himself to death if that's what he wanted.

You know who I blame for it all going bad? Not Jim and not even those reporters who spread it all over the newspapers and TV. I blame Dr Lund and that writer guy, Flexible Sandy. They encouraged Len right from the beginning. No one can say they're not guilty, no matter what slick language they use to deny it.

A week after Jim's funeral, Stephenie's cousin Billy had to deliver some lumber to Len's ranch, and he asked me to ride along with him. Said he didn't want to go up there on his own, and his regular man was down with that puke virus that was hitting the county. Reba asked me to take along some of her canned peaches. 'For the children out there.'

It'd been a while since I'd last been to Len's ranch, must have been near Christmas or thereabouts. I'd seen all those new people of course, driving around in their pick-ups and SUVs with dented sides, and part of me was curious to see what was going on up there. Billy said it made him uneasy being around them. Most were from the state, but others had driven up from as far away as New Orleans.

We got up to the gate, saw that there were a couple of men standing there. One of them was that Monty guy, the one Reba took against. They waved us down, asked us what we wanted, like they were sentries. Billy told them and they stood back, let us go through, but they stared at us real suspicious.

There weren't as many trailers or tents as I expected, but there were enough. Kids were running everywhere; women huddled in groups. As we drove up, I could sense them watching us. I said to Billy that Grayson Thatcher, who used to work the place before Len came, would've near had a heart attack if he'd seen what had happened to his ranch.

Soon as we drew up, Pastor Len came striding out of the ranch-house, this big grin on his face, and a couple of guys appeared from the barn, started unloading the wood.

I greeted him as polite as I could, handed over the peaches Reba had sent.

'Thank her for me, Lorne,' he said. 'She's a good woman. Tell her I'd be mightily glad to see her out here on Sunday. I was sorry to close the church in town, but God has shown me that my path leads here.'

Course, I had no intention of telling Reba any such thing.

Then, coming from the pasture out back, I heard gunfire. Sounded like automatic weapons, too. 'What you doing out there, Len? Hunting season's closed.'

'We gotta keep sharp, Lorne. God's work isn't only about prayers.'

It's everyone's God-given right to protect himself. I taught my girls how to shoot, same as me and Reba have been encouraging them to be prepared for any of those solar flares they're predicting will occur. But this sounded like a whole nother rodeo – like they were fixing for some sort of battle. The more I looked around, the worse I got to feeling. It was clear they were fixing to set up some kind of secure compound. Rolls of barbed wire stacked up next to the old feed barn, and Billy said they were more than likely going to be using that wood to build some kind of fence.

Billy and I got out of there as fast as we could. 'You think we should tell Sheriff Beaumont 'bout what they're doing out here?' Billy asked.

You could see it was going to go bad, you could smell it as if it was two-day-old roadkill.

So we went and saw Manny Beaumont. Asked him if he knew what was going on up at that ranch. Manny said that until the Pamelists broke any laws, there wasn't nothing he could do about them. Lots of questions were asked later. Why weren't the FBI monitoring his emails, things like that, like they do with those Islamofascists? Guess they didn't reckon on a backwater preacher being able to reach out into the wider world and cause the trouble that he did. Or maybe they were worried they'd have another Waco on their hands if they tried to shut him down.

Before Private First Class Jake Wallace left Okinawa Island, he sent the following email to his parents in Virginia on 11 June 2012. It was released to the press after his body was formally identified.

Mom, Dad,

I'm doing this for you and Cassie.

Someone has to become God's Soldier in the Fight for Souls and I have stepped up to do my duty. The signs are getting clearer. Those floods in the Philippines, the war that's going to happen in North Korea. The fourth Horseman they found down in Africa.

I got to work fast now as time is running out.

I am writing this to beg you to go and get Saved and take Jesus into your hearts before it is too late.

Dad, I know you don't believe, and I am begging you as your son to please look at the evidence. God would not lie to us. You used to tell me that 9/11 was a government conspiracy and you would get pissed when none of us agreed with you. Please, Dad. Take Mom and Cassie to church and take the Lord into your heart. TIME IS RUNNING OUT.

I will see you in heaven when Jesus takes us up to his bosom.

Your Son,
Jake

Monty Sullivan, the only Pamelist who agreed to speak to me, is currently incarcerated in the North Infirmary Command Protective Custody section at Rikers Island, where he is awaiting trial. We spoke via phone.

EM: *When did you first hear about Pastor Len Vorhees and his theory about the horsemen?*

MONTY SULLIVAN: I guess it was right at the beginning. I was a truck driver back then, delivering chickens from Shelby County to all over the state. The CB was quieter than usual, and I'd started playing the radio dials, looking for a rock station. Back then, I wasn't into those religious shows at all. Heck, I didn't even like country that much. When I was crossing into Sannah County, I came across Pastor Len's show. Something about his voice got my attention.

EM: *Can you be more specific?*

MS: He sounded like he truly believed what he was saying. A lot of pastors and preachers you hear on the radio and TV, you get the idea that all they're after is poor folks' hard-earned cash. I was never much into religion back then, got turned off it when I was younger because of my ma. She was a real believer, sent off a monthly tithe to one of those super-church preachers down in Houston even when we didn't have food in the house. I could tell Pastor Len was different, he didn't once ask folks to send him any cash. And what he was

saying, it caught my attention straight off. Course, Black
Thursday was all over the news, and lots of preachers,
specially the evangelicals, were saying it was another
sign that we were all heading for Armageddon. Said
the same thing after 9/11, so that wasn't new. But Pastor
Len's point of view hit home. What he said about Pamela
May Donald's last words . . . The evidence was just too
strong. All those colours on the planes matching up with
the colours of the horsemen that John saw in Revelation;
the facts that those kids shouldn't have got away unhurt.
When I finished my run a couple of days later, I went
straight on the Internet, found Pastor Len's site,
pamelaprophet.com. He'd put all the evidence right there,
in black and white. I read it all, then dug out my ma's
Bible which was the only thing of hers I still had. I'd sold
the rest, though she didn't leave me much. Guess you
could say I was pretty wild in those days. I wasn't into
drugs or anything heavy, but I liked a drink back then, so
that's where the money went.

After I heard Pastor Len's show and read that website,
I don't think I slept for three days. I could feel something
growing inside me. Course, Pastor Len told me later it
was the Holy Spirit.

I sent him an email, saying how I'd been real impressed
by what he was saying. I didn't think there was much of a
chance I'd hear back from him. But I'm damned if he
didn't send me a message within the hour. And a personal
one, not one of those automated messages lots of people
use. I know it off by heart. Must've read it a million times:
'Monty, I sure appreciate you contacting me. Your faith
and honesty proves that I am on the right path, the path to
saving more good folks just like yourself.'

I waited till my day off, then I drove through the night, straight to Sannah County and Pastor Len's church. Waited in line to get saved. Had to have been fifty people that day and there was a real festive atmosphere. We all knew we were doing the right thing. When I introduced myself to Pastor Len as he came along the line, thanking us for coming to his church, I never thought he would recall who I was, but he knew me straight off. 'You're the fella who wrote me from Kendrick!' he said.

The way he explained things so clear, I realised that I'd been blind for years. It broke my ma's heart that I turned my back on the church when I was younger, and I wished that she could have lived long enough to see that I went back to Jesus' fold. How can I not have seen we were heading for the End of Days? How can the Lord not have been priming to bring down His judgement on us after what was going on in the world? The more I looked into it, the more it made my head spin. Do you know that children in America are made, *made* to read the Koran in schools? But not the Bible, no ma'am. Intelligent Design is banned, but not the handbook of the infidels? Then there's the gays and the baby murderers and the liberals conspiring to turn America into a godless nation. Dr Theodore Lund was right about that, even if he did turn his back on Pastor Len's truth afterwards. Turned out that Dr Lund just wanted all the glory that came from Pamela's message for himself. He wasn't dedicated to saving souls; not like Pastor Len was.

EM: *When did you decide to move to Sannah County?*

MS: After I was saved, I came home and wrote Pastor Len almost every day for a few weeks. I felt a calling to move closer to his church round about early March and become one of his Messengers. It wasn't a hard decision, the Lord was nudging me in that direction. When Pastor Len invited me to move to the ranch, I didn't think twice. Jacked in my job, sold my truck and hitched all the way to Sannah County. He needed me as his good right hand.

EM: *Do you have a history of violence?*

MS: Not really, ma'am. Just the odd schoolyard fight, couple of bust-ups back when I used to drink. Not saying I was squeaky clean, but I was never a violent individual. Never ran into any trouble with the law.

EM: *Where did the weapon you used to shoot Bobby Small come from?*

MS: That particular gun belonged to Jim Donald. Wasn't the one he used on himself, but one he'd given to us for safe-keeping. But I knew how to shoot. My father taught me how to use a gun before he cut out and left me and my ma, back when I was twelve.

EM: *Did you know Jim Donald?*

MS: Not well, ma'am. I met him once or twice. Pastor Len said he was struggling to come to terms with the death of his wife. Pastor Len did what he could to help him, but you could see Jim was real cut up about that. He was a real martyr, just like Pamela. He saw the truth about the destruction the horsemen had wrought on the world, and how they'd murdered those innocents on the planes.

EM: *Did Pastor Len instruct you to travel to New York to kill Bobby Small?*

MS: I did what anyone who cares about saving souls would have done. I was acting as God's soldier, doing what I could to eradicate the threat and give people more time to be saved before the Rapture. If we can stop the signs in their tracks, halt the horsemen's work, then we have more time to spread Jesus' message and bring more people into the fold. Now that they've found that fourth horseman, now that fire and brimstone is falling upon the earth with all those natural disasters – the floods in the Philippines and Europe, and those tsunami warnings in Asia – we don't have long.

EM: *But if you believe that the four horsemen are God's messengers, weren't you concerned that by attempting to murder Bobby Small you would be punished by God?*

MS: Now wait just one minute, ma'am. No one's talking about murder. When the Antichrist comes, when that sixth seal is broken, there's no going back. There's no guarantee that you'll get a second chance during the Tribulation. I am on God's side; He knows that Pastor Len and the Pamelists are working hard to bring more people into his fold. And those children were unnatural. Everyone could see that. After a while they started using their power and flaunting it. They may have started off as God's messengers, but I firmly believe what Jim told us – that they became tools of the Antichrist in the end.

EM: *Did Pastor Len Vorhees instruct you to shoot Bobby?*

MS: I can't answer that, ma'am.

EM: *Many people believe that you acted under Pastor Len Vorhees's influence and that he should be as accountable as you.*

MS: Jesus was punished for spreading God's truth. It doesn't matter to me what they say. I'll be in Jesus' arms soon. They can lock me up, they can put me in the chair, it's all the same to me. And maybe it's all part of Jesus' plan. I'm locked in here with sinners, and here's my chance to save as many of them as I can.

PART NINE

SURVIVORS

MAY–JUNE

In the weeks since Ryu first appeared on the 2-chan forum, the speculation over whether his princess was actually Hiro Yanagida's cousin grew to fever pitch. Ryu eventually returned to the forum under his Orz Man avatar.

NAME: ORZ MAN POST DATE: 2012/05/01 21:22:22.30
Hi guys. Don't know if any of u who were on the thread I started a while back are online. Blown away by the way u guys have jumped on my story.
   Just wanted to say thanks again.

NAME: ANONYMOUS23
Orz! Cool to have u back. So????? Did it work??? Did u get yr princess? （＾人＾）

NAME: ORZ MAN
Simple answer: Yes. We r now together.
[This is followed by at least a hundred variations on 'w00t', and 'u r such a Bad Ass Mutherfucker/Boss/ Man/The Dude' etc. Ryu goes on to explain how he sprayed an ORZ symbol outside Chiyoko's house to get her attention, much to the Netizens' glee.]

NAME: ANONYMOUS557
Orz. Got to know. Is the princess Android Boy's cousin?

NAME: ORZ MAN
I was waiting for you to ask me that…I've been following some of the threads. I can't confirm for obvious
reasons.

NAME: ANONYMOUS890
Orz, u met Android Boy yet?

NAME: ORZ MAN
See above. _|7O

NAME: ANONYMOUS330
How hot is the princess, dude?

NAME: ORZ MAN
How to answer this and be honest…
When I first saw her…She wasn't the person I thought
she was. But somehow, that didn't matter.

NAME: ANONYMOUS765
So she's the fat chick who was at the memorial service
and not the one who looks like Hazuki? Bummer, dude.

NAME: ANONYMOUS111
Welcome back, Orz. Ignore 765

NAME: ANONYMOUS762
Dude, get to the good bits. Have you done her yet????

NAME: ANONYMOUS111
Don't be crude. Let Orz Man speak

NAME: ORZ MAN

I'm going to sound soppy here, but guys, being with her has changed my life.

Even though she is a princess, we have more in common than I thought possible. She has also had a hard time in the past like me. We have the same views on everything: society, music, gaming, even politics. Yeah, we have heavy conversations sometimes!

Even started telling her stuff I haven't told anyone before.

She helped me find a job at a Lawsons outlet, so I now have some money coming in (not much, but enough to keep me from starving).

This is going to sound lame...but sometimes I have this dream that we are married and living together in an apartment and we never have to go out.

NAME: ANONYMOUS200

Aw. Yr making me jealous here, Orz.

NAME: ANONYMOUS201

Sounds like lurve.

NAME: ANONYMOUS7889

Come on, Orz Man, tell us about Hiro. Have you met his surrabot yet?

NAME: ANONYMOUS1211

What does he think about the Cult of Hiro?

NAME: ORZ MAN

Guys, no offence, but this is a public message board

and I can't talk about this in detail. The princess will freak out if anything I said got into the magazines.

NAME: ANONYMOUS111
U can trust us, Orz, but see yr point.

NAME: ORZ MAN
Let's just say that a certain person is soothing to be around. Not like anyone I have ever met.
That is all I am going to say.

NAME: ANONYMOUS764
How often do you see the princess?

NAME: ORZ MAN
Almost every night. Her parents are kind of strict, and they wouldn't approve of her seeing someone like me so we have to sneak around.

There's a small children's playground opposite her house and I wait there for her. There's an apartment block next to it, so sometimes I feel like I'm being watched, but I can stand it.

NAME: ANONYMOUS665
Orz smokes another cigarette, waiting for his princess to come out and join him. He knows he looks cool. Maybe tonight will be the night. Some of the neighbours look out of their windows at him but he knows they won't mess with him. He flexes his muscles and they disappear.

NAME: ANONYMOUS9883
The ice princess runs out of the door wearing nothing but a short dress that is see thru…

NAME: ANONYMOUS210
The princess falls into his arms and she doesn't care who is watching her...
[The thread is disrupted by graphic descriptions of a sexual nature]

NAME: ORZ MAN
blushes
Can u imagine if she ever read that?

NAME: ANONYMOUS45
Dude, tell us that you did it with her for reals.

NAME: ORZ MAN
I got to go. She's waiting for me.

NAME: ANONYMOUS887
Orz, don't leave us out of it. We're there with u every step of the way. A geek getting a princess? How often does that happen outside of galge?

NAME: ANONYMOUS2008
Yeah Orz u owe it to us to let us know how the story goes.

NAME: ORZ MAN
I know. Knowing u guys are there for us makes all the difference even if you are deranged sex fiends.
   It's good to know we r not alone.

I spoke to graphic artist and Greenpoint resident Neil Mellancamp via Skype in June 2012.

After all those whackos started showing up, no one in the neighbourhood came right out and said they wished Lillian and Bobby would move somewhere else, but you could see most of us were thinking it.

I live a few blocks from Lillian's place, on the other side of McCarren Park, and the neighbourhood became a circus pretty much day one after they found out where Bobby lived. Whole area was buzzing. First there were the reporters and the guys who wanted a soundbite for one of their blogs or tweets or whatever: 'What's it like living so close to the miracle child?' etc., etc. I always told them to go fuck themselves, although there were lots of guys in the neighbourhood who saw this as a chance for their fifteen minutes. Assholes. Then came the UFO crowd. They were totally mondo bizarro, but you could tell most of them were harmless. They'd hang out outside Bobby's building shouting shit like, 'I wanna go with you, Bobby!' but the cops cleared them out. They weren't as tenacious as the religious whack-jobs. Those ones came in waves. There were freaking scores of the fuckers when the news broke about Lillian's husband, a whole contingent who wanted Bobby to heal them – looked to me like they'd hired themselves a bus and driven down especially from Nutsville Carolina or wherever. 'Bobby! Bobby!' you could hear them shout, even after it got dark. 'I got cancer, touch me and heal me.' Those weren't anywhere near as bad as the nasty ones, who'd hang around the park

and harass people. 'God hates fags,' they'd shout, but
what that had to do with a six-year-old is anyone's guess.
There were others that looked like they'd fallen straight
out of a comic strip: 'The End is Near,' and 'Have YOU
been saved?' on their T-shirts and placards. Soon it felt
like I couldn't step outside the apartment without running
into one of them. You know the neighbourhood, right? It's
a mix, like a lot of Brooklyn, you got your arty crowd,
hipsters, Hasidics, lots of guys from the Dominican
Republic, but the nut-jobs stood out a mile.

Don't get me wrong, much as it all got old really
quickly, I felt sorry for Lillian. Most of us did. My girlfriend reported a couple of the nastier ones for hate
speech, but what could the cops do? Those freaks didn't
care if they were arrested. They wanted to be martyrs.

That morning, I was heading to work, and for some
reason, I decided to take the L train rather than the bus,
which meant I had to walk through the park and on past
Lillian's building. In the early mornings, a lot of what my
girlfriend calls the 'hipster dad gang' jog through the
park while pushing their baby buggies, but the guy I saw
hanging around the benches near the sports centre was
definitely not a stay-at-home dad who dabbled in pop-up
restauranteuring or whatever in his spare time. This dude
was just sitting there, but I could tell something was off
with him, and not just because of how he was dressed. It
was a warm morning – not hot and humid like it sometimes gets – but muggy, and this guy was dressed for winter, long black army-style trenchcoat, a black beanie hat. I
nodded at him as I passed by, but he looked straight
through me. I tried to shrug it off, but when I reached
Lorimer I just got this feeling that I should hang around,

check what he was doing in the neighbourhood. For all I knew, he could just be some poor homeless guy or whatever, but something told me to be sure. I looked around for the cops that were sometimes parked outside Lillian's building, but I couldn't see them. I'm not a spiritual person or anything, but this voice inside me said, Neil, go get yourself a coffee, check the dude out, and then head to work. So that's what I did. I grabbed a large black Americano from Orgasmic Organic and started on back to the park.

When I got back to Lillian's street, I could see the creepy dude heading towards me, walking really slowly. That feeling came back, and I knew there was something seriously wrong with him. The street wasn't empty, there were lots of people heading out to work, but I focussed on him and sped up my pace. The door to Lillian's apartment opened, and an old woman with dyed red hair and a kid in a baseball cap stepped out onto the pavement. I knew it was them straight away. Whoever thought up that disguise didn't use their imagination.

'Watch out!' I screamed. The next bit happened fast, but also like in slow motion, if that makes sense. The creepy guy pulled out a gun – I don't know guns so I couldn't have told you what it was – and just started crossing the road, ignoring the traffic. I didn't think twice. I ran straight for him, flipped the lid off the top of my coffee, and threw it right at the fucker. Right in his face. He still got a shot off, but it went wide, hit a Chevrolet that was parked in the street.

Everyone was screaming and yelling, 'Get down, get the fuck down!'

Next thing I know, this dude came out of nowhere –

found out later he was an off-duty cop who'd just gotten off work – and shouted at the gunman to 'drop his fucking weapon'. The freaky dude did as he said, but by then you could see he wasn't a threat. He was blubbering and rubbing at his eyes and face. That coffee was hot and his skin was bright red. He dropped to his knees in the middle of the road and the cop kicked his gun away and got straight on his radio.

I ran over to Lillian and Bobby. Lillian's face was ashen, and I was scared she was going to have a heart attack or a stroke or something. But Bobby, I don't know if it was the shock or whatever, but he'd started giggling. Lillian grabbed his hand and pulled him inside. Seemed like seconds later the street was full of police cars. That freaky dude was hauled to his feet and taken away. I hope the fucker rots in hell.

That cop called me later, said I was a hero. Mayor's office said I was looking at a civilian medal for bravery. But I did what anyone would've done, you know?

I didn't see Lillian and Bobby around the neighbourhood after that. They went to that safe house, right? That's what the old lady who lived in their building said. Lillian sent me this really cool email, saying as how she'll never forget what I did that day. I teared up when I read it. The next time I saw them was on the news.

This is the last email I received from Lillian Small, dated 29 May.

We're doing the best we can, Elspeth. I'm still shaken, who wouldn't be after something like that? But I'm trying to be strong for Reuben and Bobby. Bobby is fine – I don't think he was really aware of what was going on.

I think I've given you all you wanted to know. If, in your book, you could please say that we don't know why Reuben started talking again, but it isn't anything to do with Bobby. I thought about denying it, after those evil men started saying it was another sign, but Betsy knows the truth and so does Bobby. I don't want him to read this book and the news reports when he's old enough and see that his Bubbe is a liar. I believe in my heart that Reuben made one last effort to kick Al out of his consciousness so that he could spend time with his grandson. It was the force of his love that made this possible.

They're insisting that we move to a safe house now. There isn't much choice if I want to keep Bobby safe. There's talk of putting Reuben in a care facility in a different state, but I won't have that.

No. We're a family and we're going to stick together whatever happens.

14 May, 5.30 a.m.

I can't get rid of the smell. That fishy smell. The one Stephen leaves when he comes. I've tried everything; even resorted to scrubbing the walls with Domestos. The bleach made my eyes burn, but I couldn't stop.

Jess didn't take any notice as usual. She sat in the lounge watching *The X Factor* while her mad uncle flitted through the house with a bucket of toilet cleaner. Couldn't give a toss, as Geoff would say. I invited Mrs E-B around; I was hoping maybe she had some old-lady wisdom about getting rid of lingering odours (I lied and said that I'd burned Jess's fish fingers). But she said she couldn't smell anything, apart from the eye-watering sting of bleach. She took me outside into the garden for a cigarette, patted my hand again, and said that maybe I was trying to do too much, especially with all the pressure from the media. She said I should try to cry more, get my grief out that way instead of bottling it up. Went on and on about how cut up she was when her husband died ten years ago. She said she didn't think she'd be able to go on, but God helped her find a way.

Hello, God, it's me, Paul. Why the fuck aren't you listening?

It's like I'm split in two. Rational Paul and Going Mental

Paul. It's not like it was before. That was just a depressive episode. More than once I've picked up the phone to call Dr K or Darren to beg them to take Jess away from me. But then Shelly's voice pops into my head, 'All they need is love, and you've got buckets to spare, Paul.'

I can't let them down.

Could it be Capgras Syndrome? Could it?

I've even...God. I even made an excuse to take Jess over to Mrs E-B's place so that I could see how Mrs E-B's dog reacted to her. In the movies, animals can always sense if there's something wrong with someone. If they're possessed or whatever. But that dog didn't do anything. It just lay there. Got to take it a day at a time.

Got to.

But the pressure of acting normal when I'm screaming inside...Jesus. The Discovery Channel wants me to do some kind of interview about how I felt when I heard the news about the crash. I can't. Turned them down flat. And I completely forgot about a *Sunday Times* photo shoot that Gerry organised weeks ago. When the photographers showed up I slammed the door on them.

Gerry's tearing his hair out, and he's no longer buying my 'I'm still grief-stricken' card. He says your publishers are going to sue, Mandi. Let them. Fuck, what do I care? It's all falling apart.

And the pills don't work.

How the fuck did she know the Dictaphone was in her room?

21 May, 2.30 p.m.

While Jess was at school I did some more Internet research. Googled the crap out of the Pamelists, the alien theorists, even the ones who believe the kids are possessed by demons (there are a lot of these).

Because the kids. The other kids. Bobby Small and Hiro whatshisname. They're not normal, either, are they? I could tell Lillian was hiding something when I phoned her, and now I know what it was. There's no cure for Alzheimer's. Everyone knows that. No. There's something up with Bobby. And the other one, talking through an android. What the fuck is that all about?

Couldn't find much on Kenneth Oduah apart from what I was expecting – a shedload of hysterical religious sites (The Final Proof We Need!), several satirical articles, and some bumf about him being kept at a safe house in Lagos 'for his own safety'.

What if they are the horsemen? I know, I know. Mel especially would freak if she heard me talking like this. But just hear me out. Sane Paul won't even take this on board, but I think we need to keep an open mind. There's definitely something wrong with Jess. And weird shit is happening around the other two. Or three. Who the fuck knows what gubbins the other one is up to?

Aliens, horsemen or demons – oh my!

(*Starts sobbing*)

Should I call Lillian again? I just don't know.

28 May, 10.30 p.m.

I know I should feel sorry for Bobby after being attacked like that, but I only feel sorry for Lillian.

It's all over the news of course. Every bloody channel. In the old days I'd try to stop Jess watching it. Keep her away from it, but why bother? It doesn't seem to affect her either way.

On the Sky report they had a collage of photographs of the crashes and giant blown up pics of The Three. I found Jess sitting inches from the screen, her My Little Ponies littered around her, watching as Sky did a 'time-line' of events and brought pundits in to discuss it ad nauseam.

I made myself approach her. 'Do you want to talk about this, Jess?'

'Talk about what, Uncle Paul?'

'Why that little boy is on the news. Why your photo-graph is on the news.'

'No thanks.'

I hovered around for a few more seconds, then ran out-side for a fag.

Darren says it's likely that the police will be keeping a close eye on the house, just in case the religious nutters decide to jump across the Atlantic and target Jess.

Tonight after she has gone to bed, I'm going to try one last time to get Stephen to talk to me. 'How could you let that thing in here?' He has to mean Jess, right?

I should have done it ages ago.

I'm going to stay up all night, drink enough coffee to fell a horse, and when Stephen comes I'm going to *make* him talk to me.

30 May, 4.00 a.m.

I must've dropped off. Because when I woke up, there he was. All the lights were on, but he looked like he was in the dark. Sitting in shadow. Couldn't see his face.

He shifted his position, and the smell was so strong I gagged.

'What do you want? Please tell me,' I begged him. 'Please!'

I reached out to grab him, but there was nothing there.

I ran into Jess's room, shook her, thrust a photo of Polly in her face. 'This is your sister! Why don't you fucking care?'

She turned over, stretched, and smiled at me. 'Uncle Paul, I need to sleep. I've got school in the morning.'

Jesus. Could it be that she's the rational one?

God help me.

1 June, 6.30 p.m.

A couple of cops came to see me today, showed up this morning before I was even dressed. Actually, they're not police, but Special Branch. Sane Paul, the me before all this fucked-up shit happened, was squeeing inside. Calvin and Mason, they're called. Calvin and Mason! Like the title of a butch cop show. Calvin's black, speaks with a public school accent, and has shoulders like a prop forward. Totally Sane Paul's type. Mason is older, a silver fox.

I made them tea, apologised for the lingering bleach smell (after Mrs E-B's reaction I've learned not to mention the fishy rotten stench). They wanted to know if I'd had any threatening phone calls lately, like the ones we got right at the beginning when Jess first came home. I said no. Told them the truth. That the only hassle we were getting these days was from the press.

Jess was on its best behaviour of course. Smiling and laughing and acting like a charming little celebrity. Hot they may be, but I don't think much of Mason and Calvin's detection skills. They fell for it, of course. Hook, line and sinker. Mason even had the gall to ask if he could have a photo with her to show to his daughter.

They said they'd be keeping an eye on the house, and to give them a call if I was worried about anything. I almost said, 'Would you mind giving my brother a warning, and telling him to leave me the fuck alone?' My dead brother! And IT, of course. Imagine how that would have gone down.

Must stop calling Jess 'it'. Not right, just feeds the monster.

When they left, I tried to call Lillian again. No answer.

2 June, 4.00 a.m.

(*Sobbing*)

Okay.

Woke up. Felt that familiar weight on the bed. But it wasn't Stephen. It was Jess, although she's not heavy enough to make a dent in the mattress, is she?

'Do you like your dreams?' she said. 'I've given them to you, Uncle Paul. So that you can see Stephen whenever you like.'

'What are you?' It was the first time I'd come out and said it.

'I'm Jess,' she said. 'Who do you think I am? You're such a silly billy, Uncle Paul.'

'Get out!' I screamed at her. 'Get out get out get out.' My throat is still sore.

She laughed and skipped away. I locked the door behind her.

I'm running out of options. They'll take Jess away from me if find out what I'm thinking. Some days I think that would be a good thing. But what if the real Jess is still in there, trying to get out, trying to get help? What if she needs me?

It's time to be proactive. Explore my options. Keep an open mind. Do more research. Cover all bases.

I don't have any other choice.

Gerhard Friedmann, a 'secular exorcist' who works throughout Europe, agreed to talk to me via Skype in late June after I made a donation to his organisation.

Before I begin to answer your questions, I would like to make something clear. Exorcism is not a word I like to use. It has too many connotations. No, I exact 'inner healing and spirit deliverance'. That is the service I offer. I also want to make it clear that I do not charge a fee for this service, but merely ask for a donation, of whatever amount the subject or client chooses to provide. I am also not affiliated with any particular church or religious institution. I just go about my practice in a slightly different manner. And business is very good at the moment. Let us just say that it is rare that I do not fly first class. At around the time I was contacted by Mr Craddock, I would say that I was doing up to three spirit deliverances and cleanses a day, all around Europe and the UK.

I ask Gerhard how Paul Craddock contacted him.

I have a number of ways in which prospective clients can get in touch with me. Mr Craddock contacted me through one of my Facebook accounts. I have several. I am also on Twitter, of course, and have a website. As his circumstances did not allow me to come to his residence, we agreed to meet at a location that I sometimes use for spirit deliverance.

(He refuses to reveal this location)

I ask him if he was aware who Paul Craddock was before they met.

Yes. Mr Craddock was very candid about this, but I assured him that our relationship would be confidential – akin to that of a doctor/patient agreement. I was aware of the theories about Jessica Craddock and the other children, but did not let these influence my diagnosis. I am only talking to you now because the news that Mr Craddock contracted my services was leaked by his defence team.

I tell him that I have been on his website, where he states that there is a spirit that manifests itself as homosexuality. I ask if he was aware that Paul Craddock was gay.

Yes, I knew of this. But I knew that in his case this wasn't the root of the problem.

He was concerned that he or his niece was infested with bad energy, possessed, if you like. When we met, he was agitated, but not overly so. He kept saying, over and over again, that he had contacted me in order to 'rule out this option', and asked me to investigate this possibility. Mr Craddock told me that he was having extremely disturbing dreams, in which his dead brother would come to him, and that he was having difficulty relating to his niece. These are both symptoms of spirit possession and/or sickness induced by overexposure to negative energy.

I ask him if he was aware of Paul Craddock's mental health issues.

Yes. He was very upfront about this. I am always careful not to confuse, for example, a schizophrenic episode with possession, but I knew immediately that this was not what I was dealing with. I am extremely intuitive when it comes to this.

I ask him how he usually goes about his spirit deliverance.

The first thing I do is settle the subject, make sure they're comfortable. Then I anoint their forehead with oil. Any oil will do, but I prefer to use extra-virgin olive oil, as this seems to get the best results.

Next, I must decipher if I am dealing with bad energy poisoning or entity possession. If it is possession, the next step is to discover what kind of entity has attached itself to the client and call it out by name. Entities are disturbing and powerful phenomena that have made their way to earth from a different plane. They attach themselves to someone who is already weakened, perhaps because of abuse or because they have been poisoned by someone else's bad energy, which has allowed their defences to be compromised. There are many many types of entities; the ones that I specialise in are those that have found doorways into this realm through sites where much negativity has taken place.

I also do object cleansing, as objects can also harbour negative energy. This is why I always encourage people to be careful when handling antiques and artefacts from museums.

I ask him why, if Paul Craddock believed Jessica was also possessed, he didn't request that she also be cleansed.

That was not possible because of his current situation. He said he was under surveillance from the press, who followed him and Jess everywhere.

But when he went into more detail about his symptoms, which included being plagued by the sense that Jess wasn't the real Jess but a facsimile, I was certain that if it was an entity that was causing the problem, then it had attached itself to him, and not to his niece. The grief and anguish he would have suffered after his family was killed in the plane crash would have weakened his defences enough for him to be a prime candidate for possession. He also expressed concern that Jess could be an alien being, but I assured him that aliens don't exist and he was more than likely dealing with a bad energy influx.

And, as soon as I tuned into him, I did indeed find that he was suffering from severe malaise caused by an over-toxification of bad energy. I assured him that once we had gone through the cleansing ritual – which involves anointing with oil and transference of bad energy via touch – he would no longer be plagued by the dreams he was experiencing or the belief that his niece was a changeling.

Afterwards, I warned him that although he had been cleansed, he was still compromised, and there would still be traces of bad energy inside him that could eventually attract an entity. I encouraged him to avoid stressful situations at all costs.

He thanked me, and as he left, he said, 'There can only be one explanation now.'

I ask him if he knew what Paul Craddock meant by this.

Not at the time.

PART TEN

END GAMES

Joe DeLesseps, a salesman who regularly travels through Maryland, Pennsylvania and Virginia, agreed to talk to me via Skype in late June.

I operate in three states, selling just about anything that you can care to think of in the hardware line; there are still people out there who prefer to deal with a human being rather than a computer. I keep off the turnpike when I can. I prefer the back roads. Like my grandson Piper would say, that's just how I roll. Over the years I've carved out several routes for myself, got my favourite places to stop off for coffee and pie, some of which I've been visiting for years, though more and more mom and pop outlets have been hit by the recession. I'm not a fan of those chain motels either, prefer the family-run joints. You may not get cable and Taco Bell on tap, but the company and the coffee's always better and the rates are competitive.

I was running behind schedule that day. Wholesaler I'd seen in Baltimore liked to talk, and I'd lost track of time. Almost decided to take the interstate, but there's this little roadhouse just before Mile Creek Road – one of my favourite routes which takes you near Green Ridge Forest – where the coffee's good and the pancakes even better, so I decided to take the long way instead. My wife Tammy is always nagging me to watch my cholesterol, but I figured that what she didn't know wouldn't hurt her.

I made it there round about five, half-an-hour before closing time. Pulled up next to a new Chevy SUV with tinted windows. Soon as I walked in, I figured it had to belong to the small group sitting drinking coffee in one of the booths by the window. At first glance I thought they were just an ordinary family: a couple with their child, on a road-trip with grandma and grandpa. But when I looked closer, I could see they didn't seem to fit together. There wasn't that companionable ease you see with most families or holidaymakers; the younger couple especially looked on edge. Could practically see the creases on the younger fellow's shirt where he'd just pulled it out of its packaging.

I knew Suze, the short-order cook, would be wanting to head home, so I ordered my pancakes real quick and put extra cream in my coffee so that I could chug it down faster.

'Po Po wants to go to the bathroom,' the little kid said, pointing to grandpa. But the old fella hadn't said a word. I could see there was something not right with him. Had a vacant look in his eyes, like my pa got right at the end.

The older woman helped the old fella shuffle his way to the bathroom. I greeted her as she passed my table, and she gave me a weary smile. Red hair you could see was dyed, an inch of grey roots. Tammy would have said that there goes a woman who hadn't found the time to take care of herself in quite a while. I could feel eyes on me; the younger fella was checking me out. I nodded at him, said something about how we could do with some rain, but he didn't respond.

They left a few minutes before I did, but they were still helping that old-timer into the SUV when I made my way outside.

'Where you headed?' I asked, trying to be friendly.

The younger fella gave me a look. 'Pennsylvania,' he said. I could tell he'd just pulled that answer out of his ass.

'Uh-huh. Well, drive safe.'

The older, red-haired woman gave me a tentative smile.

'Come on, Mom,' the younger woman said to her, and the redhead jumped as if she'd just been pinched.

The little kid waved at me and I winked back at him. Cute little guy.

They took off at a clip, heading in the wrong direction for Pennsylvania. That SUV would've been equipped with GPS, and I could see the young fella knew what he was doing. Guess I thought, none of my business.

I didn't see it happen. I came around the bend; saw the broken glass. The Chevy was on its roof on the wrong side of the road.

I pulled over, dug in the back for my first-aid kit. Driving as much as I do, you're apt to encounter a lot of accidents, and I'd been keeping a kit in the car for years. Even did a course a couple a years ago.

They'd hit a deer. I figure the young fella musta yanked too hard on the wheel and flipped the car. Could see straight off that the two at the front – the driver, that young fella, and the young woman with the hard eyes – were gone, and it would have been quick. You couldn't tell which parts was deer, which parts was human.

The old fella in the back was gone, too. No blood, but his eyes were open. Looked like he was at peace.

The woman with the red hair was a different story. There wasn't much blood on her, but I could see her legs were trapped. Her eyes were open, and they were dazed.

'Bobby,' she whispered.

I knew she must mean the boy. 'I'll look for him, ma'am,' I said.

Couldn't find him anywhere at first. Figured he must have been flung out of the back window. Found his body two hundred yards from the vehicle. He was in the culvert, lying face up, as if he was watching the sky. You can tell when the soul is gone. There's an emptiness. Looked like there wasn't a scratch on him.

There was no way I could get the woman out of there – needed the Jaws of Life to do that – and I was worried she might have spinal injuries. She'd stopped crying by then and I held her hand as she drifted away. I listened to the sound of the engine ticking and waited for the cops.

I only found out who they were the next day. Tammy couldn't believe I hadn't figured it out sooner; that boy's face was always plastered over the magazines she gets.

Didn't seem right. What are the chances of that poor kid being in two fatal accidents? I'd been planning to keep on going right till Tammy forced me to retire, but maybe this whole thing is a sign that it's time to quit. A sign that enough is enough.

I thought long and hard about whether or not to include Bobby Small's autopsy report in this book. I decided to include an extract after various conspiracy sites insisted that his death was faked. It should be noted that according to pathologist Alison Blackburn, the State of Maryland's Chief Medical Examiner, no anomalies were found when she conducted a thorough internal examination.

Bobby Small was formally identified by Mona Gladwell, who declined to talk to me again.

(Sensitive readers may wish to skip over this. It can, however, be found in its entirety at *http://pathologicallyfamous.com/*)

OFFICE OF THE CHIEF MEDICAL EXAMINER
STATE OF MARYLAND

Decedent: Bobby Reuben Small	Autopsy number: SM 2012–001346
Age: 6 years	Date: 11/06/2012
Sex: Male	Time: 9.30 a.m

Examination and summary analysis performed by: **Alison Blackburn, MD, Chief Medical Examiner**

Initial examination: **Gary Lee Swartz, MD, Deputy Chief Medical Examiner**

Osteological examination: **Pauline May Swanson, Ph.D., ABFA**

Toxicology examination: **Michael Greenberg, Ph.D., DABFT**

ANATOMIC FINDINGS

Young, male boy with superficial abrasions of forehead, nose and chin. Complete dislocation between C6, C7 and C7, T1. Severing of inter-vertebral disc and anterior ligament C6, C7. Fractured spinal process C6. Partial tearing of posterior root filaments and multiple bleeding points observed.

CAUSE OF DEATH

Traumatic disruption of cervical cord.

MANNER OF DEATH

Accidental death consistent with ejection from a motor vehicle.

CIRCUMSTANTIAL SUMMARY

Bobby Small, a 6-year-old male, was the sole survivor of a plane crash 6 months ago, in which his mother was killed. He suffered minor injuries in the crash from which he made a full recovery. He was being targeted by a religious group and a decision was made to move him to a place of safety with his grandparents. All three were being transported in a Chevrolet Suburban SUV by two FBI agents. Bobby was seated between his grandparents in the rear of the vehicle where he was secured by a lap seat belt. At approximately 5 p.m. they stopped at Duke's Roadside Diner in Maryland. The group were observed there by Mr Joseph DeLesseps, a travelling salesman. They stirred his interest as he thought them a strange group. The adults had coffee and Bobby had a strawberry milkshake and a plate of fries. The group left around 5.30 p.m. followed soon after by Mr DeLesseps, who saw the Suburban drive off at speed. At approximately 5.50 p.m. Mr DeLesseps rounded a bend in a wooded section of the road and spotted the Suburban crashed at the side of the road. He found the vehicle against a large tree with a dead deer partially on the hood of the car and partially through the shattered windshield. In the vehicle were two dead people in the front seats and a dead elderly man in a rear seat. There was a severely injured elderly woman in the other rear seat. There was no sign of the little boy he had seen in the diner, so Mr DeLesseps searched around the vehicle. He found the body of the boy in a small culvert two hundred metres from the SUV. There was no sign of life. He called 911 immediately.

DOCUMENTS AND EVIDENCE EXAMINED

1. Report from vehicle examination centre re Chevrolet Suburban. Evidence of damage to hood and front windshield consistent with impact from a deer. Crumpling of rear of vehicle consistent with impact with a tree trunk. Shattered rear window and damaged central lap belt. No evidence of any pre-accident damage or faults to the vehicle.

2. Report from RTA examination team. Skid marks indicate likelihood of sudden braking secondary to impacting with deer at moderate to high speed with resultant spinning off the road of vehicle and rear off-side impact with tree. Adult seat belts remained in place, but central, rear lap belt open and partially damaged, resulting in the ejection of the male child casualty through the shattered rear window.

IDENTIFICATION

On 11/06/2012 at 9.45 a.m. a complete post mortem examination was performed on the body of Bobby Small, who was identified by the Norfolk County Chief Medical Examiner's Office. David Michaels was present as autopsy assistant.

CLOTHING AND VALUABLES

Bobby Small was wearing a bright red baseball cap (retrieved at the scene), blue jeans, a red *Night at the Museum* T-shirt, a pale grey hooded sweatshirt, and a pair of red Converse sneakers.

EXTERNAL EXAMINATION

The body is that of a well-nourished white young male consistent with a stated age of 6 years.

Body length 45 inches Weight 46lbs.

Light blonde, medium length slightly curly scalp hair. No nevi or tattoos. A small scar on the forehead. Superficial abrasions to forehead, nose and chin. Pupils equal and regular. Light blue irides. Healthy milk teeth with absent two upper front incisors.

Although Paul Craddock attempted to destroy his computer's hard drive, several documents and some email correspondence were recovered, including the following, which was leaked to the press.

(The spelling errors have been left uncorrected to illustrate his frame of mind)

List of Weird Shit Jess said today (8 June)

(more on the new obsession with boredom). Uncle Paul, do you get bored being you? I'm bored being me. (goes back to watching her new favourite show, fucking *TOWIE*). These people are bored being them. (I ask her wtf that means). Being bored is like being a cup that can't be filled (v fucking zen, where'd she hear that??????? Certainly not on Celeb Big Brother).

(10 June)

I hand her her supper she says, Uncle Paul, does Stephen smell as bad as these fish fingers now? (I scream, she laughs). I leave she turns channel to the news. I hear her laughing at something else. Almost throw up when I see it's a report that Bobby Small has been killed in a car accident. I ask whats funny she says, he's not dead he's just playing silly-billy. Like mummy and daddy and polly.

(I'm in the kitchen, thinking about the pills again ie how many would it take to be sure). She glides in without me seeing her. Moves too close to my face. She says, am I special paul? They say I am at school. It's so easy.

(14 June)

It finds me crying. Do you want to come play my little pony with me? You can be princess luna again and stephen can be princess celestia (laughs).

1) POSESSION: FOR: she alwaqsy seems to know what I'm thinking, knows things she couldn't know like about sexual ortienattion, knows aboput the stephen dreams ssays she sent them

2) POSSESSION AGAINST: NOT RATIONAL I KNOW THIS WHAT AM I THINKING and she doesn't have fits or anything like on the checklist on the inetrnet or speak in funny voices and that prick gerhard said it was unlikely although i don;t trust his opinion

3) HORSEMAN THEORY FOR: colours of the planes, signs lots of no way thwy could have survived, other children acting weird too there's Bobby's seniles granddad talking and Hiro talking through a fucking robot and how can so many be wrong because so many believe this is the truth and nw they have found the fourth child altho that could all be more bullshit

4) HORSEMAN THEORY AGAINST: batshit crazy, even archbishop of canturbury and that top iman say it is utter bullshit and they also believe in sky fairies and if there is a horseman inside her wehere is the real jess and why does she look like hersefl. Signs they have put on the website could have happend anyway and the foot and mouth thing blown over now anyway and aniomals bite people all the time anyway same as floods etc etc

5) CAPGRAS SYNDROME FOR: my history of mental illness although that was stress related only and would be nice

as is a medical cpondition that woould explain why i don't think shes jess evben though she looks just like jess amnd sometimes talks like her. I wish it is this

6) CAPGRAS SYNDROME AGAINST: never had it before, no head injury (unless I was drunk and hit my head and didn't realise it) its very very very fcking rare

7) ALIENS FOR: same as possession and would explain how some-tiems she seems to be watching me like i'm an expriment

8) ALKIENS AGAINST: because it s not rationla altho the eveidence can be persuasive and this is the only one I haVen't discounted yet needto look into moerew okay paul

To: **actorpc99@gmail.com**
From **openyreyes.com**
Subject: **RE: Advice in confidence**
Date: 14/06/2012

Paul, thanks for your email, happy to help in any way I can.

As I said when we spoke telephonically, the commonest way in which they work is by implanting a MICROCHIP inside the subject. I believe that at the moment of the crashes, the children were put into stasis, which is why they were not injured. Then they were implanted. Through 'voice to skull' manipulation, the Others (ALIENS) are able to control and influence those they have chosen. This is a new type of technology that is LIGHT YEARS away from what we can yet do in our realm.

You say you have checked out all the options and have proved this is NOT a case of demonic possession. I applaud you for being so thorough.

I'm not at all surprised that Jess is showing disturbing symptoms, or out of character behaviour – this is to be expected. Remember, a change in PERSONALITY is NOT actually a symptom of PTSD. As you say, look at what's happening with the boy in Japan (talking through a mechanism, a ROBOT) and the boy in America, who was no doubt experimenting with his grandfather's cognative [*sic*] functioning. It is very unlikely he is dead. This is a government ruse as they are in cahoots with the OTHERS. They receive immunity from experimentation and have made a treaty with the aliens so that they can have free rein to feed off our energies.

Your questions about the Pamelist theory are very interesting. I believe that there are a LOT of similarities with the truth. Very close to what WE believe. They are wrong, but MORE RIGHT THAN THEY KNOW.

And what you are feeling mustn't be confused with Capgras syndrome. That is a psychological anomoly [*sic*].

How to proceed? I would be cautious around Jess, it's unlikely she will do anything to harm you. The dreams and visions you are having are probably interference from the chip. I would advise you to watch her carefully, and be careful what you let on to her.

Let me know if there's anything else I can help you with.

Best,

Si

Noriko Inada (not her real name) resides on the fifth floor of the apartment block opposite Chiyoko Kamamoto's house. This account was collated by *Tokyo Herald* journalist Daniel Mimura, who interviewed her two days after Hiro Yanagida's murder. (Translation by Eric Kushan.)

I usually wake very early, at around five, and as I wait for daylight to come, I often watch the clock next to my bed. This is how I knew the exact time of the first gunshot. Although my block is situated only two hundred metres from the busy Hatsudai expressway, it's well insulated from noise, but that sound made its way into my room. A muffled bang, which made me flinch, then another, then two more. I had never heard a gunshot before, except on television, so I did not know what to think. Perhaps that it was fireworks? And I couldn't be sure where it was coming from.

It took me several minutes to climb into my wheel-chair, but gradually I made it over to the window where I spend most of each day. I don't go out very often. There is a lift in the apartment building, but it's hard to get through the door without help, and my sister can only find the time to visit me once a week, when she brings me groceries. I lived here for many years with my husband, and when he died I decided I would stay. This is my home.

It was not yet light, the sun was still struggling into the sky, but because of the streetlights I could see from my position that the Kamamoto family's front door was open. It was too early for Kamamoto-san to leave for work; he left every day at six, so that did give me some cause for concern. No one else in the neighbourhood had stirred. When I was questioned by the police later that day, they said that my neighbours who'd heard the gunshots assumed they were hearing a car back-firing.

I opened my window to let in some fresh air, then waited to see if the sound would come again or if anyone would emerge from the house. Then, I saw two figures walking towards the house from the direction of the Hatsudai. When they passed beneath my window, I recognised the girl as Chiyoko Kamamoto and I could tell by his long hair that her companion was the boy I'd seen hanging around in the children's playground many times before. Once, I'd seen him spray-painting a message on the pavement, but he'd cleaned it off, so I did not complain. Those two were very different types of people. Chiyoko walked upright as if she owned the streets; he would hunch over as if he was trying to appear smaller than he was. I had seen Chiyoko slipping out of the house many times at night to meet him, but this was the first time I had seen her returning. They were talking quietly, so I could not hear the details of their conversation. Chiyoko laughed and nudged the boy with her elbow and he bent down to kiss her. Then she playfully pushed him away and turned to walk into her house.

She hesitated when she saw the door was open and turned back to say something to her companion. She went inside and thirty seconds later I heard a scream. Not just a scream, a howl. The anguish in that sound was terrible to hear.

The man, who was still waiting outside, jerked as if he had been slapped, then ran into the house.

Several neighbours started emerging from their doorways, disturbed by the screams, which sounded as if they would never stop.

Chiyoko staggered out into the street, the boy in her arms. I thought at first she was covered in black paint, but as she stumbled into the light beneath my window, it became red. The little boy, Hiro, was limp in her arms, and…and… I couldn't see his face. Just blood and bone where it should be. The tall boy tried to help her, as did the neighbours, but she screamed at them to leave her alone. She was yelling at Hiro to wake up, to stop pretending.

He was such a dear little boy. Whenever he left the apartment, he would always look up at me and wave. My sister didn't believe me at first when I told her that the miracle child was living in the house across the street from me. The whole of Japan took that boy into their hearts. Sometimes there were photographers waiting in the street; once, one knocked on the door and asked if he could film the house from my apartment, but I refused.

It couldn't have been more than five minutes later that I heard the ambulance arriving. It took three paramedics to take Hiro's body away from Chiyoko; she fought and hit and bit them. The police attempted to drag her towards one of their vehicles, but she twisted out of their grasp, and before they could stop her, she started running away, still drenched in blood. The long-haired boy sprinted after her.

The crowd of onlookers and reporters grew as the news spread. There was a hush as the bodies, encased in their black plastic shrouds, were removed from the house. That was when I turned away from the window.

I didn't sleep at all that night. I thought that I would never sleep again.

The 2-chan message board erupted minutes after the news of Hiro's murder was released.

NAME: ANONYMOUS111 POST DATE: 2012/22/06 11:19:29.15
Fuck! U guys hear about Hiro?

NAME: ANONYMOUS356
Can't believe it.
   The Android Boy is dead. Fucking bastard American marine broke into their house. Shot the princess's parents as well as Hiro.

NAME: ANONYMOUS23
U seen the stuff on Reddit? Marine was one of those religious freaks. Like the dude who tried to shoot the kid in the US.

NAME: ANONYMOUS885
Orz was there. Orz and the princess found the body. I'm cryin inside for Orz. U see the pictures of him? He was fighting to get to the Princess while the cops were tryin to keep him away.
   I was cheering him on.

NAME: ANONYMOUS987
We all were, dude. So happy they got away in the end. Go Orz!

NAME: ANONYMOUS899
The princess isn't as hot as I thought she'd be. Orz looks like a typical otaku, just like I imagined him.

NAME: ANONYMOUS23
That's cold. Fuck u 899.

NAME: ANONYMOUS555
Where do u think Orz and the princess have gone? Cops will want to talk to them.

NAME: ANONYMOUS6543
You think Orz is ok?

NAME: ANONYMOUS23
Don't be such a fucking noob 6543! Of course he's not ok!!!!
[Much speculation followed about what this could mean for Orz and the princess's future. Then, three hours later, Ryu appeared on the board.]

NAME: ORZ MAN POST DATE: 2012/22/06 14:10:19.25
Hi guys.

NAME: ANONYMOUS111
Orz??? That really u?

NAME: ORZ MAN
It's me.

NAME: ANONYMOUS23
Orz, u ok? How is the princess? Where are u?

NAME: ORZ MAN
I don't have long. The princess is waiting for me.

I showed her yr messages and she says it doesn't matter now that u know who we really are. She says that u should never forget what they did.

She is broken.

I am broken.

But wanted to say thanx for giving us all that support.

This isn't easy…

Wanted to let u know that u won't hear from me again.

We're going to be together forever going somewhere where they can't hurt us any more.

I wish I could meet every one of u. Wouldn't have had the balls to leave my room without all yr encouragement.

Goodbye.

Your friend, Ryu (aka Orz Man)

NAME: ANONYMOUS23
Orz??????

NAME: ANONYMOUS288
Orz!!!! Come back, man.

NAME: ANONYMOUS90
He's gone.

NAME: ANONYMOUS111
Netizens, this isn't good. That sounded like a suicide note to me.

NAME: ANONYMOUS23
Orz would never do something like that...would he?

NAME: ANONYMOUS57890
If u think about it, if Orz and the princess hadn't been out together that night then the marine might have shot her too.

NAME: ANONYMOUS896
Orz saved her life.

NAME: ANONYMOUS235
Yeah. And if 111 is right, they're going to kill themselves together. A suicide pact.

NAME: ANONYMOUS7689
There's no proof this is what they're gonna do.

NAME: ANONYMOUS111
Those US fuckers. They were behind this. They murdered Hiro and destroyed Orz's happiness. They can't be allowed to get away with it.

NAME: ANONYMOUS23
Agreed. Orz is one of us. They need to pay.

NAME: ANONYMOUS111
Netizens, for once in yr lives it's time to do something that counts.

Melanie Moran agreed to talk to me via Skype shortly after Jessica Craddock's funeral in mid-July.

I blame myself. Geoff says I mustn't but some days I can't help it. 'You've got enough on your plate, petal,' he keeps saying. 'What could you have done in any case?'

Looking back now, with the benefit of hindsight and that, I can't help feeling that I should have seen it coming. Paul had been acting strange for a while, so much so that even Kelvin and some of the others had picked up on it. He'd missed the last three 277 Together meetings, and he hadn't asked me or Geoff to fetch Jess from school or babysit for a good couple of weeks before it happened. To be honest, me and Geoff were relieved to get a bit of a break. We had a lot on our plate, what with our own grandchildren to look after, especially after Gavin went for the police exams early. And Paul did have the tendency to take over, make himself the centre of attention. He could be quite needy, self-obsessed. But that said, I should have done more. I should have made more of an effort to go and check up on him.

I heard that social worker of his being interviewed on the radio, trying to explain himself. He was saying how it was no wonder everyone was fooled, Paul was an actor, played different personas for a living. But that's just an excuse. Fact is, the social weren't doing their job. They dropped the ball on that one. So did that psychologist. As Geoff keeps saying, Paul wasn't *that* good an actor, was he?

When we first started 277 Together, a few of the others – not many mind – felt that because Paul was the only one of us who had a relative who'd survived the crash, that he should take a back seat, let the others talk. Me and Geoff, we didn't go along with that. Paul had lost his brother, hadn't he? And his niece and sister-in-law. The first time Paul brought Jess to a meeting, it was hard for most of them to look at her; how do you behave towards a miracle child? Because that's what she was. A miracle, only not in the way those fundies say. You should hear Father Jeremy go off about them, 'Putting Christianity into disrepute'.

We babysat Jess quite a few times while Paul was out doing what he needed to do. Lovely little girl, really bright. I was relieved when Paul decided to send her back to school. Get her right back into a normal way of life. The primary school where she went, it looked like a good supportive place, they had that lovely memorial service for Polly, didn't they? I suppose in some ways it was harder for Paul than it was for us. He had a member of his family who was still alive, but then again, he had a constant reminder that the others were gone, didn't he?

You can tell I'm putting off getting to the next bit. The only people I've told in detail are Geoff and Father Jeremy. It's what my Danielle would have called a total mind-fuck. She had a right mouth on her. Took after me.

Don't mind me; tears are always close to the surface. I know people think of me as a coper, as a tough old bitch, and I am…but it gets to you. All this misery, all this death. It's all needless. Jess didn't need to die and Danielle didn't need to die.

I'd turned my phone off that day. Just for a couple of hours. We were coming up for Danielle's birthday, and I was feeling down. Decided to treat myself and have a long soak in the bath. When I switched my mobile back on, I saw I had a message from Paul. First up he apologised for keeping his distance, said he'd had a lot to think about and deal with over the last few days. His voice sounded flat. Lifeless. In retrospect I suppose I should have felt a sense of foreboding then. He asked me if I could come over to his place for a chat. Said he'd be in all day.

I tried calling him back, but it went straight to voice-mail. The last thing I felt like doing was going over to Paul's, but I was feeling guilty that I hadn't called to see why he hadn't been at the 277s lately. Geoff was over at Gavin's, watching the little ones, so I went on my own.

When I got there, I rang the bell, but there was no answer. I tried again, and then I realised that the front door was slightly open. I knew something was wrong, but I went inside anyway.

I found her in the kitchen. She was lying sprawled, face up, next to the fridge. There was red everywhere. Spattered on the walls, on the fridge and the other white goods. I didn't want to believe it was blood at first. But the smell. They don't tell you that on the shows, the crime shows. How bad blood can smell. I knew straight away that she was dead. It was hot outside and already a few big bluebottles were buzzing around her, crawling on her face and that. The places where…oh Lord…the places where he'd cut into her…deep gashes, right to the bone in places. A pool of blood was spreading out beneath her. Her eyes were open, staring up, and they were full of blood, too.

I was sick. Just straight away. All down my front. I started praying and my legs felt like they were weighed down with cement blocks. I assumed that a lunatic must have broken in and attacked her. I pulled out my phone, called 999. I still can't believe I managed to make myself understood.

I'd just hung up when I heard a thump coming from upstairs. It wasn't me who made my body move. I know that doesn't make sense. It was like I was being pushed forward. For all I knew, whoever had attacked Jess could still be in the house.

I walked up those stairs like I was some kind of robot, stubbed my toe on the top step, but hardly felt it.

He was lying on the bed, white as a sheet. Empty booze bottles scattered all over the carpet.

I thought he was dead at first. Then he groaned, making me jump, and I saw the packet of sleeping pills clutched in his hand; the empty bottle of Bells next to him.

He'd left a message on the side table, written in large angry letters. I'll never be able to get those words out of my head: 'I had to do it. It is the ONLY WAY. I had to cut the chip out of her so that she would be FREE.'

I didn't pass out, but the time until the police arrived is a blank. That neighbour, the snobbish one, she took me straight inside her house. You could tell she was also beside herself with shock. She was kind to me that day. Made a cup of tea, helped me get cleaned up, called Geoff for me.

They said that it must have taken a long time for Jessie to bleed out on that floor. It goes through your head, all the time. If only I'd visited Paul earlier. If only, if only, if only.

And now... it's not anger I feel towards Paul, but pity. Father Jeremy says that forgiveness is the only way forward. But I can't help thinking that it might have been better if he'd died. Locked up like that, in one of those places, what sort of future is he going to face?

The following article, written by journalist Daniel Mimura, was published in the *Tokyo Herald Online* on 7 July 2012

Western Tourists targeted by Orz Movement

Yesterday afternoon, a tour bus packed full of American tourists was pelted with buckets of red paint and eggs when it pulled into the parking lot of the Meiji Shrine in Shibuya. The perpetrators fled before police arrived, but were heard shouting, 'This is for Orz,' as they left the scene. No one was injured in the attack, although several of the elderly tourists were reportedly deeply shaken.

There are also unconfirmed reports of several American language students being harassed in an electronics store yesterday evening in Akihabara and another unconfirmed verbal assault on a British tourist in Inokashira Park.

It is believed that these incidents were perpetrated by the Orz Movement, a group protesting the murder of Hiro Yanagida, which is responsible for defacing several Western outlets and religious institutions with graffiti. On 24 June, two days after the murder of Hiro Yanagida, cleaning staff arrived at the Tokyo Union Church in Ometsando, located next to the iconic Louis Vuitton store, to discover a painting of a blood-soaked handbag daubed next to the entrance. That evening, a stencil of a man spewing vomit appeared on the walls of Toyko's two Wendy's outlets and a McDonald's in Shinjuku, causing both disgust and hilarity. A week later, a masked man was caught on CCTV defacing the sign outside the American Embassy.

The tag signature ORZ is left at every scene. ORZ – an emoticon or emoji – which resembles a figure bashing its head on the ground, signifies depression or despair and was popularised on chat-forums such as 2-channel.

So far, police have been frustrated in their efforts to curb the increasingly radical behaviour, and with copycat ORZ stencils beginning to pop up in cities all over Japan – including as far away as Osaka – all indications are that it is spreading fast.

A spokesperson from the Japanese National Tourism Organisation has stressed that Japan is not a nation known for 'violent protests', and that it should not be judged on the actions of a 'misguided minority'.

The Orz Movement has now attracted a vocal and high-profile supporter. Aikao Uri, the head of the rapidly growing and controversial Cult of Hiro, issued the following statement: 'Hiro's unforgivable murder, and the fact that the US government is unconcerned about bringing those behind it to justice, is a clear sign that we need to break ties immediately. Japan is not a child who needs its American nanny watching over it. I applaud what the Orz Movement is doing. It is a shame that our government is too afraid to follow their example.' Unlike many hardline Nationalists, Aikao Uri has called for ties to be strengthened with Korea and the People's Republic of China, going so far as to insist that reparations be made for Japanese World War II war crimes against these nations. She is at the forefront of the campaign for the historic Treaty of Mutual Cooperation and Security between the United States and Japan to be overthrown, and all US troops based on Okinawa Island to be removed. She is married to politician Masamara Uri, who is widely tipped to be the next prime minister.

AFTERWORD TO THE FIRST EDITION

The following article was published in the *Tokyo Herald* on 28 July 2012.

'Orz Man's' Remains Found in Jukei

Every year, volunteers from the Yamanashi Prefecture police and the Fujisan Rangers undertake a thorough sweep of the notorious Aokigahara forest, searching for the bodies of those who have chosen to end their lives in this 'sea of trees'. This year, over forty bodies were discovered, including the remains of a man who police suspect could be Ryu Takami (22), who achieved notoriety after his story of heartbreak captured the imagination of the 2-chan message board. Takami, who used the avatar Orz Man, was believed to be in a relationship with Chiyoko Kamamoto (18), the cousin of Sun Air Flight 678 survivor, Hiro Yanagida. Chiyoko and Ryu disappeared on 22 June 2012, the same day that Hiro and Chiyoko's parents were shot to death by Private Jake Wallace, an American soldier based at Camp Courtney on Okinawa Island. Private Wallace shot himself at the scene. Shoes, mobile phone and wallet belonging to Chiyoko Kamamoto were found next to the decomposed body. Chiyoko Kamamoto is also believed to have ended her life in the forest, although her body has not yet been discovered.

In a strange twist of fate, the remains were discovered by Yomijuri Miyajima (68), the volunteer suicide monitor who rescued Hiro Yanagida from the scene of the crash on 12 January 2012. Miyajima, who says he was devastated when he heard about Hiro's untimely death, came across the partially decomposed body during a search of the area near to the ice cave.

Takami's disappearance sparked off the ongoing and increasingly violent anti-US protests spear-headed by the Orz Movement and the Cult of Hiro, and authorities are worried that the discovery of his remains could inflame an already volatile situation.

Journalist Vuyo Molefe attended the press conference called by the South African branch of the Rationalist League on 30 July 2012 in Johannesburg. Follow him at @VMtruthhurts.

Vuyo Molefe @VMtruthhurts
Credentials checked again at joburg convention centre entrance. 3rd time now. #chilloutwerenotterrorists

Vuyo Molefe @VMtruthhurts
Lots of speculation going on. Rumours flying that Veronica Oduah is going to pitch.

Vuyo Molefe @VMtruthhurts
@melanichampa Don't know. Been here for an hour. If yr coming bring coffee and doughnuts plis sisi

Vuyo Molefe @VMtruthhurts
FINALLY. SA Rational League spokesperson Kelly Engels appears. Goes on about upcoming US election

Vuyo Molefe @VMtruthhurts
KE: worried bout growing int. support for religious right – could have global implications

Vuyo Molefe @VMtruthhurts
Rumours on point. Veronica Oduah is here! Looks older than 57. Has to be helped to front of room

Vuyo Molefe @VMtruthhurts
VO v nervous. Voice wobbles. Says shes here to come clean. Room gasps. Only one meaning to this

Vuyo Molefe @VMtruthhurts
VO: 'he is not my nephew. They've been keeping him a safehouse away from me for weeks. I told them that when i 1st saw him.'

Vuyo Molefe @VMtruthhurts
VO: 'They offered me money to keep quiet but i did not want to take it.' Says K's dad's cousin did take cash tho

Vuyo Molefe @VMtruthhurts
BBC journo: 'who offered money?' VO: 'The Americans. I don't know their names.'

Vuyo Molefe @VMtruthhurts
Room seriously buzzing. Kelly Engels: 'also have proof from Jozi lab whistleblower that Ken's mitrochondrial DNA not a match.'

Vuyo Molefe @VMtruthhurts
Whistleblower also bribed to keep quiet. Says SA g'ment and religious right faction in cahoots #surprisesurprisecorruptionagain

Vuyo Molefe @VMtruthhurts
And another surprise guest! Zimbo journo next to me says this is better than Transport Minister Mzobe's corruption trial.

Vuyo Molefe @VMtruthhurts
New person woman from eastern cape – Lucy
Inkatha. Says 'Kenneth' is her grandson Mandla

Vuyo Molefe @VMtruthhurts
LI: 'Mandla ran away from home to find father in
cape town. 8-yrs-old has severe learning difficulties'

Vuyo Molefe @VMtruthhurts
Kelly Engels: 'we're all working to get Mandla home
asap.'

Vuyo Molefe @VMtruthhurts
Veronica Oduah: 'It is hard, but I have to accept that
Kenneth is dead.' Some reporters getting upset.

Vuyo Molefe @VMtruthhurts
KE: 'Now that the truth is out there, people will see
exactly how self-serving politicians can be.'

Vuyo Molefe @VMtruthhurts
KE: 'Would like to thank everyone who has been
brave enough to come forward and speak up for the
truth.'

Vuyo Molefe @VMtruthhurts
RT @kellytankgrl FINALLY some sanity in this mess
#dontletthebastardswin

Vuyo Molefe @VMtruthhurts
RT@brodiemermaid Rel.R PR team gonna need another
miracle to get out of this #dontletthebastardswin

Vuyo Molefe @VMtruthhurts
Place now in uproar. Waitin for reaction from end
timers. Could this influence their majority?
#dontletthebastardswin

EDITOR'S NOTE: AFTERWORD TO THE SPECIAL ANNIVERSARY EDITION

When Elspeth Martins' agent first sent me the proposal for *From Crash to Conspiracy* in early 2012, I was immediately intrigued. I had read and admired Elspeth's first book *Snapped*, and I knew that if anyone could come up with a fresh perspective on the events surrounding Black Thursday and The Three, it was Elspeth. As the book started taking shape, it was clear we had something very special on our hands. We decided to rush it into production, choosing to publish in early October before the landmark 2012 election.

Within a week it went into a second, then a third printing. To date, despite the worldwide recession and a massive drop in book sales overall, more than 15 million print and digital editions have been sold. And no one – least of all Elspeth herself – could have foreseen the furore the book would cause.

So why an anniversary edition? Why republish the book that the Rationalist League has dubbed 'inflammatory and dangerous' in these deeply troubled times?

Apart from the most obvious reason – that the book itself has cultural and historical significance as it undoubtedly influenced the 2012 US presidential election – we were granted the rights to some exciting new material that forms the appendix to this edition. Many readers will be aware that on the second anniversary of Black Thursday, Elspeth Martins disappeared. The facts are these: after travelling to

Japan, Elspeth left her hotel in Roppongi, Tokyo on the morning of 12 January 2014. We can only speculate what transpired afterwards, as later attempts to trace her last movements have been hampered by the escalating tension in the area. It does not appear that her credit cards or phone were used after this date, although a self-published book, *Untold Stories from Black Thursday and Beyond*, by 'E. Martins', appeared on Amazon in October 2014. Speculation is rife as to whether the author is actually Elspeth herself or an impostor eager to cash in on *FCTC*'s notoriety.

For this anniversary edition, we have permission from Elspeth's former partner, Samantha Himmelman, to publish her last known correspondence, which is included below.

Elspeth, if you are reading this, please get in touch.

Jared Arthur
Editorial Director
Jameson & White
New York
(January 2015)

TO: **<Samantha Himmelman>** samh56@ajbrookside agency.com
FROM: **<Elspeth Martins>**elliemartini@fctc.com
SUBJECT: **Please read**
12 January 2014, 7.14 a.m.

Sam,
    I know you asked me not to contact you again, but it seems fitting to send this to you on the second anni-

versary of Black Thursday, especially as tomorrow I'm going to the Aokigahara Forest. Daniel – my contact in Tokyo – is desperately trying to dissuade me, but I've come this far, may as well go all the way. I don't want to sound melodramatic, but people do have a habit of going into that forest and not coming out again, don't they? Don't worry – this isn't a suicide note. Not sure what it is. Guess I thought I deserved a chance to make things right, and someone needs to know why I'm here.

No doubt you think I'm crazy travelling to Japan right now, specially with the spectre of the tri-Asian alliance on the horizon, but the situation here isn't as dire as you might have heard. I didn't pick up any hostility from the customs officials or from the people milling around the airport Arrivals area; if anything, they were indifferent. That said, my hotel in the 'Westerners' Sector', which used to be a mega-star Hyatt – gargantuan marble lobby, designer staircases – has seriously gone to seed. According to a Danish guy I spoke to in the immigration queue, the hotels assigned to Westerners are now being run by Brazilian immigrants on limited visas and minimum wage – i.e., zero initiative to give a crap about standards. Only one of the elevators is working, several of the light bulbs in the corridors are dead (I was seriously spooked walking to my room) and I don't think anyone's bothered to vacuum the carpets for months. My room stinks of stale cigarette smoke and there's black mould on the shower tiles. On the upside, the toilet – a sci-fi style thing with a heated seat – works like a dream (thank you, Japanese engineering).

Anyway – I'm not writing to you to whine about my hotel room – see attached. I can't make you read it, for all I know you'll scan the subject line and delete it. I know you won't believe me, but despite all the cut n pasted stuff and transcripts in it (you know me, old habits die hard), I swear I'm not planning on using the content in another book – or at least I'm not now. I'm done with all that.

   xx

Letter to Sam

11 January. 6 p.m. Roppongi Hills, Tokyo

Sam – I have so much to tell you, I'm not sure where to start. But seeing as there's no way I'm getting any sleep tonight, I guess I'll take it from the top, see how far I get before I flag.

Look, I know you think I 'ran away' to London last year to escape the flak I was getting after the book was published, and that was part of it, sure. The Haters and Rationalists still send emails accusing me of being solely responsible for putting a Dominionist in the White House, and no doubt you still think I'm getting everything I deserve. Don't worry – I'm not going to try to defend myself or trot out my tired justification that there was nothing in *From Crash to Conspiracy* (or, as you insisted on calling it, *From Crap to Conservatism*) that wasn't a matter of public record. Just so you know, I still feel guilty for not showing you the final manuscript; the fact that it was rushed into production as soon as I'd signed off on the final interviews with Kendra Vorhees and Geoffrey and Mel Moran is no excuse.

Incidentally, in August there was a new flurry of one-star reviews on Amazon. You should check them out – I know how much of a kick you get out of them. This one caught my eye, probably because it's unusually restrained and grammatically correct:

Customer Review

1.0 out of 5 stars Who does Elspeth Martins think she is???
22 August 2013
By zizekstears (London, UK) – See all my reviews

This review is from: From Crash to Conspiracy (Kindle Edition)

I'd heard about the controversy that this so-called 'non-fiction' book caused last year but assumed it was exaggerated. Apparently the Religious Right quoted parts of it in their campaign during the run-up to the election as 'proof' that The Three were not just normal children suffering from PTSD.

I am not surprised the US Rationalist League came down so hard on the author. Ms Martins has framed and edited each interview or extract in a deliberately manipulative and sensationalist manner ('eye-bleeding'?????? and that awful mawkish stuff about the old man with dementia). She shows no respect for the families of the children or the passengers who died so tragically on Black Thursday.

IMHO Ms Martins is nothing but a lame Studs Terkel wannabe. She should be ashamed for publishing such trash. I will not be buying any more of her work.

Ouch.

But the backlash from the book wasn't the only reason I left. I made the actual decision to get the hell out of the States on the day of the Sannah County Massacre – two days after you'd kicked me out and told me never to contact you again. I first saw those aerial shots of the ranch – the bodies strewn everywhere, black with flies, the gore in the dust – in the anonymity of a Comfort Inn, which seemed as good a place as any to hole up and lick my wounds. I'd been working my way through the bar fridge miniatures and channel surfing when the news broke. I was drunk, couldn't quite make sense of what I was seeing on CNN at first. I actually threw up when I read the strap line: 'Mass suicide in Sannah County. Thirty-three dead, including five children.'

I sat frozen for hours, watching as reporters jostled for position outside the compound gate, spouting variations on the theme: 'Out on bail while he awaited trial for incitement to induce violence, Pastor Len Vorhees and his followers turned their stockpiled weapons on themselves...' Did you see the interview with Reba, Pamela May Donald's frenemy? As you know, we'd never met in person, and from her voice, I'd always pictured her as overweight and permed (felt a weird disconnect when I realised she was actually skinny with a grey braid snaking over her shoulder). Reba had been a nightmare to interview – always off on a tangent about the 'Islamofascists' and her prepping activities – but I felt sorry for her then. Like most of Pastor Len's ex Inner Circle, she was of the opinion that Pastor Len and his Pamelists thought that by following in Jim Donald's footsteps they'd be martyred: 'I pray for their souls every day.' You could see in her eyes that she'd be haunted by their deaths for the rest of her life.

This isn't fun to admit, but empathy for Reba aside, it didn't take me long to start fretting about the consequences the Sannah County Massacre would have on me personally. I knew that the Pamelists' mass suicide would result in another wave of requests for comments and begging letters from hacks pleading with me to put them in touch with Kendra Vorhees. It was never going to be over. I guess what finally tipped me over the edge was Reynard's address to the nation, his movie-star features carefully arranged for optimum piety: 'Suicide is a sin, but we must pray for those who have fallen. Let us use this as a sign that we must work together, grieve together, strive together for a moral America.'

There was nothing keeping me in the US any more. Reynard, Lund, the End Timers, and the corporate fuckers who'd backed them could have it. Sam, do you blame me? Our relationship was shattered, our friends were pissed at me (either for publishing *FCTC* in the first place, or for wallowing in self-pity after I was called out for it) and my career had imploded. I thought about the summers I spent staying with Dad in London. Decided that England was as good a place as any.

But Sam, you have to believe me – I'd convinced myself that Reynard's wet dream of a nation governed by biblical law was just that: a dream. Sure, I knew that Reynard and Lund's Make America Moral campaign would unite the disparate fundamentalist factions, but I swear I underestimated how quickly the movement would spread (guess that was partly down to the Gansu Province Earthquake – another SIGN of God's wrath).

If I'd known that Reynard's fear-mongering would infect the purple as well as the red states, and how bad it would get, I wouldn't have left without you.

Enough excuses.

So.

I exchanged my Lower East Side hotel room for a flat in Notting Hill. The neighbourhood reminded me of Brooklyn Heights: a mix of brisk professionals with shiny hair, rich hipsters, and the occasional bum rooting through the trash. But I'd given no thought to what I'd actually *do* in London. Writing a sequel to *FCTC* was out, of course. I still can't believe I'm the same woman who was so fired up about writing *Untold Stories from Black Thursday*. Interviews with the crash victims' families (Captain Seto's wife, and Kelvin from 277 Together, for example); profiles on the Malawian refugees still searching for their missing relatives in Khayelitsha; an exposé on the new wave of fake 'Kenneths' who popped up after the Mandla Inkatha debacle.

I moped around for the first few weeks, living on a diet of Stoli and take-out Thai. Barely spoke to anyone except the cashier in the off-licence and the To Thai For delivery guy. Did my best to turn into a hikikomori like Ryu. And whenever I did venture out I tried to disguise my accent. The Brits were still incredulous that Reynard could have won the election after the Kenneth Oduah scandal – and the last thing I wanted was to be dragged into political discussions about the 'failure of democracy'. I guess the Brits thought we'd learned our lesson after Blake's tenure. I guess we all did.

I tried to avoid the news, but I caught a clip about the anti-Biblical Law protests in Austin on my Mindspark feed. Jesus, that scared me. Scores of arrests. Tear gas. Riot police. I knew from stalking you on Twitter (I'm not proud of this, okay?) that you'd gone to Texas with Sisters Together Against Conservatism to join up with the Rationalist League's contingent, and I didn't sleep for two days. In the end I called Kayla – I needed to know you were safe. Did she ever tell you that?

Anyway, I'll spare you more details about my self-inflicted London isolation and get down to what you would call 'the juicy bits'.

A few weeks after the Austin riots, I was en route to Sainsbury's when the headline on a *Daily Mail* placard caught my eye: 'Murder House Memorial Plans.' According to the story, a council employee was pushing for Stephen and Shelly Craddock's house – the place where Paul had stabbed Jess to death – to be turned into another Black Thursday memorial. When I flew to the UK to meet with my British publishers and interview Marilyn Adams, I'd avoided visiting it. Didn't want that picture in my head. But the day after that story came out, I found myself waiting on a freezing platform for a delayed train bound for Chislehurst. I told myself it was my last chance to see it before it got the National Trust treatment. But it wasn't just that. Remember when Mel Moran said she couldn't stop herself from going upstairs to Paul's bedroom, even though she knew it was a bad idea? That's how I felt – as if I *had* to go. (Sounds hokey and Paulo Coehlo-esque, I know – but it's the truth.)

It lurked in a street full of pristine mini-mansions, its windows boarded up; the walls smeared with blood-red paint and graffiti ('beware the DEVIL lives here'). The driveway was choked with weeds and a 'for sale' sign leaned mournfully next to the garage. Most disturbing of all was the mini-shrine of mildewed soft toys piled outside the front door. I spotted several My Little Ponies – some still in their packaging – littered on the steps.

I was thinking about climbing over the locked garden gate to check out the backyard, when I heard a voice shouting: 'Oy!'

I turned to see a stout woman with stern grey hair striding up the driveway towards me, dragging a small elderly dog on a lead. 'You are trespassing, young woman! This is private property.'

I recognised her immediately from the photographs taken at Jess's funeral. She hadn't changed a bit. 'Mrs Ellington-Burn?'

She hesitated, then straightened her shoulders. Despite the military stance, there was something melancholy about her. A general who'd been decommissioned before her time. 'Who wants to know? Are you another journalist? Can't you people stay away?'

'I'm not a journalist. Not any more, at any rate.'

'You're American.'

'I am.' I walked up to her and the small dog collapsed at my feet. I scratched its ears and it looked up at me through smoky, cataracted eyes. It resembled Snookie (both in appearance and smell), which made me think of Kendra Vorhees (the last time I heard from her – just after the Sannah County Massacre – she said she'd changed her name and was planning to move to Colorado to join a vegan commune).

Mrs Ellington-Burn's eyes narrowed. 'Wait...Don't I know you?'

I cursed the giant photo the marketing people had slapped on the back of *FCTC*. 'I don't think so.'

'Yes I do. You wrote that book. That ghoulish book. What do you want here?'

'I was just curious to see the house.'

'Prurience, is it? You should be ashamed of yourself.'

I couldn't stop myself from asking: 'Do you still see Paul?'

'What if I do? What's it to you? Now leave, before I call the police.'

A year ago I would've waited until she'd returned to her house and poked around a bit more, but instead, I got out of there.

A week later the phone rang, which was something of an event – the only people who had my new number were my soon-to-be-ex-agent Madeleine and the spammers. I was completely thrown when the guy on the other end of the line introduced himself as Paul Craddock (I later discovered that Madeleine's new PA had been taken by his British accent and given him my number). He said that Mrs E-B had mentioned I was in London, and told me matter-of-factly that in a rather controversial move, one of his consultant psychiatrists had encouraged him to read *FCTC*, in order to help him 'come to terms with what he'd done'. And Sam, this man – who let's not forget had stabbed his niece to death – sounded completely sane: coherent and even witty. He brought me up to speed on Mel and Geoff Moran (who'd moved to Portugal to be closer to their daughter Danielle's resting place) and Mandi Solomon, his ghost writer, who'd joined a splinter End Times sect in the Cotswolds.

He asked me to apply for a visitation order, so that 'we could have a little chat face to face'.

I agreed to visit him. Of course I did. I may have been in the midst of a self-pitying, depressive funk, I may have moved to London to get away from the fallout of the goddamned book, but how could I pass up that opportunity? Do I need to explain why I jumped at the chance, Sam? You know me better than that.

That night I listened to his voice recordings again (I'll admit I got spooked – had to leave the bedroom light on). I replayed Jess saying, 'Hello, Uncle Paul,' over and over again, trying to detect something other than playfulness in her tone. I couldn't.

According to Google Images, Kent House – the high security psychiatric facility where Paul was incarcerated – was a dour, grey-stone monolith. I couldn't help but think that insane asylums (okay, I know this isn't the PC term) shouldn't be allowed to look so stereotypical and Dickensian.

I had to sign a waiver saying that I wouldn't publish the details about my meeting with Paul, and my police clearance and visitation order came through on the last day of October – Halloween. Coincidentally the same day that Reddit first aired the rumour that Reynard was planning to repeal the First Amendment. I was still avoiding Sky and CNN, but I couldn't avoid the newspaper billboards. I remember thinking, how could it be unravelling so fast? But even then, I didn't allow myself to believe that Reynard would manage to secure Congress and the two thirds majority he'd need. I assumed we'd just have to ride out his presidency, deal with the fallout after the next election. Stupid, I know. By then the Catholic church and the Mormons had pledged their support to the Make America Moral campaign – even a moron could have seen where it was heading.

I decided to shell out for a taxi rather than play Russian Roulette with the train service, and I was right on time for my meeting with Paul. Kent House was as forbidding in real life as it looked on Google Images. A recent addition – a brick and glass carbuncle tacked onto the building's exterior – somehow made the whole place look more intimidating. After being searched and scanned by a couple of incongruously cheerful security staff, I was escorted to the carbuncle by a jovial male nurse with skin as grey as his hair. I'd been picturing meeting Paul in a stark cell, bars on the doors, a couple of grim-faced jailors and several psychiatrists watching our every move. Instead, I was buzzed through a glass door and into a large airy room furnished with chairs so brightly coloured they looked insane. The nurse told me that there would be no other visitors that day – apparently the bus service to the institution had been cancelled that afternoon. That wasn't unusual. The UK wasn't immune to the recession caused by Reynard's meddling in the Middle East. But I have to say, there was an admirable lack of grumbling when the electricity and fuel rationing was proposed; maybe the end of the world is Prozac for the Brits.

[Sam – I couldn't record our conversation as I'd had to leave my iPhone at security, so this is all from memory. I know you don't care about these sorts of details, but I do.]

The door on the opposite side of the room clicked open and a morbidly obese man dressed in a tent-sized

T-shirt and carrying a Tesco's bag waddled in. The nurse called out, 'All right, Paul? Your visitor's here.'

I immediately assumed there must have been a mix-up. 'That's Paul? Paul Craddock?'

'Hello, Miss Martins,' Paul said in the voice I recognised from the recordings. 'It's a pleasure to meet you.'

I'd checked out the YouTube clips of Paul's acting roles just before I left, and I searched in vain for any sign of his conventionally handsome features in the sagging jowls and doughy cheeks. Only the eyes were the same. 'Please, call me Elspeth.'

'Elspeth, then.' We shook hands. His palm was clammy and I resisted the urge to wipe mine on my trousers.

The nurse clapped Paul on the shoulder and nodded to a glass-fronted cubicle a few yards from our table. 'I'll be over there, Paul.'

'Cheers, Duncan.' Paul's chair squeaked as he sat down. 'Ah! Before I forget.' He rummaged in the plastic bag and pulled out a copy of *FCTC* and a red sharpie pen. 'Will you sign it?'

Sam – it was going from the bizarre to the surreal. 'Um . . . sure. What do you want me to put?'

'To Paul. I couldn't have done it without you.' I flinched, and he laughed. 'Don't mind me. Put what you like.'

I scribbled, 'Best Wishes, Elspeth,' and pushed the book back across the table to him. 'Please excuse my appearance,' he said. 'I'm turning into a pudding. There's not much to do in here except eat. Are you shocked that I've let myself go like this?'

I murmured something about a few extra pounds not

being the end of the world. My nerves were on edge. Paul certainly didn't look or act like a raving lunatic–(not entirely sure what I'd been expecting, maybe some kind of strait-jacketed madman with rolling eyes) – but if he suddenly lost it, lunged across the table and tried to throttle me, there was only one weedy nurse to stop him.

Paul read my mind: 'Are you surprised at the lack of supervision? Staff cut-backs. But don't worry, Duncan's a black belt in karate. Aren't you, Duncan?' Paul waved at the nurse who chuckled and shook his head. 'What are you doing in London, Elspeth? Your agent said you'd moved here. Did you leave the States because of the unfortunate political climate?'

I said that that was one of the reasons.

'I can't say I blame you. If that prick in the White House gets his way, soon you'll all be Living with Leviticus. Where the gays and naughty children are stoned to death and the acned and menstrual are shunned. Lovely. Almost makes me grateful to be in here.'

'Why did you want to see me, Paul?'

'Like I said on the phone, I heard you were in England. I thought it would be nice to meet face to face. Dr Atkinson was in agreement that it might do me good to meet one of my biographers.' He belched behind his hand. 'He's the one who gave me your book to read. And it's lovely to see a fresh face in here. Mrs E-B comes once a month, but she can get a bit much. Not that I'm short of requests for visitation.' He glanced at the nurse in the booth. 'Sometimes I get as many as fifty a week – mostly from the conspiracy nuts, of course, but I've had a fair few marriage proposals. Not as many as Jurgen has, but close.'

'Jurgen?'

'Oh! You must have heard of Jurgen Williams. He's in here too. He murdered five school children, but you'd never know it to look at him. He's actually rather dull.' I had no clue how to respond to that. 'Elspeth, when you put my story in the book...Did you listen to the original recordings, or just read the transcripts?'

'Both.'

'And?'

'They scared me.'

'Psychosis isn't pretty. You must have lots of questions for me. You can ask me anything.'

I took him at his word. 'Please let me know if I'm crossing the line here...but what happened in the last few days before Jess died? Did she say anything to you that made you...made you...'

'Stab her to death? You can say it. Those are the facts. But no. She didn't. What I did was unforgivable. She was put in my care, and I killed her.'

'In your recordings...you said she taunted you.'

'Paranoid delusions.' He frowned. 'All in my head. There was nothing strange about Jess. It was all me. Dr Atkinson has made that very clear.' He glanced at the nurse again. 'I had a psychotic break, brought on by alcohol abuse and stress. End of. You can put that in your next book. May I ask you a favour, Elspeth?'

'Of course.'

He rummaged in the plastic packet again, this time extracting a slim exercise pad. He handed it to me. 'I've been doing some writing. It's not much...some poetry. Would you mind reading it and letting me know what you think? Maybe your publishers would be interested.'

I decided not to mention that I didn't have a publisher

any more, although I suspected they would jump at the opportunity to publish poetry written by a notorious child murderer. Instead I said I'd be happy to and shook his hand again.

'Make sure you read all of it.'

'I will.'

I watched him waddling away, and the grey-skinned nurse escorted me back to the security entrance. I started reading the book on the taxi ride home. The first three pages were filled with short, appalling verse with titles like: *Cavendish Dreams* (Reading a line/For the twentieth time/Makes me reflect/We are all actors) and *Flesh Prison* (I eat to forget/Yet it makes my soul sweat/I think … will I yet/Ever say no?).

The other pages were blank, but on the inside of the cardboard back cover were the words:

Jess wanted me to do it. She MADE ME do it. Before she went she said that they've been before and sometimes she decides not to die. She said that sometimes they give people what they want, sometimes they don't. Ask the others, THEY KNOW.

Sam, what would you have done with this? Knowing you, you would have contacted Paul's psychiatrist immediately, let him know that Paul was still in the midst of some sort of psychotic break.

That would have been the right thing to do.

But I'm not you.

After *FCTC* came out, I thought maybe I was the only person in the world who didn't think there was something supernatural (for want of a better word) about The Three. I've lost count of the number of whack-jobs who pleaded with me to puff their self-published books on how The

Three were still alive and living with a Maori woman in New Zealand/being experimented on in a secret Cape Town military base/hanging out with aliens in Dulce Air Force Base New Mexico (I have proof, miss martins!!!! Why else is the world still going to hell!!!!!). And then there are the countless conspiracy sites that use quotes or extracts from *FCTC* to 'prove' their theories that The Three were possessed by aliens or were multi-dimensional time-travellers. (The following are the ones they tend to fixate on:)

BOBBY: 'One day *I'll* bring [the dinosaurs] back to life.'

JESS: 'It doesn't work like that. A fucking wardrobe. As if, Uncle Paul.'
   'It was a mistake. Sometimes we get it wrong.'

CHIYOKO: [Hiro] says he remembers being hoisted up into the rescue helicopter. He said it was fun. 'Like flying.' He said he was looking forward to doing it again.

There are even several websites dedicated to discussing the implications of Jess's obsession with *The Lion, the Witch and the Wardrobe*.
   But the rest of us have to admit that there's a rational explanation for all of it: the kids survived the crashes because they got lucky; Paul Craddock's version of events re Jess's behaviour was just the ramblings of a lunatic; Reuben Small could easily have been in remission; and Hiro was simply aping his father's

obsession with androids. The kids' changes in behaviour
could all have been a result of the trauma they'd suffered.
And let's not forget the hours of material I chose *not* to
include in the book – Paul Craddock's lengthy complaints
about not getting laid; the minutiae of Lillian Small's
daily life – where absolutely nothing happened. That
Amazon reviewer was spot on when he accused me of
being manipulative and sensationalist.

But…but… '*She said that they've been before and
sometimes she decides not to die. She said that sometimes
they give people what they want, sometimes they don't.*'

I had a number of options. I could visit Paul again, ask
him why he'd chosen to give me this information; I could
ignore it as the ramblings of someone who was mentally
ill; or I could throw rationality out of the window and
look into what the words could possibly mean. I tried the
first option, but I was told that Paul wasn't interested in
having any further contact with me (no doubt because he
was concerned I might reveal what he'd given me to his
psychiatrist). The second option was tempting, but
presumably Paul had passed this on to me for a reason:
Ask the others, THEY KNOW. I guess I thought that
looking into it wouldn't hurt – what else did I have to do
with my time apart from delete abusive emails and
wander around Notting Hill in a vodka-fuelled haze?

So I threw reason out of the window and decided to
play devil's advocate. Say that Paul was repeating
something Jess had told him just before he'd killed her,
what *did* it mean? The conspiracy nuts would have a
trillion theories about *they've been before and sometimes
she decides not to die*, but I wasn't about to contact any of
them. And what about: *sometimes they give people what*

they want, sometimes they don't. After all, The Three *had* given people – or at least the End Timers – what they wanted: apparent 'proof' that the end of the world was nigh. Then again, Jess had given Paul what he thought he wanted – fame; Hiro gave Chiyoko a reason to live, and Bobby . . . Bobby had given Lillian her husband back.

I decided it was time to break a promise.

Sam, I know it used to drive you crazy when I kept things from you (like the entire first draft of *FCTC*, for example), but I gave Lillian Small my word that I wouldn't reveal that she'd survived the car crash that killed Reuben and Bobby. Out of all the people I'd interviewed for the book, her story affected me the most – and I'd been touched that she trusted me enough to contact me when she was in hospital. The FBI had offered to relocate her, and we decided after that it would be best to break contact – she didn't need any further reminders of what she'd lost.

I doubted the FBI would simply pass on her phone number, so I decided to give Betsy – her neighbour – a shot.

The phone was answered with a '*Ja*?'

'I'm looking for Mrs Katz?'

'She no live here no more.' (I couldn't place the accent – it might have been Eastern European.)

'Do you have a forwarding address? It's really important.'

'Wait.'

I heard the thunk of the handset being dropped; the thump of bass in the background. Then: 'I have a number.'

I Googled the area code – Toronto, Canada. Somehow I couldn't imagine Betsy in Canada.

[Sam – the following is the transcript of the call – yeah, I know, why would I have recorded it and transcribed it if I wasn't planning on using it in a book or article? Please, trust me on this – I swear you will not be seeing *Elspeth Martins' Truth about The Three* on sale in a store near you anytime soon:]

ME: Hi...is that Betsy? Betsy Katz?

BETSY: Who is this calling me?

ME: Elspeth Martins. I interviewed you for my book.

[*long pause*]

BETSY: Ah! The writer! Elspeth! You are well?

ME: I'm fine. How are you?

BETSY: If I complain, who will listen? What do you think about what is happening in New York? Those riots on the news and the fuel shortages. Are you safe? Are you keeping warm? You have enough food?

ME: I'm fine, thanks. I was wondering...do you know how I can get hold of Lillian?

[*longer pause*]

BETSY: You don't know? Well, of course how would you know? I'm sorry to tell you this, but Lillian has passed. A month ago, now. She went in her sleep – a good way to go. She didn't suffer.

ME: [after several seconds of silence while I fought not to lose control – Sam, I was a fucking mess] I'm so sorry.

BETSY: She was such a good woman, you know she invited me to stay with her? When the first of the blackouts hit New York. Out of nowhere she called me and said, 'Betsy, you can't live there on your own, come to Canada.' Canada! Me! I miss her, I won't lie. But there's a good community here, a nice Rabbi who takes care of me. Lily said she appreciated how you made her sound in your book – smarter than she was. But what Mona said – what poison! Lily found that hard to read. And what do you think about what is happening in Israel? That schmuck in the White House, what does he think he is doing? Does he want all the Muslims down on our heads?

ME: Betsy...before she passed, did Lillian mention anything...um...particular about Bobby?

BETSY: About Bobby? What would she say? Only that her life has been a tragedy. Everyone she ever loved taken away from her. God can be cruel.

I hung up. Cried for two hours straight. For once they weren't tears of self-pity.

But say that I had spoken to Lillian, what *would* she have said anyway? That the Bobby who came home after the crash wasn't her grandson? When I interviewed her all those months ago, whenever she spoke about him I could hear the love in her voice.

Ask the others, THEY KNOW.

So who else was there? I knew Lori Small's best friend

Mona was out (after the *FCTC* furore she denied ever having spoken to me), but there was someone else who'd encountered Bobby and hadn't come away unscathed.

Ace Kelso.

Sam, I can just picture your face as you read this: a mixture of exasperation and fury. You were right when you said I should have put his reputation first. You were right when you accused me of not fighting hard enough to have his admission that he saw blood in Bobby Small's eyes taken out of the later editions (another nail in the coffin of our relationship). And yeah, I should have destroyed the recording refuting Ace's claim that he'd said it off the record. Why the fuck didn't I listen to you?

The last time I'd seen him was in that soulless boardroom in the publishers' lawyers' offices, when he was told he didn't have a case. His flesh hung loose on his face, his eyes were bloodshot, he hadn't shaved in days. His threadbare jeans sagged at the knees; his tatty leather jacket stank of stale sweat. The Ace I'd interviewed for the book and seen on TV was square-jawed, blue-eyed – a real Captain America type (as Paul Craddock once described him).

I had no clue if Ace would even talk to me, but what did I have to lose? I Skyped him, fully expecting that he wouldn't answer. When he did, his voice was blurry, as if he'd just woken up.

ACE: Yeah?

ME: Ace...Hi. It's Elspeth Martins. Um...how are you?

[*a pause of several seconds*]

ACE: I'm still on extended sick leave. A euphemism for permanent suspension. What the hell do you want, Elspeth?

ME: I thought you should know...I've been to see Paul Craddock.

ACE: So?

ME: When I met with him, he was adamant that what he'd done to Jess was the result of a psychotic break. But as I was leaving he handed me a note. Look, this is going to sound crazy, but in it he said that – among other things – Jess told him she'd 'been here before' and 'sometimes she decides not to die'.

[*another long pause*]

ACE: Why are you telling me this?

ME: I thought...I dunno. I guess...what you said about Bobby...Like I say, it's crazy to even think like this, but Paul said, 'ask the others' and I—

ACE: You know something, Elspeth? I know you got a lot of criticism for what you included in that book, but far as I'm concerned you were lambasted for the wrong reasons. You published all that inflammatory stuff about the kids' personalities changing, dropped the bomb and just walked away. You didn't take it further; you assumed everything had a rational explanation and naively thought everyone who read it would also see it like that.

ME: My intention wasn't to—

ACE: I know what your intentions were. And now you're sniffing around to see if there really *was* something up with those kids, am I right?

ME: I'm just looking into things.

ACE: [a sigh] Tell you what. I'm gonna email you something.

ME: What?

ACE: Read it first, then we'll talk.

[The email came through immediately and I clicked on an attachment entitled: SA678ORG

At first glance I thought it was an exact copy of the Sun Air Cockpit Voice Recording transcript that I'd included in *FCTC*. And it was exactly the same, apart from this exchange that occurred a second before the plane ran into trouble:

Captain: [expletive] You see that?

First Officer: Hai! Lightning?

Captain: Negative. Never seen a flash like that. There's nothing on TCAS, ask ATC if there's another aircraft up here with us—]

ME: What the fuck is this?

ACE: You gotta understand, we didn't want to fuel the panic. People needed to know that the causes of those crashes were explainable. The grounded planes had to get back in the air.

ME: The NTSB faked the Sun Air transcript? You're telling me that you guys seriously believed you were dealing with an alien encounter?

ACE: What I'm telling you is that we were confronted by facts that we couldn't explain. Sun Air aside, the only disaster that had a definite cause was the Dalu Air crash.

ME: What the hell are you talking about? What about the Maiden Air disaster?

ACE: We had a multiple bird strike with no snarge. Sure, possibly explainable if the engines had been consumed by fire – but they weren't. How in the hell do two jet engines get imploded by birds – without a trace of matter? And look at the Go!Go! incident. We were grasping at straws with that one – but one thing's for sure – it's pretty damn unusual for pilots to fly into a storm of that magnitude in this day and age. And answer me this, how in the fuck did those three kids survive?

ME: Look at Zainab Farra, the little girl who survived that crash in Ethiopia. The Three were like her, they got lucky—

ACE: Bullshit. And you know it.

ME: This transcript...why did you send it to me? Do you actually want me to publish it?

ACE: [a bitter laugh] What's the worst that can happen now? Reynard will give me a medal – more proof that

The Three weren't just normal kids. Do what you want with it. The NTSB and JTSB will deny it anyway.

ME: So you're seriously saying you think there's something... I don't know... otherworldly about The Three? You're an investigator – a scientist.

ACE: All I know is what I saw when I went to see Bobby. It wasn't an hallucination, Elspeth. And that photographer, the one who ended up being dinner for his goddamned reptiles, he saw something as well.

[*another sigh*]

Listen, you were just doing your job. I shouldn't have gone after you for publishing what I said about Bobby. Maybe I said it was off the record, maybe I didn't. But it was the truth. Fact is, you gotta be blind not to see that there was something wrong with those kids.

ME: So what do you suggest I do now?

ACE: Up to you, Elspeth. But whatever you do, I suggest you make it quick. The End Timers are hell-bent on fulfilling their own prophecies. How in the hell do you negotiate with a president who's convinced that the end of the world is nigh and that the only way to save people from eternal damnation is to turn the US into a theocracy? Simple. You can't.

Of course I struggled to believe that the NTSB would actually doctor the record – even if it was concerned about people panicking about the causes of the disasters. Could the transcript be Ace's revenge for the eye-bleeding debacle? If I made something like this public, the Rationalist League would have another reason to string me up.

But you know where this is going, right? I had Paul's note, Ace's (possibly faked) transcript, and his assurances that he really had seen blood in Bobby's eyes.

It could all be bullshit – probably was. But there was one child left.

I spent the next few days researching Chiyoko and Hiro. Most of the links led to new material on Ryu and Chiyoko's tragic love story, among them a recent article on a spate of copycat suicides, but there was surprisingly little on Hiro. I contacted Eric Kushan, the guy who'd translated the Japanese extracts in *FCTC,* to see if he could give me any leads, but he'd left Japan a few months earlier after the Treaty of Mutual Cooperation between the States and Japan was overturned, and all he could suggest was that I look into the Cult of Hiro.

I thought it might have morphed into something approximating the Moonies or Aum Shrinrikyo, but rather than becoming a hardcore nationalist cult, it had fizzled into little more than a bizarre celebrity trend. Now that her husband had won the election, Aikao Uri appeared to have dumped her alien theories and surrabot, focusing her energies on campaigning for the tri-Asian alliance. The Orz Movement had gone completely underground

Do you remember Daniel Mimura? He was one of the *Tokyo Herald* journalists who'd given me permission to use a couple of his articles for *FCTC*. He was one of the few contributors (along with Lola – Pastor Len's 'fancy woman' – and the documentary filmmaker Malcolm Adelstein) who'd sent me a supportive note after the shit hit the fan. He sounded delighted to hear from me, and we chatted for a while about how the Japanese people were coping with the spectre of a possible alliance with China and Korea.

I transcribed the rest of our conversation:

ME: You think Chiyoko and Ryu really did die in Aokigahara?

DANIEL: Reckon Ryu did for sure, they did an autopsy, which is quite unusual for Tokyo – they aren't done automatically in every suspicious death. Chiyoko's body was never found, so who knows?

ME: You think she could be alive?

DANIEL: Possibly. You heard the rumours about Hiro? They've been circulating for a while.

ME: You mean the usual 'The Three are still alive' bullshit?

DANIEL: Yeah. You want me to go into it?

ME: Sure.

DANIEL: This is crazy conspiricist stuff but…Look, to start with, the cops shut down that scene really fast. The paramedics and forensics guys were instructed not to talk to the press. Even the police agency guys couldn't get much of a story out of them, except for the official statement.

ME: Okay... but why would they fake his death?

DANIEL: The New Nationalists could have planned it, maybe. I mean, what better way to turn the public against the US? S'pose at a push, if you were that way inclined, you could say they set the whole thing up, staged the scene, killed the Kamamotos and that soldier, made it look like Hiro was dead.

ME: That doesn't make sense. Private Jake Wallace was a Pamelist – he had a motive to kill Hiro. How would they get him involved in a scheme like that?

DANIEL: Hey, don't shoot the messenger. I'm just telling you about the rumours. Hell, I dunno, maybe they got wind about what he was gonna do, set him up. Hacked into his emails like those other guys did.

ME: But the witnesses said that they saw Chiyoko carrying Hiro's body.

DANIEL: Yeah. But have you seen those surrabots Kenji Yanagida makes? They're eerie. Unless you're close up to them, they look seriously convincing.

ME: Hang on... wouldn't that mean that Chiyoko would've been in on it?

DANIEL: Yeah.

ME: So let's say what you're saying did happen. Chiyoko sat back and allowed her parents to be murdered... why?

DANIEL: Who knows? Money? So that she and Hiro could go off to some unknown country and live out their lives in luxury? And poor old Ryu got caught up in it and ended up another casualty.

ME: You any idea how often I've heard these kinds of theories?

DANIEL: Sure. Like I say, all bullshit.

ME: You ever looked into it?

DANIEL: Dug around a bit, nothing major. You know how these things go. If there was anything to it, someone would have leaked it by now.

ME: Didn't Kenji Yanagida identify Hiro's body?

DANIEL: So?

ME: If anyone knows the truth, it's him. Would he talk to me?

DANIEL: [a laugh] No fucking way. It's all bullshit, Ellie. The kid is dead.

ME: Is Kenji Yanagida still in Osaka?

DANIEL: Last I heard he left the university after being hounded by the Cult of Hiro – they were desperate for him to be one of their high-profile mascots. Apparently he moved to Tokyo, changed his name.

ME: Can you track him down for me?

DANIEL: You have any idea how many people have tried to talk to Kenji Yanagida and been stonewalled?

ME: But I have something they don't have.

DANIEL: What?

I didn't tell Daniel about Ace's transcript. It might be my way into speaking to Kenji Yanagida, it might not.

I know what you're thinking: that I didn't tell Daniel about it because it was my exclusive and I wanted to use it for my own ends – maybe shove it in another book. But again, I'm done with all that, Sam, I swear.

I didn't do anything for the next few weeks. The world was holding its breath after that group of renegade End Timers tried to set fire to the al-Aqsa Mosque at the Temple Mount in another effort to step up the race to the Rapture. Not even I was stupid enough to fly to Asia on what could be the cusp of World War III.

And the news we were getting in from the States was just as depressing. I may have been sticking my head in the sand, but the reports of escalating attacks on gay teenagers; the mass closure of reproductive health clinics; the Internet blackouts; the GLAAD and Rationalist League leaders being apprehended under so-called state security laws, filtered through. There were anti-US protests in the UK, too. The UK was cutting its ties with Reynard's regime, and MigrantWatch were campaigning to stem the tide of US émigrés. And I don't want you to think I wasn't worried about you. That's all I thought about over the holiday season (I'm not going to whine about spending Thanksgiving alone in my freezing flat eating take-out jalfrezi). Thought of you when those UK celebs joined the US A-listers in their 'Save Our Bill of Rights' campaign – it would have brought out your cynical side. All the YouTube clips and supergroup iTunes songs in the world weren't going to change the convictions of people who honestly believe that by wiping out 'immorality', they'll be saving others from burning in hell for all eternity.

But I couldn't let it go.

Remembering what Ace said about not dragging my feet, I called Daniel in early December and told him I needed help getting into Tokyo. He thought I was crazy, of course – his contract had just been cancelled (he said it was happening to Westerners all over Japan, 'their way of saying we're no longer welcome'). Even with my British passport, thanks to new regulations, I'd need a visa, a valid reason for travel and a Japanese citizen willing to stand as my sponsor and representative. He reluctantly said he'd ask one of his friends to help.

I tracked down Pascal de la Croix – Kenji's old buddy – and begged him to ask Kenji to see me. I told him the truth – that I had new information regarding the Sun Air crash that Kenji needed to know. I told him I was flying into Tokyo especially to see him. Pascal was reluctant of course, but he finally agreed to email Kenji for me on the proviso that if I did get to see him, I wouldn't publish anything about our meeting.

I reckon I checked my inbox about fifty times a day after that – filtering through the hate mail and spam – for a response.

It came through on the same day as my visa. An address, nothing more.

Sam, I'll be honest. Before I left I took a long, hard look at myself. What the hell did I think I was doing? Didn't following this up make me as crazy as the End Timers and the conspiracy freaks? And let's say my batshit insane Kenji Yanagida wild-goose chase did lead me to Hiro. Say he was still alive and I managed to talk to him. And he told me that The Three were all possessed by the horsemen out of Revelation, or were all psycho aliens, or were three of the Four fucking Tops, what then? Did I have a duty to 'let the truth be known'? And if I did, would it make any difference? Look what happened with the Kenneth Oduah scandal. Solid proof that his DNA results were faked, but still millions bought into Dr Lund's bullshit that 'it is God's will that the fourth horseman may never be found'.

The flight was a nightmare. I got the total Pamela May Donald heebies before we even took off. Kept imagining how she must have felt in the minutes before her plane went down. I even found myself composing an *isho* in my head just in case. (I won't embarrass you with it.) It didn't help that half-an-hour into the flight, 90% of the other passengers (all Westerners, mostly Brits and Scandinavians) were already drunk. The guy next to me, some kind of IT specialist who was heading to Tokyo to help disband IBM's Roppongi branch, filled me in on what to expect when we arrived. 'See, it's not that they're openly hostile or anything like that, but it's best to stay in the "Westerners' section" – Roppongi and Roppongi hills. It's not bad, lot of pubs.' He downed his double JD and breathed bourbon fumes over me. 'And who wants to hang out with the Japs anyway? I can show you around if you like.' I declined, and thankfully he passed out shortly afterwards.

When we landed at Narita, we were funnelled to a special holding area where our passports and visas were scrutinised with forensic precision. Next, we were herded onto coaches. At first, I couldn't see any signs that Japan was heading, like the rest of the world, towards economic collapse. It was only as we cruised over the bridge that led into the heart of the city, that I realised the trademark billboards, signage, and even the Tokyo Tower were only half-illuminated.

Daniel met me at the hotel the next day, and painstakingly wrote down step-by-step directions describing how to get to Kenji's address in Kanda. As it's in the old part of the city and outside the Westerners' Approved areas he suggested that I hide my hair, wear glasses and cover my face with a surgical flu mask. It seemed a bit over-the-top, but while he assured me that he doubted I'd run into trouble, he said it was best not to draw too much attention to myself.

Sam, I'm exhausted, and I have a big day ahead of me. It's getting light now, but I have one last scene to relate. I haven't had time to transcribe my conversation with Kenji Yanagida – I only saw him yesterday – so you're getting it in Proper Writing.

Without Daniel's detailed directions, I would
have been lost within seconds. Kanda – a labyrinth
of criss-crossing streets lined with tiny restaurants,
minuscule book stores and smoke-filled coffee shops
packed with black-suited salarymen – was bewildering
after Roppongi's comparatively soulless Western-style
architecture. I followed the directions to a narrow alley
teeming with overcoated people, their faces hidden
behind scarves or flu masks. I paused outside a door set
between a tiny shop selling plastic baskets of dried fish
and one displaying several framed paintings of children's
hands, and checked the kanji on the sign outside it
against the lettering Daniel had written out for me.
Heart in my mouth, I pressed the intercom button.

'*Hai*?' a man's voice barked.

'Kenji Yanagida?'

'Yes?'

'My name is Elspeth Martins. Pascal de la Croix put
me in touch with you.'

After a beat, the door clicked open.

I stepped into a corridor that stank of mildew, and
with no other option, started down a short stairway. It
ended at an anonymous, half-open door. I pushed through
it and into a large cluttered workshop. A small group of
people were hanging around in the centre of the room.
Then my brain hitched (Sam – I can't think of another
way to put it) and it hit me that these weren't people at
all, but surrabots.

I counted six of them – three women, two men and
(horribly) a child, propped up on stands, the halogen
lights bouncing off their waxy skin and too-shiny eyes.
There were several more sitting on plastic chairs and

frayed armchairs in a gloomy corner – one even had its legs crossed in an obscenely human pose.

Kenji stepped out from behind a worktop covered in wires, computer screens and soldering equipment. He looked a decade older and twenty kilos lighter than on his YouTube clips – the skin around his eyes was creased; his high cheekbones looked as prominent as a skull's.

Without greeting me, he said: 'What information do you have for me?'

I told him about Ace's confession and handed him a copy of the transcript. He scanned it without any change in expression, then folded it and slid it into his pocket. 'Why did you bring this to me?'

'I thought you had a right to know the truth. Your wife and son were on that plane.'

'Thank you.'

He stared at me for several seconds, and I got the impression he could see straight through me.

I gestured at the surrabots. 'What are you doing here? Are these for the Cult of Hiro?'

He grimaced. 'No. I am making replicas for people. Mostly Koreans. Replicas of the loved ones they have lost.' His eyes strayed to a pile of wax masks lying on the bench. Death masks.

'Like the one you made of Hiro?' He flinched (who can blame him? It was hardly a sensitive thing to say). 'Yanagida-san... your son, Hiro... when he was killed, was it you who identified him?'

I steeled myself for a barrage of invective. But instead he said: 'Yes.'

'I'm sorry to ask this... it's just there are rumours that maybe he isn't... maybe he...'

'My son is dead. I saw his body. Is that what you wanted to know?'

'And Chiyoko?'

'Is this why you came? To ask me about Hiro and Chiyoko?'

'Yes. But the transcript – that's the truth. You have my word on that.'

'Why do you want to know about Chiyoko?'

I decided to tell him the truth. I suspected he would see straight through bullshit. 'I'm following a series of leads regarding The Three. They led me to you.'

'I cannot help you. Please leave.'

'Yanagida-san, I have come a long way—'

'Why can you not leave this be?'

I could see the grief in his eyes. I'd pushed him too far, and to be honest, I was disgusted with myself. I turned to leave, but as I did, I spied a surrabot in a darkened corner, half-hidden behind the facsimile of a corpulent man. She sat in her own private area, a serene figure dressed in a white kimono. She was the only one who appeared to be breathing. 'Yanagida-san . . . is that the copy of your wife? Hiromi?'

A long pause, then: 'Yes.'

'She was beautiful.'

'Yes.'

'Yanagida-san, did she . . . did she leave a message? An *isho*, like some of the other passengers?' I couldn't stop myself. I needed to know.

'Jukei. She's there.'

For a second I thought he meant his wife. Then it clicked. 'She? You mean Chiyoko?'

'*Hai.*'

'The forest? Aokigahara?'

A minuscule nod.

'Where in the forest?'

'I don't know.'

I wasn't going to press my luck any further. 'Thank you, Yanagida-san.'

As I made my way back to the staircase, he said: 'Wait.' I turned to face him. His expression remained as unreadable as the surrabot next to him. Then he said: 'Hiromi. In her message, she said, "Hiro is gone."'

So that's it. That's all I've got. I have no idea why Kenji told me the content of his wife's *isho*. Maybe he really was grateful for the transcript; maybe, like Ace, he thinks that there's no point keeping it to himself any more.

Maybe he was lying.

I'd better send this now. The wifi here is crap – got to go down to the lobby to do it. The forest is going to be cold – it's starting to snow.

Sam – I'm aware that the chances you've actually read this are slim, but just so you know, I've decided I'm coming back home after this. Back to NYC – if the governor isn't bullshitting about holding a referendum for secession, I want to be there. I'm not going to run away any more. I hope you'll be there, Sam.

I love you,

Ellie

HOW IT ENDS

Elspeth's disguise of sunglasses and the now slightly soggy flu mask is just as effective in the suburbs as it was in the city – so far, none of her fellow passengers have spared her a second glance. But as she alights at Otsuki – a rickety station that looks like it's stuck in the 1950s – a uniformed man barks something at her. She feels a momentary panic, then realises he's only asking for her ticket. Stupid. She bobs her head, hands it over and he waves her towards an elderly locomotive waiting at an adjacent platform. A whistle blows and she scrambles on board, relieved that the carriage is empty. She sinks onto the bench seat and tries to relax. As the train jolts, shudders, then finds its stride, she looks through grimed windows onto snow-dusted fields, slope-roofed wooden houses and a series of small frozen allotments, barren but for a crop of ice-rotten cabbages. Icy air seeps through cracks in the train's sides; a light drift of snow brushes against the windows. She reminds herself that there are fourteen stops to Kawaguchiko – the end of the line.

She concentrates on the clack of the wheels; tries not to think too deeply about where she's headed. At the third stop, a man with a face as rumpled as his clothes climbs into her carriage, and she stiffens as he chooses the seat opposite hers. She prays that he won't try to engage her in conversation. He grunts, digs in a large shopping bag, and hauls out a packet of what look to be giant nori rolls. He stuffs one in his mouth, then offers her the bag. Deciding that it would be rude to refuse, she murmurs 'Arigato,' and takes one. Instead of rice encased in seaweed, she bites into some sort of light crispy candy that tastes of Splenda. She takes her time eating it in case he offers her another (she's already nauseous) then drops her head as if she's taking a nap. It's only partly an act; she's exhausted after a sleepless night.

When she next looks up, she's stunned to see a giant roller-coaster filling the window, its rusting frame shaggy with icicle teeth. It must be attached to one of the now-defunct Mount Fuji resorts Daniel told her about; an incongruous dinosaur stuck in the middle of nowhere.

Last stop.

Giving her an enormous smile that makes her feel guilty for pretending to sleep, the old man departs. She hangs back, then follows him across the tracks and into the deserted station, a wooden structure clad in shiny pine that looks as if it would be more at home in an Alpine ski resort. Hurdy-gurdy music plays from somewhere, loud enough to follow her when she exits into the station fore-court. The tourist booth to her right has the aura of a mau-soleum, but she spies a single taxi parked next to a bus stop, smoke pouring out of its exhaust.

She digs out the scrap of paper on which Daniel had (reluctantly) written her destination, folds it around a ten thousand yen note and approaches the car. She hands it to the driver, who shows no emotion as he glances at it. He nods, tucks the money into his jacket and stares straight ahead. The taxi's interior reeks of stale cigarette smoke and despair. How many people has this man ferried to the forest, knowing that more than likely they wouldn't be returning? The driver guns the engine before she's even managed to secure her seat belt, and whips through the deserted village. Most of the stores are boarded up; the gas station pumps are padlocked. They pass a single vehicle – an empty school bus.

Within minutes they're skirting a wide glassy lake, and Elspeth has to cling to the door handle as the driver throws the car around the narrow road's curves; clearly he's as keen to be done with the journey as she is. She takes in the sagging skeleton of a large shrine, a forest of neglected grave markers in front of it; a row of rotting kayaks and the burned limbs of several holiday shacks peeking gamely through the snow. Mount Fuji looms in the background, mist cloaking its top.

They leave the lake behind, and the driver swings onto a deserted highway before turning sharply and speeding down a narrower road, lumped with snow and slick with ice. The forest creeps up around them. She knows it has to be Aokigahara – she recognises the bulbous roots that sit above the forest floor's volcanic base. They pass several snow-shrouded cars abandoned by the side of the road. In one, she's almost certain she can discern the shape of a slumped figure behind the wheel.

The taxi driver spins the car into a parking lot and jerks to a stop next to a low shuttered building that screams neglect. He points to a wooden sign strung across a pathway that leads into the forest.

There are several vehicle-shaped humps here, too.

How in the hell is she going to get back to the station? There's a bus stop on the other side of the road, but who knows if they're even running?

The driver taps the steering-wheel impatiently.

Elspeth has no choice but to try to communicate with him. 'Um...do you know where I might find Chiyoko Kamamoto? She lives around here.'

He shakes his head. Points at the forest again.

What now? What the fuck did she expect to find? Chiyoko waiting for her in a limousine? She should have listened to Daniel. This was a mistake. But she's here now – what would be the point of going back to Tokyo without exploring all her options? She knows there are villages around here. She'll have to make her way to one of them if the buses aren't running. She murmurs, '*Arigato*,' but the driver doesn't respond. He accelerates away the second she closes the back door.

She stands still for several seconds, letting the silence settle around her. Glances at the pathway's dark mouth. Shouldn't the hungry spirits who lurk in the forest be attempting to lure her into the trees by now? After all, she thinks, they target the vulnerable and damaged, don't they? And what is she if not vulnerable and damaged?

Ridiculous.

Trying not to look too closely at the abandoned vehicles, she picks her way through several deep drifts, and heads towards the snow-covered mounds, which are arranged in a circle in front of the building. She's read that there are several memorials to the crash victims in the area, and she brushes ice crystals from the top of one of them, revealing a wooden marker. Behind it, partially hidden behind another drift, she spots the shape of a Western-style cross. Elspeth wipes away the snow, the melting ice starting to seep through her gloves, and reads the words, 'Pamela May Donald. Never Forget.' She wonders if Captain Seto has a marker here; she's heard that despite the evidence, some of the passengers' families still blamed him for what happened. Perhaps that really would have been a story worth pursuing. *Untold Stories from Black Thursday.* Sam was right: she is *so* full of shit.

A voice behind her makes her jump. She whirls, sees a stooped figure in a bright red windbreaker trudging towards her from behind the building. He snarls something at her.

There's no point hiding. She whips off her sunglasses, the light making her blink.

He hesitates. 'What are you doing here?' His English is tinged with a slight Californian accent.

'I came to see the memorial,' she finds herself lying – she's not sure why.

'Why?'

'I was curious.'

'We do not get Westerners coming here any more.'

'I'm sure. Um... your English is very good.'

He smiles suddenly and fiercely. His teeth are ill-fitting and there's a gap between them and his gums. He sucks them back into his mouth. 'I learned it many years ago. From the radio.'

'Are you the custodian?'

He frowns. 'I do not understand.'

She gestures at the dilapidated building. 'Do you live here? Take care of the place?'

'Ah!' Another teeth-snapping smile. 'Yes, I live here.' She wonders if he could possibly be Yomijuri Miyajima, the suicide monitor who rescued Hiro and came across the remains of Ryu. But that would be too serendipitous, wouldn't it? 'I go into the forest to collect the things that people leave behind. I can trade them.'

Elspeth shivers violently as the cold bites into her cheeks, making her eyes water. She stamps her feet. It doesn't help. 'You get a lot of people coming here?' She nods at the cars.

'Yes. You want to go in?'

'To the forest?'

'It is a long walk to the site where the plane crashed. But I can take you there. You have money?'

'How much?'

'Five thousand.'

She digs in her pocket, hands him a note. Does she really want to do this? She finds that she does. But this isn't why she's here. What she *should* be doing is asking him if he knows the whereabouts of Chiyoko, but... she's come this far, why not go into the forest?

The man turns and strides towards the pathway and Elspeth scrambles to catch up. His legs are bowed and he's at least three decades her senior, but he appears to have the vigour of a twenty-year-old.

He unclicks a chain strung across the pathway and skirts a wooden sign, the writing on it peeling and faded. The trees shower her with snow blossoms, the flakes finding their way into her neck where her scarf has slipped. She can hear her own breath, ragged in her ears. The old man cuts across the main path, heading into the depths of the forest. Elspeth hesitates. No one, except for Daniel, knows she's here (Sam might not even read the email she sent her this morning) and he'll be leaving Japan in a few days. If she runs into trouble, she's screwed. She checks her phone. No signal. Of course. She tries to take note of her surroundings, searching for landmarks that might help her find her way back to the parking lot, but within minutes the trees swallow her whole.

She's surprised when she doesn't feel the sense of foreboding she was expecting. It's actually, she thinks, quite beautiful. There are brown pockets of earth where the forest's canopy blocks out the sky, and there's something charming about the trees' knobby roots. Samuel Hockemeier – the marine who'd been on the scene a couple of days after the crash – had said they were otherworldly and forbidding.

Still, as she crumps her way through the snow, following in the old man's footsteps, she can't forget that this is where it all started. A sequence of events that was kicked off, not by three children surviving plane crashes, but by a seemingly innocuous message left by a Texan housewife as she died.

The man stops suddenly, then veers off to the right. Elspeth hangs back, not quite sure what to do. He doesn't go far. She steals forward cautiously, stopping dead when she sees a flash of dark blue in the snow. There's a figure curled in a foetal position at the foot of a tree. The remains of a rope snake into the branches above the body, the frayed end crisp with ice crystals.

The man sinks to his haunches next to it, and starts rooting through the pockets of its dark blue windbreaker. Its head is bowed, so she can't tell if it's male or female. The backpack next to it is half-unzipped, revealing a cellphone and what looks to be some kind of diary. Its hands are blue and furled, the nails white. The sweet roll the old man on the train gave her lumps in her gut.

Elspeth stares at the body with a kind of morbid fascination, her brain unable to process what she's seeing. With no warning, a hot rush of bile floods into her mouth and she turns away, gripping a tree trunk as she dry heaves. She drags air into her lungs, wipes her eyes.

'You see?' the man says matter-of-factly. 'This man died two days ago, I think. Last week I found five. Two couples. We get many who choose to die together.'

Elspeth realises she's shaking. 'What will you do with the body?'

He shrugs. 'They will only come to collect it when the weather is warmer.'

'What about his family? They might be looking for him.'

'It is possible.'

He pockets the cellphone and straightens. Then he turns and walks on.

Elspeth has seen all she wants to see of this place. How could she have found it beautiful?

'Wait.' She calls after him. 'I'm looking for someone. A young woman who lives around here. Chiyoko Kama-moto.' The man stops in his tracks, but doesn't turn around. 'Do you know where she lives?'

'Yes.'

'Will you take me to her? I can pay you.'

'How much?'

'How much will it take?'

His shoulders slump. 'Come.'

She steps back to allow him to pass, then follows him towards the parking lot.

She doesn't look back at the corpse.

Jogging to catch up to him, she flails as she hits a patch of ice, managing to catch her balance at the last moment.

He hauls open a pair of double doors at the side of the building, disappears inside and seconds later Elspeth hears the stutter of an engine trying to start.

A car backs out, its engine chugging asthmatically.

'Get in,' he snaps through the window. It's clear that

she's offended him in some way – because she didn't want to go up to the crash site, or because she mentioned Chiyoko?

She climbs in before he can change his mind. He pulls out of the parking lot and onto the road, as heedless of the snow and ice on the road as the taxi driver. He appears to be keeping to the edges of the forest, and as they round a bend, she makes out the snow-dusted roofs of several wooden houses.

The old man slows the car to a crawl, and they creep past a series of draughty-looking single-storey residences. She notes a rusting vending machine, a child's tricycle half-hidden in the snow next to the side of the road, a pile of icicled wood slumped against the side of one of the houses. As they reach the outskirts of the village, he doubles back towards the forest's edge. The road here is hidden beneath untouched snow – not a footstep or animal print marring it.

'Does anyone live here?'

The man ignores her, revs the accelerator and the car lurches awkwardly up a slight incline, and stops a hundred yards from a small structure constructed out of peeling boards that lurks in its own gloomy pocket adjacent to the forest. If not for the sagging veranda huddled around it and the shuttered windows, it would resemble a shed. 'This is the place you want.'

'Chiyoko lives here?'

The old man sucks his teeth, stares straight ahead. Elspeth pulls off a sodden glove and scrabbles in her pocket for the money. '*Arigato*,' she says, handing it over. 'If I need a ride back can I—'

'Go.'

'Have I offended you?'

'You have not offended me. I don't like this place.'

This from a man who strips corpses for a living. Elspeth shivers again. He takes the money and she climbs out. She waits while he backs away, the car farting a black cloud of exhaust smoke. She resists the urge to scream 'wait!' after him. The engine's whine fades quickly; too quickly, as if the atmosphere is greedily absorbing every sound. In some ways the forest was more hospitable. And she's getting that crawly sensation at the back of her neck, as if eyes are on her.

She climbs up onto the wooden porch in front of the house, noting with relief that the floor is littered with cigarette butts. A sign of life. She knocks on the door. Her breath condenses, and for the first time in years she finds herself wishing for a cigarette. She knocks again. Elspeth decides that if no one answers this time, she'll get the hell out of here.

But a second later, the door is opened by an overweight woman dressed in a grubby pink yukata. Elspeth tries to dredge up a memory of the photographs she's seen of Chiyoko. She recalls a pudgy, hard-eyed teenager, her expression defiant. Elspeth thinks the eyes might be the same. 'Are you Chiyoko? Chiyoko Kamamoto?'

The woman's broad face splits into a grin and she gives a small bow. 'Come in, please,' she says. Her English is flawless, and like the old man's, holds a trace of an American accent.

Elspeth steps into a narrow entrance room – the frigid air is no more forgiving in here – and kicks off her sodden boots, wincing as the cold wood bites through her tights. She places her boots on a shelf next to a pair of blood-red high heels and several grimy slippers.

Chiyoko (if it is Chiyoko – Elspeth still isn't sure) waves her through a door and into an equally chilly interior, which appears to be far smaller than it looked from the outside. A short corridor bisects two areas partially hidden behind screens; at the far end, Elspeth can make out what looks to be a small kitchen.

She follows Chiyoko through the screen to her left and into a dimly lit square room, the floor covered in tattered tatami mats. A low stained table squats in the middle of it, several faded grey cushions scattered around it.

'Sit.' Chiyoko gestures to one of the cushions. 'I will bring you some tea.'

Elspeth does as she is told, her knees popping as she kneels. It's only slightly warmer in here, and the air smells faintly of fish. The coffee table is smeared with sauce and wormed with dried noodles.

She hears the murmur of voices, followed by a giggle. A child's giggle?

The woman returns, carrying a tray containing a teapot and two round cups. She places it on the table, then sinks to her knees with more grace than her bulk should allow. She pours the tea, hands Elspeth a cup.

'You *are* Chiyoko, aren't you?'

A smirk. 'Yes.'

'You and Ryu…What happened? They found your shoes in the forest.'

'Do you know why you must remove your shoes before you die?'

'No.'

'So you don't track mud in the afterlife. That's why there are so many ghosts without feet.' A giggle.

Elspeth takes a sip of the tea. It's cold, tastes bitter. She makes herself take another, barely stops herself from gagging. 'Why did you move here?'

'I like it here. I get visitors. Some of them come before they go into the forest to die. Lovers who think they are being noble and will never be forgotten. As if anyone cares! They always ask me if they should do it. And do you know what I tell them?' Chiyoko gives Elspeth a sly sidelong smile. 'I tell them do it. Most of them bring me an offering – food, wood sometimes. As if I am a shrine! They have written books about me, songs about me. There's even a fucking manga series. Have you seen it?'

'I've seen it.'

She nods, grimaces. 'Oh yes. You mentioned it in your book.'

'You know who I am?'

'Yes.'

Elspeth jumps as a high-pitched yell sounds from behind the screen door. 'What was that?'

Chiyoko sighs. 'That is Hiro. It is almost time to feed him.'

'*What*?'

'Ryu's child. We only did it once.' Another giggle. 'It wasn't very good. He was a virgin.'

Elspeth waits for Chiyoko to get up and go to the child, but it appears she has no intention of doing so. 'Did Ryu know he was going to be a father?'

'No.'

'*Was* that his body they found in the forest?'

'Yes. Poor Ryu. An otaku without a cause. I helped him get what he wanted. You want me to tell you how it went? It's a good story. You can put it in a book.'

'Yes.'

'He said he would follow me anywhere. And when I said I wanted to die, he said he would follow me to the afterlife, too. He joined an online suicide group before we met, did you know that?'

'No.'

'Nobody knew. It was just before we started talking. He couldn't go through with it. He needed to be pushed.'

'And I'm guessing you pushed him?'

A shrug. 'It didn't take much.'

'And you? You tried too, didn't you?'

Chiyoko laughs and pushes up her sleeves. There are no scars on her wrists or forearms. 'No. Fanciful stories. Have you ever felt like that? Like you wanted to die?'

'Yes.'

'Everyone has. It is fear that stops people in the end. The fear of the unknown. Of what we might find in the next world. But there is no reason to be afraid. It just keeps on going and going.'

'What does?'

'Life. Death. Hiro and I have spent many hours talking about this very thing.'

'You mean your son?'

Chiyoko laughs in derision. 'Don't be ridiculous. He is just a baby. I mean the other Hiro, of course.'

'Hiro Yanagida?'

'Yes. Would you like to talk to him?'

'*Hiro* is here? How can Hiro be here? He was killed by that marine. Shot.'

'Was he?' Chiyoko gets smoothly to her feet. 'Come. You must have many questions for him.'

Elspeth stands, her thigh muscles aching from crouching on the floor. Her vision wavers, her stomach cramps, and for a horrible moment she wonders if Chiyoko has drugged her. The woman is definitely unhinged and if what she's saying about Ryu and the suicidal people who visit her is the truth, she's dangerous. And she can't forget the old man's reaction to the place. Her mouth fills with saliva and she pinches her left arm, refusing to give in to her faintness. It passes. She's light-headed from exhaustion. Worn out.

She follows Chiyoko to the other screened-off room across the passageway.

'Come,' Chiyoko says, opening the screen wide enough for Elspeth to slip through. It's dark in here; the wooden shutters are closed. Elspeth squints, and as her eyes adjust, she can make out a crib on the left side of the room, and a futon piled with pillows beneath the windows. The fishy odour is stronger in here. She shudders, remembering Paul Craddock's delusion about his dead brother. Chiyoko plucks a toddler out of the crib, and the child wraps his arms around her neck.

'I thought you said Hiro was here?'

'He is.'

Slinging the toddler on her hip, Chiyoko opens one of the shutters, letting in a shaft of light.

Elspeth was wrong – the pillows on the futon aren't pillows at all, but a figure slumped against the wall, its legs outstretched.

'I will leave you two alone,' Chiyoko says.

Elspeth doesn't respond. As she stares at the surrabot of Hiro Yanagida, it blinks, a fraction too slowly to be convincingly human. Its skin is nicked in places; its clothes are frayed.

'Hello.' The voice – unmistakably a child's – makes Elspeth jump. 'Hello,' the android says again.

'Is that you, Hiro?' Elspeth says. The sheer insanity of her situation finally hits her. She's in Japan. Talking to a robot. She's talking to a fucking robot.

'It's me.'

'Can I...can I talk to you?'

'You are talking to me.'

Elspeth steps closer to it. There are small brown droplets on the dull skin of its face – dried blood? 'What are you?'

The android yawns. 'I'm me.'

Elspeth's feeling that same kind of disconnect she felt when she was in Kenji Yanagida's workshop. Her mind goes blank. She has no idea what to ask first. 'How did you survive the crash?'

'We chose to. But sometimes we get it wrong.'

'And Jessica? And Bobby? Where are they? Are they actually dead?'

'They got bored. They usually do. They knew how it would end.'

'And how does it end?' It blinks at her again. After several seconds of silence, Elspeth asks: 'Is there...is there a fourth child?'

'No.'

'What about the fourth plane crash?'

The robot's head jerks slightly to the side. 'We knew that would be the day to do it.'

'Do what?'

'Arrive.'

'So...why children?'

'We're not always children.'

'What does that mean?'

The thing's head twitches and it yawns again. Elspeth

gets the impression it's intimating: *figure it out, bitch*. Then it makes a sound that could be a laugh, its jaw opening just a fraction too wide. There's something familiar about the way it's been framing its words. Elspeth knows how it works. She's seen the footage of the camera capturing Kenji Yanagida's facial movements. But there's no sign of a computer in the room. And...wouldn't that require some kind of signal? There's no signal here, is there? She checks her phone again to be sure. But Chiyoko could be operating the android from another room, couldn't she?

'Chiyoko? Is that you? It is, isn't it?'

The surrabot's chest rises and falls, then stills.

Elspeth runs from the room, her feet slipping on the tatami mats. She hauls open the door next to the empty kitchen, revealing a tiny bathroom, the small tub swimming with filthy cloth nappies. She backtracks and rips back the screen to the only other room. Chiyoko's son looks up at her from where he's lying on the floor, playing with a dirty stuffed animal, and laughs.

She opens the front door and sees Chiyoko standing on the porch, cigarette smoke coiling around her head. Could she have made it out here while Elspeth was searching the house? She's not sure. She pulls on her boots and joins her.

'Was that you, Chiyoko? Talking through the android?'

Chiyoko stubs her cigarette out on the balustrade; lights another one. 'Did you think it was me?'

'Yes. No. I don't know.'

The cold air isn't helping to clear her head and Elspeth is sick of all this talking in riddles. 'Okay...If it wasn't you, what were – are – they? The Three, I mean?'

'You've seen what Hiro is.'

'All I've seen is a fucking android.'

A shrug. 'All things have souls.'

'So is that what he is? A soul?'

'In a sense.'

Jesus. 'Can you please just give me a straight answer?'

Another infuriating smile. 'Ask me a straight question.'

'Okay...Did Hiro – the real Hiro – tell you why The Three, whatever the fuck they are, came here and took over the bodies of the kids?'

'Why would they need a reason? Why do we hunt when we have enough to eat? Why do we kill each other over trifles? What makes you think they needed any more motivation other than to simply see *what might happen*?'

'Hiro implied that they've been here before. I've also heard that from Jessica Craddock's uncle.'

A shrug. 'All religions have prophecies about the end of the world.'

'So? What does that have to do with The Three being here before?'

Chiyoko makes a sound somewhere between a sigh and a snort. 'For a journalist, you are very bad at thinking things through. What if they came here before in order to plant the seed?'

Elspeth starts. 'No way. Are you trying to say that they came here thousands of years ago and set this whole thing up – just so that they could return years later and see if the so-called *seed* they planted causes the goddamned end of the world? That's insane.'

'Of course it is.'

Elspeth has had enough. She's so tired the marrow in her bones aches. 'Now what?'

Chiyoko yawns; several of her back teeth are missing.

She wipes her mouth with her sleeve. 'Do your job. You're a journalist. You have found what you were looking for. Go back and tell them what you've seen. Write an article.'

'You really think anyone's going to believe me if I say that I've spoken to a goddamned android harbouring the...soul or whatever of one of The Three?'

'People will believe what they want to believe.'

'And if they do believe it...They'll think...they'll say...'

'They'll say Hiro is a god.'

'And *is* he?'

Chiyoko shrugs. '*Shikata ga nai*,' she says. 'What does it matter?' She stubs her cigarette out on the top of the balustrade and walks into the house.

Elspeth stands stock still for several minutes, and with no other option, she zips up her jacket and starts walking away.

HOW IT BEGINS

Pamela May Donald lies on her side, watching the boy as he flits with the others in the trees.

'Help me,' she croaks.

She fumbles for her phone. It's somewhere in her fanny pack, she's certain of that. *C'mon, c'mon, c'mon*. Her fingers stroke it, she almost has it…*so close, you can do it*…but she can't quite seem to…There's something wrong with her fingers. They won't work, they're numb, dead, no longer belong to her.

'Snookie,' she whispers, or maybe she only thinks she says it aloud. Either way, it's the only word that comes into her mind before she dies.

The boy skips over to her, tiptoeing around the roots and wreckage. He looks down at Pamela May Donald's body. She's gone. Snuffed out before she could record the message. He's disappointed, but it's happened before and he was starting to get bored with this game anyway. They all were. It doesn't matter. Even without the message, it always ends in the same way.

He sinks to his haunches, wraps his arms around his knees, and shivers. He can hear the distant thwupping sound of the rescue helicopters approaching. He always enjoys being hoisted up into the helicopter's belly. This will be fun, no matter what.

But next time, he'll do it differently. And he thinks he knows how.

ACKNOWLEDGMENTS

Huge appreciation goes to Agent Extraordinaire Oli Munson of A.M. Heath, who took one look at the synopsis, said 'go for it', and basically changed my life.

The novel would be far weaker without the outstanding editorial guidance of my super-hero editor Anne Perry who took a chance on me, made me a stronger writer, and taught me how to accessorise – all without losing her sense of humour. Many thanks are also due to Oliver Johnson, Jason Bartholomew and the fantastic team at Hodder; Reagan Arthur and her excellent team at Little, Brown; and Conrad Williams and all at Blake Friedmann.

The following folk kindly shared their expertise, personal experiences, dealt with my endless questions or opened their homes to me: Captain Chris Zurinskas, Eri Uri, Atsuko Takahashi, Hiroshi Hayakawa, Atsushi Hayakawa, Akira Yamaguchi, David France Mundo, Paige and Ahnika at the House of Collections, Darrell Zimmerman at Cape Medical Response, Eric Begala and Wongani Bandah. Thank you all for being so patient and generous. The responsibility for mistakes made and liberties taken (both geographical and factual) is mine and mine alone.

Christopher Hood's superb academic text, *Dealing with Disaster in Japan: Responses to the Flight JL 123 Crash* was an invaluable resource and introduced me to the terms *isho* and *izoku*. I'm also indebted to the authors of the following non-fiction books, blogs, articles and novels which helped shed light on the issues I chose to deal with in the novel: *Welcome to Our Doomsday* by Nicholas Guyatt; *God's Own Country* by Stephen Bates; *Shutting out the Sun* by Michael Zielenziger; *The Otaku Handbook* by Patrick W. Galbraith; *Quantum: A Guide for the Perplexed* by Jim Al-Khalili; *Train Man* by Nakano Hitori; *Are We Living in the End Times?* by Tim LaHaye and Jerry B. Jenkins; *Understanding End Times Prophecy*, by Paul Benware; *Below Luck Level* by Barbara Erasmus; *Alzheimer's from the Inside Out* by Richard Taylor; sherizeee.blogspot.com; www.dannychoo.com; www.tofugu.com; 'Apocalypse Now,' Nancy Gibbs (time .com 2002). Many thanks go to the anonymous artists of asciiart.en.com for inspiring Ryu's ascii.

The following generous people read the manuscript and gave insightful and honest feedback: Alan and Carol Walters, Andrew Solomon, Bronwyn Harris, Nick Wood, Michael Grant, Sam Wilson, Kerry Gordon, Tiah Beautement, Joe Vaz, Vienne Venter, Nechama Brodie, Si, and Sally Partridge. Eric Begala, Thembani Ndzandza, Siseko Sodela, Walter Ntsele, Lwando Sibinge and Thando Makubalo kindly weeded out the majority of my stupidity in the South African sections. Jared Shurin, Alex Smith, Karina Brink, ace photographer Pagan Wicks and Nomes helped keep me sane. You all rock.

Lauren Beukes, Alan Kelly (thank you for the naughty bits!), Nigel Walters, Louis Greenberg and my fellow porn elf Paige Nick went above and beyond with their support and feedback. I owe you guys big time. As usual, my friend and editor Helen Moffett pulled my arse out of the fire again and again (may your life be forever rich in artisanal baked goods).

And last but not least, my husband Charlie and daughter Savannah put up with hours of brain-storming, neuroses and plot-solving, and brought me coffee at 3 a.m. I couldn't have written word one without you – thank you for always having my back.

ABOUT THE AUTHOR

SARAH LOTZ is a novelist and screenwriter with a fondness for the macabre. She lives in Cape Town with her family and other animals.

. . . AND HER NEXT NOVEL

Hundreds of pleasure seekers stream aboard *The Beautiful Dreamer* cruise ship for five days of cut-price fun in the Caribbean sun. On the fourth day, disaster strikes: smoke roils out of the engine room and the ship is stranded in the Gulf of Mexico. Supplies run low, a virus plagues the ship, and there are whispered rumors that the cabins on the lower decks are haunted by shadowy figures. Soon, irritation escalates to panic, the crew loses control, factions form, and violent chaos erupts among the survivors.

When at last the ship is spotted drifting off the coast of Key West, the world's press reports that it is empty. But the gloomy headlines may be covering up an even more disturbing reality . . .

Following is an excerpt from *Day Four*.

Welcome on Board The Beautiful Dreamer!

Congratulations on choosing a Status Cruise, your one-way ticket to Relaxation and Fun! Fun! Fun!

Start your Holiday of a Lifetime by treating yourself to a cocktail at one of our many sun-drenched bars while our musicians delight with their signature sounds. Then cool down in the pool and take a spin on Status's WaterWonder™ slides. Hungry? No problem! Our dining room and buffets will provide feasts galore, from five-star fare to yummy comfort food like momma used to make! And hey, don't forget to pamper yourself at our superb spa – you deserve it! Our cabaret performances will delight, so settle into your seats and prepare to be entertained like never before! Soak up the sun during one of our many exciting excursions, where you can shop til you drop at our many concessions, snorkel in turquoise seas, horse-ride along beautiful beaches, and enjoy al fresco dining on our fabulous private island. And why not take a spin in the Delectable Dreamer Casino? Who knows? It could be your lucky day!

DAYS 1, 2, 3

Cruise is relatively uneventful.

DAY 4

The Witch's Assistant

Maddie waited until Celine was midway into her opening monologue, then threaded her way through the capsule chairs, making for the empty area at the back of the Starlight Dreamer Lounge. She'd almost made it when the cruise director's voice boomed over the PA system, drowning out Celine's patter with his reminder that the New Year's festivities would kick off in 'T minus two hours'.

'Voices from above,' Celine quipped, but Maddie wasn't fooled by this show of good humour. Celine had been like a Rottweiler with a sore tooth all day, sniping at the backstage tech after he'd snagged her dress attaching the microphone's receiver to her wheelchair, and complaining that the spotlight wasn't in the correct position to halo her hair.

'Know this,' Celine continued once the announcement had petered away. 'When you all return home, rested and suntanned and maybe a few pounds heavier' – she waited for a ripple of laughter to die down – 'you won't be alone. Friends, in all my years of helping people connect with those who've crossed over, there are two things I can tell you for sure – One: there is no death; and two: the souls of those who've left the physical world are always with us...'

With Celine back on track, Maddie allowed herself to relax. She leaned against a pillar and massaged her neck, trying and failing to dissolve the headache that had dogged her since day one of the cruise. It was probably just a side effect of the anti-nausea medication she was taking, but the garish environment wasn't helping. Whoever had designed the ship's decor had a hard-on for Vegas-inspired neon and naked male angels; you couldn't go anywhere without being blinded by an illuminated palm tree or leered at by a cherub. Still – just one more night to get through and she'd be free of this floating hell-hole. The first thing she was going to do when she got back to her apartment was run a bath and scrub the ship off her skin. Then she'd treat herself to a takeout from Jujubee's – splurge on the crab special with glass noodles and extra garlic. She could afford the calories; she must have lost at least five pounds this week.

'Hey, baby,' a voice stage-whispered in her ear. She turned to see Ray, his eyes fixed to her breasts. He'd jettisoned his usual shorts and navy T-shirt combo in favour of Levi's and a flimsy cream shirt, which gave him the appearance of a seedy lounge singer.

'Shouldn't you be on the door, Ray?' Tonight's event was strictly for 'Friends of Celine' only – the select group who'd paid through the nose to cruise with 'America's Number One Psychic Medium' – and Ray knew as well as she did that Celine would flip if a non-paying passenger wandered in.

He shrugged. 'Yeah, yeah. So listen – you know when we stopped at Cozumel yesterday?'

'So?'

'So I got one of the waiters to smuggle me in a bottle of high-end tequila. The good stuff.'

A Friend sitting on the outskirts of the group scrunched around in her chair and shushed them. Maddie shot her an apologetic smile and hissed at Ray to keep his voice down.

'Whatever. So, hey – party later, my cabin. You in?'

More heads were turning in their direction. 'Seriously, Ray, shut the –'

'Think about it.' He smirked. 'Going to grab a frosty while the boss does her *thang*.' Maddie watched him saunter off towards the bar, checking out a waitress en route.

Arsehole.

The atmosphere grew taut as Celine moved on to the highlight of the evening. She licked her lips, touched her chest, and said: 'I'm getting…Who's Caroline? No, wait…Katherine? Someone with…it's a C or a K. Nope…it's definitely Katherine. Kathy, maybe.'

Maddie smothered a jab of guilt as Jacob, one of the older Friends, wobbled to his feet. She had a soft spot for Jacob. She admired his sense of style (he tended to dress as if he was a guest at a gay wedding), and he wasn't as pushy as some of the others. Celine had feigned illness for much of the cruise, barely showing her face at the various meet 'n greets and cocktail events, so Maddie had been left to pick up the slack. Part of her job was schmoozing with Celine's fanbase, but there was a world of difference between trading messages with the lonely and desperate online and contending with their neediness face to face. Listening to the Friends' hopes that Celine would connect with their loved ones, missing relatives, and, in some cases, deceased pets had worn her ragged. 'Kathy's my sister!' Jacob called.

'That's what I'm getting.' Celine nodded. 'Know this, she's stepping forward right this second. Hey…Why can

I smell turkey?' She chuckled. 'And sweet potato pie. Good pie at that.'

Jacob gasped and wiped at his eyes. 'She disappeared in the late seventies, round about Thanksgiving. Is she... is she at peace?'

'Yes. Know this. She has left the physical world and has gone into the light. She wants you to know that every time you think of her, her soul is with you.'

Jacob waited for more, but Celine just smiled blandly back at him, and he nodded and sat down.

Celine touched her chest again. 'I'm getting... It's getting harder to breathe. There's someone here who's... they passed before their time. I'm talking about a suicide. Yes.'

Leila Nelson, a bony woman with mild hair loss, squealed and jumped out of her chair. 'Oh my *Lord!* My husband killed himself two years ago.'

'I want you to know he's stepping forward, my darling. What's with the breathing? I'm thinking... did he asphyxiate? Does this make sense to you? I'm tasting carbon monoxide here.'

'Oh my *Lord*. That's how he did it! In the garage, in his Chevy.'

'In his Chevy.' Celine paused to ram this home to the Friends. 'What's the significance of April?'

'His birthday was in April.'

'So April's his birthday. Yeah, that's what I'm getting from him. A tall man, does that make sense?'

Leila hesitated. 'John was five eight.'

'That's tall if you're me, my darling,' Celine rallied. 'I'm getting that... Was John unhappy at work? Does that make sense to you?'

'Yes! He lost his job. He was never the same after that.'

'What's with the shoes?'

'Oh my *Lord,* he was always particular about his shoes. Always polishing them, been like that since he left the marines.'

'That's what I'm getting. A feeling like he was a very particular, precise sort of person. Know this, he wants you to know that what happened to him, the way he died, it was nothing you did. He needs you to move on with your life.'

'So he doesn't mind that I'm getting remarried?'

Shit. That was one detail Leila hadn't mentioned during last night's Friends of Celine cocktail event, but Celine didn't skip a beat. 'Know this, he's proud that you're doing so well.'

'He was such a jealous man, though. What I need to know is if he –'

'My darling, I'll have to interrupt you there, as Archie is coming through.' Celine pressed a hand to her throat. 'I can feel the weight of him. He's coming through strongly now.' Maddie suppressed a shudder. Fake or not, Archie, Celine's primary spirit guide – an urchin who'd supposedly died of consumption in late-nineteenth-century London – gave her the screaming heebies. There weren't many mediums who channelled the voices of their guides these days, and secretly Maddie thought Celine sounded like Dick Van Dyke gargling caustic soda whenever Archie's voice 'came through'.

Celine paused for dramatic effect. 'There's a bloke 'ere who wants a word with Juney,' Archie's voice rattled from Celine's throat.

Juanita, the Friend who'd shushed Ray, sprang to her feet. 'That's me! Juney is my nickname!'

Celine reverted to her normal voice: 'Juney, don't feel bad about leaving the insulin out of the fridge. He knows you didn't mean it.'

Goosebumps popped up on Maddie's arms. Juanita hadn't said anything about insulin last night. Celine was adept at cold-reading, but that was an unusually precise detail. She tended to stick to generalities.

Juanita's face creased. 'Jeffrey? Jeffrey, is that you?'

A blade of light sliced through the gloom as a man slipped through the doors on the far side of the lounge. He was two decades younger than Celine's core demographic, his legs clad in skinny jeans and boots, his arms scrawled with tattoos. Ray hadn't noticed the intruder; he was slumped on a bar stool, his back to the doors.

'Celine del Ray!' the guy shouted, striding towards the stage and pointing a camera phone in Celine's direction. 'Celine del Ray!'

Shit. The week after Celine had signed up as the cruise's guest celebrity, Maddie had heard via Twitter that there might be a blogger on board, and it looked like he'd finally decided to pitch up.

'Who is that?' Celine called, squinting into the audience.

'Any comment about the fact that Lillian Small is planning to sue you?'

A collective gasp. There were too many obstacles for Maddie to get to the guy easily, and she couldn't count on the waitstaff to intervene. Thankfully Ray had realised what was going on and was hustling towards him.

'You know the story, right?' the man crowed to the Friends gaping at him. 'This so-called *medium,* this *predator,* bombarded Mrs Small with messages saying that her daughter and grandson were alive in Florida, when DNA proves that–' he faltered. 'Proves that–' he clamped a hand to his mouth. 'Oh *fuck*.' With that he whirled, shoved past Ray, and ran out, the doors hissing closed behind him.

Ray glanced at Maddie and she gestured at him to follow.

Celine chuckled again, but it sounded forced. 'Uh. I tell you, that was…Give me a minute here.' She took a slug of Evian from the bottle in her wheelchair pocket. The room settled into an uneasy silence. 'You know, there are always gonna be doubters. But I can only repeat what Spirit tells me. That situation…you know…Wait…I'm getting something else here. You know, sometimes the spirits come through so strong that I can taste what they're tasting, feel what they're feeling. I'm getting…Smoke. I can smell smoke.…I'm hearing…Someone here lose a loved one in a fire? Does that make sense to anyone?'

No one spoke up. Maddie squirmed.

'It could be…yeah, you know, I'm smelling gas, think it might be a car accident. I'm getting…What is the significance of the I-90?'

A Friend called out that his second cousin had been killed in a head-on collision on that highway years earlier. Maddie allowed herself to breathe again. Ray crept back into the room and gave Maddie the A-OK sign. She checked her phone. Five minutes to go. She edged towards Celine, signalling that it was time to wrap it up. Ray had better do his bloody job and usher everyone out as fast as possible. The Friends were booked to eat at the second sitting, so they'd have to leave straight away if they didn't want a rubbery lobster tail.

Celine wished the Friends a Happy New Year and ran

through her usual schtick about visiting her website where there were links to purchase her eleven books. Maddie leapt onto the stage before her boss could be engulfed in a tsunami of well-wishers. Celine's wheelchair wasn't strictly necessary (although she could propel it with the skill of a Para-Olympian if an over-zealous fan threatened to approach), but Maddie was glad of it this evening. Close up, Celine was really showing her age; her waxy skin had the look of an apple left too long in cold storage, her lips were the colour of old deli meat.

Maddie unplugged the mic and handed it to the tech before Celine recovered and lambasted him for the PA system screwup.

'You okay, Celine?' she murmured.

'Get me the fuck outta here now.'

'Celine?' Leila bustled up to them before Maddie could intervene, waving a copy of part two of Celine's autobiography, *Medium to the Stars and Beyond*. 'I meant to ask you last night at the cocktail evening, but you were there so briefly...could you sign this?'

Celine smiled icily. 'It'd be a pleasure, my darling.'

'Can you put, "To Leila, my biggest fan"? I've got all your books. E-editions and audio as well.'

Maddie handed Celine a pen, glancing at Leila to see if she'd noticed Celine's shaking hands; fortunately she was far too busy staring rapturously at her face. 'You've helped me so much, Celine. You and Archie, of course.' Leila pressed the book to her chest. 'You've really brought me peace. John...he wasn't the easiest and...I don't know how you do it.'

'It's a God-given gift, my darling. Know this, your faith and support mean a lot to me.'

'And you mean a lot to me. That awful man who burst in here doesn't have a –'

'Celine is very tired,' Maddie interrupted. 'Connecting with Spirit takes a lot out of her. I'm sure you understand.'

'Oh, I do, I do,' Leila said, bobbing and bowing and scurrying off to join the other Friends bottlenecking the exit.

Ray approached. 'Sorry about that, Celine.'

Celine's eyes – already unnaturally hooded from a screwed-up eyelift in the eighties – narrowed. 'Yeah? What the hell, Ray? I pay you for *that?*'

'How was I supposed to know he was gonna show up? I checked out everyone else.'

'You should have been at the goddamned door, Ray.'

'Celine, like I say, I fucked up. Won't happen again.'

Celine snorted. 'Damn right it won't. Where'd he go anyway?'

'Ran into the restroom. Looked like he was gonna puke.'

Maddie's stomach rolled over. After stupidly reading a *Huff Post* exposé about ship-borne viruses, she'd only been able to cope by washing her hands at every opportunity and popping probiotics like an addict. Still, that explained why they hadn't been hounded by the blogger before. He must have been holed up in his cabin praying to the porcelain god for the duration of the cruise.

'You want me to escort you back to your cabin?' Ray asked.

'It's a suite,' Celine snapped. 'And no. Get out of my sight. Madeleine can do it.'

Ray nodded miserably and slunk away. Maddie knew very little about his personal life, but he'd mentioned something about having to pay child support to one of his exes. He may be a letch and a bullshitter, but she almost pitied him – he'd be lucky if he still had a job when they reached Miami. Celine's bodyguards never lasted long.

'Goddamned bloggers and undercover journalists,' Celine griped, twirling a hand in the air to indicate they should get going. 'Forty years I've been doing this. It's my god-given gift...'

Maddie let Celine ramble on as she manoeuvred the wheelchair out via the stage door exit, blinking as her eyes were blasted by the pink and gold neon signage splayed all over the Promenade Dreamz deck. Passengers streamed towards the staircase for the second dinner sitting, and twenty-somethings in tight white shorts and 'Status = Fun! Fun! Fun!' T-shirts flitted around, rumbaing to the calypso music in the background and hawking plastic angel wings and devil horns for tonight's Heaven 'n Hell–themed New Year's Eve party. Maddie had no intention of going anywhere near the festivities. She planned on putting Celine to bed, ordering a grilled cheese sandwich from room service (her gut clenched at the thought of eating the mass-produced slop in the dining room and buffets), then heading up to the jogging track above the Lido Deck. She hadn't yet found a gap to do her five miles today.

A trio of meaty men with fluorescent halos attached to their shaven heads made way for them as Maddie inched Celine into the elevator, which, as usual, smelled faintly of vomit. She pressed the button for the Verandah Deck with her elbow and wheeled Celine as far away from the damp patch on the carpet as she could get. A reggae rendition of 'Rehab' plinked as they were propelled upwards through the atrium, the glass sides gradually revealing the lobby and cocktail bars below.

'Christ, I need a drink,' Celine said.

'Nearly there.'

Maddie dragged the wheelchair out of the elevator and headed in the direction of the VIP staterooms. A couple of giggly elderly women squeezed themselves against the corridor wall to allow them to pass. Maddie smiled brightly at them to make up for Celine's surly 'whatever' response to their happy new year wishes, and waved at Althea, the deck's cabin steward, who was exiting a neighbouring suite, a bunch of towels tucked under an arm.

'Good evening, Mrs del Ray and Maddie!' Althea called. 'Do you need any help?'

Celine ignored her, but Althea's smile didn't falter. Maddie had no clue how Althea remained so cheerful while mopping up after arseholes like Celine. Most of the staff exuded an exhausting (obviously fake) joviality, but Maddie was certain Althea's constant good mood wasn't a front.

After swiping the room card several times until the lock finally flashed green, Maddie hefted the wheelchair into the narrow entrance area and pushed Celine towards the balcony and her collection of booze.

Celine jabbed a talon at the TV. 'For Christ's sake change the goddamned channel. How many times have I told that goddamned woman not to touch it?'

On-screen, Damien, the cruise director – an Australian with the fixed gaze of someone dangerously bipolar – was once again running through his tour of the ship. Maddie flicked past a *Saturday Night Live* parody of failed Republican nominee Mitch Reynard and a shopping channel, where two middle-aged women were gushing over a reversible jacket, before settling on footage of the run-up to the Times Square ball drop. Without being asked, she scooped ice into a glass and poured Celine a double J&B.

Celine snatched it out of her hand and took a gulp. 'Christ, that's better. You're a good girl, Madeleine.'

Maddie rolled her eyes. 'Did I just hear you correctly?'

'Archie says you're thinking of quitting.'

'Celine, I'm always thinking of quitting. Maybe I wouldn't if you stopped calling me a useless bitch.'

'You know I don't mean it.' She gestured at the TV again. 'I don't need reminding that another year's over. Put one of my films on.'

'Which one?'

'*Pretty Woman.*'

Maddie connected the hard drive and scrolled through the menu until she reached the Julia Roberts folder. She still couldn't reconcile Celine's hard-bitten outlook on life with her addiction to '90s romcoms; Maddie had lost count of the number of scratchy motel chairs she'd sat in, waiting for her boss to fall asleep while *When Harry Met Sally* or *French Kiss* played out to their predictable conclusions.

Celine rattled the glass for a refill. 'So. What are we gonna do about Ray?'

'You're the boss.'

'You know he's got a thing for you, Madeleine.'

'Ray's got a thing for everyone with a vagina. He's a dickhead.'

Celine sighed. 'I know. The cute ones always are. He'll have to go. But that doesn't solve your problem, does it?'

'I've got a problem?'

'You need a man in your life, Madeleine. It's about time you put your past to rest.'

'Not this again. What the hell am I going to do with a man?'

Celine cackled. 'Well, if I have to tell you...'

'You want to tell me how I'm supposed to maintain a relationship when I'm on the road with you nine months out of the year?'

'Yeah, yeah, guilt-trip the old woman. You should go to the party tonight. See if you can snag yourself one of those cute crew members in their tight white pants. How long has it been? You know, since you last...'

'None of your business.'

'That's not an answer. You want me to ask Archie what he –'

'Enough with the personal stuff, Celine.'

'Just saying, you deserve better outta life.'

'Okay if I use your bathroom?' If she took her time in there, with any luck Celine would pass out in front of the movie and she'd be able to slip away without too much of an ear-bashing.

'Go right ahead.'

Maddie fled inside it and locked the door. It was three times the size of the one in her cabin, with a whirlpool bath and a pyramid of rolled white towels. She sat on the toilet lid and rubbed her temples. Thanks to that hipster guy, Celine would be in a funk for the next week at least. And no doubt the footage he'd taken would already be all over YouTube. Celine had only signed up for the cruise to get away from the heat after the Lillian Small debacle, but they'd both known it could backfire on them.

After it had all blown up, Maddie had never said 'I told

you so.' She'd warned Celine not to go on Eric Kavanaugh's Black Thursday Remembrance Show; the shock-jock was notorious for skewering psychics, scientologists, and spiritualists. Plus, Celine had been one of the much-maligned 'Circle of Psychics' who'd joined together to 'use their combined energy' to ascertain the apparently mysterious causes of the four plane crashes that had occurred back in 2012. Kavanaugh had gleefully ripped the psychics a new one when the NTSB released its findings and it transpired that the psychics had struck out on all counts. To be fair, Celine had been holding her own until the subject of the Florida crash had come up. Maddie still had no clue what had possessed her boss to insist that Lori Small and her son Bobby, two of the passengers aboard the aircraft that had plummeted into the Everglades, were alive. Even when Bobby and Lori's DNA was discovered amongst the wreckage, Celine continued to proclaim that the mother and son were out there somewhere, wandering the streets of Miami, suffering from amnesia. She'd gone too far to back down. Tragically, Lori's mother, Lillian Small, had spent all her savings hiring private detectives to follow this dubious lead, and now an enterprising lawyer had taken on her case and was gunning for Celine.

It wasn't the first time Celine had got it wrong – but it was certainly the most high-profile of her blunders. But then... Maddie wasn't being entirely fair, was she? Celine *had* occasionally been right, hadn't she? There was tonight's insulin revelation for a start (but it was possible Ray had passed on that nugget – she'd have to check). She knew that statistically Celine had to hit on some facts that weren't fed to her by Maddie or whichever hapless ex-cop she'd hired to play the part of her bodyguard, but it still made her feel uneasy. And the guilt she usually managed to keep at bay was getting to her. Needling at her. It was a mistake getting to know the Friends. Maybe she should just quit. *And do what?* A shitty minimum-wage job was the best she could hope for with her record. She could always move back to the UK, slink back with her tail between her legs. Her sister would love that: *I told you so, Maddie, I told you it would all end in tears.*

'You fallen in?' Celine shouted.

'Coming!' Maddie called. So much for Celine passing out. She was about to get up, when the floor lurched, forcing her to grab on to the toilet roll holder. Her knees began juddering, a strong vibration hummed under her feet. The lights flickered, there was a long mechanical yawning sound, and then ... silence.

Pulse thumping in her throat, Maddie unlocked the door and hurried into the suite. 'Celine? I think there's something wrong with the ship.'

Maddie was expecting Celine to say something along the lines of: 'You're goddamned right something's wrong with the ship, it's a shithole,' but her head was slumped forward; her arms hung listlessly over the chair's sides. The glass lay on the carpet where it must have slipped from her fingers.

On-screen, Richard Gere rolled down Hollywood Boulevard. Then the television blinked off.

'Celine? Celine, are you okay?'

No answer.

Maddie crept forward and touched the crepey skin on Celine's forearm. No response. She moved around to face her and sank to her knees. 'Celine?' Without lifting her head, Celine sucked in a breath, then began humming a jaunty, jazzy tune that reminded Maddie of Lizzie Bean, another (albeit less vocal) of Celine's spirit guides. 'Celine?' It was becoming difficult to swallow. 'Hey...Come on, Celine.'

Celine raised her head, a look of such raw terror in her eyes that Maddie yipped and fell back on her haunches. 'Jesus!'

Maddie leapt to her feet, meaning to lunge for the phone, but then the lights went out again, and she stumbled as the ship listed to the left. She fought to control her breathing, had almost done so when a voice cut through the silence. 'Ho-hum me old ducky,' Archie cackled. 'This is going to be fun.'